SEA OF
AKERI

KINGDOM OF
VENDA

A TERR

MARABELLA

★ SANCTUM

EUX

FALWORTH

GREAT RIVER

KINGDOM OF
DALBRECK

REUX
LAU

CRUVAS

DANCE OF THIEVES

OF

NEW YORK TIMES–BESTSELLING AUTHOR OF THE REMNANT CHRONICLES

MARY E. PEARSON

Henry Holt and Company

NEW YORK

For my fierce and unstoppable girls,
Ava, Emily, and Leah

Henry Holt and Company, *Publishers since 1866*
Henry Holt® is a registered trademark of Macmillan Publishing Group, LLC
175 Fifth Avenue, New York, NY 10010 • fiercereads.com

Text copyright © 2018 by Mary E. Pearson

Map copyright © 2018 by Keith Thompson

Library of Congress Control Number: 2017957735

ISBN 978-1-250-15901-4

Our books may be purchased in bulk for promotional, educational, or business use.
Please contact your local bookseller or the Macmillan Corporate and Premium
Sales Department at (800) 221-7945 ext. 5442 or by e-mail at
MacmillanSpecialMarkets@macmillan.com.

First edition, 2018 / Designed by Rebecca Syracuse

Printed in the United States of America

1 3 5 7 9 10 8 6 4 2

Write it down, he had told me.

Write down every word once you get there,

Before the truth is forgotten.

And now we do, at least the parts we remember.

—Greyson Ballenger, 14

CHAPTER ONE

KAZIMYRAH OF BRIGHTMIST

THE GHOSTS ARE STILL HERE.

The words lingered in the air, each one a shimmering spirit, cold whispers of caution, but I wasn't afraid.

I already knew.

The ghosts, they never go away. They call to you in unexpected moments, their hands lacing with yours and pulling you down paths that lead nowhere. *This way.* I had learned to mostly shut them out.

We rode through Sentinel Valley, ruins of the Ancients looking down upon us. My horse's ears pricked, watchful, a rumble deep from his throat. He knew too. I rubbed his neck to calm him. It had been six years since the Great Battle, but the scars were still visible—overturned wagons eaten up with grass, scattered bones dug from graves by hungry beasts, the skeletal ribs of giant brezalots reaching skyward, birds perched on their elegant bleached cages.

I felt the ghosts hovering, watching, wondering. One of them slid a cool fingertip along my jaw, pressing a warning to my lips, *Shhh, Kazi, don't say a word.*

Natiya led us deeper into the valley, unafraid. Our gazes scanned the rugged cliffs and the crumbling devastation of a war that was slowly being consumed by earth, time, and memory, like the awkward swallowing of a fat hare by a patient snake. Soon, all the destruction would be in the belly of the earth. Who would remember?

Midway, as the valley narrowed, Natiya stopped and slipped from her saddle, pulling a folded square of white cloth from her saddlebag. Wren dismounted too, her thin limbs gliding to the ground as silently as a bird. Synové hesitated, watching me uncertainly. She was strongest of us all, but her round hips remained firmly planted in her saddle. She did not care for talk of ghosts, even in the brightness of a high sun. They frequented her dreams too often. I nodded to reassure her, and we both slid from our horses and joined them. Natiya paused at a large green mound as if she knew what lay beneath the woven blanket of grass. She absently rubbed the fabric between her delicate brown fingers. It was only for a few seconds, but it seemed to last forever. Natiya was nineteen, only two years older than us, but she suddenly looked much older. She had actually seen the things we had only heard stories about. Her head shook slightly, and she walked toward a scattered pile of rocks. She began picking up the fallen stones and puzzling them back into place on the humble memorial.

"Who was it?" I asked.

Her lips rolled tight against her teeth. "His name was Jeb. His body was burned on a funeral pyre because that's the Dalbretch way, but I buried his few belongings here."

Because that's the vagabond way, I thought, but said nothing. Natiya didn't talk much about her life before she became Vendan and a Rahtan, but I didn't talk much about my earlier life either. Some things were better left in the past. Wren and Synové shifted uncomfortably on their feet, their boots pressing the grass into small, flat circles. Natiya wasn't prone to sentimental displays, even if they were quiet ones like this, especially if they delayed her well-planned schedule. But now she lingered, just like her words that had ushered us into the valley. *They are still here.*

"He was special?" I asked.

She nodded. "They all were. But Jeb taught me things. Things that have helped me to survive." She turned, giving us a sharp glance. "Things I have taught all of you. *Hopefully.*" Her scrutiny softened, and her thick black lashes cast a shadow beneath her dark eyes. She studied the three of us as if she were a seasoned general and we were her ragtag soldiers. In some ways, I supposed we were. We were the youngest of the Rahtan, but *we were Rahtan.* That meant something. It meant a lot. We were the queen's premier guard. We didn't rise to these positions because we were bumbling fools. Not most of the time, anyway. We had training and talents. Natiya's gaze rested on me the longest. I was lead on this mission, responsible for making not just the right decisions, but perfect ones. That meant not only achieving success, but keeping everyone safe too.

"We'll be fine," I promised.

"Fine," Wren agreed, impatiently blowing a dark curl from her forehead. She wanted to be on her way. The anticipation was wearing on all of us.

Synové anxiously twisted one of her long persimmon braids between her fingers. "Perfectly fine. We're—"

"I know," Natiya said, putting her hand up to stop Synové from embarking on a long explanation. "Fine. Just remember, spend some time at the settlement first. Hell's Mouth comes after. Only ask questions. Gather information. Get what supplies you need. Keep a low profile until we get there."

Wren snorted. A low profile was certainly one of my specialties, but not this time. Getting into trouble was my goal for a change.

Galloping broke the tense exchange. "Natiya!"

We turned toward Eben, his horse kicking up soft clods of grass. Synové's eyes brightened like the sun had just winked at her from behind a cloud. He circled around, his eyes fixed only on Natiya. "Griz is grumbling. He wants to leave."

"Coming," she answered, then shook out the square of fabric she was holding. It was a shirt. A very handsome shirt. She touched the soft fabric to her cheek, then laid it over the rock memorial. "Cruvas linen, Jeb," she whispered. "The finest."

We reached the mouth of the valley, and Natiya stopped and looked back one last time. "Remember this," she said. "Twenty thousand. That's how many died here in a single day. Vendans, Morrighese, and Dalbretch. I didn't know them all, but someone did. Someone who would bring a meadow flower to them if they could."

Or a Cruvas linen shirt.

Now I knew why Natiya had brought us here. This was by the queen's order. *Look. Take a good long look and remember the lives lost. Real people that someone loved. Before you go about the task I have given you, see the devastation and remember what they did. What could happen again. Know what is at stake. Dragons eventually wake and crawl from their dark dens.*

I had seen the urgency in the queen's eyes. I had heard it in her voice. This wasn't only about the past. She feared for the future. Something was brewing, and she was desperate to stop it.

I surveyed the valley. From a distance, the bones and wagons blended back into a calm sea of green, hiding the truth.

Nothing was ever quite what it seemed.

Griz's grumbling to break camp was nothing new. He liked to make camp early and leave early, sometimes even when it was still dark, as if it were some sort of victory over the sun. His horse was already packed when we returned, and the campfire doused. He watched impatiently as the rest of us buckled up bedrolls and bags.

An hour's ride from here, we would go our separate ways. Griz was headed to Civica in Morrighan. The queen had news she wanted to share with her brother, the king, and she trusted no one else to deliver it, not even the Valsprey she used for other messages. Valsprey could be attacked by other birds or shot down and messages intercepted, whereas nothing could stop Griz. Except, perhaps, a quick side trip to Terravin, which was probably why he was in such a hurry. Synové liked to tease that he had a sweetheart there. It always made him explode in denial. Griz was old-school Rahtan, but the Rahtan was not the elite, rule-bound ten it once was. There were twenty of us now. A lot of things had changed since the queen came to power, including me.

When I began folding my tent, Griz came and stood over my shoulder and watched. I was the only one who used a tent. It was small. It didn't take up much room. He had balked the first time he had seen me use one on a mission to a southern province. *We don't use tents*, he'd said with utter distaste. I remembered the shame I felt. In the weeks that followed, I turned that humiliation to determination. Weakness made you a target, and I had promised myself, long ago, I would never be a target again. I buried my shame deep beneath carefully crafted armor. Insults couldn't penetrate it.

Griz's brooding stature cast a mountainous shadow over me. "Doesn't my folding technique meet with your approval?" I asked.

He said nothing.

I turned and looked up at him. "What *is* it, Griz?" I snapped.

He rubbed his bristled chin. "There's a lot of open territory between here and Hell's Mouth. Empty, *flat* territory."

"Your point?"

"You'll be . . . *all right?*"

I stood, shoving my folded tent into his belly. He took it from me. "I've got this, Griz. Relax."

His head bobbed in a hesitant nod.

"The real question is," I added, long and drawn out for effect, "do *you?*"

He eyed me, his brow furrowed in a question, and then he scowled, reaching for his side.

I smiled and held his short dagger out to him.

His scowl turned to a reluctant grin, and he replaced the dagger in its empty sheath. His bushy brows lifted, and he shook his head in approval. "Stay downwind, Ten."

Ten, my hard-won nickname. It was his acknowledgment of confidence. I wiggled my fingertips in appreciation.

No one, especially not Griz, would ever forget how I had earned it.

"You mean upwind, don't you?" Eben called.

I glared at Eben. And no one, especially not Eben, would ever forget that my life as Rahtan began the day I spit in the queen's face.

CHAPTER TWO

KAZI

THE QUEEN HAD BEEN WALKING THE NARROW, DIRTY STREETS of the Brightmist quarter when I spotted her. I hadn't planned it, but even events unplanned can whisk us down paths that we never expected to travel, changing our destinies and what defines us. Kazimyrah: orphan, invisible street rat, girl who defied the queen, Rahtan.

I had already been shoved down one path when I was six, and the day I spit in the new queen's face I was sent reeling down another. That moment had not only defined my future, but the queen's unexpected response—a smile—had defined her reign. Her sword hung ready in the scabbard at her side. A breathless crowd had waited to see what would happen. They knew what would have happened *before*. If she were the Komizar, I would have already been lying headless on the ground. Her smile had frightened me more than if she had drawn her sword. I knew at that moment, with certainty, that the old Venda I knew how to navigate was gone, and I would never get it back again. I hated her for it.

When she learned I had no family to summon, she told the guards who had grabbed me to bring me along to Sanctum Hall. I thought I was so very clever back then. Too clever for this young queen. I was eleven years of grit and grovel by then, and impervious to an interloper. I would outwit her just as I did everyone else. It was *my* realm after all. I had all my fingertips—and a reputation to go with them. In the streets of Venda, they called me "Ten" with whispered respect.

A complete set of fingers was legendary for a thief, or an *alleged* thief, because if I had ever been caught with stolen goods, my nickname would have been Nine. The eight quarterlords who dispensed the punishment for stealing had a different name for me. To them, I was the Shadowmaker, because even at high noon, they swore, I could conjure a shadow to swallow me up. A few even rubbed hidden amulets when they saw me coming. But just as useful as the shadows was knowing the strategies of street politics and personalities. I perfected my craft, playing the quarterlords and merchants against one another as if I was a musician and they were crude drums rumbling beneath my hands, making one boast to another that I had never pulled anything over on him, making them all feel so very smart, even as I relieved them of items I could put to better use elsewhere. Their egos were my accomplices. The twisting alleyways, tunnels, and catwalks were where I learned my trade, and my stomach was my relentless taskmaster. But there was another kind of hunger that drove me too, a hunger for answers that were not as easily plucked from the wares of a bloated lord. That was my deeper, darker taskmaster.

But because of the queen, almost overnight I witnessed my world dissolving. I had starved and clawed my way to this position. No one was going to take it from me. The cramped, winding streets of Venda were all I had ever known, and its underworld was all I understood. Its members were a desperate coalition who appreciated the warmth of horse dung in winter, a knife in a burlap sack and the trail of spilled grain it left behind, the scowl of a duped merchant realizing he was short an egg in his basket—or, if I was feeling punitive, the whole chicken who had laid it. I had walked away with bigger and noisier things.

I liked to say I stole only because of hunger, but it wasn't true. Sometimes I stole from the quarterlords just to make their miserable lives more miserable. It made me wonder, if I ever became a quarter-lord, would I cut off fingers to secure my place of power? Because power, I had learned, could be just as seductive as a warm loaf of bread, and the small bit I wielded over them was sometimes all the food I needed.

With new treaties signed among the kingdoms allowing settlement of the Cam Lanteux, one by one those whom I thieved for and with left to go live in wide-open spaces to begin new lives. I became a plucked bird flapping featherless wings, suddenly useless, but moving to a farming settlement in the middle of nowhere was something I would not do. It was something I *could* not do. I learned this when I was nine and had traveled just a short distance beyond the Sanctum walls in search of answers that had eluded me. When I looked back at the disappearing city and saw that I was a mere speck in an empty landscape, I couldn't breathe and the sky swirled in dizzy currents. It hit me like a smothering wave. There was nowhere to hide. No shadows to melt into, no tent flaps to duck behind or stairs to disappear under—there were no beds to hide beneath in case someone came for me. There was no place to escape to at all. The structure of my world was gone—the floor, the ceilings, the walls—and I floated loose, untethered. I barely made it back to the city and never left again.

I knew I would not survive in a world of open sky. Spitting in the queen's face had been my futile stab at saving the existence I had carved out. My life had already been stolen once. I refused to let it happen again, but it happened just the same. Some rising tides cannot be held back, and the new world slipped around my ankles like water at the shore and pulled me into its current.

My first months in Sanctum Hall were turbulent. Why no one strangled me I still wasn't certain. I would have. I stole everything in sight, and out of sight, and hoarded it in a secret passage beneath the East Tower staircase. No one's private chambers were immune. Natiya's favorite scarf, Eben's boots, the cook's wooden spoons, swords, belts, books, armory halberds, the queen's hairbrush. Sometimes I gave them back, sometimes I didn't, bestowing mercies like a capricious queen. Griz roared and chased me through the halls the third time I stole his razor.

Finally, one morning, the queen applauded me as I walked into the Council gallery, saying it was evident I had mastered thieving, but it was time I learned additional skills.

She rose and handed me a sword I had stolen.

I locked eyes with her, wondering how she had gotten hold of it. "I know that passage well too, Kazimyrah. You aren't the only sneak in the Sanctum. Let's put this to better use than rusting in a dark, damp stairwell, shall we?"

For the first time, I didn't resist.

I wanted to learn more. I didn't just want to possess the swords, knives, and maces I had acquired. I wanted to know how to use them too, and use them well.

The landscape was getting flatter now, as if huge hands had anticipated our passing and smoothed out the wrinkles of hills. The same hands must have plucked the hills clean of ruins. It was strange to see nothing. I had never traveled long on any path where some evidence of an earlier world wasn't in view. The Ancients' ruins were plentiful, but here there wasn't so much as a single crumbling wall to cast a measly shadow. Nothing but open sky and unfettered wind pressing on my chest. I forced in deep, full breaths, focusing on a point in the distance, pretending it held a magical shadowed city waiting to greet me.

Griz had stopped and was conferring with Eben and Natiya about meet-up sites. It was time to part ways. When he was finished, he turned and cast a suspicious eye at the vastness ahead of us like he was searching for something. His gaze finally landed on me. I stretched and smiled as if I were enjoying a summer outing. The sun was high and threw sharp shadows across his battle-scarred face. The lines around his eyes deepened.

"One other thing. Watch your backs through this stretch. I lost two years of my life near here because I wasn't looking over my shoulder." He told us how he and an officer from Dalbreck had been pounced upon by labor hunters and dragged off to work in a mining camp.

"We're well armed," Wren reminded him.

"And there's Synové," I added. "You've got this covered, right, Syn?"

She fluttered her eyes like she was seeing a vision, and nodded. "Got it." Then she flicked her fingers in a sweeping motion and whispered happily, "Now go enjoy your time with your sweetheart."

Griz bellowed and threw his hand in the air, waving away the notion. He mumbled a curse as he rode away.

We managed to depart with no further instructions from Natiya. It had all been laid out already, both the ruse and the real. Eben and Natiya were going south to Parsuss, the seat of Eislandia, to speak with the king and make him aware we were intervening on his soil. He was a farmer first, like most Eislandians, and his entire army consisted of a few dozen guards who were also laborers in his fields. He was short on resources to deal with disturbances. Griz had also described the king as meek, more of a handwringer than a neck one, and at a loss for how to control his distant northern territories. The queen was sure he wouldn't object, but she was bound by protocol to inform him. It was a diplomatic precaution in case something went wrong.

But nothing would go wrong. I had promised her.

Even then, the Eislandian king would only be told the ruse of our visit, not our real mission. That was too closely guarded a secret, not to be shared even with the ruling monarch.

I tucked the map away and nudged my horse forward in the direction of Hell's Mouth. Synové looked back, watching Eben and Natiya go their own way, judging how far apart they rode and whether they were exchanging words. Why she had an affection for him I didn't know, but there had been others. Synové was in love with love. As soon as they were out of earshot, she asked, "Do you think they've done it?"

Wren groaned.

I was hoping she meant something else, but I asked anyway. "Who did what?"

"Eben and Natiya. You know, *it*."

"You're the one with the knowing," Wren said. "You should know."

"I have *dreams*," Synové corrected. "And if you both tried a little harder, you'd have dreams too." Her shoulders shivered with distaste. "But that's one dream I don't care to have."

"She does have a point," I said to Wren. "Some things shouldn't be imagined or dreamed."

Wren shrugged. "I've never seen them kiss."

"Or even hold hands," Synové added.

"But neither is exactly the affectionate type either," I reminded them.

Synové's brow squiggled in contemplation, none of us saying what we all knew. Eben and Natiya were devoted to each other—in a very passionate way. I suspected they had done far more than kissing, though it wasn't something I dwelled upon. I really didn't care or want to know. In some ways, I supposed I was like Griz. We were Rahtan first, and there was time for little else. It only created complications. My few brief dalliances with soldiers I had pledged with only led to distractions that I decided I didn't need—the risky kind, ones that stirred a longing in me and made me think about a future that couldn't be counted on.

We rode along, with Synové doing most of the talking, as she always did, filling the hours with multiple observations, whether it was the waving grass brushing our horses' fetlocks or the salty leek soup her aunt used to make. I knew at least part of the reason she did it was to distract me from a flat, empty world that sometimes bobbed and weaved and threatened to fold me into its open mouth. Sometimes her chatter worked. Sometimes I distracted myself in other ways.

Wren suddenly put her hand out as warning and signaled us to stop. "Riders. Third bell," she said. The sharp edge of her *ziethe* sliced the air as she drew and spun it, ready. Synové was already nocking an arrow.

In the distance, a dark cloud skimmed the plain, growing larger as it sped toward us. I drew my sword, but then suddenly the dark cloud veered upward, into the sky. It flew close over our heads, a writhing antelope in its claws. The wind from the creature's wings lifted our hair, and we all instinctively ducked. The horses reared. In a split second, the creature was already gone.

"*Jabavé!*" Wren growled as we worked to calm our horses. "What the hell was that?"

Griz had neglected to warn us about this. I had heard of these creatures, a rumor really, but thought they were only in the far north country above Infernaterr. Apparently not today.

"Racaa," Synové answered. "One of the birds that eat Valsprey. I don't think they eat humans."

"*Think?*" Wren yelled. Her brown cheeks glowed with fury. "You're not sure? How much different could we taste than an antelope?"

I slid my sword back into its scabbard. "Different enough, we can hope."

Wren recomposed herself, putting her *ziethe* away. She wore two of them, one on each hip, and kept them razor sharp. She was more than capable of taking on two-legged attackers, but a winged attack required a moment of reassessment. I saw the calculations spinning in her mind. "I could have taken it down."

No doubt. Wren had the tenacity of a cornered badger.

The demons that drove her were as demanding as mine, and she had honed her skills to a sharp, unforgiving edge. She had watched her family slaughtered in Blackstone Square when her clan made the deadly mistake of cheering for a stolen princess. The same with Synové, and though Syn played the cheerful innocent, there was a lethal undercurrent that ran through her. She had killed more raiders than Wren and I put together. Seven by last count.

With her arrow back in its quiver, Synové resumed her chatter. At least for the rest of our ride she had something else to talk about. Racaa were a whole new diversion.

But the racaa's shadow sent my thoughts tumbling in another direction. By this time next week, it would be us swooping down on Hell's Mouth, casting our own shadow, and if all went well, within a short time I would be departing with something far more vital than an antelope in my claws.

Six years ago a war was waged, the bloodiest the continent had ever seen. Thousands died, but only a handful of men were its architects. One of those men was still alive, and some thought he was the worst—the Watch Captain of the citadelle in Morrighan. He betrayed the very kingdom he had sworn to protect, and slowly infiltrated the fortress with enemy soldiers in order to weaken Morrighan and help it to fall. Some soldiers who had been under his command had simply disappeared, maybe because they became suspicious. Their bodies were never found. His crimes were numerous. Among them, helping to poison the king and murder the crown prince and thirty-two of his comrades. The Watch Captain had been the most hunted fugitive on the continent ever since.

He had twice escaped the kingdoms' clutches, and then he seemed to have vanished completely. No one had seen him in five years, but now a chance sighting and a merchant eager to share information had become a hopeful lead. *He gave over his own kingdom*, the queen had told me, *and the lives of thousands to feed his greed for more. Hungry dragons may sleep for years, but they do not change their eating habits. He must be found. The dead demand justice, as do the living.*

Even before I visited the valley of dead, I already knew the cost of lurking dragons, ones who crept through the night, crashing into a world and devouring whatever pleased them. The queen's fugitive would pay because he stole dreams and lives without ever looking back, not caring about the destruction he left in his wake. Some dragons might slip away forever, but if Captain Illarion, who betrayed his countrymen and brought about the death of thousands, was there, Tor's Watch could not hide him. I would steal him away, and he would pay—before his hunger killed more.

I need you, Kazimyrah. I believe in you. The queen's belief in me had meant everything.

It was a job I was uniquely qualified for, and this mission was an undeserved chance to redeem myself. A year ago, I'd made a mistake that almost cost me my life and put a blemish on the near perfect record of the queen's premier guard. *Rahtan* meant "never fail," but I had failed dismally. Hardly a day passed that I didn't think of it.

When I had mistaken an ambassador from Reux Lau for someone

else, it had unleashed something wild and feral in me that I didn't know was there—or maybe it was a wounded animal I had been secretly feeding for a long time. My hands and legs were not my own, and they propelled me forward. I hadn't intended to stab him, at least not immediately, but he lunged unexpectedly. He survived my attack. Luckily my knife hadn't slashed deeply. His wound only required a few stitches. Our whole crew was arrested and thrown in prison. As soon as it was determined I acted alone, they were released—but I sat in a prison cell in a southern province for two months. It took the queen herself to smooth it over and obtain my release.

Those months gave me a lot of time to think. In a split second, I had abandoned my control and patience—the very things I took pride in and that had saved my skin for years. And maybe worse, the mistake made me question my own memory. Maybe I didn't remember his face anymore. Maybe it was gone like so many other memories that had faded, and that possibility terrified me even more. If I didn't remember, he could be anywhere and anyone.

Once we returned, it was Eben who told the queen about my past. I didn't know how he even knew. I had never told anyone, and no one really cared about where a street rat came from. There were too many of us.

The queen had called me into her private chamber. "Why didn't you tell me about your mother, Kazimyrah?"

My heart beat madly, and a sick, salty taste crawled up my throat. I forced it down and locked my knees, afraid they might buckle.

"There's nothing to tell. My mother is dead."

"Are you certain she's dead?"

In my heart I was certain, and I prayed to the gods every day that she was.

"If the gods are merciful."

The queen asked if we might talk about it. I knew she was only trying to help me, and I did owe her a fuller explanation after all she had done for me, but this was a confused knot of memory and anger I hadn't untangled myself yet. I excused myself without answering her.

When I left her chamber, I cornered Eben in the stairwell and lashed out. "Stay out of my business, Eben! Do you hear me? Stay out!"

"You mean stay out of your past. There's nothing to be ashamed of, Kazi. You were six years old. It's not your fault that your—"

"Shut up, Eben! Don't ever bring up my mother again or I'll slit your throat and it will happen so quickly and quietly, you won't even know you're dead."

His arm shot out, and he blocked my way so I couldn't pass. "You need to confront your demons, Kazi."

I lunged at him, but I was out of control and he wasn't. He expected my attack and whirled me around, pinning me to his chest, squeezing me so tightly I couldn't breathe even as I railed against him.

"I *understand*, Kazi. Believe me, I understand what you feel," he had whispered in my ear.

I raged. I screamed. No one could understand. Especially not Eben. I hadn't yet come to grips with the memories he stirred. He couldn't know that every time I looked at his stringy black mop of hair hanging over his eyes, or his pale, bloodless skin, or his dark, menacing gaze, all I saw was the Previzi driver who had crept into my hovel in the middle of the night, holding a lantern in the darkness asking, *Where is the brat?* All I saw was myself cowering in a pool of my own waste, too afraid to move. I was not afraid anymore.

"You've been given a second chance, Kazi. Don't throw it away. The queen stuck her neck out for you. She can only do that so many times. You're not powerless anymore. You can make other things right."

He held me tight until there was no struggle left in me. I was weak when I finally pulled free, still angry, and I skulked away to hide in a dark passage of the Sanctum where no one could find me.

I learned later from Natiya that maybe Eben did understand. He was five when he witnessed an ax being planted in his mother's chest and he watched while his father was burned alive. His family had tried to settle in the Cam Lanteux before there were treaties to protect them. He was too young to identify who did it or even to know what kingdom they were from. Finding justice was impossible for him, but his parents' deaths remained etched in his memory. As I got to know Eben better and worked with him more, I no longer saw the Previzi driver when I looked at him. I just saw Eben along with his own quirks and habits—and someone who had his own scarred past.

Make other things right.

It was a turning point for me, yet another new start. More than anything I wanted to prove my loyalties to someone who had not only given me a second chance, but had also given all of Venda a second chance. The queen.

There was one thing I could never make right.

But maybe there were other things that I could.

Gather close, my brothers and sisters.
We have touched the stars,
And the dust of possibility is ours.
But the work is never over.
Time circles. Repeats.
We must ever be watchful.
Though the Dragon rests for now,
He will wake again
And roam the earth,
His belly ripe with hunger.
And so shall it be,
For evermore.

—The Song of Jezelia

CHAPTER THREE

JASE BALLENGER

AS FAR AS YOU CAN SEE, THIS LAND IS OURS. NEVER FORGET THAT. It was my father's and his father's before that. This is Ballenger territory and always has been, all the way back to the Ancients. We are the first family, and every bird that flies overhead, every breath that is taken, every drop of water that falls, it all belongs to us. We make the laws here. We own whatever you can see. Never let one handful of soil slip through your fingers, or you will lose it all.

I placed my father's hand at his side. His skin was cold, his fingers stiff. He'd been dead for hours. It seemed impossible. Only four days ago, he'd been healthy and strong, and then he gripped his chest as he got up on his horse and collapsed. The seer said an enemy had cast a spell. The healer said it was his heart and nothing could be done. Whichever it was, in a matter of days, he was gone.

A dozen empty chairs still circled his bed, the vigil ended. The sounds of long good-byes had turned to silent disbelief. I pushed back my chair and stepped out to the balcony, drawing in a deep breath. The hills reached in hazy scallops to the horizon. *Not one handful*, I had promised him.

The others waited for me to emerge from the room wearing his ring. Now *my* ring. The weight of his last words flowed through me, as strong and powerful as Ballenger blood. I surveyed the endless landscape that was ours. I knew every hill, every canyon, every bluff and river. *As far as you can see.* It all looked different now. I backed away from the balcony. The challenges would come soon. They always did when a Ballenger died, as if one less in our numbers would topple us. News would reach the multiple leagues scattered beyond our borders. It was a bad time for him to die. First harvests were rolling in, the Previzi were demanding a greater take of their loads, and Fertig had asked for my sister's hand in marriage. She was still deciding. I didn't like Fertig, but I loved my sister. I shook my head and pushed away from the rail. *Patrei.* It was up to me now. I'd keep my vow. The family would stand strong, as we always had.

I pulled my knife from its sheath and returned to my father's bed. I cut the ring from his swollen finger, slipped it on to my own, and walked out to a hallway full of waiting faces.

They looked at my hand, traces of my father's blood on the ring. It was done.

A rumble of solemn acknowledgement sounded.

"Come on," I said. "It's time to get drunk."

Our steps echoed through the main hall with singular purpose as more than a dozen of us headed toward the door. My mother stepped out from the west antechamber and asked me where I was going.

"Tavern. Before the news is everywhere."

She slapped me on the side of the head. "The news was out four days ago, fool. The vultures sniff death before it arrives and circle just as quickly. They'll be picking at our bones by next week. Now go! Alms at the temple *first*. Then you can go drink yourself blind. And keep your *straza* at your sides. These are uncertain times!" She shot a warning glower at my brothers too, and they dutifully nodded. Her gaze turned back at me, still iron, thorns, and fire, *clear*, but I knew behind them a wall had been painfully built. Even when my brother and sister died, she didn't cry, but channeled her tears into a new cistern for the temple instead. She looked down at the ring on my finger. Her head bobbed slightly. I knew it unsettled her to see it on my hand after twenty-five years of seeing it on my father's. Together, they had strengthened the Ballenger Dynasty. They had eleven children together, nine of us still living, plus an adopted son, a promise that their world would only grow stronger. That is what she focused on, instead of what she had lost prematurely. She lifted my hand to her lips, kissed the ring, then pushed me out the door.

As we walked down the porch steps, Titus whispered under his breath, "Alms first, fool!" I shoved him with my shoulder, and the others laughed as he tumbled down the steps. They were ready for a night of trouble. A night of forgetting. Watching someone die, someone who was as full of life as my father, who should have had years ahead of him, was a reminder that death looked over all our shoulders.

My eldest brother, Gunner, sidled close as we walked to our waiting horses. "Paxton will come."

I nodded. "But he'll take his time."

"He's afraid of you."

"Not afraid enough."

Mason clapped me on the back. "Hell with Paxton. He won't come until the entombment, if he comes at all. For now, we just need to get you snot drunk, *Patrei*."

I was ready. I needed this as much as Mason and everyone else. I needed it to be over with and all of us moving on. As weak as my father had been before he died, he managed to say a lot in his last breaths. It was my duty to hear every word and vow my allegiance even if he'd said it all before—and he had. He'd been telling me my whole life. It was tattooed inside my gut as much as the Ballenger seal was tattooed across my shoulder. The family dynasty—those both blood and embraced—was safe. Still, his final labored instructions dug through me. He hadn't been prepared to let go of the reins this soon. *The Ballengers bow to no one. Make her come. The others will notice.* That part might prove a little harder.

The other vultures who came circling, hoping to take over our territory, were what I needed to crush first, Paxton foremost among them. It didn't matter that he was my cousin—he was still the misbegotten progeny of my long-ago uncle who had betrayed his own family. Paxton controlled the smaller territory of Ráj Nivad in the south, but it wasn't enough for him. Like the rest of his bloodline, he was consumed by jealousies and greed. Still, he *was* blood and would come to pay honor to my father—and to calculate our strength. Ráj Nivad was a four-day ride from here. He hadn't heard anything yet, and if he had, it would take him just as long to get here. I had time to prepare.

Our *straza* shouted to the tower, and they in turned called down to the gate guards, clearing our passage. The heavy metal gates creaked open, and we rode through. I felt the eyes on me, on my hand. *Patrei.*

Hell's Mouth sat in the valley just below Tor's Watch, only parts of it visible through the canopy of tembris trees that circled it like a crown. I had told my father once that I was going to climb to the top of every one. I was eight years old and didn't realize how far they reached into the heavens, even after my father told me the top of the tembris was the realm of the gods, not men. I didn't make it far, certainly not to the top. No one ever had. And as high as the trees stretched, the roots reached to the foundations of the earth. They were the only thing more rooted in this land than the Ballengers.

Once we were at the base of the hill, Gunner shouted and took off ahead of the pack. The rest of us followed, the trampling of hooves pounding in our bones. We liked to make our arrivals into town well announced.

The bell chimed softly, as delicate as crystal goblets meeting in a toast. The ring echoed up through the stone arches of the temple unchallenged. As disorderly and loudly as we pounded into town, the family respected the sanctity of the temple even if cards, red-eye, and barrels of ale swam in our visions. Five more bells and we would be done. Gunner, Priya, and Titus knelt on one side of me, Jalaine, Samuel, Aram, and Mason on the other. We took up the whole front row. Our *straza*—Drake, Tiago, and Charus—knelt behind us. The priest spoke in the old tongue, stirring the ashes with calf's blood, then placed a wet, ashy fingertip on each of our foreheads. Our offerings were taken by the sober-faced alms bearers into the coffers, deemed acceptable by the gods. More than acceptable, I would guess. It was enough to fund another healer for the infirmary. Three more bells. Two.

One. We stood, accepting the priest's blessing, and walked solemnly in a single file out of the dark hall. Chiseled saints stood on lofty pillars looking down upon us, and the cantillating benediction of the priestess floated after us like a protective ghost.

Outside, Titus waited until he was at the bottom of the steps before he pealed out a shrill whistle—the call to the tavern. Drinks were on the new *Patrei*. Decorum in the face of death brought emotion too near the surface for Titus. Maybe for all of us.

I felt a tug on my coat. The seer was huddled in the shadow of a pillar, her hood covering her face. I dropped some coins in her basket.

"What news have you?" I asked.

She pulled on my coat until I knelt to eye level with her. Her eyes were tight azure stones, and appeared to float, disembodied, in the black shadow of her hood. Her gaze latched on to mine, her head tipping to the side like she was slipping deep behind my eyes. "*Patrei*," she whispered.

"You heard."

She shook her head. "Not from without. Within. Your soul tells me. From without . . . I hear other things."

"Such as?"

She leaned close, her voice hushed as if she feared someone else would hear. "The wind whispers they are coming, *Patrei*. They are coming for you."

She took my hand in her gnarled fingers and kissed my ring. "Gods watch over you."

I gently pulled loose and stood, still looking down at her. "And over you."

Her news wasn't exactly news, but I didn't begrudge the coins I had tossed her way. Everyone knew we would face challenges.

I hadn't gotten to the bottom step when Lothar and Rancell, two of our overseers, dragged someone over and threw him to his knees in front of me. I recognized him, Hagur from the livestock auction.

"Skimming," Lothar said. "Just as you suspected."

I stared at him. There was no denial in his eyes, only fear. I drew my knife.

"Not in front of the temple," he pleaded, tears flowing down his cheeks. "I beg you, *Patrei*. Don't shame me before the gods."

He grabbed my legs, bowing his head and sobbing.

"You're already shamed. Did you think we wouldn't find out?"

He didn't answer, only cried for mercy, hiding his face in my boots. I shoved him away, and his gaze froze onto mine.

"No one cheats the family."

He nodded furiously.

"But the gods showed mercy to us," I said. "*Once*. And that's the Ballenger way. We do the same." I sheathed my knife. "Stand, brother. If you live in Hell's Mouth, you are part of our family." I held out my hand. He looked at me as if it were a trick, too afraid to move. I stepped forward, pulled him to his feet, and embraced him. "*Once*," I whispered into his ear. "Remember that. For the next year, you will pay double the tithe."

He pulled away, nodding, thanking me, stumbling over his steps as he backed up, until he finally turned and ran. He would not cheat us again. He would remember he was family, and one did not betray one's own.

At least, that was the way it was supposed to work.

I thought about Paxton and the seer's words again. *They are coming for you.*

Paxton was a nuisance, a bloodsucking leech who had developed a taste for wine. We would handle him, just like we handled everything else.

The scavengers have fled, our supplies now theirs.

Gone? he asks.

I nod.

He lies dying in my arms, already dust and ash and a ghost of greatness.

He presses the map into my hand.

This is the true treasure. Get them there. It's up to you now. Protect them.

He promises there is food. Safety. He has promised this since the first stars fell. I do not know what safety is anymore. It is from a time before I was born. He squeezes my hand with the last of his strength.

Hold on to it, no matter what you have to do. Never give it up. Not this time.

Yes, I answer because I want him to believe in his last moments that all his effort and sacrifice are not wasted. His quest will save us.

Take my finger, he says. *It's your only way in.*

He pulls a razor from his vest and holds it out to me. I shake my head. I can't do this to my own grandfather.

Now, he orders. *You will have to do worse things to survive.*

Sometimes you must kill. This, he says, looking at his hand, *this is nothing.*

How can I disobey? He is the chief commander of everything. I look at those surrounding us, sunken eyes, faces streaked with dirt and fear. I barely know most of them.

He shoves the razor into my hand.

> *Out of many, you are one now. You are family. The Ballenger Family. Shield one another. Survive. You are the surviving remnant that Tor's Watch was built for.*

I am only fourteen and all the rest are younger. How can we be strong enough to withstand the scavengers, the winds, the hunger? How can we do this alone?

Now, he says again.

And I do as he orders.

He makes no sound.

Only smiles as he closes his eyes and takes his last breath.

And I take my first breath as leader of a remnant, charged by my grandfather and commander to hold on to hope.

I am not sure I can.

—*Greyson Ballenger, 14*

CHAPTER FOUR

KAZI

LIVESTOCK PENS WERE BROKEN AND SCATTERED LIKE TINDER, and the stink of scorched grass burned our lungs. Rage blazed beneath my skin as I took in the destruction. Wren and Synové rumbled with fury. Our task suddenly fractured and multiplied like an image in a shattered mirror. In the end, the anger would serve us. We all knew it. Our sham excuse for coming here—investigating treaty violations—had suddenly grown, full-bodied, sharp, all teeth, claws, and venom.

The settlement consisted of four homes, a longhouse, a barn, and multiple sheds. They had all suffered damage. The barn was completely destroyed. We spotted a stooped man, furiously hoeing a garden, seemingly oblivious to the carnage around him. When he saw us coming, he raised his hoe as a weapon, then lowered it when he recognized Wren's cloak made with the patched fabrics of the Meurasi clan. My leather waistcoat was embossed with the revered thannis found on the Vendan shield, and Synové's horse had the tasseled nose band of the clans who lived in the eastern fens. All distinctly Vendan if you knew what you were looking for.

"Who did this?" I asked when we reached him, though I already knew.

He straightened, pushing on his bowed back. His face was lined with years in the sun, his cheekbones tired hills in a sagging landscape. Partial faces peeked around doors and between cracked shutters in the dwellings behind him, more settlers too afraid to come out. His name was Caemus, and he explained that the marauders had come in the middle of the night. It was dark and they couldn't see their faces, but he knew it was the Ballengers. They had come just a week earlier with a warning to the settlers to keep their shorthorns off their land. They took one as payment.

Wren looked around. "Their land? Out here? In the middle of the Cam Lanteux?"

"It's all theirs," he answered. "As far as they can see, according to them. Every blade of grass belongs to them."

Synové's knuckles whitened with rage.

"Where's your livestock?" I asked.

"Gone. They took the rest. I guess as payment for the air we breathe."

I noticed there were no horses either. "And the Ravians that Morrighan gifted you?"

"Everything's gone except for one old dray horse for our wagon. A few of the others went into town to buy more supplies. They won't be able to get much. Vendans pay a premium."

His jaw was set hard, his fingers tight around the hoe. Vendans didn't scare off easily, but he said he was afraid some might be too fearful to return to the settlement.

"You won't be paying a premium to anyone, nor payment for the air you breathe," I said. I took a last look at the damage. "It may take a while, but reparations will be made to you."

"We don't want more trouble from—"

"The other settlers will return, and it is you who will receive payment."

He looked at me, doubtful. "You don't know the Ballengers."

"True," I answered. "But neither do they know us."

And they were about to.

Hell's Mouth was twenty miles away. It was a remote, mysterious city, far from the seat of Eislandia, that few knew anything about, other than it was a growing trading center. Until a few months ago, I had never heard its name. But it was supposedly a large enough town that it offered the opportunity for buying and trading for the settlement. I was tired and irritable as we rode. I hadn't slept well last night, even in my tent. This miserable flat wilderness pecked at me like a relentless sour bird, and it seemed impossible that any sizable town existed way out here. It felt like I hadn't taken a deep breath in days. Synové chattered nonstop, and I snapped at her like a shrill crow when she brought up the racaa again.

"I'm sorry," I said after a long silence. "I shouldn't have jumped on you."

"I'm afraid I've run out of fresh subjects," Synové answered.

I was truly wretched. And she was right—*she knew*. I didn't like the silence, and she was only trying to fill it for me. I was used to the noise of the city, the constant hum, the bang, the wail, the sound of people and animals, the tinny patter of rain on roofs and the slosh of wagons in muddy puddles, the chant of street peddlers trying to entice someone to buy a pigeon, an amulet, or cup of steaming thannis. I longed to hear the roar of the river, the jingle of soldiers as they marched down a lane, the heave of a hundred men pulling the great bridge into place, the sounds of remembrance bones clacking as they swung from a thousand belts, all of it teeming together like something alive and whole on its own.

All those things helped me to hide. They were my armor. The wind-swept silence left me naked. "Please," I said, "tell me about how they give birth again."

"Eggs, Kazi," Wren interrupted. "You weren't listening."

Synové cleared her throat, her signal for us to be quiet. "I'll tell you a story instead."

Wren and I both raised our brows, dubious, but still, I was grateful.

It was one she had told many times before, but she often added an unexpected twist to make us laugh. She told the story of the devastation, the way the Fenlanders told it. She reverted to her thick, easy drawl. The angel Aster played large in this version. The gods had become lazy, not tending to the world as they should, and the Ancients had elevated them-selves to godly positions, soaring among the heavens, ravenous in power but weak in wisdom, crushing all in their path, and so Aster, who was guardian of the heavens, swept her hand through the galaxy, gathered a fistful of stars, and threw them to earth to destroy the wickedness that dwelled there. But there was a Remnant on the earth she found to be pure of heart, and to them she showed mercy, leading them away from the devastation to a place of safety behind the gates of Venda. "And to the Fenlanders, of course, supreme over all, she gave a fat roasted pig with a glittering star in its mouth." Every time she told the story, Aster always bestowed the Fenlanders with a different gift—usually a fat, juicy one—depending on how hungry Synové was at the moment.

Wren took a turn too, telling the story with the details from her own clan. There were no roasted pigs in her version, but plenty of sharp blades. I had no version of my own, no clan that I belonged to—even among Vendans I was anchorless—but one thing was constant in all the versions I heard, the gods and angels destroyed the world when men aspired to be gods and mercy had fled their hearts.

No one was spared except for a small Remnant who found favor, and that was how all the kingdoms began, but as the queen often warned, *The work is never over. Time circles. Repeats. We must ever be watchful.*

Now it seemed, we needed to be watching the Ballengers.

Wren had the eyes of a hawk and called out first. "There it is!"

Hills rippled the plain in the distance, and scattered ruins finally appeared, flecking the landscape with rich, lush shadows, but far beyond them, tucked at the foot of a misty lavender mountain, a dark blotch grew larger. It took form and color as we got closer and sprawled like a giant beast lying at the feet of its brooding master. What kind of beast was Hell's Mouth, or, maybe more important, who was its master? An oval of deep green appeared to hover over it all like a foreboding spiked tiara. Trees? Strange, unearthly trees. Nothing like I had ever seen before.

Synové sucked in a breath. "*That* is Hell's Mouth?"

My pulse quickened, and I stepped up in my stirrups. Mije snorted, ready to break into a gallop. *Not yet, boy. Not yet.*

Glimpses of ancient streets began to appear, like the backs of subterranean snakes surfacing as if they traveled just below us.

"By the gods," Wren said. "It's as big as Sanctum City."

I took a deep relaxed breath and sat back in my saddle. This was going to be easy.

The city was just inside the border of Eislandia, a Lesser Kingdom shaped like a large falling tear, and Hell's Mouth was at its apex, distant and remote from the rest of the kingdom. Just outside the border, the Ballenger stronghold overlooked it all, but their fortress was impenetrable according to a report the queen had received. We would see.

Unlike the Sanctum in Venda, there were no walls around this city, no Great River to hold it prisoner. It ambled with the boldness of a warlord, nothing daring to hold it back. Its homes and hamlets reached out with strong crooked fingers, and the whole city seemed to be hemmed in only by the circle of trees that towered over it like a mystical wreath. There were multiple points of entry, and far off we could see many other travelers making their way into the city too. While still a good distance away, Wren picked out a suitable abandoned ruin as we passed, and she and Synové stowed some packs there before we continued on.

Though many travelers entered the city, when we rode in we drew stares. It could be they saw the Vendan crest on our tack, or maybe they saw something in our faces. We weren't there to buy or sell goods. We weren't there for any reason they perceived as good. They were right.

Wren hissed. Shook her head. Grumbled. "I don't like it." She pulled out her *ziethe*, spun it, and shoved it back in its scabbard, the hilt snapping against the leather.

Synové and I exchanged a glance. We knew this was coming. It was Wren's ritual, as she recalculated every risk in the minutes before we actually took the risks. "You sure? They're a powerful family. If they lock you up—"

"Yes," I answered before she could propose something else. It was the only way this was going to work. "Like I told Griz," I said, our gazes meeting, "I've got this. So do you."

She nodded. "Blink last."

"Always," I confirmed.

There were all kinds of unwritten laws that we lived by on the streets.

Wren knew that was one of mine. Blinking last wasn't just an occupational tip to reel in a target, it was a survival aspiration.

We proceeded forward, gawking at the strange city, taking turns pointing out oddities, like the web of rambling structures looming overhead where the thick, muscled arms of tree branches held them securely aloft, rope suspension bridges connecting them to more structures—homes, shops, even a large, sprawling inn that ascended into the trees—shadows upon shadows and endless paths to follow. The architecture of the city was a mix of old and new, ruins repurposed into homes and shops. The pitted ancient stones of another time were joined and fitted with newly polished marble. In some places, the giant trees were a staunch troop of sentries huddled close together, their trunks as wide as two wagons, and only dappled light danced through their soaring canopies. In the center of town, the sentries took a step back, leaving an opening for the sun to shine unobstructed into Hell's Mouth. It shone now on a white marble building ahead, giving it an ethereal glow.

A temple.

It was the focal point of a wide, circular plaza that was thick with people, bustle, noise, and—and everything I loved. I paused, taking it all in, and then for a handful of seconds I held my breath. It was a fruitless habit I couldn't shake, and I scanned the crowd for a face that haunted me but was never there. I sighed with both relief and disappointment when I didn't see it. As we circled around, I noticed that the avenues were laid out like the spokes of a wheel with the plaza at its center. We found a livery to feed and water our horses, and while Wren and Synové got our horses settled in stalls, I asked the stable master for directions to the magistrate's office.

"Right here. You're looking at him."

The magistrates I had met in Reux Lau didn't muck stables on the side. "You also enforce the law here?"

"I keep watch. There's ten of us." His shoulders pulled back and he squinted one eye. "What's this all about?"

I told him who I was, here by the authority of the King of Eislandia, which was only a slight stretch of the truth, and also by the Queen of Venda to investigate treaty violations.

He didn't try to disguise his slow perusal of me from my boots to the sword and knives belted at my side. His gaze lingered there. "Don't know anything about violations."

Sure you don't.

I moved closer and he eased back a step. Apparently even he knew of Rahtan. "As an enforcer of the law for your king, I instruct you to tell us anything you know."

He shook his head and shrugged. Nothing. I was ready to twist the little weasel into a braided loaf, but it was too soon for that. I had bigger game to hunt. "There are Vendans here in town buying supplies. Have you seen them?"

He seemed relieved to see me on my way. "Sure," he answered, now eager to talk again. "Saw them headed that way this morning." He pointed down an avenue across the plaza. "There's a mercantile there—"

"Where Vendans have the privilege of paying double?"

He shrugged his indifference. "Don't know anything about that either, but I'll tell you, folks here are loyal, and the Ballengers own this town. They always have."

"Interesting," I said. "Are you aware that Hell's Mouth is part of Eislandia, and not the Ballenger dynasty?"

A smirk lifted the corner of his mouth. "Hard to tell the difference sometimes. Half those here have some relation to them, and the other half are in debt to them."

"Really. And which are *you*, Magistrate?"

His taciturn demeanor bloomed again, and he only grinned. I turned and left but was only a few steps away when he called after me. "Just a friendly warning. Be careful whose toes you go stepping on."

Friendly.

I gathered up Wren and Synové, and we asked a few questions as we made our way to the mercantile. The responses we garnered were similar to the magistrate's. They knew nothing. I wasn't sure if it was because we were Rahtan or if they were too afraid to speak about the Ballengers to any form of law.

Outside the mercantile, a striped awning stretched over barrels and crates brimming with food—grains, dried beans, salted meats, pickled hocks, colorful fruits and vegetables—all displayed in neat rows. The abundance surprised me, but it always did when I traveled to other cities. Inside, the store appeared to sell more food and other wares. Through the windows, I viewed shovels, bolts of fabric, and a wall full of tinctures. A dray pulled by an old draft horse was parked nearby, and I wondered if it belonged to the Vendan settlers. As we approached, I watched a clerk chase off children who were playing near stacked crates of oranges. My tongue prickled. *Bright, luscious oranges.* I had tasted only one in my whole life—when I stole into the home of a quarterlord. I was searching for something else but found it sitting on the middle of his table like a revered ornament. I sniffed it, then joyously peeled it, scattering the dimpled skin across the tabletop so the quarterlord would see that his treasure was appreciated. With every tear of the peel, I breathed in the heavenly spray of its scent. As soon as it passed my lips, I knew it was divinely inspired and had to be the first food the gods ever created.

My cheeks ached with the memory of golden wedges bursting in my mouth. Even the way it was fashioned had fascinated me, impossibly organized into neat little half-moons packaged in gilded perfection. It was the first and last time I had had one. Oranges rarely made their way to Venda on Previzi wagons, and when they did they were a luxury reserved only for quarterlords or governors—usually as a gift from the Komizar—like the other rarities that only he could conjure. I understood the children's lust for the mysterious fruit.

A woman leaving the mercantile called to the children, and they ran to the dray, jumping into the back, taking the goods she carried from her arms. Once the goods were stacked, their eyes turned longingly back to the oranges.

Wren called to the woman in Vendan, and her eyes immediately widened, surprised to hear her own tongue. Here they spoke Landese, which was essentially identical to Morrighese, the predominant language of the continent.

Once we were close, Synové asked, "Are you from the settlement?"

The woman glanced nervously around her. "Yes," she said quietly. "I'm afraid we had some trouble. Some of our provisions in an outbuilding were burned, so we had to come to the city for more."

She told us that this had used up the last of their money. I heard the fear in her voice. Her group had come here to avoid the starving seasons of Venda where life could not be scraped out on the devastated and fallow land. A colossal Vendan army had been disbanded in hopes of something better, but the something better was turning into something else for them, a harshness of a new kind.

I explained that we were Rahtan sent by the queen to check on their welfare and asked about the raiders. Her story was the same as Caemus's—it was dark so they couldn't see—but the Ballengers had demanded payment. "Where are the others you came to town with?" I asked.

She pointed down the street and said they were gathering what they needed from various shops and they all planned to leave as soon as possible. When I asked if the mercantile had charged her double, she looked down, afraid to answer, saying softly, "I don't know."

I eyed an empty burlap sack in the back of the dray. "May I borrow that?" Her eyes pinched with worry but she nodded.

I shoved it into Wren's hands and signaled for her to follow me. She immediately knew why and rolled her eyes. *"Now?"*

"Oh, yes. Now," I answered, and walked over to the clerk who supervised the merchandise under the awning. I pointed at the crate of oranges.

"How much?" I asked.

His response wasn't quick, instead inventing an answer just for me. He had seen me talking to the Vendan woman and by now had probably guessed I was Vendan too.

"Five gralos each."

Five. Even as a foreigner in these parts, I knew that was a fortune. "Really," I replied, as if contemplating the price, then I grabbed one and tossed it into the air. It landed with a firm slap back into my hand. The clerk's brows pulled down in a deep V and his mouth opened, ready to bark at me, but then I grabbed another and another and still another, juggling them in the air, and the clerk forgot what he was going to say. His mouth hung agape, his eyes twirling along with the spinning oranges.

I smiled. I laughed. Even as a knife slid through me, the same knife that had slid through me a hundred times, and the more I smiled, the more I bled, the faster the oranges twirled, the hotter my anger burned, but I laughed and chattered as I had so many times because that was part of the trick. *Make them believe. Smile, Kazi. It is just an innocent game.*

It was a trick I reserved for the most suspicious quarterlords, those who had no mercy or compassion for any of the street rats like me. Even though the prize was only a half-rotten turnip or a square of hard cheese to fill an empty belly, it was worth the risk of a lost finger. Each victory would get me through another day, and that was another trick of sur-viving in Venda. Make it one more day. Die tomorrow was another one of my rules. How many times had I hypnotized merchants this way? Smiling to deceive them, spinning to rob them, drawing crowds to their stands to make them forget, using near misses, calls to those in the crowd, and tossing the same fruit into their arms to distract them so they never noticed the ones that disappeared.

The clerk was sufficiently mesmerized as I continued to grab orange after orange, juggling, tossing, and redistributing them into a tall neat stack in another crate, even as I discussed the wonder of oranges and how fine his were, the best I had ever seen. One thrown to a crate, one dropped into the waiting burlap sack at Wren's feet. Once four were safely ensconced in the bag, I juggled the last piece of fruit onto the pile, making a perfect pyramid. The clerk laughed and admired the stack in wonder, never noticing a single missing orb.

"Your oranges are lovely, but I'm afraid too steep for my pocket." It didn't pass his notice that several townspeople had wandered over to watch the show and now were perusing his goods. He handed me one of the smaller, scarred oranges. "With my compliments."

I thanked him and returned to the dray, Wren following close behind with the sack.

Even the children were not aware of what was inside. I sniffed the scarred orange, inhaling its perfume, then dropped it in with the others, tucking the sack between other supplies for them to discover later. We continued down the street to talk with more Vendans we saw leaving the apothecary. That was when I spotted trouble coming.

A throng of young men, full of swagger—and a night of carousing, judging by their disheveled appearance—walked toward us. The one in the middle hadn't even bothered to button his shirt, and his chest was half exposed. He was tall, his shoulders wide, and he walked like he owned the street. His dark-blond hair hung in disarray over his eyes, but even from a distance it was easy to see they were bloodshot with drink. I looked away, exchanging knowing glances with Synové and Wren, and we moved on. Karsen Ballenger, patriarch of the lawless family, was my ticket into Tor's Watch and the center of our target. This sloppy group was not the kind of trouble I could be bothered with.

CHAPTER FIVE

JASE

I FELT A SHOVE AND MY FACE SLAMMED INTO THE FLOOR.

"Wake up."

I rolled over and saw the bench I had fallen from and Mason looming over me. I squinted against the bright light streaming in through the tavern windows and reached up to feel my skull, certain a cleaver was lodged in it.

I cursed Mason and reached for a hand up, then noticed my bare arm.

"Where's my shirt?"

"Anyone's guess," Mason answered as he hoisted me up. He looked as bad as I felt.

I'd bought drinks for half the city last night, and I was certain just as many had bought them for me. There were no grand coronations when a new *Patrei* was named, though at the moment it seemed a far better idea than the rites that had passed last night, and I didn't remember half of them. Everyone wanted to be part of a ritual that only occurred once every few decades—if we were lucky. This one had come too soon. I spotted my shirt strewn across the bar and stumbled over to it, kicking the boots of Titus, Drake, and others sprawled on the floor as I went. "Get up."

Gunner groaned and grabbed his head just as I had, then vomited across the floor. The smell made my own stomach lurch. *Never again*, I swore beneath my breath. *Never.*

"Up!" Mason yelled to them all, then said more quietly to me when I winced at the noise, "There's visitors in town. Vendan soldiers—Rahtan—at least that's what one of the magistrates is saying. They're asking questions."

"Son of a bitch," I hissed, but not too loudly, still rubbing my temple. I grabbed a half-empty pitcher of water and splashed my face, then threw on my shirt. "Let's go."

The avenues were crowded. The first harvest had come in, and farm workers swelled in the streets, spending the fruits of the season on everything Hell's Mouth had to offer—and the Ballengers made sure no need was unmet. Traders from other kingdoms rolled in too. Everyone was welcome into Hell's Mouth, except Vendan soldiers—especially not ones asking questions. *Rahtan.* The queen's elite guard. Maybe I could turn this to our favor after all.

"There. Up ahead. That must be them," Mason said, his eyes still bleary. Half of our crew still lay on the floor back at the tavern, but I put my hand out to stop Gunner, Titus, and Tiago, who followed behind us. I wanted to observe these Vendans first, see just what they were doing, and they didn't seem to be asking questions. There were three of them outside the mercantile—women—and one of them was *juggling*. I blinked, thinking the magistrate had made a mistake. This was a girl I might have eagerly bought a drink for last night, but there was no mistaking she was outfitted for trouble, a sword hanging from one hip and two knives from the other. Her long black hair hung loosely over her shoulders, and she laughed and chatted with the store clerk as she continued to juggle, and then—

I jabbed Mason. "Did you see that?"

"See what?"

"She just nicked an orange!" At least I thought she did. I rubbed my eyes, uncertain. *Yes! She did it again.*

"Let's go," I said, moving toward her. She spotted me, her eyes connecting with mine, slowly perusing me like I was a bug, then nodded to those with her and they walked away.

Like hell.

CHAPTER SIX

KAZI

We intercepted the Vendans leaving the apothecary—a husband and wife. Their eyes were lined with fatigue. Leaving Venda for the unknown was not an easy choice, and yet it was their only hope for something better. The fact that they were still here, trying, showed how desperately they wanted to make it work. The settlement locations had been carefully chosen, approved by every kingdom in advance, usually near sizable cities so there was a greater potential for trade and growth—and protection. But they were receiving the opposite here.

It wasn't only the major powers of Morrighan and Dalbreck who wanted the Vendans divided and dispersed, the Lesser Kingdoms did too, afraid of their numbers and the strength they had once amassed, but the queen had never held it out as threat, only that it was the right thing to do. These were people who hoped for a brighter future.

Troops would come if disputes couldn't be resolved, but before troops came, a darker trouble needed to be uncovered here—discreetly. Any whiff of what we were really after and our prey might vanish entirely, as he had before. *Not this time*, the queen said. I saw the ghosts in her eyes. *Even for her*, I thought, *they never go away.*

"So you can't identify the attackers either?" I asked.

"No, we—"

"What's going on here?"

I sighed. The bevy of bacchanals had followed us. I turned and faced them, eyeing the bloodshot leader of the group. "Move along, boy," I ordered. "This doesn't concern you."

His eyes went from bloodshot to flaming. "Boy?" He stepped closer, and in one swift movement, I brought him to his knees and slammed him up against the apothecary wall, a knife to his throat.

His crew jumped forward but then stalled when they saw the blade firm against his skin.

"That's right, *boy*. Call off your misbegotten posse and move along as I ordered, and maybe I won't cut your pretty neck."

His muscles strained beneath my grasp, his shoulder a knot of rage— and yet the knife was snug against his jugular. He considered carefully.

"Back off," he finally told his friends.

"Sensible," I said. "Ready to move along?"

"Yes," he hissed.

"Good boy," I said, though it was now clear to me that there was nothing boyish about him.

I pulled the knife from his belt and shoved him away. He didn't protest or try to double back, but instead took his time to stand. He faced me and waved back the others, who were ready to jump to his defense now that his neck was safe from my knife. Seconds stretched and he studied me as though he was memorizing every inch of my face. Revenge burned in his gaze. He lifted his arm and Wren and Synové tensed, raising their weapons, but he only raked his thick hair back from his face, and then, his eyes still boring into mine—he smiled.

A chill danced up my spine. Smiles like his unsettled me. I had a history with them. They meant something else, but he only dipped his head in good-bye, and said, "I wish you a pleasant stay in Hell's Mouth." He turned and walked away by himself, his friends going in the opposite direction, as though he had sent them some private communiqué. I knew about subtle signals—Wren, Synové, and I often used them to silently communicate our moves—but if he had used one, I hadn't seen it.

I puzzled over it for a moment then returned my knife to its sheath, eyeing him as he disappeared down an avenue. Synové and Wren did like-wise with their weapons, and the noise around us, which had hushed with the commotion, slowly resumed. I turned back to the couple, but they both stood stiff, their eyes wide with horror.

"It's all right," I said. "They're gone—"

"Do you know *who* that was?" the woman asked, her voice trembling.

"It was—"

"The *Patrei*," her husband answered before I could finish.

I had a very clear description of Karsen Ballenger—a robust man, somewhere near forty, dark brown hair, dark eyes, a scar across his chin—and the swaggering dirty blond was not remotely him.

"The *Patrei* is Karsen Ballenger," I said. "He's—"

"Karsen Ballenger is dead," the man replied. "He died yesterday. That was Jase, his son, the new *Patrei*."

New Patrei? Karsen Ballenger dead? Yesterday? No. They were mistaken. I was told that Karsen was young, fierce, and healthy. How could—

The ring.

My stomach spun. *The gold signet ring. It was on his finger.* I caught a glimpse of gold when I held him against the wall, but I didn't think any-thing of it. It was supposed to be on an older man.

My mind whirled, and I felt myself being whisked down an

unexpected path. I could see Natiya raging already, Griz roaring, and the queen burying her face in her hands.

I sucked in a deep breath. *There is still time to save this.* If I was going to get under anyone's skin other than Karsen Ballenger, his son was the next best choice. This could still work. In fact, maybe it was perfect timing.

I looked in the direction he had walked. *Alone.*

He had wanted me to follow him. I was told that Karsen Ballenger had a large ego. It was obvious his son did, too—maybe bigger. He wasn't going to let this humiliation go.

"Guard the end of the street," I told Wren and Synové. "Don't let his crew follow me," and I went after him.

———

It was a quiet avenue, strangely void of anyone, lined with the back sides of shops, trash bins, and the trunks of giant trees. Shadows crisscrossed the buckled and rutted cobbled street. I couldn't see him, but I knew he was here. Somewhere. I felt the hot trail of rage he left behind. Yes, I wanted him angry but not so much that he would kill me—that was not part of the plan. It was eerily calm, and I pulled my sword halfway from its scabbard, scouring the shadows on either side. I listened for sounds, and a little farther down the road I heard a scuffling noise, a grunt, a soft clatter. A repeat of the same sounds. I turned my head, trying to pinpoint where it came from. I took another step and determined it came from an intersecting lane only a few yards ahead. I stepped forward, cautiously, and saw him, but not in the way I expected. He was bound and gagged, blood running from his temple, and he was in the grips of an enormous man almost the size of Griz. They both spotted me, and I stepped out into the middle of the lane.

"What do you think you're doing?" I called. I didn't think it could be a trick. The blood was real.

"No concern of yours, missy. Just cleaning up street trash. Go about your business."

I pulled my sword free. "Let him go," I ordered.

"Nah, I don't think so. He's a strong one. We'll get a lot for him."

And then I spotted a hay wagon not far behind them both, with tall sides and a heavy tarp thrown over the top. *Labor hunters?* A vision swirled before my eyes. A long-ago voice I couldn't block out punched the air from my lungs. I blinked, trying to force the memories away.

"By order of the Queen of Venda, I demand that you release him now. He is in my custody for treaty violations."

Jase Ballenger's eyes grew wide, and he groaned and struggled beneath his gag but the man's arm was a vise around him. For a moment, I regretted taking his knife. He might have avoided this quandary.

The man grinned. "You mean he's under arrest? Well, if you put it that way . . ."

His voice was thick with sarcasm, and the memories clawed me again. *You'll bring a nice profit.*

Jase groaned louder.

"Release him! Now!" I ordered.

It was then that I heard a sound behind me. I whirled but it was too late. Something hard and heavy struck my head, and my feet flew out beneath me. My cheek crashed into the muddy cobbles, and I caught a hazy glimpse of boots shuffling near me, stepping on the sword that was still in my hand. I felt him pull it from my grip, his boots scuffling closer, the toe of one nudging my shoulder, and then the cloudy haze darkened until it was black.

I thought it couldn't get worse. I didn't open my eyes when I first woke, trying to get my bearings, listening instead to the noises around me, feeling the rock and sway beneath my back, sweat trickling between my breasts, the throb of my head, something sharp cutting into my wrists. I slivered my eyes open. My wrists were chained, but worse, my boots were gone and my ankle was shackled to Jase Ballenger.

He sat across from me, his gag gone, swaying with the wagon, the side of his face crusted with dried blood, the rest shining with perspiration. He saw that I was awake. His expression was grim. He was probably far beyond angry now, and most certainly fantasizing about how slowly he would kill me if he ever got the chance. His scrutiny was smothering, and I turned my head. That was when I caught the view out the back of the wagon. There were no trees, no streets, no mountains or even hills. We were in the middle of a wide-open plain, with nowhere to hide, and nowhere to run. How long had I been unconscious?

This was more than an unexpected turn.

It was an unchecked slide into hell.

CHAPTER SEVEN

JASE

THE LAST THING GUNNER AND THE OTHERS WOULD HAVE expected was for me to disappear in a hay wagon. *Keep the straza at your sides.* My mother had said it a hundred times. Her order was as matter-of-fact as brushing the hair from our eyes every time we left Tor's Watch. I had heard it since I was a child. *These are uncertain times.* She said it to my father too. It was her good-bye. We had become numb to it. The times were always uncertain, and our *straza* were always there, a presence at our sides like a knife or sword. They only had to be seen, not used. The main difference between *straza* and everyone else was their title, and maybe the severity of their scowls. My brothers and I were all capable of fighting our own battles, and we had one another's backs. Usually.

But we didn't see this battle coming. I was blind with rage when I signaled Mason. The faintest nod to the side that he read and understood. *Go with the others or she won't follow. Circle around and meet me at the livery. This Rahtan is going to cool her heels.* I was still blind with rage as I walked down that alley. *Boy.* She didn't know who I was, I figured that much, but I also knew it would be only a matter of seconds before the dawning came and she'd be trailing after me. *Move along and I won't cut your pretty neck.* She said it with venom—and sincerity. She would have done it. There was no doubt that she was driven, by what I wasn't sure. She didn't even know me.

But I was driven too. This was my town, and she wasn't going to spit out orders.

As soon as I started down the alley, I should have known. My father had always warned me, *If something doesn't feel right, it probably isn't. Trust your gut.*

In those first steps, something seemed off, but my gut was woozy with a night of ale, and halfway down the alley my stomach caught up with my rage and I doubled over to vomit. As I wiped my mouth, an anvil pounded in my head and I blamed it on her—that was when the labor hunter hit me, knocking me to the ground. I hadn't heard him approach and didn't even understand who or what he was at first. As he gagged and bound me, I thought maybe he was Rahtan too, but then he called to another man farther down the alley, saying I'd bring a good price.

And then she appeared and demanded my release.

I looked at her now, lying across from me. She hadn't stirred all morning, and I wondered if she would wake at all. I didn't know why I tried to warn her that the brute was sneaking up from behind. Maybe because I saw her as a chance to get away. I'd seen how fast she could move when she kicked my legs out from under me back in Hell's Mouth. I mulled that over too, or maybe it was more like I seethed over it.

My stomach was still raw, empty. The hunters hadn't given us anything but water since they took us yesterday. I watched her chest barely rise, her breaths so shallow sometimes I thought she wasn't breathing. He'd hit her hard, and I guessed she had a good-sized egg on the back of her head. She had hesitated in the alley when she spotted me, as if something had distracted her. Her demands had disappeared and a puzzled expression had crossed her face. Maybe it was only seeing her prey snatched from beneath her nose.

Rahtan. I turned the word over and what I had thought it meant. I had seen Rahtan before in Ráj Nivad, but none had been like her. They looked like killers and brutes, and they were *big*. She barely reached past my shoulder. And they sure as hell never *juggled*. Nothing about this added up. Could she be an imposter? Someone sent by Paxton? But I had overheard her speaking Vendan when we first approached. No one spoke like that around here, except other Vendans.

Her lids fluttered. She was finally coming to, but her eyes remained closed, even though her chest rose and her breaths became fuller. She was awake. Just assessing her predicament. I could tell her. It was bad. Very bad.

Scum like this hadn't ventured close to Hell's Mouth in years. They feared the Ballengers. But with settlements moving in, they probably thought they could too. *Give up a handful and you will lose it all.* My father was right. All the Ballenger generations had been right. We would give up no more; not a single fistful of soil would be shared.

Her eyes opened and her gaze shot to her chained hands first, then our shackled ankles, and finally her eyes rose to mine. I said nothing, just stared at her, letting it all sink in.

Still plan to arrest me? Maybe not.

I had already spent the whole night trying to loosen the chains or pick the locks with a sliver of wood I had pried from the wagon. The locks were secure, and we were stuck. She turned her head, staring out the back of the wagon, and for the first time, she flinched. If it was fear, she muffled it quickly and pulled herself up to sit against the side of the wagon. She winced as she rose. I wondered if she had broken anything when she slammed against the cobbles. Half of her face was still covered with dirt. She looked around, finally taking note of the others chained in the wagon—six of us altogether.

"Welcome to the party," I said.

She looked at me, unflustered. Her eyes were smoky golden moons, her pupils pinpoints, shrewd, scheming, or maybe it was just the blow to her head that made her look that way. Her focus turned back to her chained hands, and then she stared at our shackled ankles again, examining them for long, studious minutes. I suspected that rankled her the most. If she hoped to jump out of the back of the wagon and run, I was her anchor. She slowly surveyed the others. We were the only ones with leg shackles, maybe because of our position at the back of the wagon, but all their hands were similarly bound like ours. Their expressions were empty, despondent. I recognized two of them from Hell's Mouth, one from the cooperage and another from the smithy. Her gaze shifted to the driver. She studied him for a long while too, and then her chin lifted as it had when she told me to move along. I knew something was coming.

"Driver!" she called. "Stop the wagon. I have to pee."

The driver laughed and called over his shoulder. "You missed piss break, darling. You gotta go, you do it right there."

"I'd rather not," she called back.

"And I'd rather not listen to your caterwauling. Shut up!"

Her eyes narrowed.

I nudged her with my foot. *Don't,* I mouthed. He had pummeled one of the other prisoners senseless when he wouldn't stop moaning, and I didn't want her messing up my own plan for escape. I had spotted an ax under the driver's seat. Easy to get to, if the opportunity arose.

A grin lit her eyes. *A grin.* What was the matter with her? She was going to push him.

"*Let it go,*" I whispered between gritted teeth.

"Driver, I really need to pee."

He whipped around, furious, but before he could speak, she said, "I'll give you a gift for your trouble?"

His rage turned to a chuckle. "I already got all the valuables off you. Sword. Knives. Vest. Those fancy boots."

She leaned forward. "What about a riddle? Something to occupy your mind for all these long, dreary miles? That's a treasure in itself, no?"

His expression changed. No doubt any proposal containing the word *treasure* caught his greedy attention. When there was nothing tangible left to take, this prize appealed to him.

"Give it to me," he demanded.

"Pee first."

"Riddle first."

She sat back. "Very well. But I warn you, you won't get the answer until I pee."

He nodded, happy with his deal, and told her he was ready for it.

I watched her expertly pushing him against a wall, but I wasn't even sure what the goal was. All this to pee? I didn't think so.

"Listen up," she instructed, her voice cheerful, like it was a fun diversion for her.

"My gaze is sharp, my scales thick,
I jump, I pounce, but I'm still not quick.
I have two feet, yet cannot stand,
My head is full of rocks and sand.
I breathe out fire, but my light is dim,
I'm easy prey to chance and whim.
My chest is empty, the treasury bare,
I do not grieve, for it was never there.
I am less than nothing, and more of the same,
A white chit tossed in a high-stakes game."

"A lizard!" the driver guessed immediately. He made more guesses, focusing on only one clue at a time, not putting any of them together. *A desert! A horse! A dragon!* She answered no to every guess, and he shifted angrily in his seat. He ordered her to repeat the riddle several times. She did, but all his guesses only garnered a no from her. The more his frustration grew, the more at ease she became. Her hands stretched, fingers wiggled, as if anticipating something.

"*Tell me!*" he demanded.

"Pee break," she replied.

He roared a string of curses then yelled, "Whoa!" pulling on the reins. He shouted to the hunters ahead of us who were scouting the path, "Hold!" His face was purple with rage. He jumped down from his seat and stomped to the back of the wagon. I had no doubt he intended to beat the answer out of her.

"*Tell him,*" I whispered. "*Now! I don't want to be chained to a bloody pulp.*"

She peered at me and smiled. "I've got this, pretty boy." I wondered if she had lost all sense when she was hit in the head. She reached up and pulled her shirt from her trousers so it was loose, just as the driver appeared at the back.

"Tell me," he growled. "Now! Pee break *after.*"

"How do I know that—"

He grabbed her shoulders, jerking her forward. She leaned into him and in a single move, as smooth as air, she palmed the keys hooked at his side without so much as a tug or jingle, and slid them beneath her shirt. "All right!" she said, caving to his demand. "All right! Here is your answer."

He pushed her away, waiting.

"A fool. An empty-headed fool." She tweaked her head coyly to the side. "And I was so certain *you* would get it."

For once, he didn't miss her point and his arm swung, the back of his fist meeting with her jaw. She fell back, and he glared at her. "Who's the fool now? I got the answer, and you got no pee break. Piss your pants, bitch."

He stomped back to his seat and drove the wagon forward again.

She sat up, getting her bearings, blood trickling from the corner of her mouth, and her eyes met mine. Even the others hadn't seen what she did. She motioned toward my hands. I leaned forward and she slipped the keys from her shirt and with a slow, guarded motion, unlocked my chains. I quietly laid them on the floor of the wagon. The others noticed, and I pressed my finger to my lips so they wouldn't make a sound. I took the keys from her and did the same with the chains on her wrists. The others rustled anxiously, seeing what was going on, and thrust their hands out to be freed too, the clinks of their strained chains making a ruckus. The driver thundered back over his shoulder, "Quiet!" We all froze and then I cautiously unlocked the man next to me. He took the keys and did the same for the man next to him.

The girl kicked my foot and nodded at our legs as the keys traveled out of our reach. Our ankles were still chained together. I waved to the last two men to pass them back, but they were panicking, unable to get the key in the locks, afraid the driver would turn and see them. I pressed my fingers to my lips again warning them, but one began struggling and sobbed to the other, "Hurry!" The other prisoner freed him at last, but not before the driver turned and saw what was happening.

"Scatter!" I yelled, hoping for distraction as I lunged for the keys that had fumbled from the last man's fingers to the floor. The others ran over us, jumping from the back of the wagon, kicking the keys from my reach.

The driver was screaming, alerting the men who rode ahead, and I saw him reach down for the ax beneath his seat. The girl lunged too, as the keys were kicked in the bedlam of the prisoners stampede for freedom. I almost had them in my hand when the girl screamed, "Above you!" I rolled just as an ax splintered the wagon floor where my head had been. I grabbed the handle as he pried it free, and we battled for its control. I made it to my feet, but I had less leverage with one leg chained.

"Keep it, you bastard fool!" I yelled and let go of the ax, pushing him. As he stumbled for balance, my arm shot forward, my fist crushing his throat, caving it inward. His eyes bulged and he fell from the wagon onto his back, his throat wheezing, unable to draw a breath. He was as good as dead, but then another hunter on horseback, with a spiked mace in hand, doubled back toward us after taking down one of the other prisoners. His eyes were fixed on me.

The girl had snatched up the keys in her fist and was trying to fit the key into the lock at our ankles to free us, but I yelled, "Run!" There wasn't time for locks. I grabbed her arm and pulled her with me. We stumbled onto the dirt as the hunter's mace swung over our heads, his horse trampling around us. We scrambled together beneath the wagon just as the mace split the wood over our heads. We crawled to the other side and ran, our paces clumsy with the chain between us. "This way!" I shouted.

The hunter was close behind us, but I knew what was up ahead, and I only prayed she could keep step with me. If we stumbled, we were finished. She managed to keep pace, the chain rattling between us, the keys still firm in her grip. The flat plain gave way to a long, steep incline that led to the river below. In one jump, we leapt and rolled, head over heels, tumbling, the shackles cutting into our legs as we pulled apart and came together in what felt like an endless cascade down the loose dirt, unable to break our fall until we hit a flat crest above the river.

"The keys!" the girl shouted. Her hand was empty. She had lost them in the long tumble.

We untangled ourselves and got to our feet, both of our ankles bleeding where the irons had cut into them. We looked back up the incline, hoping to see the glint of a rusty key.

"Devil's hell!" I hissed. The hunter was traversing the steep embankment on his horse, *still* coming after us.

"*Fikat vide*," the girl growled and glanced behind us for escape. There was nowhere to go but the river, and it was a long way down.

"Can you swim?" I asked. "I don't want your dead weight dragging me under."

"Let's go, pretty boy," she said, glaring at me, then jumped, pulling me with her.

CHAPTER EIGHT

KAZI

SWIM?

Not well. There were few opportunities in Sanctum City for swimming. The Great River was too cold and too violent. I'd had some training as Rahtan but didn't get past the basics of floating. There was simply nowhere to practice.

But his accusing question galled me. Dead weight dragging *him* under? He was the one who passed the keys to others before freeing us. He was the one who pushed us down an embankment, making me lose the keys. The hunter was quickly approaching, another just behind him with their weapons poised to bash in our heads, or at least disable us enough to drag us back to the wagon. There was no other choice. The river was a long way down, but this time I would be the one doing the pushing. I grabbed his arm and jumped.

It seemed forever before we hit, the surface surprisingly hard as we broke through. It viciously slammed into my ribs, and then we were tumbling in the current. I didn't know which way was up, and my lungs were bursting searching for a breath. I kicked, struggled to find the surface, find air, find the way up, but there were only thousands of bubbles, flashes of light, swirls of darkness, and a vise clamping down on my chest, the last breath I had gulped seeping away as I kicked desperately, and then I felt something gripping my arm, fingers digging in, jerking me upward, and I broke the surface, gasping for air.

"Lean back!" he yelled. "Cross your legs! Feet forward!" Jase pulled me so I was between his arms, leaning back against his chest, rapids splashing over us, spinning us, but each time he righted our course and we shot down the river like aimless leaves swept away on its surface. The riverbanks on either side weren't far away, but they were lined with boulders and we were moving too swiftly to risk grabbing on to one. I choked as rapids splashed into my mouth and up my nose. His arms held me tight, pulling me backward when I tried to lean up. "Relax against me," he ordered. "Go with the current. When it widens and calms, we'll make our way to the side." His survival depended on mine and mine on his. We truly were anchors to each other. The only good thing about the fearsome ride was it was taking us far from the labor hunters. The current finally slowed, and stretches of sandy banks began to appear. "A little farther," he said, his face tucked next to mine, "to make sure they can't follow."

We had already gone a mile down the river, or more. My legs throbbed, and I was relieved when he started maneuvering us toward a sandy bank. I finally felt my feet touch bottom, and we both stumbled out. We collapsed on the bank, gasping. My hair was a mass of tangles in front of my face, my heart still pounding. I glanced to the side. He lay next to me on his back, his eyes closed, his chest heaving, and his hair dripping in wet strings.

I may have put one threat behind me, but now I was chained to another—in the middle of nowhere. There was no pretending that we were friends, and now I had no weapon. Neither did he, but he was undeniably bigger and stronger than me, and I had seen what his fist could do. It was clear I needed to strike at least a temporary truce.

Once I caught my breath, I asked, "What now?"

His head rolled to the side and he looked at me, a long searing stare. His eyes were clear, bright, the haze of drink long vanished from them, and his irises were the same deep brown as the earth he was lying on.

"Did you have something in mind?" he asked.

I wasn't sure if it was sarcasm or humor. Maybe both, but his eyes remained locked on mine. An uneven breath squeezed my lungs.

"I'm just saying, I know you don't like me, and I don't like you, but until we can be free of each other, I guess we'll have to make the best of it."

He blinked. Long and slow.

Definitely sarcasm. And distaste.

He turned away and looked up into the sky as if he was thinking it over. "You have a name?" he finally asked, without looking at me.

I paused. I wasn't sure why it felt risky to tell him. It was strangely personal, but I was the one who suggested we make the best of it. "Kazi," I said, waiting for him to deride it.

"And your family name?"

"Vendans don't use surnames. We're known by where we're from. I'm known as Kazi of Brightmist. It's a quarter in Sanctum City."

He quietly repeated my name but said nothing more, staring upward. I was sure he was conjuring all the possible ways he could be rid of me. If only he had that ax to hack away my foot that bound me to him. He finally stood and held his hand out, waiting for me to take it. I cautiously grabbed hold of his wrist and he helped me to my feet, but he didn't release my arm, tugging me closer instead. He looked down at me. "And I do have a name too, even though you're fond of calling me pretty boy.

Jase Ballenger," he said. "But you probably already knew that, didn't you? Considering you intended to *arrest* me." Uneasy seconds passed, his grip still strong. Dark clouds flashed in his eyes. Our truce was off to a shaky start.

"The arrest wasn't imminent," I replied. "There were still more questions to ask, accusations to review, and then I would have called you in for further discussion."

"*You call me in?* Hell's Mouth is *my* city. Just who do you think you are?"

Your worst nightmare, Jase Ballenger, I fumed, but I molded my words into a calm reply. "Do you want to make the best of this or not?"

He sucked in a slow, heated breath and swallowed his next words. He released my arm and turned, taking in our surroundings as though he was appraising our situation. "All right, then, Kazi of Brightmist, let's see if we can make the best of it and get out of here." His gaze jumped to the ridge on the opposite bank, then back to the forest behind us. He pointed to his left. "I think . . ." He shook his head and his finger shifted slightly to the right. "I think there's a settlement in that direction. Closest civilization we're going to find that doesn't put us right back in the hunters' path. Maybe a hundred miles."

A hundred miles? Chained, barefoot, with no weapons or food?

And with someone who was about as trustworthy as a merchant's wink. But I was sure survival was on his mind too. "What kind of settlement?" I asked.

"The only kind that's out here. One of *yours*."

There was no attempt to hide his disapproval. I looked in the direction he had pointed, still uncertain. "Where's Hell's Mouth from here?" I asked.

"Other side of the river, where the hunters are. And more than a day's ride east."

A day? Had I been knocked unconscious for that long? My stomach rumbled in confirmation, and his conclusion rang with some truth. There was another Vendan settlement far west of Eislandia. Casswell was one of the first and largest settlements—several hundred strong. They would have the supplies and resources to help me, in one way or another.

The chain rattled between us, and he shifted on his feet. "Well?" he asked. "You have a better idea?"

Not at the moment. "We'll head toward the settlement," I answered.

"But . . ." he said, taking a step closer, his eyes narrowing, "here's the real question: *If* I get you back to civilization, you still think you're going to call me in for further discussion?"

Was that a veiled threat? *If I get you back?* The chain firmly connecting us now seemed like a blessed assurance I wouldn't be bludgeoned the minute I turned my back. Everything about his stance was smug confidence. This was a game for him. A challenge. I'd bite.

"I'd be a fool to answer that, now, wouldn't I, considering my predicament?"

An amused huff jumped from his chest. "I'd say you'd be a fool not to."

I stared at him, trying to judge how much was bluster and how much genuine threat. "Then shall we simply agree to go our separate ways, once we reach the settlement? No foul, no gain."

"Separate ways," he said. "Agreed."

We got our last drinks at the river since we didn't know when we would come across fresh water again, and then I stopped to toe some small rocks I spotted on the bank. I picked one up, turning it over in my hand.

"That for me?" he asked.

I glanced up. This time, humor. A grin lit his eyes. He was impossible to predict, which only added to my misgivings. Quarterlords and their greedy egos were as easy to forecast as a snowy day in winter. Every exchange of words between Jase and me seemed like a dance, a step forward, a step back, circling, both of us leading, anticipating, wondering what the next move would be. He didn't trust me any more than I trusted him.

"Flint," I answered. "And my buckle is firesteel. The hunters may have relieved me of my valuables, but at least my belt was worthless to them. A fire will be welcome tonight."

He looked at my buckle, a brown oval of metal shaped like a serpent, and nodded his approval of this development. A step forward.

"Then I better keep my eyes open for some dinner." He stepped toward the forest to leave.

"Hold up," I said. "Before we go, I need you to turn around."

"What?"

"I need to pee. Turn around."

"We just got out of a river. Why didn't you pee there?"

"Maybe because I was doing this little thing called fighting for my life."

"You mean I was fighting for your life. You just went along for the ride."

"*Turn around*," I ordered.

"Turn my back on you?"

I smiled. "Don't worry," I answered, spitting his own words back into his face, "I wouldn't want to be chained to a *dead weight*. You're safe, pretty boy."

"I don't even get a riddle first?"

I narrowed my eyes.

He slowly turned. "Hurry."

I had done more humiliating things I supposed, but at the moment I couldn't remember what they were. I took care of my business quickly. Making the best of it was not going to be easy.

When he turned around again, he reached toward me and I flinched. My hand shot up ready to strike.

"Whoa! Hold on," he said, pulling back. "I was just going to take a look at your face. You've got quite a shiner blooming there."

I reached up and touched my jaw, feeling the heat of a fresh bruise.

He shrugged. "I'm not saying it wasn't worth it—you got your hands on the keys—but it makes me wonder, is there anything you won't do to get what you want?"

I eyed him cautiously. "Some things," I answered.

But not many.

CHAPTER NINE

JASE

I GRABBED A LONG BRANCH OF DRIFTWOOD TOSSED UP ON THE bank and broke it in two, handing one to her. It would serve as both walking stick and protection if we needed it. I doubted the hunters would cross the river after us. We were only a commodity to them and it would cost them less time and trouble to ensnare new victims, but there were four-legged threats out here too. "We'll sharpen them later," I said.

We set out through the forest, maneuvering through the dense maze of yellow ringed spirit trees. The trunks were thin, none much wider than my arm, but they grew closely, making our path an ever-constant zigzag. The floor of the forest was a thick mat of decaying leaves, a soft cushion on our bare feet. Other parts of the journey wouldn't be this easy. We faced a river of scorching sand ahead, but if I paced it right, we would travel over it in the cool of night.

It was a gamble when I told her about the direction of the settlement. I wasn't sure how well she knew the terrain. Even if she did, it was easy to confuse one forest or plateau with another out here, and she'd been unconscious the whole time in the hay wagon. My gamble paid off. She didn't know where we really were—east or west of Hell's Mouth.

I thought she'd go along easier if she thought she was headed for a Vendan settlement. The alternative was to carry her trussed up over my shoulder the whole way, which would take even longer. It was already going to take too long as it was. The river had taken us way off course, and we wouldn't be able to move fast with this chain between us—especially without shoes.

She wouldn't like where we were going, which brought me some satisfaction as there was little else to be satisfied with at the moment. I needed to get home fast. More than ever, this was a time the family needed to be pulling together, showing a unified front. We needed to be fortifying our positions. Scouts had already been sent to outlying posts, watching for threats. Other leagues were always vying for a piece of Hell's Mouth's lucrative trade, hoping to displace the Ballengers. Paxton was a wolf sniffing the air for blood every time he came to town. If I wasn't there, he'd sense weakness and whistle for more of his pack to follow. The same with the other league leaders. They would know something was wrong. The town would become restless too, wondering where I was. Every day, every minute I was gone only made my problems multiply. The others would be covering for me, searching, hoping for the best and putting on a show that all was well. Funeral plans would have to proceed. My fingers curled into my palm, wishing I could hit something.

Today would be the preparation and wrapping of my father's body. My family would be doing it without me. Tomorrow the tomb would be opened and cleaned, a lantern lit and a daily prayer offered up by family in anticipation of his entombment, and in two weeks his body would be laid on the internment stone for the final good-bye, viewing, and sealing ceremony. And then, once the tomb was shut and sealed, the priestess would say a blessing over the new *Patrei*. But I wouldn't be there. Visitors gathered to pay their respects would wonder at my absence, and the fears and whispers would run rampant. So would the wolves. My family was at risk. So was the town—all because of her.

I wondered if she was truly Rahtan. Yes, she was skilled, but she didn't exactly possess brawn—even if she had managed to overtake me and slam me up against the wall. But juggling? Riddles? *Her age.* Her poise and demeanor was that of a cynical tested soldier, but her appearance—she was young, younger than me, I was certain. Her black hair fell in thick, long waves, and her hands were delicate, her fingers more suited for a piano than a sword.

Or for slipping keys from a belt.

My doubts doubled and I glanced sideways at her. Her cheeks were flushed with warmth, but she kept step with my brisk pace.

I thought about the queen who had sent her and my father's last words.

Make her come. The leagues will notice. It will validate our position on this continent.

The Lesser Kingdoms and territories hadn't been part of the battle, but everyone knew of the war between the Greater Kingdoms and the queen who had led a vastly outnumbered army to an astonishing victory. She could have plucked from any number of skilled soldiers or chosen assassins from three kingdoms to investigate treaty violations. Why this girl?

"Do you actually know the queen?" I asked.

Her glance at me was sharp, but her one word answer was languid. "Yes."

Even in one simple word, I heard a hundred nuances—most of them haughty, condescending, and superior.

"How did you meet?"

She paused, considering her reply. "I met her when I pledged as a soldier."

A lie.

"You know her well?"

"Quite well."

More questions only produced more terse answers, and I wasn't sure any were true.

I stopped abruptly and stepped in her path to block her, the question I promised myself I wouldn't ask bubbling up anyway. "Why don't you like me?"

She stared at me, confused. "What?"

"Back at the river, you said that you don't like me. I want to know why."

She rolled her eyes like it was obvious and tried to sidestep around me. Again, I moved to block her path. She looked at me then, her eyes as smooth and calm as a summer sea, and said without blinking, "Because you're an opportunist. You're a cheat. You're a thief. Shall I go on?"

My back stiffened, but I forced myself to deliver an unruffled reply. "Wouldn't those all be the same thing?"

"There are differences. Can we walk and talk at the same time?"

"Maybe you're right," I replied, and we fell back into step. "I guess it would take a real thief to know the subtleties. I saw you steal those oranges."

She laughed. "Did you, now? I *paid* for those oranges. You and your bunch of thugs were too drunk and full of yourselves to see anything beyond your own inebriated noses. I can see your kind coming a mile away."

"*My kind?*" I squared my shoulders, struggling to remain calm. She had no respect or fear for the Ballengers, and I wasn't used to it. "You don't know anything about me."

"I know enough. I've read the long list of your violations. Skimming merchants. Caravan raids. Stealing livestock. Intimidation."

I stepped in front of her path, blocking her again. "Ah, so there you have it—a list with the Vendan twist. Do *your kind* have any idea how hard it is to survive out here in the middle of everything and everyone? Surrounded by kingdoms on all sides? Everyone thinking it's their right to enter your territory and take what they want? Moving in at the slightest sign of weakness? My world is not your world." My temples burned and my voice rose. "Vendans sit behind their high, safe walls at the far edge of a continent, scribbling out new treaties and training their pretty, smart-mouthed, elite soldiers who have no idea what it's like to fight to survive!" I lowered my voice to a growl. "And you, Kazi of Brightmist, have no understanding of the trouble you've caused me. I should be home with my family, protecting *them*, and instead I'm out here, chained to you!"

My chest heaved with anger, and I waited for a caustic comeback, but instead she blinked slowly and replied, "I may know more about survival than you think."

Her pupils were deep black wells floating in a calm circle of amber, but her hands betrayed her, stiff at her sides, ready to strike. A war raged inside her, one she held back, biting it off like a poisonous snake with disturbing self-control.

"Let's go," I said. Our worlds had an impassable gulf between them. It was useless to try to make her understand.

We walked in silence, the clank of the chain between us suddenly amplified.

Her steely control made me angry at myself for losing mine. It wasn't like me. That was one of the reasons my father gave for naming me *Patrei*. I wasn't the oldest, but I was the least impulsive. It was a strength my father valued. I weighed the advantages and costs of every word and action *before* I acted. Some saw me as aloof. Mason said, with admiration, that it made me a stone-cold bastard, but this girl had pushed me to a reckless burning edge I didn't even recognize, and her calm reply only pushed me further.

She knew something about survival. I wondered if she might even know more than me.

Each other. Hold on to each other because that is what will save you.

I hold back tears because others are watching, already terrified. I pile handfuls of dirt, brush, rocks, thing upon thing until his body is hidden. It is the best I can do, but I know animals will find him by nightfall. By then he will be far behind us.

How many more will I have to bury?

I shout into the air, a rush of tears and anger breaking loose.

No more of us, I scream.

The anger feels good, saving, a weapon when I have nothing else.

I shove a stick into a hand. And then another, and another, until even the youngest holds one. Miandre balks. I squeeze my hand around hers until she winces, forcing her to take hold of her club. If we die, we will die fighting.

—Greyson Ballenger, 14

CHAPTER TEN

KAZI

I SHOULD BE WITH MY FAMILY.

He'd been silent for an hour now.

His father's death had come as a surprise to me, and now I guessed it had been unexpected for him too. Even if Karsen Ballenger was the ruthless outlaw who harbored a stable of ruffians as the King of Eislandia had reported, he was still Jase's father and he'd only been dead for two days.

I doubted that Jase cared whether I liked him or that I called him a thief—but he did care about his family and he was not there with them to bury his father, or whatever it was they did with the dead in Hell's Mouth.

In the last months of the Komizar's reign, I had watched Wren when she grieved her parents' deaths. I saw her fall on their bloody bodies, slaughtered in the town square, screaming for them to get up, hitting their lifeless chests and begging for them to open their eyes. I had seen Synové days after her parents' deaths, her eyes wide, unseeing, numb and beyond tears.

It had been odd to envy their grief, but I had. I envied the explosion and finality of it—their sobs and tears. At that point, my mother had been gone for five years and I had never grieved her death, never cried, because I never saw her die. Her passing came slowly, over months and years, in the dull bits, pieces, and mundane hours that I worked to stay alive. Day-by-day she faded, as every stall I searched turned up nothing, and another piece of her drifted away. Every hovel and home I snuck into held no part of her, no amulet, no scent, no sound of her voice. The memories of her became disconnected blurred images, warm hands cupping my cheeks, a tuneless hum as she worked, words that floated in the air, her finger pressed to my lips. *Shhh, Kazi, don't say a word.*

I wondered if Jase had missed his chance to grieve too. A one night drunk was hardly a good-bye.

"I'm sorry about your father," I said.

His steps faltered, but he kept walking, his only reply a nod.

"How did he die?"

His jaw clenched and his reply was quick and clipped, "He was a man, not a monster, as you imagine. He died the way all men die, one breath at a time."

He was still angry. He still grieved. His pace quickened, and I knew the topic was closed.

———

Another hour passed. My legs ached trying to keep pace with him, and my ankle was raw from the shackle. The thin fabric of my trousers was little protection against the heavy metal. I kept my eyes open for some bay fern or wish stalks to make a balm, but this forest seemed to have only trees and nothing else.

"You're limping," he said, suddenly breaking the silence. Those weren't the first words I expected from him, but everything about him was unexpected. It made me wary.

"It's only the uneven terrain," I answered, but I noticed his pace slowed.

"How's your head?" he asked.

My head? I reached up, gently pressing the knot and wincing. "I'll live."

"I watched you in the wagon. Your chest. For a while, I didn't see it move at all. I thought you were dead."

I didn't quite know how to respond. "You were watching my chest?"

He stopped and looked at me, suddenly looking awkward and young and not like a ruthless killer at all. "I mean—" He began walking again. "What I meant was, I was watching to make sure you were still breathing. You were out cold."

I smiled—somewhere deep inside so he wouldn't see. It was refreshing to see him flustered for a change.

"And why would you care if I was breathing?"

"I was chained to you."

The hard reality. "Oh, right," I answered, feeling slightly deflated. "No fun being attached to a corpse. Dead weight and all."

"I also knew you might be useful. I'd seen your quick—"

He paused as if he regretted the admission, so I finished his thought for him. "Takedown? When I nailed you against the wall back in Hell's Mouth?"

"Yes."

At least there was some degree of honesty in him.

<hr>

When we came upon a brook in the afternoon, we stopped to rest. The forest was thinning and there was little shade, the sun unforgiving. Jase said he thought we'd soon be out of the forest altogether and crossing the open plateau of Heethe. I looked up, judging the sun's place in the sky. Only a few hours of daylight left. The cool of night would be welcome, but the prospect of an open plateau, a wide night sky, and sleeping without a tent was already a beast running a warning claw down my back. A tent. It was ludicrous to think of that now. *Get a grip on yourself, Kazi,* I thought, but it wasn't that simple and never had been. It was not something I could just talk myself out of no matter how many times I tried.

"Maybe we should stop here for the night?" I suggested.

Jase squinted at the sun. "No. We can get a few more hours of walking in."

I reluctantly nodded. I knew he was right—the sooner to the settlement, the sooner I got back to Hell's Mouth so the others would know I was still alive and the whole mission wasn't abandoned. He was eager to get there too. In spite of dragging a three-foot length of chain between us, his pace had never lagged until he noted my limp. But sleeping out there, utterly exposed . . . it would be hard enough to sleep under the cover of these skimpy trees as it was. A loose breath skittered through my lungs.

I dipped my hands into the brook, splashing my face, taking a drink and picturing myself a week from now, back in the middle of a crowded city. Jase knelt beside me, and fully dunked his head in the shallow water, scrubbing his face and neck. When he surfaced and smoothed back his hair, I saw the gash over his brow from when the hunters trapped him. The cut was small and the dried blood that had crusted his face was gone now, but it made me wonder why he had wanted me to follow him down that empty street in Hell's Mouth. What had been his plan for me before he had been intercepted by the hunters? I didn't think it was to share a cup of tea.

I rinsed my neck and arms with more cool water, wishing the brook was deep enough to take a whole bath, but then I caught the silver flash of something even better. "Minnows!" A few feet away, dozens of shiny minnows darted in a dark pool of water created by a cluster of rocks.

"Dinner?" Jase said, his tone hopeful. We hadn't come across any berries or fungus or even a squirrel to spear with our walking sticks. Our only prospect for dinner had been water, so the fish, however small, lifted my spirits, and it seemed, his too. But catching the slippery angels was another matter.

"Take off your shirt," I said. "We can each hold a side of the fabric and corral them. We'll use it as a net."

He eagerly pulled his shirt over his head, and my excitement for the minnows was replaced with discomfort, wondering if I should look away, but we were chained in close proximity and a strange curiosity took hold. He held his shirt in his hand and I watched the water dripping from his hair trickle down, traversing his chest, abdomen, and the muscles that defined them. I swallowed. It explained the force of his punch when he killed the hunter, and his grip when he pulled me into his arms in the river and held me against him. A winged tattoo fluttered over his right shoulder, across his chest and down his arm. My mouth suddenly felt dry. Synové would have plenty to say about this if she were here, but my thoughts and words stalled on my tongue. He caught me staring.

"It's part of the Ballenger crest," he said.

Now it was me who was flustered, and I felt my cheeks flush warm.

He lifted his hand to the corner of his mouth, trying to stifle a smile, which only made me squirm more. I snatched his shirt from his hand. "Let's catch some dinner, shall we?"

CHAPTER ELEVEN

JASE

IT TOOK SEVERAL TRIES TO CATCH THE SLIMY BASTARDS. THEY were clever and easily darted past our makeshift net, but together we eventually perfected our technique, sneaking forward in unison, allowing the fabric to billow so we could scoop them up. I hooted when we snagged our first catch of two, and with several more sweeps we had a few dozen of the skinny, four-inch fish piled on the bank. They weren't much, but right now my stomach thought they looked like a juicy roasted pig.

"Cooked or raw?" she asked as she lifted one to her mouth.

I pushed her hand down before she could eat it. "Cooked," I said firmly, not trying to hide my disgust. The last thing I'd had in my stomach was a barrel of ale, and squirming fish were not going to swim in it.

"Don't look at me like I'm a savage," she snapped.

"We simply have different eating tastes, and mine include dead game." I worked on the fire while she began skewering the fish onto two sticks for roasting.

As the minnows sizzled over the fire, she looked at my chest again, this time leisurely, not looking away when I noticed. "Is that an eagle?" she asked.

"Part of one."

"Tell me about the crest. What does it stand for?" she asked. "I didn't know you even had one."

Of course she didn't. She knew nothing about us. "It's hard to tell you about the crest without telling the whole Ballenger history, and I doubt you want to hear that considering your low opinion of us."

"Try me. I like history."

I shot her a skeptical glance. But she sat there attentive and waiting.

"It began with the first Ballenger, the leader of all the Ancients."

"All?" Her brows rose, already disputing the claim.

"That's right. Years after the Last Days—"

"You mean the devastation."

I knew there were a lot of different versions and words used to describe the gods' revenge against the world. "All right, the devastation, but you can't interrupt me after every word."

She nodded and listened quietly while I told her that the leader of the Ancients, Aaron Ballenger, had gathered a surviving Remnant spared by the gods, most of them children, and was leading them to a place where they would be safe. But before they could reach Tor's Watch, they were attacked by scavengers and he died. As he lay dying, he charged his grandson, Greyson, with leading the group the rest of the way. "Greyson found this symbol," I explained, sliding my hand over my chest, "when they reached Tor's Watch—at least a version of it—at the entrance to a secure shelter, and he adopted it as the Ballenger crest."

"So he was your first leader?"

"Yes. He was only fourteen and had to look after twenty-two people he didn't know, but they became family. The crest has changed over the generations, but some parts are constant, like the eagle and the banner."

"And the words?" she asked, gesturing at my arm.

I shrugged. "We don't know what they mean exactly. It's a lost language, but to us they mean protect and defend at all costs."

"Even death?"

"All costs means all."

I glanced up at the sky. It was already a dusky purple, and a few stars were beginning to shine. "Too late to leave now. We'll have to make camp here for the night."

She nodded and almost looked relieved.

<hr />

The sun had been gone for hours, and we stared at the small fire crackling at our feet. Light flickered on the yellow-ringed trunks surrounding us.

"I've never seen trees like this, so many and so thin," she said.

"Legend says the forest grew from bone dust and that every tree holds the trapped soul of someone who died in the devastation. That's why they bleed red when you cut them."

She shivered. "That's a gruesome thought."

I told her a few other legends that were less gruesome, ones about the forests and mountains surrounding Tor's Watch, and even a story about the towering tembris, which became the footstools of the gods and held the magic of the stars.

"Where'd you learn all these stories?"

"I grew up with them. I spent a lot of my childhood outdoors exploring every corner of Tor's Watch, usually with my father. He told me most of the stories. What about you? What was your childhood like?"

Her gaze darted to her lap, a furrow deepening over her brow. She finally lifted her chin with a proud air. "Much like yours," she answered. "I spent a lot of time outdoors." She ended the conversation, saying it was probably time that we got some sleep.

But she didn't. I stretched out and closed my eyes, but time after time when I opened them she still sat there, hunched, her arms hugging her knees. Had my story about spirits trapped in trees spooked her? It was strange to see her looking so vulnerable now, and yet earlier she'd been aggressively reckless when she told the hunter a riddle, challenging him, knowing he would strike her. There hadn't been a drop of fear in her then, when all odds were against her. I wondered if this was some sort of trick. Was she up to something?

"It's hard to sleep if you don't lie down," I finally said.

She reluctantly lay down, but her eyes remained open, her chest rising in deep, controlled breaths as if she were counting them. Her arms trembled, but the night was warm. This was no trick.

"Are you cold?" I asked. "I can add more branches to the fire if you need it."

She blinked several times, like she was embarrassed that I had noticed. "No, I'm fine," she said.

But she wasn't fine at all.

I studied her for a minute, then said, "Tell me a riddle. To help me sleep."

She balked, but only a little, and it seemed she was happy to have something else to occupy her mind besides what had been lurking there. She rolled onto her side to face me, settling in, comfortable. "Listen carefully," she said. "I won't repeat it a dozen times like I did for the hunter."

"You won't need to. I'm a good listener."

She said the words slowly, deliberately, like she was imagining the world behind the picture she painted. I watched her lips as she formed each word, her voice relaxed and soft, once again confident, her golden eyes watching mine, making sure I paid attention and missed nothing.

"My face is full, but also slight,
I pale in the bright of light,
I whisper sweet to the forest owl,
I kiss the air with wolf's sad howl,
Eyes follow me from sea to sea,
Yet alone in this world . . . I will ever be."

I stared at her, swallowed, my thoughts suddenly jumbled.

"Well?" she asked. I knew the answer but I drew it out, offering several wrong answers, making her laugh once. It was the first time I had seen her laugh, genuine, without any pretense, and it filled me with a strange burst of heat.

"The moon," I finally answered.

Our gazes held, and she seemed to know what I was doing.

"Tell me another one," I said.

And she did. A dozen more, until her lids grew heavy and she finally fell asleep.

Prepare your hearts,
For we must not only be ready
for the enemy without,
but also the enemy within.

—Song of Jezelia

CHAPTER TWELVE

KAZI

I WOKE TO WEIGHT PINNING ME DOWN. THE HEAT OF SKIN ON mine. A hand over my mouth. *"Shhh. Don't move."* Jase's face hovered next to mine.

I jerked but his weight pushed harder. And then I heard it.

Footsteps.

The crunch of leaves.

A breath.

Jase's mouth pressed close to my ear. A bare whisper. *"Don't move no matter what."*

Leaves stirred, careless footsteps. Heavy steps that didn't care about noise.

The sky above us was still dark, just tinged with dawn, the black silhouette of trees barely lacing an outline above us. Jase's face was a shadow near mine, and his heart pounded against my chest.

Something large lumbered toward us, hulking, a mountain of swaying black. Each footfall trembled though me. Jase couldn't speak now; it was too close, but I felt the strain of his muscles willing me to freeze. It went against every instinct I had. *Run, Kazi, hide.* But I froze beneath his weight, sweat springing between our bodies. The creature sniffed the air, saw us, and its mouth opened wide, a gaping cavern of enormous teeth, and a terrible roar split the forest. My muscles tensed but Jase held me tight, still. It drew closer, so close that its heaving breaths touched our skin, the smell noxious and suffocating, like all the furnaces of hell bellowed from within. A warning grumble vibrated from it, its mouth tasting the air, tasting us, its tongue rolling over our skin. It huffed, as if disappointed, and turned away. We didn't move as dawn crept over us, but when the creature's footsteps had finally faded, Jase let out a long-held breath, and his hand slid from my mouth.

He looked down at me, our faces still close, and the moment splintered, out of step, tumbling into long, frozen seconds, his chest still beating against mine. He blinked as though he was finally oriented again, and rolled off, lying on the ground next to me.

"I didn't mean to crush you," he said. "There wasn't time to wake you up. Are you all right?"

Was I? The fear was ebbing, and yet my pulse still raced. I still felt the pressure of his body on mine and the burn of his skin.

"Yes," I said, my voice hoarse. "What was that?"

He explained it was a Candok bear and they preferred fish to people, but there was no outrunning or killing them if they perceived you as a threat. If you made no sudden moves, they would usually leave you alone.

Usually. I felt like Wren now, understanding the certainty she wanted when it came to racaa and their meat preferences—especially when I still had the memory of the bear's hellish wet tongue sampling my face.

"We should go in case it comes back," Jase said, getting to his feet, but in two steps he stumbled and fell, the chain jerking between us. He cursed. "I forgot about this thing."

He got back to his feet and grabbed his shirt from the rock where he had laid it to dry the night before. I watched as he put it on, seeing the inked feathers on his skin disappear beneath the fabric, and I thought about how he had forgotten about the chain and the *dead weight* he was attached to, and yet he had protectively hovered over me anyway.

Over the next few days, we fell into a surprisingly easy rhythm. There was rarely silence, and for that I was grateful. He told me about other animals that lived in this region. There were several deadly ones I hadn't yet had the pleasure to meet. He hoped we would come across a meimol mound, a sign of a meaty, tasty bird that tunneled and nested beneath the soil in this area. He eyed the sharpened end of his walking stick, saying the bird wasn't hard to spear.

"How do you know so much about this region?" I asked, my hand sweeping the horizon.

"It's Ballenger territory too."

"Way out here? This has to be more than a hundred miles from Tor's Watch."

"Could be."

I grunted but said nothing else. My silence poked and stabbed between us.

He finally sighed and a sardonic grin pulled at his mouth. "All right, Kazi of Brightmist, tell me, just what is your definition of a thief?"

His tone wasn't angry. It seemed more like a genuine entreaty to understand me, and I wondered if he had been pondering it ever since I called him a thief a few days ago.

"The Vendan definition is no different than anyone else's. You take things that don't belong to you."

"Such as?"

"Livestock."

"You're talking about the shorthorn we took from the Vendans? It was payment for trespassing."

"You weren't entitled to even one shorthorn, but it was far more than that. It was everything. You burned their fields. Destroyed their pens. Took their supplies."

He shook his head. "One shorthorn. That was it. The rest is Vendan embellishment."

"I saw the damage myself."

"Then someone else did it. Not us."

I glanced at his profile, wondering if he was lying. A vein twitched in his neck, and he seemed absorbed by what I said. This news troubled him. Or maybe it was just me who troubled him. I didn't let up. "What about the merchant caravans you raid?"

"Only under certain circumstances when they cross into our territory."

"You mean if they cross *you*?"

He stopped and faced me. "That too." There was no apology in his expression. His easy tone was gone.

"But you have no defined borders. You aren't even supposed to be settled in the Cam Lanteux at all. You're breaking the law. It's a violation of the ancient treaties. How can you lay claim to all of this?"

"Well, maybe the ancient treaties never bothered to consult us. Tor's Watch has been here longer than any of the kingdoms—including Venda. And we do have borders, but maybe our lines are drawn differently than yours. They extend as far as it takes for us to feel secure. We've lived by our laws and survived by them for centuries. Venda has no right to be meddling."

"What about *your* meddling? The businesses you skim in Hell's Mouth? Is that one of your laws too?"

The color deepened at his temples. "Hell's Mouth was ours long before it became part of Eislandia. We built the city from rubble and ruins, and we protect everyone who lives there. No one gets a free ride."

"Protect them from *what*?"

He looked down at the chain between us. "Do I really need to give you a list? Ours is a different world than yours. My family doesn't need to explain anything to Venda."

I was ready to argue more, to point out that Hell's Mouth was in Eislandia and it was their jurisdiction to protect as they saw fit—not the Ballengers who extracted fear money—but I tried to remember that my primary goal wasn't to educate him but to obtain information, and his ire was growing. Soon we'd revert to silence.

He had already told me some of the Ballenger history, but now I wondered about his family, which he had mentioned more than once. It was a driving motivation in his life, and I contemplated the prospect of meeting a whole family of thugs who possibly harbored a dangerous traitor. For what purpose would they give him refuge? It seemed everything was a transaction for the Ballengers. No free rides. What were they getting out of it?

I softened my tone, trying to redirect the conversation. I already recognized his tics, the straight, firm line of his lips, his nostrils flaring, the muscles in his neck tightening, his wide shoulders pulling back. His enormous pride and ego when it came to his family was his weakness, and I needed to understand it, because for a thief, understanding and exploiting your opponent's shortcomings was the first rule of the game. And he *was* my opponent. I needed to remind myself of that because he hadn't turned out to be what I expected, and some part of me found him—

I wasn't sure what the word was. Maybe the safest one was *intriguing*.

But as he spoke of his family, they didn't seem like a weakness at all—maybe it was just the sheer number of them that astounded me. No one had families that large in Venda. Ever. Besides his mother, he had six brothers and three sisters. There were also aunts, uncles, and cousins. More extended family lived in the city. He told me their names, but there were far too many to remember them all, save a few. Gunner and Titus were his oldest brothers, Priya his sister was the oldest of the siblings, and Nash and Lydia, who were only six and seven, were his youngest—still too young to sit in on family meetings. The meetings were a formal affair where the whole family gathered together around a table to decide on family business. They voted on all major decisions.

"And there's Mason too," Jase added. "He's another brother. Same age as me—nineteen. My parents took him in when he was only three after his parents died. We're the only family he's ever known. He votes too."

"And what's your role in this?"

"As *Patrei*, I make the final decision."

"You can overrule the vote of the family?"

"Yes—*if* I were there. But as you may have noted, I haven't even had a full day as *Patrei* yet."

"And that's the trouble you think I've caused."

His response was an affirmative silence, but then he added, "I shouldn't have gone down that alley alone, but I only expected to encounter you, not hunters, so I waved off my *straza*."

"*Straza?*"

He explained they were personal guards. The whole family had them.

"You have that many enemies?"

"When you have power, you have enemies," he answered. "What about you? Do you have family?"

My throat squeezed. Since I lost my mother, I had seen family as only a liability. Even growing close to Wren and Synové seemed like a terrible risk. The world was so much safer when you only had yourself to lose.

"Yes," I answered. "I have family. Both of my parents live in Venda."

"What are they like?"

I searched for an answer, something that would make his questions stop. "Happy. Content. And very proud of their only daughter," I said, then steered the conversation elsewhere.

Though I was no stranger to hunger, our foraging had been scant, so I was overjoyed when we came to a creek and I spotted wish stalks growing at its banks. I was surprised that he had no knowledge of them. In Venda, they were a spring treat, growing in wide thickets in bogs. My mother and I would go gather them just outside the city walls. *Make a wish, Kazi. With each one you pick, make a wish for tomorrow, the next day, and the next. One will always come true.*

The magic of the wishes, of course, was simply in making them, fishing deep for a hidden desire, molding it into words to make it real, and tossing it into a mysterious unknown that you believed was maybe, just maybe, listening. Even at six years old, I knew wishes didn't come true, but I made them just the same. It felt rich and wild and as indulgent and marvelous as a rare dinner of pigeon and parsnips. For a few minutes, a wish put a sword in my hand and gave me power over the grimness of our world.

I picked several, making silent wishes with each one. Jase looked at my handful of stalks like they were weeds. "What do they do besides grant wishes?" It was obvious that he had never skipped a meal in his life, much less a week of meals.

"You'll see," I answered. We sat down on the bank cooling our ankles in the creek, and I told him to chew. "Don't eat the stalk, just swallow the juice." I explained that the juice was not unlike nectar and just as nourishing.

"But the real magic is this," I said and took the pulpy stalk I had chewed and split it open so it lay flat. "Give me your ankle," I said, pointing to the chained one. He pulled it from the creek, and I slipped the flattened stalk beneath the shackle where his skin was cut. "You'll start to feel the difference soon," I said. "It has—" I glanced up at him and found his eyes were focused on me, not his ankle. I froze, thinking there was something he was about to say. Our gazes remained locked, and there were questions in his eyes, but not the kind I could answer. My breath stopped up in my chest.

"It's awkward, isn't it?" he said.

"What's that?" I replied, my voice far too breathy.

"These moments when we're not hating each other."

I swallowed and looked away. But it seemed there was nothing to look at and the moment only grew more uncomfortable and my jaw ached from clenching it. He was right, it *was* awkward. This was not something I was good at. I was good at running away, distance, disappearing. Not this. Not at being confronted with him over and over again, never having more than three feet of space between us, and I hated that I actually found him . . . *likable*. I shouldn't have liked him at all. And I hated the other things I noticed about him too, little things that caught my attention, like the way his hair fell over his eyes when he stooped to build a fire, the interesting quirk of his right brow when he was angry, the four small freckles on his arm that would make a *J* if a line connected them, the way the light caught the stubble on his chin. I was a connoisseur of detail, but I didn't like the details I saw. I hated that I found him—appealing. Not just his appearance, but the confidence of his strides, the calculations in his gaze, his cockiness, his damned voice. I hated the ridiculous flip-flop my stomach did just now when I caught him looking at me. I was not Synové!

Maybe most of all, I hated that I found any kindness in him at all. I hated that I'd had to swallow a knot in my throat that first night when I realized he was trying to help me sleep, as he had every night since then. Those I had tricked and stolen from in the past had never been kind. It made it easy to turn them into fools and steal from them.

"You were saying? It has . . . ?" he asked. I knew he was trying to give me some coherent thought to occupy myself.

"Healing qualities. It has healing qualities."

"Here, let me put this one on your ankle."

"I can do it myself," I said and took the chewed stalk from him, fussing over it again and again as I pressed it onto my ankle.

"I think you have it in the right position," he said, and I finally left it alone.

We sat there for silent minutes, chewing more stalks and breaking several more in half to stuff in our pockets. He leaned over, looking at his ankle. "The sting is gone. Thank you." His voice. There was no mistaking the kindness I heard.

I nodded and finally felt composed enough to look at him. "Thank you, too."

"For?"

"Keeping me still when the Candok came upon us," I answered. "I might have ended up as his breakfast."

His mouth pulled in a frown. "Nah. One bite and he'd have spit you out. You're not even close to being sweet enough."

I suppressed a smile. I was much more at ease with his disparaging remarks.

He stood and put his hand out to help me up. "We should get going, Kazi of Brightmist."

I took it and stood. "You seem to like calling me that. Why?"

"Because I'm not sure that's your real name. You appear to have a lot of hidden sides to you—juggling, telling riddles, taking down boys and threatening to cut their pretty necks."

I grimaced and shook my head, sizing up his neck. "It's not so pretty."

He rubbed his neck as if offended. "Anything else up your sleeve I should know about?"

"If I told you, it wouldn't be fun, would it?"

"Should I be concerned?"

"Probably."

They tricked us. Their voices were soft. Their heads bowed. They did not look dangerous. They looked like us, afraid.

Until we opened the gate.

They stabbed Razim and laughed. They left him for dead, and we couldn't open the door to get him until they were gone.

I heard the name of one of them as they ran away. One day I will be stronger than I am now. One day I will call his name, and I will kill him.

—Theo, 11

CHAPTER THIRTEEN

KAZI

I'M NOT SURE THAT'S YOUR REAL NAME.

Oddly, that was probably the least complicated and most true thing about me. *Kazimyrah of Brightmist.*

My mother had come from the northern province of Balwood, venturing to Sanctum City like so many others who crowded in there hoping it offered a better life than the harsh terrain beyond it, but she came there with the added burden of a baby in her belly and only a handful of coins. She never talked of my father. I didn't know if he was alive or dead, if she had loved or hated him, or if she had even known him at all. Traveling alone across the barren plains was a dangerous prospect for anyone. *He's gone, Kazi,* was all she had said, and she seemed sad so I didn't ask again.

The quarter of Brightmist was in the northern part of the city. She managed to find an unoccupied hovel there that would keep the rain off—and a midwife—so that was where she settled. Jase wasn't the first one to question my name, wondering if it was real. Most of those we encountered in the city had never heard the name Kazi. When asked about it, my mother told them it was a highland name that meant "spring." Another time she had said it meant "little bird," and another time, "god's messenger." I realized she didn't know what it meant at all, and once she was gone, the name didn't seem to matter. Who or what I was became a forgotten detail. Any name would do, and all kinds were pulled from the air to run me off. *Scat, you nasty vermin, brat, pest, crapcake!*

Until I devised a way to make them want me to stay.

The thing about a mark is they've created lies in their head, a story they've invented that they desperately want to believe, a fantasy that merely needs to be fed patiently—*you are kinder, more beautiful, shrewder, wiser, you are deserving, eat up*—like a round-mouthed fish breaking the surface of the water following after a trail of bread crumbs. Draw them closer with one morsel, two, and then hook them behind the gills, senseless and flapping, oblivious to what they have really lost because their bloated stomach is full.

Kazimyrah, I would sometimes whisper to myself as I slunk away with a meal hidden beneath my coat, because there were days even I forgot who I had once been.

———◦◦◦———

I made more of an effort to erase Jase's suspicions and convince him I was only a soldier, telling him about my training and life in the Sanctum. But even with that I had to carefully edit the truth. Training as Rahtan was different. The drills, hours, and study were endless. Probably the only thing I failed at was swimming, but only for lack of practice. I was smaller than most of the pledges and had to work twice as hard to prove myself. That part was easy to do. The hardest thing I had to learn was to sleep *in* a bed, not under it. Most nights, to save myself the anguish, I simply snuck off with a blanket to a hidden dark passage under the stairs.

One night, the queen had unexpectedly joined me. I remembered I had stared furiously at the lantern flame, focusing on it rather than her. I had felt shame for huddling in the dark. She sat on the floor next to me, the tunnel too small for us to stand.

"I came here too," she had said. "It was a dark, safe space for me. There were many days I feared would be my last here in the Sanctum. I was so afraid then. Some days, I'm still afraid. I have so many promises to keep."

"But you have kept your promises."

"Freedoms are never won once and for all, Kazimyrah. They come and go, like the centuries. I cannot grow lazy. Memories are short. It is the forgetting that I fear."

That was what I feared too.

Forgetting.

But none of this could I share with Jase.

When he asked me if juggling was part of Rahtan training, I laughed it off and said it was just something I had picked up along the way.

"What way is that?"

Digging.

I told him a friend taught me.

"You have clever friends."

"Yes, I do," I answered, offering no more information. I was self-taught. Desperation can be a good teacher, maybe the best teacher. I had to perfect new skills quickly—or starve. But his comment about friends made me think of Wren and Synové. They came to the Sanctum a few months after I did, both caught in scuffles with no immediate family to summon. Being the same ages and having known one another on the streets, we were naturally drawn together. After two years, Kaden, the queen's Keep, had the final say on who would advance to Rahtan training.

He had given us a long, stern look, trying to decide if all three of us would move on to the next level. Surprisingly, his wife, Pauline, had shot him a stern look in our favor. We'd trained and worked together ever since. I hoped they were safely tucked away, sitting tight, Synové entertaining Wren with the mundane details of the racaa. Yes, our plan had gone awry, but they were inventive and we had backup plans. By now they had probably figured out I wasn't inside Tor's Watch.

"How much farther is the settlement?"

"I'm not sure. I forgot to bring my map and compass. Why don't you dig out yours?"

"You think we're still on course?"

"Yes," he answered emphatically. I wasn't sure if he was annoyed that it was the second time I had asked or simply unhappy that we'd be walking into the Casswell settlement—and Vendan territory—whether he liked it or not.

He continued to tell me more stories about Tor's Watch that I had to admit fascinated me. I looked forward to them. This morning, he'd told me about Breda's Tears, a series of seven cascading waterfalls in the Moro mountains. They were named for the goddess Breda who had come to earth and fallen in love with the mere mortal Aris. Their love was so great that new flowers sprang up in their footsteps, flowers more beautiful than any that the gods had ever created, and the gods became jealous. They forbade Breda from returning to earth, and when she disobeyed, they struck Aris dead. Her grief was so overwhelming that rivers of tears fell from the heavens, rushing down the mountains where they once walked, creating waterfalls that still flow to this day.

"And there are flowers that grow at the base of those waterfalls, that grow nowhere else on the mountain."

"So it must be true," I said.

He smiled. "Must be. I'll show you one day."

A clumsy silence fell. We both knew he would never show me, but his words had slipped out easily before he could stop them, as if he were talking to a friend.

There were more awkward moments.

Yesterday morning, I awoke to his arm slung over me, his chest nesting close to my back. He was unaware, probably seeking some warmth in his sleep. I lay there, not moving away, thinking about the weight of his arm, how it felt, the soft sound of his breaths, the heat of his skin. It was a reckless, indulgent minute, wondering what he dreamed of, and then sense flooded back in, and I carefully nudged his arm away before he woke up. I'd made a conscious effort not to touch him. I think he had done the same, but sleep had become its own thief, stealing away our intentions.

As we walked, I plied him with questions, sprinkled carefully so they would seem offhand and casual, mostly about Tor's Watch. I learned it was a sprawling complex of homes and buildings that housed the offices of the Ballenger business empire. Their income came from multiple sources, but he didn't tell me what they all were. When I thought he sensed I was digging, I changed the topic to something else, but I did learn that a hefty portion of their revenue came from the trading arena, a large exchange where buyers and sellers from all over the continent came to trade goods. It began with the grain grown in Eislandia, but with more trade opening up between the kingdoms since the new treaties, the arena had tripled in size every year since.

"Am I hearing this right?" I asked, laying on my thickest mocking tone. "You're saying you have benefited from the new treaties?"

"In some ways. But not so much that we're willing to give up who we are."

He rubbed his bare finger just below the knuckle where his signet ring had once been. It was another tic I had noticed. He did it frequently when he talked of home. I imagined the struggle that had ensued when the hunter tried to take it from him. I was certain Jase hadn't given it up easily. I supposed he was lucky he still had his finger at all.

I pushed my hand into the bottom of my pocket and fingered the warm circle of metal and wondered if I should give it to him, but it seemed too late now. He would wonder why I had taken it in the first place, and especially why it took me so long to hand it over. The keys I had taken for survival. The ring was for an entirely different reason.

In the year before the queen came, more of my stealing had become punitive. It was an angry tax I collected for answers I never received, and a retribution for all the fingertips of children taken by quarterlords and then fed to the swine. Most of the punitive thefts were for items that held no value. They could not fill a belly, but they filled me in other ways.

The smallest, most useless thing I ever stole was a shiny brass button that made the Tomac quarterlord so very proud. It protruded from his belly among a long line of shiny buttons on his jacket, a rare treasure he had bought from a Previzi driver. To me, they looked like fat golden rivets holding his belly in place. Stealing the middle button had ruined the entire showy effect. I had stalked him for a week, knowing just when he would pass down one small, crowded alley, throngs shoving against him, and I was there, my cap pulled low, my small curved blade in the palm of my hand. He didn't know it was gone until he reached the end of the alley, and I heard his bellowing screech. I had smiled at the sweet sound. It was all the supper I needed.

Jase's ring was just as useless to me as that button had been, and I had stolen it for the same reason. It was a symbol of power, a legacy they revered, and in one quiet move I had relegated it to the bottom of my dark, dirty pocket.

CHAPTER FOURTEEN

JASE

SHE HAD AN INTENSE CURIOSITY, AND I WAS HAPPY TO FEED IT with stories about Tor's Watch, but when it came to her own life her words became reserved and calculated. Being chained to someone hour after hour, day after day, gives every pause a hidden weight. I dwelled on the details she wouldn't share.

What had her life been like in Venda? Or maybe, more precisely, what had they *done* to her? She was not the result of happy, content parents. It was like she'd been held prisoner in a cellar her whole life. She flinched at sun and an open sky. As soon as we hit the Heethe plateau, she kept her eyes straight ahead on some distant point, her focus like steel, her shoulders rigid, like she carried a heavy pack on her back. When I pointed out an eagle soaring above us, she barely gave it a glance.

I turned the conversation back to something that she seemed confident about—being a soldier. She told me about the various weapons that were forged for the Rahtan, the knives, *ziethes*, swords, rope darts, crossbows, and more. The fortress Keep assessed what best suited their strengths.

Her sword and knives were presented to her by the queen when she became Rahtan.

"Have you ever used them?"

She raised a brow. "You mean, have I ever killed anyone? Yes. Only two so far. I try to avoid it if I can."

If I can. She said it so casually, unruffled, the same girl who I had to coax riddles from each night so she could sleep under an open sky.

"Who did you kill?" I asked.

"Raiders," she answered. A frown pulled at the corner of her mouth as if she was still disgusted by the encounter. "We were rear guard on a supply train. They didn't see us hanging back. That was the point. But we saw them. What about you? Have you ever killed anyone?"

I nodded. Far more than three, but I didn't tell her how many and I was glad she didn't ask.

More than once, she caught me studying her. I tried to focus on the landscape, but my eyes drifted back to her again and again. She fascinated me, her contradictions, her secrets, and the girl that sometimes surfaced from beneath her tough soldier exterior, like when she spotted the wish stalks on the bank. The girl who forgot who I was and pressed a wish stalk to my ankle. In another world, another circumstance, I think we might have been friends. Or more.

I knew that I spent more time wondering about her than I should.

I scanned the foothills ahead, trying to concentrate. Trying to push my mind back to where it should be. I had ridden this way before but had never walked it all on foot—especially not barefoot, chained, and half starved. It was hard to judge distances. How much farther was it? Was there any chance of getting back before they sealed the tomb? What was going through all of their minds? *Where the hell is Jase?* No doubt search parties had been sent out, but no body had been found. I was certain that the Rahtan with Kazi were in my brothers' custody by now, being interrogated. Mason could squeeze information out of anyone, but even Kazi's companions wouldn't have any hunch about what had happened to us. They couldn't have known about the labor hunters any more than Kazi and I had.

Her comment, *I saw the damage myself*, kept resurfacing in my mind, the burning of the fields and the theft of all the settlers' livestock. We had meant to scare them off. They had to leave. Our visit hadn't been pleasant. The short horn had been a warning, a chance for them to gather up their things and move on, but that was all we took. Who took the rest?

Gunner was impulsive, his temper quicker than mine, and the days of standing vigil at our father's bedside had left all of our emotions ready to snap. Gunner had always voiced his objections about the settlers more loudly than any of us—but I was sure he wouldn't go off on a rampage without my approval, even if at that time I hadn't officially been *Patrei* yet. He deferred to me in these matters. But if not him, who? Were the settlers or Kazi lying?

That was another reason my father gave for naming me *Patrei*. I was usually good at spotting lies, better than my brothers. But being able to discern lies didn't necessarily reveal the truth. That took more digging— and I wanted to know what her truths were.

Dammit.

I wanted to know a lot more about her, and that was only asking for trouble. I needed her and the other Vendans out of my life sooner rather than later. Hopefully, we wouldn't be chained much longer.

I glanced at her, tireless, her dark lashes casting a determined shadow beneath her eyes, her warm skin glistening, my gaze lingering far too long.

Maybe some trouble was impossible to avoid.

"What's this?" I heard the trepidation in her voice as if she already sensed what was hidden in the half-mile-wide river of blinding sand.

We had crested a knoll, and I had misjudged when we would reach it. It was midday and the sands would be scorching and we were bootless.

"Sand," I answered.

"That is *not* sand," she said.

Not entirely. The bones were visible, small, broken, and mostly human. Dull, pitted teeth, the occasional whole vertebrae resting on top like a white lily on a shining alabaster pond. "It's called Bone Channel," I said. "They say the sand streams from a city that was destroyed in the flash of the first star. We can't cross it barefoot in the heat of day."

Shimmers of heat rippled upward. Kazi stared at it like she could see the ghosts entombed in the sand trying to claw their way to shore. Her attention rose to the distant foothills on the other side and the ruins that topped them—our first potential shelter—but a burning graveyard lay between us.

"Our shirts," she said. "We can wrap them around our feet." She began unbuttoning her shirt. "Take yours off too. We'll need them both."

"We can wait until night—"

"No," she said. "I'm not sleeping out here in the middle of nothing when there are ruins in sight."

She took off her shirt and ripped it in half. She had a thin chemise on beneath it, and I was both hoping she would and wouldn't remove it too. *Devil's hell, get hold of yourself Jase.*

"Your shirt," she reminded me.

I wasn't eager to rip it in half, but I didn't want to wait until nightfall for the sands to cool either, and with the heat of summer we didn't really need the shirts for warmth.

We wrapped our feet with several layers of fabric, tying them securely. We stepped out, the sand still feeling like a furnace beneath us, but the fabric did the job, keeping our feet from blistering.

It was harder to walk with the knotted fabric pulling at our ankles, but we synchronized our steps. I tried to make conversation, thinking of other legends to tell her, but I was distracted. It wasn't that I had never seen a bare-shouldered woman before, or one so scantily clad, but somehow this felt different. She's a soldier, I reminded myself. Rahtan. One who held a knife to my throat and was prepared to use it. It didn't help. Halfway across I said, "Tell me a riddle."

She looked at me, surprised. "Now?"

I nodded.

She thought for a moment, her hand gliding over her abdomen, then said,

> *"The less I have, the more I grow,*
> *I swirl and twirl and make a show.*
> *You can't ignore me, though hard you try,*
> *I growl, and scream, and wail, and cry.*
> *I roost in darkness, but my bite is seen,*
> *In rib and cheek, and wrist so lean.*
> *With fierce teeth, and sharper claw,*
> *None can escape my ruthless maw,*
> *But a strutting hen can strike me down,*
> *With its pretty legs in feathered gown."*

My stomach told me the answer to this one. Talk of chicken legs made the beast curled in my gut lift its sorry head. "Tonight," I said. "I promise, the beast will be fed."

She didn't seem to hear my reply. Her right brow lifted, her gaze turned puzzled. She looked past me over my shoulder. "What is . . . that?"

I turned. In the distance, stark against a clear blue sky, a single cloud exploded upward. It wasn't just any cloud. I had seen this kind before, but only when I was on safe high ground. It was a fat, bulging arm radiating miles into the sky, its muscles flayed open, purple and full, like a rampaging monster.

"Run," I said.

"But—"

"We're in a wash. *Run!*"

She trusted the urgency in my voice and ran, but we were still a long way from the other side. Silver fingers of water began shining in the distance, crawling toward us. "Faster!" I yelled.

Our steps pounded the sand and the fabric on her feet began unraveling, flapping loose at her ankles, but there wasn't time to fix it. In seconds, we saw the frothing wall of water coming toward us, a deadly churning wave. She kicked the fabric loose. "Keep going," she yelled, but I saw the agony in her face as she ran across the scorching sand. I scooped her into my arms and doubled my pace, my heart thudding in my chest, the wall getting closer, its roar like an animal bearing down, the trickling silver fingers already clawing at my ankles.

We made it to the other side, but the water was rising, already to my knees, and we still had to make it up the steep bank. I set her down, water now up to our waists, sucking to pull us into the current. The soft soil slipped beneath our feet, rain now pouring over our heads too. But we climbed, clawed, the water rising with us, both of us stabbing our walking sticks into the ground, stumbling, falling below the water, grabbing each other's hands, and we finally made it to the crest, stumbling and pulling ourselves over the top of the embankment just before the wall roared past us. We collapsed, lying on our backs, gasping for air, rain pounding the ground around us, and then she chuckled. The chuckle turned to a string of long breathless laughs, and I laughed along with her. It was relieved, feverish laughter, like we had just slayed a monster that already had us in its jaws.

And then our laughter subsided, both of us spent from our dash across the channel, and the only sound was the slap of the rain. The heat of the wet soil steamed up around us, and I turned my head to look at her. Her eyes were closed, strings of hair clinging to her cheek, drops of water collecting in the hollow at her throat, a small vein pulsing in her neck.

I sat up and reached for one of her feet to look at the sole. She flinched at first, but then let me touch it. I gently brushed my thumb over the skin. There were already blisters forming. I reached in my pocket and pulled out a wish stalk. I chewed it, then pressed it to her foot.

"Does that help?" I asked.

She blinked, her eyes avoiding mine, her chest rising in an uneven breath, then finally she answered, "Yes."

CHAPTER FIFTEEN

KAZI

THE FIRE BLAZED AND THE SMELL OF FAT DRIPPING FROM THE meimol into the flames was intoxicating, a sweet perfume finer than any found in the *jehendra*. I breathed it in, heady with its scent, and my stomach churned in anticipation.

The hot throb of the blisters was gone. More wish stalks were wrapped on my feet. Jase had used his own shredded shirt to make a bandage, then carried me up to the ruins. I told him I could walk, but he had insisted I needed to give the wish stalks a chance to do their magic. We found a snug, dark cubby among the tumbled and leaning walls of the ruins, and between the roasting meimol and the dark cave with a roof I could almost touch, I was sure the gods had finally taken mercy on that poor, miserable wretch, Kazi, or they had just tired of tormenting her.

The storm had passed quickly—gone as fast as it had come. As soon as we reached the foot of the ruins, Jase had spotted several mounds and managed to spear a meimol on his second try.

Once the meimol had sizzled to perfection, we sat and ate, savoring the juicy dark meat, sucking on each bone, licking our fingers noisily with delight, and talking about some of our other favorite foods. He mentioned many that I had never heard of before, braised rabbit with fool's sauce, huckleberry meringue puffs, and bergoo stew. I was surprised to learn that they had four cooks at Tor's Watch, but his aunt did most of the cooking. I told him about Berdi's fish stew that was a staple at Sanctum Hall. "I could eat it for every meal," I said. "And then there are sage cakes." I sighed longingly.

"Never heard of those."

"Then you've missed out. They're a heavenly vagabond specialty that can bring me to my knees."

"And oranges." His mouth pulled in a smirk, the fire casting a warm glow on his cheek. "You like oranges."

I smiled and conceded. "Yes, probably my favorite of all. I never had one as a child. It wasn't until I—" I caught myself before I revealed too much.

His brows rose. "Until you what?"

"Until I traveled to Dalbreck that I tasted one. Oranges aren't available in Venda."

His eyes drilled into me, knowing I was lying, and I hated that about him, that he was able to read beyond my face and words. He was quiet, and I suspected he mulled over what I said—or didn't say. He finally asked how my feet were doing.

"Not stinging anymore. I think they'll be fine by morning."

It was another one of those awkward moments. Our eyes meeting, lingering, looking away. After all we had been through, it seemed there should be no awkwardness left between us, but this was different. Every pause was full, like an overfilled sack of grain, the seams strained, ready to spill, filled with something we dared not explore.

"Tell me another story," I said.

He nodded. "First, let me get some more wood for the fire." He eyed the chain between us. Where one of us went, so did the other. "You up to it?"

"I told you, the pain is gone, and I have these fine shoes you made me." He stood and reached out, helping me to my feet. My soles were tender, but the discomfort wasn't unbearable, especially with the cushion of the bandages. We walked to the cave mouth and out onto the long wide ledge that rimmed it. Coming up the hill to the ruin, I had only seen the bank and brush in front of me. Now, looking out in the other direction from the ledge, I saw a dizzying sky of stars meeting an infinite empty plain lit only by a three-quarter moon.

"Look. Up there," Jase said, pointing into the sky. "That's Aris's Heart. And right next to it is—"

I turned, my head swimming, and I reached for the ruin wall. Jase grabbed and steadied me.

"I just got up too fast," I said.

He gazed down at me, I knew, not buying it. He had known about my strange uneasiness ever since that first night when he had asked me for a riddle in the forest.

"What did they do to you, Kazi?" His voice was low, earnest. Even in the dim light, I was able to see the worry in his eyes.

I pretended I didn't know what he was talking about. "Who did what?"

"Who made you afraid of an open world? An open sky? Was it Venda? Your parents?"

"No one did anything," I answered quietly.

"Then hold on to me," he said. "Let me show you the stars."

We stood on the ledge, and he told me stories. He began with the lowest star on the horizon, Thieves' Gold he called it, because it had a distinct goldish cast. I held on to his arm, only concentrating on the single star and not everything that surrounded it, concentrating on Jase's voice and the story he wove around the glimmering gold nugget and the thieves who had tucked it into the sky, forgetting where they had buried their treasure.

He moved on to another cluster of stars, Eagle's Nest, with its three bright eggs, and then another cluster, and another, until soon the whole sky was not a sky at all but a dark parchment of glittering stories, each one connected to the next. And as he spoke, some stars streaked across the sky, alive, leaving burning tails behind them, and for those he had stories too. "They're the Lost Horses of Hetisha, abandoned when she fell from her chariot to the earth. They race across the heavens now, always circling, always searching for her. It's said that if she's ever found, their stars will join with her chariot once again and be the brightest in the night sky."

I stared where a streaking star had just disappeared, and an ache grew inside me. Maybe the throbbing was for a glittering sky I had never truly seen before, or maybe it was the story he told me about the Lost Horses. Maybe it was the thought of them circling the heavens for millennia that ached beneath my ribs. *They will never find her,* I thought. *She is gone.*

"And I think . . ." He turned toward me. "That's about it." Our faces were unexpectedly close, the moonlight cutting across his cheekbone, and suddenly I wasn't thinking about stars or runaway horses.

I had forgotten that I was still gripping his arm and I loosened my hold, returning my hand to my side.

"I guess I should gather a few branches for the fire," he said.

"I'll help you." I stepped forward, both of us taking quick clumsy steps, and we bumped into each other, then tripped, the ruin wall keeping both of us from stumbling to the ground. Now his face was even closer, my back pressed to the wall, his arm braced against it. There were no more diversions, no more chances to look away. It was as though we had both given in to a moment that had been circling, waiting, trying to pounce on us all along. And now it had.

He swallowed, his face only inches from mine. Long silent seconds passed, and it felt like all the world and stars and sky were closing in on us, pressing us nearer to each other.

"Do you suppose," he finally whispered, "that this could be part of making . . . the best of it?"

My breath fluttered faintly in my chest. There were a hundred things I should have said, but instead I answered, "I think it could be."

His head tilted to the side, his face lowering, and his lips barely brushed mine, tender, slowly, leaving time for me to turn away, but I didn't. I didn't want to. His hand slid behind my back, drawing my hips to his. Rivers of heat throbbed inside me, and then his mouth pressed to mine, his tongue parting my lips, warm, sweet, gentle. His breath grew heavy and his arms closed around, drawing me closer, the heat of his touch like a fiery brand against the small of my back. My hands glided over his shoulder blades, his skin searing my fingers, his muscles tense, hard. My head spun, but in a way that I wanted to sink into, to drown in the warmth of it. I was falling into a vast dark sky and I didn't care. I wanted to disappear into it. I wanted more. Our tongues explored, soft, warm, and then he pulled away, his eyes searching mine, wondering, asking. Should he stop?

No, I thought. *No. Don't stop.*

His gaze held, waiting, as if he needed to hear me say it aloud.

My breaths shuddered, still hot in my chest. I knew I had made a big mistake, but it was a glorious one, and I wanted to make it over and over again. But there was something in his eyes, something genuine and earnest and true that made me pause. This was more than just making the best of it, this was something taking root, a seed being planted. But it was a seed that couldn't be planted.

You are Rahtan, Kazi. You have a promise to keep, and you will betray him eventually. Don't do this.

A fist tightened in my gut. It wasn't right. This was a line I couldn't cross. My hands slid around to his chest to push him away, but then I hesitated, my palms burning against his skin, and slowly they slid upward, rising, my fingers raking through his hair, lacing behind his head, and I pulled his mouth back to mine.

CHAPTER SIXTEEN

KAZI

I HAD ALWAYS HEARD THE GHOSTS.

Death was no stranger in Venda. He had walked the streets boldly, rubbing his bony elbows against passersby whose cheeks were as gaunt as his own, his wide grin spotting you from afar, whispering, *You, you are next.* And I would whisper back, *Not yet, not today.* Everyone in Venda was always just a season away from death, including me, depending on which way death turned, and his frozen grin had long ceased to frighten me.

So when I saw the ghosts in Bone Channel, their bony fingers reaching out, pawing my feet, their rattled voices warning, *Turn back, do not pass this way*, I ignored them.

Do not pass this way.

But we did.

And now we couldn't turn back. We had fallen through a hole and come out on the other side in a different world, a temporary world that was upside-down, where everything sounded, felt, and tasted different, and every fleeting flavor of it was dangerously sweet.

Jase leaned close, lifting my chin, his lips meeting mine—*the best of it*, that's what we told ourselves, over and over again as one day rolled into the next; we were only making the best of it. It was a story, a riddle, a wish stalk that we wove into every kiss, a sweet powdered sugar that would melt and disappear on the end of our tongues, but for now it was real enough. What was the harm? We were surviving.

But as the miles we walked added up, our steps whispered a different message, each one bringing us closer to the world we had left. Heaviness would crouch in my gut, a hidden animal that wasn't fooled, no matter the stories we told ourselves. He might be one kind of person out here, but back there, he *was* the enemy, the lawless head of a lawless family—a family that possibly harbored a murderous war criminal who was a threat to the entire continent, and if they did, he and his family would pay. Here, I might be a girl who had helped him escape from hunters, helped heal his wounds, the girl who loved listening to his stories, but there, in the real world, I was entrusted with a job by the Queen of Venda. I was as loyal to her as he was to his family, and I would betray him when the time came. I would bring his family and dynasty to their knees. His world was about to end.

The best of it.

We were only making the best of it.

For now.

It was our story. It didn't have to have a happy beginning or a happy ending, but the middle was a feast at a banquet, a rich soapy bath, a night's rest at an inn and a full stomach, a warm chest nestled up against my back, the soft heat of lips at my nape, stories whispered in my ear.

We stopped midmorning to drink at a spring, then rested in the shade of an alder. Foliage was growing thicker now, the plains behind us, the foothills steeper, the mountains topped with forests looming just behind them. I lay on my back and he hovered next to me, propped on one elbow. His finger traced a line along my jaw. He didn't ask anymore what had been done to me. Now it seemed he only wanted to erase it, wash it from my memory, and for now, I let him.

"Kazi," he whispered against my cheek. And then his lips slid down my neck, and I forgot once again about the world we were heading into and thought only about this one.

———❖———

Another night closed in, a midnight blanket of clouds covering the stars, making our words safer. The darkness mercifully swallowed what might be seen in our eyes.

What is this, Kazi?

I knew what he meant. *This.* What was this between us? Just what game were we playing?

I had wondered too. Because now our kisses were filled with pauses, our gazes filled with more questions instead of fewer.

I don't know, Jase.

What do you feel?

Your lips, your hands, your heartbeat.

No, Kazi, in here, what do feel in here?

His finger stroked a line down the center of my chest.

I felt an ache pressing within. A need I couldn't name.

I don't know.

I didn't want to know.

Let me taste your mouth, I whispered. *Don't make me think.*

———❖———

I screamed with joy when we came upon a deep pool to bathe in. We rushed toward it, stumbling, squealing, jumping into the cool crystal water. When I surfaced, he splashed me and an all-out war began, the pool erupting with a maelstrom of blinding water and laughter, until he finally grabbed my wrists so I couldn't move. Calm returned, but not to his eyes. They churned with a different kind of storm. I looked at his face, water dripping from his hair and chin, his lashes clumped together with wetness.

"I like you, Jase Ballenger," I said softly. "I think if you weren't a thief, we might be friends."

"And if you didn't whisk out knives and threaten to cut pretty necks, I think we might be friends too."

I wrinkled my nose. "Oh, how obsessed you are with your pretty neck."

His hands tightened on my wrists. He pulled me close, his teeth nipping at my neck and between kisses, he whispered, "It is not my neck I am obsessed with, Kazi of Brightmist."

A cooling breeze lifted my hair, the scent of pine wafting through it, high grass swaying around our knees. We had left early, the screech of a racaa startling us both awake. It flew low, its shadow nearly touching both sides of the valley. Jase confirmed that their primary diet was antelope, occasionally snatching foals or sheep, but he assured me he had never heard of them taking humans. "At least not more than once or twice. It's never worried me, though. I hear they favor black-haired beauties—with their sour, tough meat and all."

I jabbed him with my elbow. "Where I go, you go, so you better hope it finds a nice juicy antelope today."

By midmorning, the breeze was gone, the sun relentless, and the still air seemed to hold a foreboding *hum*. Maybe it was just our footsteps swishing through the grass or the endless rattle of the chain dragging between us. Maybe it sounded like a timepiece ticking off our steps.

"Let's take a break," I said, and we headed for a stand of birch and lay beneath the shade on a thick bed of summer grass. But even without the rattle of the chain and the swish of our footsteps, I still heard a per-sistent *hum* and *tick* in the stillness of the air. It vibrated through my bones like a quiet warning. "Tell me a story, Jase," I said. "Something else about your family history." Anything to block the *hum* and the *tick*.

He told me the story of Miandre. She was the first mother of all Ballengers. She came to Tor's Watch with Greyson as part of the surviv-ing Remnant when she was thirteen. She was only a child herself but was forced to lead along with Greyson because the others were even younger. Like Greyson, she had watched her last living relative murdered by scavengers, so they had a common goal to create a haven where no scavenger could hurt them again. Stone by stone, the fortress they founded grew over the centuries, but they were the beginning of Tor's Watch. "We were the first country, or as you Vendans would call it, the first kingdom." I heard the pride in his voice. Even his eyes danced with light as he spoke.

The lines of Morrighese, Vendan, and Dalbretch history had blurred and overlapped each other long ago, but it was well recognized by all the kingdoms that Morrighan was the first to be established, not a rocky out-of-the-way fortress no one had heard of until recently. And from Morrighan the other kingdoms were born. Even Venda had been only a wild territory with no official name until the first borders were drawn. Tor's Watch was small and isolated. It was little surprise that Jase knew nothing of the history of the entire continent. I only learned most of it myself after I went to live at the Sanctum.

"And all of this is written in the books you told me about?"

"Yes," he said confidently. "Every word. It was Commander

Ballenger's last order to his grandson, to write it all down, and Greyson did, along with the surviving Remnant, but it was mostly he and Miandre who recorded what had happened. It wasn't until almost a decade later that the two of them married, and the Ballenger line began. They had eight children together."

Babies. The Ballenger women seemed to be quite fertile.

I had been careful not to cross that unwanted line that might bind Jase and me together forever—out here there was no protection for that. I wasn't going to risk creating a child, not when this world we were living in would disappear in only a day or two when we fell back into the other one, and soon I would return to Venda. Jase didn't push me, as if he didn't want to cross that line either. We might be deluding ourselves for now, but he was as driven as I was and his connection to home was strong. It showed in his face and his determined pace. Even our rests he kept short, only breaking when we came to a spring, stream, or shade.

"Did it hurt?" I asked, my hand skimming the feathers tattooed across his shoulder and chest.

"Like hell. I was fifteen and too stupid to know how much it would hurt. But I was eager to get it a year early. My brothers didn't get theirs until they were sixteen."

"Why did you want it early?"

He shrugged. "To prove myself, I guess. It seemed important at the time. My younger brother and sister had died unexpectedly from an illness, we'd just gotten word about the new treaties that were already over a year old that no one had bothered to tell us about, and then there had been an attack on one of our farmsteads. They destroyed everything and killed two of our hands and my cousin. Our world seemed to be falling apart. I guess getting the tattoo was my way of trying to prove it wasn't. It was something permanent that said our family and legacy would survive. My father tried to warn me, but I was stubborn and insisted. I wailed like a baby when I got it—and that was just with the first feather."

"You? Stubborn? I never would have guessed."

He grinned, and I watched a dreamy memory float through his eyes. "Yeah, my father smiled the whole time I was getting it done. He reminded me, *Be careful what you ask for,* and he made sure the tattoo was nice and big. I had to go back for three more sessions after that to finish it up. Those were even harder, but I survived. When it was done, my father made me come to dinner without a shirt for a week to show it off. He was proud. I think that was when I knew I would be the next *Patrei.* I just didn't think it would happen so soon."

His expression turned sober, and I wasn't sure if it was because he was remembering the duties that awaited him or remembering that his father was dead.

I gently dragged my fingernail over his skin, outlining the jagged edge of feathers, trying to bring him back from that other world, at least for a few minutes. His eyes gleamed once again, and a flurry of birds flew through my stomach like they did every time he stared at me so intently. I wondered how I had not seen how beautiful his eyes were the first time we met. But then I knew—it was his kindness that had broken me, that first night when he asked for a riddle. He had perceived a weakness in me that he tried to help me overcome by bringing out my strength. Before that kindness, the color of his eyes hadn't mattered.

He looked down at me, our pauses becoming more reckless, the questions lurking behind them doubling.

"What?" I finally said as he continued to study me, like all the world's mysteries were hidden behind my eyes.

"I have a riddle for you this time," he said.

"You?" I laughed.

"Don't be such a skeptic. I'm a fast learner when I'm motivated."

Wish stalks, stories, riddles—for now it was enough. "All right, then, Jase Ballenger, go ahead."

"What is as bright as the sun,
As sweet as nectar,
As silky as the night sky,
And as irresistible as a cold, tall ale?"

"Hmm. Bright, sweet, silky, and irresistible? I give up."

"Your hair woven through my fingers."

I laughed. "That's a terrible riddle. It makes no sense."

He smiled. "Does it have to?"

He brushed a strand of my hair across his cheek, his face drawing closer, and his lips hovered, lingering at my hairline. I closed my eyes, breathing in his touch, needles of heat skimming beneath my skin, and then as slow as syrup his lips traveled over my brow, grazed my lashes, down my cheek, drawing a line all the way to my mouth, and there his lips rested gently, our breaths mingling featherlight, a searching, wondering ache between them—*How much longer?*—both of us memorizing this moment as if we feared it disappearing, until finally his lips pressed harder, hungry on mine.

It was a wild indulgent slope we had cascaded down, and I didn't care. For once in my life, I didn't care about tomorrow. I didn't care if I starved or died. I feasted on the now, and I didn't let myself think about who he was or who I was, only who we were right now in this moment and how he made me feel on this patch of earth, in this patch of shade. In this strange upside-down world, ignoring tomorrow seemed as natural and expected as breathing.

What is this, Jase? What is this?

But it was a question I didn't really want answered.

Our lips finally parted, and he rolled onto his back. He blew out a long slow breath. "Time to go," he said. "I'll think of a better riddle next time." He stood and helped me up. We got our last drinks at the stream, and he studied the path ahead. I perceived a shift in him already, counting the steps to home. The settlement was closer than I thought.

Next time.

There would be no more next times. This brief story we had created was ending. I felt it in the glint of the sun, the curl of the wind, the voices of ghosts still calling, *Turn back.* I saw it in the change of his focus. That other world, the one that held who we really were, was calling him, already whittling a hole into this one, our pasts echoing through it. Its voice was strong and I heard its call too.

The mountains on either side stepped closer, the wide valley narrowing, funneling us in the crook of its arm. I watched the way he scanned the shrinking horizon, the way he tensed as we crested every knoll, always walking a step ahead of me. My fingers danced up the knots of his spine, and his chest expanded in a deep breath. He looked sideways at me, his expression dark.

I had interrupted his thoughts.

"My father is being entombed today," he said.

The final good-bye.

I wondered how quickly his father passed, if there were things Jase didn't get a chance to say to him. We can never know the exact moment when someone will leave our lives forever. How many times had I bargained with the gods for one more day, one hour, just one minute. Was that too much to ask? One minute to say the unsaid things that were still trapped inside me. Or maybe I only wanted one more minute to say a real good-bye.

"Is there more you wished you could have asked him?"

He nodded. "But I didn't know what all my questions were until it was too late."

"How did he die, Jase?" I wondered if he would trust me enough to tell me now, instead of skirting the question like he had the last time.

"His heart," he answered, but it sounded more like a question, like he was still not quite believing it himself, or maybe this was the first time he could say it aloud. "It was unexpected. It seized in his chest, making him fall from his horse, and within a few days he was gone. There was nothing the healers could do." He stopped walking. "I've told you about my family, and you've told me nothing about yours. Can you at least be honest with me about *this*? How did your parents die, Kazi?"

The words that had been teetering on my tongue vanished. I hadn't expected this. "I never said they died."

"You've talked about Berdi and her stew, nameless people you trained with, and others you've met in distant cities, but you never mention your parents. They're either monsters or they're dead. I can see the scars, Kazi. You're not fooling me."

Be honest? I could barely be honest with myself, but after his confession, what I held back seemed like a mountain, all the larger and darker for its secrecy. I could only create a larger mountain to hold back the truth.

"Not every family is like yours, Jase. I don't see mine as often as you see yours. My parents are very important people. My father is the governor of a northern province, and my mother's a general in the army. They're always away. I rarely see them."

He was silent for a long while as if mulling over my answer, then asked, "If they weren't around, who raised you?"

The streets, hunger, fear, revenge, the merchants and quarterlords who chased me away. Desperation. A lonely world in the middle of a bustling city—a world he couldn't begin to understand.

"Friends," I answered. "Friends helped raise me."

We were the poorest of the poor. My mother was beautiful but so very young. Too young to have me, but she did, and she loved me. We were rarely apart. Whatever she did to earn a few mouthfuls of food, I was there too. She stitched garments, washed clothes, wove tethers for amulets, and sometimes at the *jehendra* she sold the useless fragments of the Ancients that she dug up in the ruins. Many Vendans thought they could ward off angry spirits.

We had a silent language between us, street language, signals that helped my mother and me survive. The subtle flick of fingers. A hand held at the side, rigid. A fist against a thigh. A finger on the cheekbone. *Run. Don't move. Say nothing. Disappear. I will return. Smile.* Because in a taut moment, some things were too dangerous to say with words.

It was the middle of the night when he came. I was awakened suddenly when I felt a finger pressed to my lips, *Shhh, Kazi, don't say a word,* and she slowly pushed me to the floor between our bed and the wall to hide me. From beneath the bed, I saw yellow flickering light dancing across walls as he approached. We had no other way out, no weapons, but she had a heavy wooden stick in the corner. She didn't reach it in time. He lunged out of the darkness, grabbing her from behind.

"I have nothing," she immediately told him. "Not even food. Please don't hurt me."

"I'm not here for food," he said as his eyes scoured the small hovel we called home, a cramped space in an abandoned ruin. "Someone's had his eye out for a girl like you. You'll bring a nice profit." The moving light from his lantern made the planes of his face jump like he wore a distorted, hideous mask. Cheekbones, chin, a shining forehead, looming close then far, twisting like a monster as I cowered in terror beneath the bed. "Where is the brat you were with today?"

That's when I knew I had seen him before, a Previzi driver, unloading his wagon of goods at the *jehendra* as merchants gathered around to admire the exotic wares. He walked by the stall later where my mother made amulets. He paused and studied us both but didn't buy anything. The Previzi never did. Vendan goods were beneath them, and they had no fear of the gods or spirits. They didn't need amulets.

"Come out, girl!" he yelled, lifting his lantern trying to see into the corners of the ruins that were our home. He shook my mother. "Where is she?"

My mother's eyes were frantic black pools. "I don't know. She's not mine. Only an orphan I let help me."

I wanted to run to her. Run for the stick in the corner, but I saw her hand, desperate, rigid at her side. Demanding. *Do not move.* Her fist against her thigh. *Say nothing.* I watched as he forced something to her lips, her hand striking him, her struggle as he made her drink, as she choked and coughed, and within seconds she went limp in his arms. I watched as he carried her away, her limp arms swinging as if saying good-bye.

Run, Kazi. Grab the stick. Save her. Now.

But I didn't. And then the flickering lantern light disappeared, darkness closed in again, and I was alone.

When the light of morning dawned, I still cowered beneath the bed, too afraid to move. I stayed there for two days, lying in my own waste, growing weak and hazy with hunger and thirst. I finally crawled out, dazed, and searched the streets for her, drinking at the washbasins, chewing bitter cuds of thannis, because wild plants were the only thing that was free. Those first months were a blur, maybe because I was half starved, but somewhere along the line I stopped being afraid of the merchants who chased me away. I was only hungry and determined.

Someone's had his eye out for a girl like you. Who? A rich merchant? A quarterlord? *You'll bring a nice profit.* I never forgot the driver's face, but it took me years to understand what his words even meant. I thought he took her to make amulets or wash clothes, so I searched every merchant tent and washbasin in the city. And once I got better at slipping into shadows, I found my way into every quarterlord's home, thinking he was making her work there. She was nowhere. She had vanished, along with the Previzi driver who had taken her, perhaps to a remote province in Venda, perhaps to a faraway kingdom on the other side of the continent. She was gone.

"You're quiet," Jase said, pulling me from my thoughts.

"So are you."

"Hungry?"

A stupid question. A placeholder for what was really on his mind. He was getting nervous. Unusually so. It made me wonder what kind of animosities the Casswell settlement might hold against the Ballengers. They were far outside the borders of Eislandia and in no way could be construed as being on Ballenger land. To my knowledge they had not been raided by them. Still, there could be grievances. Even settlements had to trade goods, and the Ballengers appeared to control the center of trading. He might have a good reason to be nervous. Just as nervous as I might be entering Tor's Watch.

CHAPTER SEVENTEEN

JASE

WE WERE ALMOST THERE. I KNEW THIS STRETCH AS WELL AS ANY.
My blood raced, and my mind sprinted from one thought to the next.
Getting home. Getting there in time. It was so close now. We just might
make it. I wouldn't let guilt get in the way of what needed to be done.
There was too much at stake. Lives. History. People who depended
on me.

I tried to keep her focused, pointing out features on the northern
range, a cluster of trees, a rock formation, a pass, anything to divert
her gaze from the southern range. I was buying minutes now, and there
wasn't a single one to spare. I had already seen our post hidden high in a
rocky outcrop overlooking the valley. It was hard to see if you didn't
know it was there, but she had a keen eye and it wouldn't stay camou-
flaged much longer.

As the valley turned, grazing horses came into view, and beyond
that our small farmstead where the caretaker lived.

"One small farmhouse?" she said. "This can't be the settlement."

"Maybe there's more at the end of the valley," I answered, still trying to delay the inevitable.

And then she spotted the three riders galloping down a trail from the outpost, heading toward us. She stopped, her walking stick jutting out in a protective stance to stop me too. "Those don't look like settlers."

"I think we'll be all right."

"No," she said, still not convinced, "settlers don't wear weapons like that at their sides. They're armed for trouble."

As they drew close, smiles evident on their faces, her shoulders pulled back and her attention turned slowly to me, her lips parting slightly, a dull realization forming. Her eyes shot back to them again, the truth settling in, my lack of concern, the recognition in their eyes when they looked at me. They pulled up short in front of us, and one of them said, "*Patrei*, we've been watching for you, hoping you'd come this way."

She turned back to me and for a few seconds her eyes were cold, deadly, but then they exploded with rage. "You filthy—" She swung her stick, but I was expecting it and grabbed hold, jerking her toward me. "What did you expect me to do?" I said. "Just dance into a Vendan settlement so you could arrest me or worse? Going separate ways was never in your plan. Your lies are easy to spot, Kazi."

Her chest heaved and she glared at me, unable to deny it. "Get away from me!" she growled, letting go of the stick. She stepped back as far as the chain would allow, still seething. I didn't have time to explain or to try and assuage her. I'd have to try later.

I looked up at Boone, our foreman. "Go back to the post for tools to get this chain off us," I ordered. "Foley, you bring back food. And an extra horse."

"Two horses?"

"No. She'll ride with me." I couldn't trust her to stay with us, and there was no spare time to go off on a chase.

"You have a messenger up there?" I asked.

"Aleski," he answered.

"Bring him down too."

While we waited for Boone and Foley to return, Tiago told me they had sent scouts out everywhere looking for me. "We finally tracked down the hunters, but the wagon was empty and tracks went off in all directions."

"There were four other prisoners," I explained. "When we escaped, everyone scattered. Did you take care of the hunters?"

He nodded. "Dead. But one did a lot of pleading for his life before we killed him. He said they'd been paid for a full load up front, and then were free to take and sell their haul to a mine for more profit that they could keep."

Paid up front? That was impossible. Labor hunters were nothing more than scavengers. No one paid them for merchandise they hadn't yet produced. Illegal mines were the only ones who dealt with them. "Maybe he was lying," I said.

Tiago shook his head. "Don't think so. Not with a knife pressed to his temple. He said they knew better than to come near Hell's Mouth, but it was too good an offer for them to resist."

"Who paid them?"

"He didn't know. Said it was a nameless fellow who approached them. He told them he'd know if they cheated him and didn't follow through."

No one would pay for merchandise they didn't want. It wasn't merchandise they were after. They were buying panic—and anger at the Ballengers for not keeping the city safe. Someone was trying to edge us out.

"Did you find any of the other prisoners?"

"Three. The smithy was dead, and the other two were in bad shape. Not sure they'll make it, but we brought them back to Tor's Watch. Healer is taking care of them."

"Good. Before you release them back to the city, make sure they know to tell no one what happened to them or that I was there."

"Already done. They know to keep quiet."

"Track down the other prisoner. He has to be out there somewhere. We don't want him stumbling back into town and talking." I gestured toward Kazi. "What about the other Rahtan who were with her? Did you find them?"

Tiago hesitated, glancing at Kazi. "We have them in custody, but they aren't talking."

Her eyes were steel. This was another development she didn't like. I wasn't going to get anything more out of her. At least not yet.

"There's been some other trouble," Tiago added.

He said that since the first night I disappeared there had been six fires in six different districts. Two homes had burned to the ground. No one died, but all the fires were suspicious and unexplained. The town was uneasy. There was also a thwarted raid on a Gitos caravan. Two drivers were injured.

I cursed. Someone was trying to create unrest in Hell's Mouth from all angles. Or maybe it was many someones.

Boone brought back awls and hammers from the post, pounding and fiddling with the rusted lock on my ankle until he broke it off. "Hers too?"

She was surprisingly silent, but her gaze was condemning, certainly calculating how she would pay me back. "Yes," I answered. "Hers too."

I rubbed my ankle where the shackle had scraped and cut into my skin. Kazi did the same as she eyed me suspiciously. We were finally separated.

Foley arrived with the fresh horse for Kazi and me, and Aleski, our post messenger, arrived just behind him. Aleski rode lean, and his Phesian colt could get there faster. As I adjusted the stirrups on my own horse, I gave him instructions. "Ride ahead. Greyson Tunnel. It's important they see us coming from Tor's Watch, not from town. Yell for clothes. Anything. Bring them down to us. We'll change on the run. We can't show up in these. Clothes for her too. Check Jalaine's room. Then get there and stall. And shoes!" I called as he rode off.

I had no choice but to bring her along. I'd talk to her as we rode. Convince her that she needed to go along with whatever I said. Try to make her understand what was at stake. The wolves were already moving in on Hell's Mouth. Tor's Watch would be next.

CHAPTER EIGHTEEN

KAZI

I GLARED AT JASE.

But inside I secretly roared with laughter.

On some level I was still furious. He talked of honesty in one breath, and two minutes later his lies were bared like a Candok's teeth. They sank into me, sharp and unexpected.

Still, once the shock had passed, I quickly had to hide my satisfaction at my astonishing good luck. He was taking me straight to where I wanted to go—Tor's Watch. I didn't have to sneak inside or create any more problems in Hell's Mouth to land me there. I was being escorted in by the *Patrei* himself. It was a rich, sweet irony that, at some point, I was going to happily shove down his throat.

From the minute we were met by the riders in the valley, I had watched him transform. He became someone else. He became the *Patrei*. His face hardened as he barked orders, and all the quiet plans he had been stewing on for the last several miles spilled out, one command after another like he was a general. His soldiers, like minions, jumped without question at each one. I had foolishly thought that in those quiet miles he had been thinking about us.

His commands didn't stop with his thugs. We wolfed down a few bites of bread, salted meat, and a swig of ale, and then he ordered me up on the horse we would share. He carefully held the reins out of my reach, got on behind me, and we left. As rushed as he seemed, he kept the horse in an even canter so it wouldn't become winded. I guessed that meant we had several miles to go yet.

I maintained my anger and silence, though I couldn't resist a smile when I knew he couldn't see. He spoke as we rode, trying to explain his ruse of the settlement destination, saying that he was afraid I wouldn't go along if I thought he was taking me into custody.

"Is that what you're doing? Taking me into custody?"

He was caught off guard by the first words I had spoken, and his answer came out in halting fits. "I—Yes, well, until we can figure this out."

Figure what out? It was clearly not me causing trouble in Hell's Mouth, nor Wren and Synové, whom they had in custody. That revelation alone shocked me. *How did that happen?* Did they stand watch at the end of that street for me for too long? And on what grounds were the Ballengers holding them? It was within their rights to investigate treaty violations. Still, I had a hard time understanding how they were taken in the first place—Wren and Synové were more than skilled, and those with Jase that day had been as bleary eyed as he had been. If they were being held at Tor's Watch—

If. Another thought wheedled into me. Maybe they didn't have them at all. Tiago had hesitated for a few seconds when Jase mentioned them. *They aren't talking.* They couldn't talk if they weren't there, and Synové did nothing but talk. Maybe his thugs were still searching for them and didn't want me to know. Another kind of leverage. They were going to hold their supposed imprisonment over my head. I suppressed another smile. I could play that game too.

I felt more like myself again. Back on track. The blurred lines became clear. I could forget these last days with Jase as easily as he could.

We slowed to cross a brook, and Jase leaned close, his chin nuzzling my cheek, "Kaz—"

I shoved him away with my shoulder, my elbow jabbing backward into his ribs.

I heard a small *oof.*

I shook my head in disbelief. Now what game was he playing?

Once across the brook, he rode faster. "Aren't you going to say anything at all?"

No.

"We're going to my father's funeral. There will be a lot of people there. I need you to back up whatever I say."

I said nothing.

"If I have to, I'll throw you off the horse right here and leave you behind. Is that what you want?"

No, he wouldn't, or he would have left me behind back at the post. He wanted me for something. I was curious enough to bite but not so much that I would serve him his wishes on a platter. And if I was too compliant, he'd grow suspicious.

"I guess you'll have to wait and see what kind of dead weight I become."

I felt his waves of anger at my back, and I wondered if I had overestimated my value, eyeing the rocky landscape around me. It wouldn't be pleasant to be thrown off a horse here.

We began climbing and the horse labored under the pace, but it was clear that Jase knew precisely how fast he could push the beast. The stallion's rest lay just ahead. When we cleared a copse of trees, the towering fortress of Tor's Watch greeted us. Multiple jagged turrets shot into the air, like sharp black spindles piercing the sky. If it was meant to intimidate, it did its job well. On one side, the lumbering behemoth teetered near the edge of a sheer drop, and around the rest a great stone wall with more turrets meandered out of sight. It was far larger than what I had imagined—and I could only see part of it. We headed for a section of the stone wall that turned and rolled down the mountain like a black weathered ribbon. A massive portcullis opened as we approached, anticipating our arrival.

As soon as we were through the entrance, I spotted Greyson Tunnel ahead. It was an engineering marvel in itself, a half-moon cut into the side of a mountain of solid granite, wide enough for an army to march through and high enough for five tall men to stand, one atop the next. The telltale signs of age wrinkled the edges of the opening, like the deep weathered lines of an old man's mouth. This was not the work of ordinary men. This was a creation of the Ancients. We rode far into the cavern, our horses' hooves echoing through the stone chamber. The air was chill and smelled of age and straw, horses, and sweat. A metallic taste permeated the air. I couldn't see how far the tunnel stretched, but it seemed endless. Somewhere, I heard the hollow ring of trickling water. The tunnel bustled with activity, wagons being loaded with goods, stable hands guiding horses, and absorbed workers hurrying down stairs that were carved in the tunnel's sides and emerging from an opening in the curved ceiling.

I made a mental map of every foot we traveled. There were not many places to disappear in here, but there were hundreds of glorious shadows, stepping stones to places yet to be explored. Partway down, a smaller tunnel jutted off in another direction and lanterns cast an eerie yellow glow from its low ceiling. On the wall next to the entrance, like a sign announcing a pub within, was a faint circular engraving, the stone edges melting away with time. A trace of an eagle's wing was the only thing that was still discernible. *The Ballenger crest?* So Jase's story wasn't just a story? Was this the same crest Greyson Ballenger had seen centuries ago? Still, one crest didn't make Jase's claim of being first any more true than seven waterfalls proved a goddess was crying over a lost lover.

A boom echoed and a pallet lowered by an elaborate pulley system jolted to the ground. My pulse thumped, like I had climbed into the belly of some dark macabre machine, its gears all turning and ticking in an orderly beat to the sound of its master's orders—and the master was Jase Ballenger. He swung down from his horse and grabbed my waist, bringing me down with him. "This way," he said.

He walked briskly ahead, expecting me to follow, peeling off his clothes as he walked, his belt falling to the ground, then his trousers. *Dear gods, not his—*

His undershorts fell by the wayside, too. He was as naked as the gods had made him, but my glimpse was quickly cut off by servants who descended upon him. They offered him wet towels to wash the grime from his face, a fresh shirt, trousers, a jacket. He dressed as he walked, hopping on one foot as he put boots on. He was driven, as if every second lost was crucial. Servants had descended on me too, and while I gratefully took the warm wet cloths to wash my face, I drew the line at stripping naked in a busy cavern with dozens looking on. Jase must have heard my grumblings behind him, and he turned around. "Just put the dress on over your trousers. I don't care!"

And that is exactly what I did. Both of us were still dirty with days of the wilderness clinging to our skin, but the wet towels scrubbed us up enough for appearance's sake, and the fresh clothes did the rest. Whoever dress I had was smaller than me. The hem hung well above my ankles, and I had to roll my trousers up to my knees. The long sleeves hit me mid-forearm, and buttoning the bodice proved impossible. I got it fastened as far as my bosom.

"Breathe out," the servant said, then tugged until it stretched tight across my breasts and the last two buttons were secure. *And when do I get to breathe in again?* I wondered. She was an older woman, her hair a striking shade of silver, and she seemed unruffled by the unusual activity. "Oleez," she said, in a simple introduction, then threw some slippers to the ground for me to step into. They were tight too, but for the short term, passable. She nodded toward Jase and I turned. He was poised before another passageway, a servant shaving the stubble from his face in quick sure strokes. "That's good enough," Jase said, wiping his face with a towel. "Let's go."

We weren't exactly transformed, our appearance still disheveled, but I supposed we presented some semblance of the picture he was trying to achieve. The passage was only wide enough for two of us to walk abreast. Jase and I led, the rumble of an army following behind us. No one spoke. I glanced sideways at Jase, and his jaw was a rigid line. We reached a door and when we stepped through it, brilliant sunlight blinded me. My hand shot up to shade my eyes, and a loud frenzy of snarling and barking erupted. My eyes adjusted to the light, and I saw two enormous black dogs charging toward me, their jaws snapping with sharp bared fangs. I gasped, and the top button of my dress popped free, plinking across the cobbles. I stepped back toward the door, but Jase's hand was at my back, stopping me.

"*Vaster itza!*" Jase shouted and the beasts immediately stopped. They lowered their heads, whimpering briefly, then lay down. "They don't know you," Jase said, unruffled, "and you made a sudden move."

Shading my eyes?

Besides the forbidding walls, this was one of the reasons Tor's Watch was impenetrable. I had never had to deal with dogs in Venda. There were none. They had all been eaten.

This was not a home. It was a formidable stronghold and those who manned the turrets and gates were not just guards—they were warriors committed to taking down any trespasser who even blinked in a manner that didn't suit them.

We stepped out into a large courtyard and continued our pace toward a guarded gate that was reinforced with metal plates—and then my breath caught—to our right, the fortress, Tor's Watch, which I had only seen from a distance, now loomed directly over us. Jase saw me looking up, my steps faltering. He eyed the missing button of my dress.

"Are you all right?"

"Shut up," I answered. He had no right to ask that now. But as we walked, I made another mental note: He was paying more attention to me than I thought.

We walked down a long road that traversed the mountain, and all of Hell's Mouth was laid out below us, a sprawling, spectacular sight, the circular formation of the tembris trees more apparent from this vantage point and appearing more unearthly.

When the road switched back, we were suddenly upon our destination, a tree-shaded graveyard full of tombs, statues, and gravestones. The crowds that gathered on the green lawns saw us coming. *Dear gods, what was I doing here?* What possible purpose did Jase have for me? Human sacrifice? Was I to be enclosed in the tomb with his father? I knew my imagination was pushing the limits of possibilities, but he was taking a huge chance bringing me here with him. Somehow, he trusted I wouldn't reveal that the *Patrei* had been taken captive in his own town by some bumbling fools. He was wrong to trust me, especially now. Whatever we had shared was behind us.

My pace slowed as we drew near and heads turned to watch our approach, but Jase's hand was firm at my back, pushing me forward. Still, I managed to skim the faces as I always did, not just looking for one from my past, but also the one carefully described by the queen. Neither materialized. Hundreds were gathered, and they parted as we reached the outer edge, making room for Jase to pass, a human seam silently and respectfully rippling open, until finally it revealed a cluster of people standing near the entrance of a large tomb.

They stood shoulder to shoulder, stoic, proud, but two children broke from the group when they spotted Jase and ran to him, calling his name. He knelt, gathering them into his arms, hugging them tight, his face nestling against one head and then the other, soaking them in. I watched their small, pale hands curling into his jacket, holding on to the folds like they'd never let go. It looked like Jase would never let go either. I could feel the knot in his throat, the ache in his chest, and my own chest tightened. Finally, he loosened his grip and wiped the boy's tears from his cheek with his thumb and whispered softly, "You're all right. Go on now." He tweaked the girl's chin and told them both to return to the group. The boy glanced up at me, his wet lashes clumped together, his eyes the same brown as Jase's, then turned and did as his brother ordered. The little girl followed.

His family. I knew that now. His mother. His brothers and sisters. Three I recognized from Jase's descriptions. Gunner was tall and angular, his dark-brown hair slicked back in waves. Titus was stout and muscled, with sandy hair that curled around his ears. Mason had long black hair woven into multiple braids, and a rose-colored scar on the side of his neck left a jagged line against his dark brown skin. These were the ones I had seen walking beside Jase on the first day we met. I tried to recall the names of the rest.

Unlike the youngest siblings, the others knew Jase was not supposed to have been missing at all, so they stood, calm, waiting, at if he had just come from Tor's Watch. But his mother's rigid jaw said everything. I watched her breathe in what was probably the first full breath she'd had since her son disappeared. Jase left my side and went to her, embracing her, reserved, with respect, whispering something briefly in her ear. He did the same with his brothers and sisters. The emotion that had spilled out with the youngest two was kept in check by the older Ballengers—this was a respectful greeting only—presumably they had all just seen him hours earlier, and the crowds surrounding them watched everything.

One of his sisters peered at me and my dress, and I guessed that it most likely belonged to her. She looked younger than me and several inches shorter. *Check Jalaine's room*, I think Jase had said. I stood in the middle of the open seam, distant from Jase and everyone else, awkwardly alone and wondering what I should do. When Jase hugged his last brother, he turned to the priest who was waiting at the end for him. They spoke a few quiet words, and then the priest, adorned in flowing red robes trimmed in gold, turned to the crowd and said he would prepare the tomb with blessings before the viewing procession would begin. He went into the tomb and the family and crowd seemed to relax, Jase's back still to me as he spoke to his mother. Other quiet conversations started up again, but then a man stepped out into the open seam.

"Jase, so good to finally see you. I thought you might not come at all." A deep silence fell as the man walked forward. He was young and tall, the sides of his dark-russet hair trimmed close to his head, the rest pulled back in a ponytail. His snug black jacket showed off his wide shoulders, and his boots were polished to a high sheen. "You've been scarce since your father's death. No one's seen you. You'd think a new *Patrei* would be more visible considering all the necessary preparations for today."

Jase's back stiffened and he turned, eyeing the man. Every angry tic of his that I had come to know—the controlled lift of his chin, the tight quirk of his upper lip, his unblinking stare—were instantly chiseled across his face. "Greetings, Paxton. I guess I shouldn't be surprised to see you. I thought I heard the howls of a few wolves."

"*Jase*, we're family. I appreciate that now. I hope you aren't still harboring grudges for my youthful arrogance and missteps. I know my place now, and today that place is here. It's only right that I pay respects to my blood kin."

"Only right," Jase repeated. "And my father did deserve your respect."

"As Jase does now," Mason added.

Paxton nodded and took a few steps closer. He wore a weapon at his side. Jase did not. I quickly scanned the crowd, wondering how many might be here with this man whom I already distrusted. He lifted a finger, tapping the air as if thinking. "One thing, though. I understand you missed the wrapping of the body. Did something urgent call you away? Where have you been, cousin?"

Jase remained silent, his face like stone, but I knew his anger was surging. He didn't like accusing questions, and it was clear he didn't like this cousin either, but still, others waited to hear his answer too, and those who listened mattered more to Jase than his cousin. He somehow managed to smile, then leisurely turned to me and put his hand out for me to join him. Though everything about him appeared to be assured and composed, his eyes were fixed on mine with a wildfire of need. His gaze burned through me. He said nothing, but I read the words in his expression, *Please, Kazi, trust me.* But I couldn't. I looked away but only found the same intensity in Jalaine's stare, his mother's, and then little Nash's, whose eyes were wide circles, waiting, as though he knew his family was at risk.

I looked back at Jase, his eyes still blazing, his hand still outstretched. I walked forward, feeling every eye that rested on me, my bones stiff, my steps self-conscious and not my own. When I was close, Jase grabbed my hand and pulled me snug to his side. His arm slid around me, holding me warmly at my waist, and his attention turned back to Paxton.

"I was doing exactly what my father asked me to do—ensuring that there are many more generations of Ballengers to come. Our legacy will continue."

A rumble of approving titters flitted through the crowd, and my cheeks warmed. Apparently no one but me thought the comment unsuitable for a funeral. I reached behind Jase's back and jabbed him with my thumb. He pulled me closer. "And as you can see, I made sure that all the preparations were well taken care of too."

Paxton scrutinized me, beginning at my exposed ankles. He spotted the suspicious scabs where the shackles had rubbed and cut into my flesh, his imagination probably racing in tawdry directions. His gaze rose slowly, taking in my sleeves that did not quite reach to my wrists, my tight bodice with the missing button, and then my face and disheveled hair. I met his ogling with an icy stare.

A man standing behind him leaned forward and whispered something. Paxton smiled.

"So you're warming your sheets with a Rahtan, no less. Is this the one who burst into town and you had that unfortunate *incident* with?"

"Only a misunderstanding," Jase said. "It's been cleared up."

But now everyone was eyeing me anew, recalling what they had heard, or where they had seen me before, remembering the Vendan clothes they had seen me storm into town with, and the weapons I had worn at my side. Paxton's doubtful insinuation had its desired chilling effect.

Gunner shifted nervously, noting the whispers, and stepped forward. "Of course, Rahtan! She brought word that the Queen of Venda is coming here to formally recognize the authority of the Ballengers and their territory."

Paxton blanched, shaken off balance by this news—just as the rest of us were. Jase stared at Gunner like he had gone mad. A pleased rumble ran through the crowd.

"Coming here? To you? That is quite a development." Paxton's tone conveyed his genuine surprise, but he didn't seem as pleased by this news as the rest of the crowd.

Quite a development, I silently agreed, but said nothing. Paxton watched me, searching for confirmation. I gave him nothing. I wasn't going to sink into this quagmire the Ballengers were creating and make the queen look like a fickle liar when she didn't come. His focus suddenly dropped to Jase's hand still curled around my waist, and his brows shot up.

"The signet ring? You've lost it already?" His tone was condescending, as though he were shaming a careless child. Heat flared at my temples.

Jase withdrew his hand from my side and rubbed his knuckle where the ring should have been. He had told me it had been in his family for generations, gold added, reworked, and repaired as it wore away, but always the same ring. Once it was put on, it never came off. Until now. Paxton was publicly chipping away at Jase's credibility bit by bit, first making note of his absence, then missing the wrapping ceremony, and now recklessly misplacing his ring, which symbolized his rule like a crown on a king. Or Paxton was outright digging to expose where Jase had been. Could he know? For my purposes, it was too soon for things to unravel. I still needed to get back to Tor's Watch and didn't need to get in the middle of a personal play for power, or take on some new unknown thug who wanted to displace the Ballengers.

"The ring is—" Jase began, I knew searching for a plausible explanation.

"Jase!" I said, shaking my head, as if something had just dawned on me. "I forgot to give it back to you." I looked back at Paxton and explained, "It's a bit large on him, but he didn't want to have it refitted until after the funeral. He handed it to me this morning as he bathed." I smiled at Jase. "I'll get it for you." I turned for privacy sake, facing his mother as I hiked up the front of my dress, then reached down into my grimy pocket, searching for it among the crumbled remains of wish stalks. His mother's gaze was hard, disbelieving, wondering what I was up to, but a glimmer of hope resided in her blue irises too. My fingers circled around the ring, and I nodded to her. I turned and held out the ring to Jase. "You'll have to call on the jewelsmith soon," I said. He looked at me like I had just pulled a Candok bear out of my ear. *How? When?* But those answers would have to wait. He leaned forward, and gently kissed my cheek as if we were happy lovers, then slid the ring back onto his finger, his gaze still considering me.

Wondering.

CHAPTER NINETEEN

JASE

I CLOSED THE HEAVY DOUBLE DOORS BEHIND ME, SECURED THE bolt against interruptions, and turned to face my family. Everyone was present except for Lydia and Nash, who were too young to hear most of what I had to say. The family had maintained our charade all the way back to Tor's Watch, even through the front entrance and into the hall. When Gunner began to ask questions, I shut him down and said, "*Family meeting room. We'll speak there.*"

As soon as I turned, Jalaine ran to hug me, and my mother came forward and slapped my face in the way only she could. "*Straza!* What have I told you a hundred times!" And then she held me too. I looked over her shoulder at my brothers and sisters, who patiently waited for answers.

When she finally let go, everyone took a seat at the long table filling the center of the room, and I told them everything about where I had been and what I had done. Almost everything. I didn't include some of the parts with Kazi.

"How did she get your ring?" Mason asked. "Do you think she was working with the labor hunters?"

"No. She stumbled into them, the same as me. And ran for her life the same as me."

"It could have been a trick," Samuel offered.

I told them no again, it was no trick, but I still couldn't figure out how she got the ring either. I had seen the hunter dump all the goods they had taken from us into a box beneath the wagon seat. When we escaped, there was no time to dig through it. "I'm not sure how she got it, but I'll be asking."

"Can she be trusted?" Aram asked.

Titus laughed. "Of course she can't be. Not if Jase had to post two men outside her room."

For now, she was in my room while guest quarters were prepared for her. I had posted Drake and Charus at the end of the hall so as not to be obvious. I still had made it clear to everyone at Tor's Watch what the limits to her wandering were. There were some places no one went but the family.

"She can be trusted in some ways," I answered. "But she is Vendan, and she did come here to investigate treaty violations. We'll have to be careful."

"*Violations*," Gunner grumbled. A seething rumble echoed from the others.

"So, just what happened out there between you two?" Priya asked.

"We were chained at the ankles. We had to work together to—"

"Don't be coy, Jase. You know what I mean."

Titus chimed in, "There were a hundred other things you could have said to Paxton to explain your absence. Why imply that you were holed up with her?"

"Because that excuse could not be refuted," my mother said. "No witnesses."

"Nor delicately discussed in depth," Mason added. "It did end Paxton's interrogation."

"He could have said he was sick," Samuel said.

My mother shook her head. "No. The healer would have been summoned, and the last thing we want to suggest is that another *Patrei* is in poor health."

Everyone jumped in with their own opinion on why it was or wasn't a good excuse. Priya finally held her hand up to stop the discussion. "Jase, you still haven't answered me. What happened between you two? You think I didn't see how you looked at her?"

I didn't remember looking at her in any particular way, only with a long moment of trepidation when I stretched out my hand, wondering if she would take it. I had taken a calculated risk that she would help me again, just like she had in that alley the first day we met, that she would choose me over wolves like Paxton, just as she had chosen me over labor hunters. She could have walked away that day, as the hunter had ordered. Instead she drew her sword. She may have hated me, but she hated some people more, and maybe I hoped that after all we had been through I wasn't just the lesser of two evils. Maybe I gambled that she would choose me because she wanted to. "If you imagine you saw me looking at her in any way, it's only because we managed to stay alive together."

Jalaine pouted like she was disappointed, but her eyes were lit with a smile. "So, you weren't really making little Ballengers?"

Aram and Samuel snickered.

Mason shrugged. "I was convinced."

I shot them a frigid stare to let it go.

"Well, we need her now," Priya said. "She's going to have to write a letter to the queen and actually tell her to come now that Gunner—"

"No," I said. "We're not going down this path again. After Father—"

"We have one of the queen's premier guards in custody," Gunner argued. "She'll come! We are through being snubbed by the kingdoms."

My mother nodded in agreement. "And now the citizens are expecting it. Did you hear the murmurs from the crowd?"

Mason sighed as if reluctant to concur. "It's spread to the whole town by now, Jase. Getting her to come might help the leagues back off."

"And they were all there today," Priya said, "supposedly paying their respects, but mostly licking their chops."

Make her come. It was my father's last request. That's what they were all thinking about. Him. What he wanted. What he never got.

When we had gotten word of the new treaties, my father wasn't concerned at first—our world had nothing to do with the outside one. We didn't care about them and what they did. We had always been isolated. But when heavily guarded settlement caravans began crossing our territory en route to other places, he took note. I told my father he needed to go to Venda and speak with the queen like every other kingdom. *We are not a kingdom!* he had raged. *We're a dynasty! We were here long before Venda, and we bend a knee to no one. She will come to us.* And he sent a letter telling her to come to Tor's Watch. There was no reply. It was a mistake, because now it was an insult that made him look weak. It was an insult he never forgot. Neither had the rest of my family.

Making the queen come here was as much about restored pride as making the leagues back off, but it could lead to other problems—bigger ones.

"We can't take the queen's guard hostage. If she came at all, it would be with an angry army behind her. Is that really what we want?"

"Not if the letter is worded carefully, commending us," Gunner argued.

Titus snorted. "Which I'm sure he's already written."

"No," I answered. "We don't need a queen's acknowledgment to be legitimate or to control those encroaching on our territory. There are challenges every time there's a shift in power or a weakness is perceived. We'll show our strength as we always have."

"Then what do we tell people when they ask when the queen's coming?" Priya asked.

I shook my head, blowing out a long, angry breath. "You should have kept quiet, Gunner! Why'd you have to go shoot off your mouth?"

Gunner pounded his fist on the table and stood. "Because she's Rahtan! The town's been buzzing about how she threw you up against a wall and brought you to your knees! *They saw it with their own eyes!* A *Patrei* on his knees with a knife at his throat! You think dismissing that as a mere misunderstanding is going to erase their doubts? And believe me, they have them! They needed something big to hold on to, and I gave it to them!"

Our angry gazes remained locked, the silence long and stifling.

Arguments around the table were not unusual. That was one of the reasons we held meetings behind closed doors, so our differences were aired in privacy, but once we walked out we were a unified front. That was one of the things that kept us strong.

"What about Beaufort?" Aram asked. "He's made big promises. Is he ever going to cough up the goods?"

"It's a long-term investment," Gunner told him. "Father knew Beaufort couldn't produce for us overnight. He's getting close."

"It's been almost a year," Priya said, "as he and his friends drink up our goodwill and wine. I don't like it. Playing with the Ancients' magic is like playing with fire."

"But it will secure our position with every kingdom on the continent— not just the leagues," I reminded her.

"And it will keep us and our interests safe," Mason added. "Trade could triple."

Jalaine grunted. "If he ever follows through."

"He will," my mother said firmly. There was more that we hoped to achieve than just security. But these were only more promises. Sometimes I thought that was all my father was trying to give her when he gave Beaufort sanctuary. Hope.

"Until then," she went on, "we need to do something *now*, Jase. We can't wait for promises to be fulfilled. The wolves have left their calling cards. Six suspicious fires in as many nights."

"Could it be the Rahtan who were with her?" Mason asked.

I got Tiago's hidden message loud and clear and knew when he claimed he had them in custody that they were still on the loose. The fact that two Rahtan had gone into hiding was suspicious and made speaking in front of the third one more risky. Where were they hiding and why? I didn't like it. But my gut told me that destroying homes and businesses with fires was not a Rahtan tactic, and scaring the citizenry was definitely the wolves' approach. "I don't think it's the Rahtan who did it, but we need to find them. They're around somewhere, maybe even hunkered down at that Vendan settlement. I know enough about them already to know they wouldn't run off too far with one of their own missing. Samuel, Aram, take a crew out to the settlement tomorrow and sniff around."

"We already did that. We turned up nothing."

"Do it again. The first time, they were expecting a visit. This time they won't be. We also have to find out who paid labor hunters up front to come stir trouble."

"Think it was Paxton?" Priya asked, her tone filled with distaste. He had always been sickeningly sweet to her, and it made her dislike him all the more. I suspected that he saw Priya and marriage as a way back into the Ballenger family—and its power.

"Could be," I answered, not sure myself, but I knew Paxton hated labor hunters too, and I wasn't sure even he would stoop that low.

"Or it could be a love letter from any of the leagues," Jalaine said. "They've seen the arena prospering and are hungry for a bigger piece of it. I hear them grumbling when they come into the office looking for their cuts. Truko's hawker practically ignites every time."

I looked at Mason. "Find out. However you have to do it, whoever you have to strong-arm or bribe, find out who paid off the hunters. Concentrate on Truko and his crew. Check with Zane too—see if he's seen any unusual activity." Zane had a sharp eye for faces and logged all deliveries at the arena. "As for the fires, Titus, post more guards on every incoming artery—day and night—and tell the magistrates that all new faces are suspect."

"And how do we address doubts?" Gunner asked. He wouldn't let it go. But then he had heard the buzzing and I hadn't. Gunner might be more impulsive than me, but he did have a good ear.

"I'll make myself more visible this next week. The *Patrei* is not cowering on his knees for anyone. I'll make a show of confidence and strength. We all will. Uncles, aunts, everyone. Tell them. Everyone walks the streets of Hell's Mouth this week. The Ballengers still run this town and keep it safe."

"What about her?"

The very Rahtan who took me down, walking the streets of Hell's Mouth with me? It could blow up in my face, but it could also reinforce my claim that it was a mere misunderstanding. And if any leagues were skulking, it would be a clear message that a great power was not moving in on us, but instead, recognizing our authority. Given a few weeks, doubts and fears would be calmed and everyone would forget about the queen coming.

"She'll walk too. With me."

My mother told me not to cry. She told me not to forget kindness.

She told me to be strong. She told me to believe in tomorrow.

Every day I try to remember what else she told me.

Something about shoes; something about birthdays and baths; something about whistling and roses. I cannot remember what she said.

I was only eight when she died. I hope the things I've forgotten don't matter.

—Miandre, 13

CHAPTER TWENTY

KAZI

I SOAKED IN A TUB OF LUXURIOUS *HOT* WATER. THE BATH chamber was excessively large, as was the tub. Sweet lavender oils swirled on top in a shimmering bubbled tapestry. My toes wiggled beneath the surface, reveling in the decadent silky oils slipping between them. Oleez had lit a candle in the corner and left me a plate of cheese, flatbread, and berries to nibble on while she scouted out some other clothes for me to wear. If this was being in custody, I was all for it.

There was no reason I couldn't soak up the Ballenger hospitality while I went about my work. Jase asked Oleez to escort me here while he went directly to a meeting with his family. I was sure after his absence they had a lot to catch up on—including me. His family had walked behind us on our return to Tor's Watch, and I felt their eyes on my back with every step. They were as protective of him as he was of them. Jase was quiet the whole way, but his hand rested on the small of my back because no doubt Paxton and others watched as we departed. As soon as we were through the gates of Tor's Watch, his hand fell and he gave orders for me to be escorted elsewhere. He didn't say good-bye, and I had to silently applaud him on how well he massaged appearances. But it wasn't appearances when he embraced Lydia and Nash. Something about that moment circled back through my head again and again. *The tenderness.* That was real. Some parts of Jase were—

I slipped beneath the water, scrubbing my scalp, wishing hot water could wash away not just dirt, but these past days too. When the viewing was over and the tomb door was finally pushed shut, the family remained stoic, but their eyes glistened and his mother's eyes puddled with tears, her stony façade cracking at last. I found myself envying the finality of a door shutting, a certainty that I would never get.

I broke the surface and gasped for a breath. Warm candlelight danced on the wall, and the only sound was the gentle sloshing of the water. I lifted my foot, listening to the drips cascading down, and surveyed my clean pickled toes and the scabs that still circled my ankle like a thorny wreath. A matching wreath circled Jase's ankle. The chain was gone now, but the connection still jingled through corners of my mind. I stood and rinsed with the pitcher of fresh hot water Oleez had left on the table for me. The thick white robe that was laid out was luxurious too, and I brushed it to my cheek before shrugging it on. Wren loved soft things. She would relish this as much as me, *if* she and Synové were here. Were they? Or were they in hiding, waiting for me to show up? That was the first thing I'd have to find out.

When I left the bath chamber, it felt strange not to have Jase within a few feet of me, strange not to hear his footsteps, his voice, and I found myself glancing to the side out of habit, expecting him to be there. It was surprising how quickly habits could form, and I wondered how long it would take for them to disappear. Then a faint voice inside me whispered, *Is he a habit you really want to disappear?*

"Yes," I whispered back. Yes was the only answer I could afford.

His bed had heavy, dark curtains that could be drawn—like a tent, only better—a perfect enclosed cave for sleeping. I think I loved it more than the tub. Heavy drapes covered the windows, and the walls were covered with polished wood panels on three sides. Another wall was full of books. Everything about it was dark and luscious.

Oleez returned with borrowed clothing that she thought would be closer to my size than Jalaine's dress and told me my other quarters were ready.

"Thank you, but I'll be staying here. This chamber suits me."

She paused, quirking her head, as though I hadn't quite understood her. "But this is the *Patrei*'s room."

"I'm aware of that. I'm sure he'll be as comfortable in the guest quarters as I would be."

She frowned, giving me a chance to change my mind. I remained firm.

"I'll let him know," she said and left. She was passing this battle on to Jase.

The guards he had posted at the end of the hall were an amusing touch, but I wasn't going to be put away in a room that would certainly be more restrictive than this one. This room had four windows, not to mention that Jase had all kinds of items to pilfer. I had already found a forgotten grooming kit in the bottom of his wardrobe with a long, thin tool that could be useful for many things besides grooming. A small black satin bag that had probably once contained an expensive gift became a sleek, discreet pocket tied beneath my clothes. I was sure the nooks and corners had more to offer, but mostly I simply liked his dark cavelike bed. I wanted to crawl into it now and draw the curtains tight.

I went to the bookshelf and pulled a thick volume out. It was carefully handwritten, the penmanship itself mesmerizing, gracefully riding across the page in bold strokes like horses with wings. I replaced the book and my hand skimmed along the spines of the others as I thought about the stories Jase had told me—Breda's Tears, Hetisha's Lost Horses, Miandre and the first Ballengers, and I wondered if he had read them here.

A knock startled me from my thoughts.

"Yes?"

"It's Jase."

My pulse jumped like a snared rabbit, and I paced several steps, trying to shake it off. I pulled the robe tighter around me. "I'm not dressed," I called.

"I need to talk to you."

I quickly combed my wet hair with my fingers. "Come in."

He opened the door hesitantly. He had properly bathed and changed this time, shaved all the stray stubble, and a crisp white shirt accentuated his burnished skin, bronzed by days in the sun. His blond hair was trimmed and combed back. He paused, looking at me, but said nothing. Unwelcome emotion surged through me, as if a bit of that world we had left behind had somehow slipped through the door with him.

He took a few steps forward, his gaze never leaving mine. "I'm sorry, Kazi," he finally whispered. "I'm sorry I didn't tell you."

He was only making things worse. "You owed me nothing. I know that now. I was a means to an end. Get me here with as little fuss as possible, and maybe get something out of it along the way."

"It wasn't like that—"

"Then how was it, Jase? There were miles. *Miles* that you could have come clean and told me where we were really going. All those times—"

"What about you? You had my ring all that time and didn't tell me? How did you get it?"

"You're welcome, Jase Ballenger. I wasn't expecting a thank-you!"

"Kazi—" He shook his head and stepped impossibly closer, his hand lifting, gently stroking the wet strands of hair from my cheek, then cupping it, everything about his touch familiar but new, and my skin was instantly on fire, wishing for more. His eyes searched my face and slowly he leaned in, his lips bare inches from mine. Heat swirled through me like a summer windstorm.

You are too close now, Kazi. Don't cross this line again.

But I wanted to, more than I had wanted to the first time, because now I knew what was on the other side of that line. I knew a side of Jase that I hadn't before, a side hidden beneath everything else, the tenderness that lay there. I knew what his lips tasted like on mine. I knew how he made me feel, and I wanted to feel it all again.

But my head spun with other thoughts too. *Know what is at stake.*

Just before his lips met mine, I turned my head. "What do you want this time, Jase?"

He stiffened at my clipped words, and his hand returned to his side. "Dinner is in two hours. That's all I wanted to tell you. I'll come back to get you once you're dressed."

He turned to leave, but when he reached the door I stopped him. "Your ring was in the hunter's vest."

He faced me again, waiting for the rest of my explanation. "I'd seen him up in the driver's seat patting his pocket every few minutes. That's a sure sign of a treasure within. When I leaned in to the get the keys, I grabbed that too."

"I didn't see you take it."

You weren't meant to, I thought, but my reply was only a shrug.

"And you didn't give it to me because?"

"I did give it to you, Jase. I gave it to you when it mattered."

The opulence wasn't overt. There were no gilded moldings, no gleaming marble floors, no ornate crystal chandeliers or servants dressed in impressive uniforms as I had seen in palaces in Reux Lau and Dalbreck. Simplicity seemed to rule here, but the expansive stone walls, wooden floors, and massive iron chandeliers exuded a wealth of their own, something sure and confident and ageless.

Instead of Jase, it was his sister who had come to get me and take me to dinner. "Jase is busy," she explained. She introduced herself as Priya, the oldest sibling. She wore a sleeveless dress, and her upper arm was tattooed with the wing of an eagle. Unlike earlier today at the entombment when none of the family wore weapons, I noted that she now wore a low-slung belt with a dagger at her side. Was this the usual attire for dinner or a message to me?

"Did something come up for him?" I asked.

"That is for Jase to tell you, not me."

Her curt reply made it obvious she was not happy with my presence nor with being saddled with this chore. We walked silently until she stopped abruptly midway down the hall and faced me. She was taller than me, and her expression was undeniably hostile. I anticipated something unpleasant, and I hoped she would not draw her dagger because I really did not want to hurt her. It could cause all kinds of complications.

"Do you care for my brother?" she asked, a crease deepening between her brows, and it dawned on me what her iciness was all about. Protectiveness ran hot in the Ballenger blood.

"No, I do not care for your brother, at least not in the way I think you're suggesting. We have reached an understanding and that is all."

I thought she'd be pleased by this answer, that her brother was not entangled with one of those distasteful Vendan Rahtan, but her expression only darkened.

"But the way he kissed your cheek and looked at you."

She was stubborn, just like her brother.

"Surely you, Priya, can discern a show when you see one. Your brother doesn't care one rat's whisker for me either. We were only working together in the face of Paxton's clear effort to plant doubts about Jase's character. And it is apparent, even to me, that Paxton is the kind of trouble no one needs."

Her eyes narrowed. "I'm more than able to discern a show when I see it—and I've seen my brother with plenty of girls. But I also know I saw something in him that wasn't like my brother at all." She fingered her dagger.

Don't do it, I thought, *or you'll be sorry and so will I.*

She leaned closer and said, "Let's just call this a friendly warning. If you hurt my brother, I'll make sure that you regret it."

She stepped away, and I breathed with relief, sliding the knife I gripped behind me back beneath my bodice. "Friendly warning accepted," I said. It wasn't just an idle threat. I believed she would do her best to make good on her word.

When we arrived at the dining room, Jase, Mason, Gunner, and Titus weren't there yet, apparently still *busy,* but the rest of his family was there talking and laughing as Nash tried to stand on his hands. They didn't notice Priya and me standing in the doorway. Besides the immediate family, Priya pointed out their uncle, aunt, and two cousins. Twelve of us already, but the dining room was large and could clearly hold many more. It was the *many more* that I wondered about.

Where were Wren and Synové if they were in custody? And the captain we searched for was definitely not among those present. I had a clear description of his distinct features—tall, square-shouldered, thick black hair, with a cleft chin and a small moon-shaped scar over his left brow from where he'd been kicked by a horse. As the queen had said, *If only he'd been kicked a little harder.* "Is this everyone at Tor's Watch?" I asked.

"Not nearly. But we don't eat with everyone. Only family and some-times close friends—and of course, our *guests* join us from time to time."

Her message was clear that I didn't fit in with the former, and had only provisional status on the latter. But at least now I knew that *others* were somewhere here at Tor's Watch.

Within seconds, Nash and Lydia, only six and seven and overflow-ing with curiosity, dashed over and asked the first awkward questions. "Are you and Jase sweethearts?"

Their mother jumped in quickly. "That's an impolite thing to ask, Lydia."

"I'm only a guest," I said. "Here to pay my respects for your father's passing."

"But Jalaine said—"

"I said *nothing*, Nash," Jalaine cut in sternly, "except that Jase's friend was joining us for dinner."

Nash's head swiveled instantly back to me. "Then are you our friend too?"

His and Lydia's eyes were wide and innocent and not part of this game the adults played.

Everyone waited expectantly. I knelt so I was eye level with Nash and Lydia. "Of course I am," I answered, taking their hands in mine. "I'm pleased to make your acquaintance, Nash Ballenger. And yours too, Lydia."

Further introductions were made. Each extended a cautious hand to me. Now that I had faces to put to the names that Jase had already men-tioned, it was much easier to remember them. First the twins, Samuel and Aram, who were impossible to tell apart. Both had dark brown hair that brushed their shoulders, dark eyes, and easy smiles. I made an effort to find some distinguishing mark and could only find a temporary one—a scratch on the back of Aram's hand. Next, I met Jase's Uncle Cazwin and Aunt Dolise, and their boys, Bradach and Trey.

Lastly, Vairlyn, Jase's mother, with whom I had already had an eye-to-eye moment at the entombment, stepped forward and introduced herself. The tight coils she had worn earlier today were pulled free and her blond hair hung in loose waves around her shoulders now, softening her appearance. She seemed too young to be the mother of this extensive brood.

She directed me to a seat at the table. The tone of the room had shifted, reserved and controlled, but polite. I had helped Jase today, but they still weren't quite sure what to make of me. Was I friend or foe?

"Your quarters are comfortable?" Vairlyn asked, as if trying to fill in the silence.

"Yes. Quite. Thank you."

"I'm sure it will be good to sleep in a bed again," Jalaine said.

"Yes, it will." Especially Jase's little cave.

Lydia sat up on her knees and leaned across the table asking softly, thinking the others wouldn't hear. "Did you two kiss?"

"Lydia," Vairlyn said firmly.

Her innocent question pinched something painful inside me. *Many times, Lydia,* I wanted to say. *A hundred times and every kiss was better than the last. I still taste his lips on mine; I still feel his breaths as my own.* Maybe that I could never say those words aloud is what hurt—more words that would have to remain beneath the surface, crowding for room with all the rest.

"She's at that age," Vairlyn said apologetically. "Always full of questions."

I smiled. "It's a good age. Questions are important."

Jalaine looked at me expectantly, as though she still hoped I would answer. I didn't.

"Jalaine has a beau," Nash said proudly.

"No, I do not, Nash." I watched Jalaine's frustration with her loose-lipped sibling grow.

"But Fertig asked you to marry him," Lydia countered.

"And I haven't said yes," she answered between gritted teeth.

"Yet," Priya mumbled under her breath.

Thankfully, the first course was brought in by Aunt Dolise, and it provided a welcome distraction for both me and Jalaine. A servant followed with two large baskets of bread. I remembered Jase saying that his aunt did most of the cooking for the family. She set a large tureen of soup on the table, and Uncle Cazwin began filling bowls and passing them. I was surprised we were starting without everyone present.

"Will Jase and the others be joining us?" I asked.

"Jase said he might be a little late," Aram answered. "He and the others were called away with business."

"And my friends?" I asked. "Jase said they were guests here too. Will they be coming?"

"I haven't seen anyone else here," Nash said.

"Me either," Lydia chimed in.

A cluster of quick tight glances were exchanged between the older Ballengers.

"I believe you're mistaken," Vairlyn answered. "They're being accommodated somewhere else. Not here."

"But we'll let Jase know that you asked," Samuel said. "Maybe he can bring them over tomorrow."

Sure he can.

They were a finely tuned machine, working together and finishing one another's thoughts. The only wrenches in the works were Lydia and Nash. I was feeling more certain that Wren and Synové were free and safe. Suddenly my appetite doubled.

When everyone was served, Vairlyn said a prayer to the gods, not unlike the acknowledgment of sacrifice that was given at Sanctum Hall meals. But here no platters of bones were passed in remembrance.

"*Meunter ijotande,*" I said quietly to myself as the others echoed Vairlyn's final thanks.

"What was that?" Priya asked, missing nothing I said or did.

"Just part of a Vendan prayer of thanks."

"What does it mean?" Aram asked.

"Never forgotten. It refers to the sacrifice that brought the meal to the table."

Samuel raised a suspicious brow. "Sacrifice?"

"The labor. The animal. All gifts, including food, come with a cost to someone or something."

"You speak Vendan?" Nash asked. "Will you teach me?"

I looked at Vairlyn. She nodded approval.

"*Le'en chokabrez. Kez lo mati,*" I said slowly, waiting for him to repeat.

He struggled to repeat the words that were foreign to his tongue but smiled with accomplishment when he finished. "What did I say?"

"I'm hungry. Let's eat."

"I'm all for that," Uncle Cazwin said and began eating.

Everyone dug in, and Lydia and Nash practiced the words over and over as they giggled and slurped mouthfuls.

"You are clever," Vairlyn said abruptly.

I lowered my spoon and eyed her, uncertain if it was a compliment or an accusation.

"Jase told me," she added. "He said you were resourceful in the wilderness."

"As was he," I answered. "We worked together and made the best of it."

Jalaine smiled. "I'm sure you did."

I couldn't see it, but I was certain Priya kicked Jalaine beneath the table because Jalaine jumped in her seat, then shot Priya an angry scowl.

A rumble of heavy footsteps echoed just outside the dining room, and the doors flew open. Mason walked in, looked around, his eyes landing on me first, then Vairlyn. "Sorry," he told her. "We won't make dinner tonight."

She asked for no further explanation, as if she had already expected this. "We'll keep your plates in the warmer."

Mason turned back toward me. "Jase would like to see you."

I spied two tiny crimson dots on his sleeve. Blood. A spray of blood to be precise.

"Sounds ominous," I said, expecting him to laugh it off. He didn't.

"Ready?" he asked.

I pushed my chair back, my mind spinning with possibilities. Everyone watched me leave like I was on my way to an execution.

"How do you say good-bye in Vendan?" Lydia called.

"*Vatrésta*," I answered, "if it's a final good-bye."

"Is this a final good-bye?"

I didn't know, and Mason shuffled me out before I could answer.

CHAPTER TWENTY-ONE

KAZI

*I HAVE SOMETHING FOR YOU TO STEAL, KAZIMYRAH. I WOULD
do it myself, but as you can see, I'm unable to travel. And the truth is, regardless of
my passion for this quest, you are the preeminent thief in Venda. But the prize I
want is not a square of cheese or a soup bone. It is loud and large. What is the
largest thing you've ever stolen?*

I had sensed that she already knew—it was spoken of in whispers on
the streets. *Did Ten really steal that? No, impossible. Why would she?* But ano-
nymity was essential in what I did, if I wanted to keep doing it. The
queen didn't question the *if* or the *what*—she wanted to hear *the how.*
Could I do it again? I thought back to my large, loud, and very dangerous acquisition. It had taken me more patience than I had thought I pos-
sessed, more than a month of many skipped meals, saving and stashing,
and favors procured by stealing numerous other much smaller things.
There was no doubt I had seen it as a challenge. But there was more to it
than just that.

The tiger had drawn a large crowd when the Previzi driver rolled into the *jehendra*. No one had seen one before or even knew what it was, but it was obvious it had to be one of the magical creatures of legend, and when it suddenly lunged and roared, the thunderous sound vibrated through my teeth. I watched three men fall back, wetting themselves. I also saw the thick iron collar and chain that kept the tiger from leaping from the back of the dray, and on closer inspection, I noticed that its glorious striped fur hung like a loose coat over its ribs. The Previzi driver was, amazingly, unafraid of the beast. He shouted a command, then laughed and scratched the animal behind its ear when it lay down.

The butcher had stepped forward, lusting for an animal that was good for soup bones at most. I watched him as he pulled on his beard, the skin puckered to attention around his eyes, his lips glistening as he licked them over and over again. And then he asked the Previzi driver if he could make the beast bellow again. *The roar.* The fear it induced, the enormous white fangs. *That* was what the butcher lusted for, and it came as no surprise. And that was when I knew I would steal the tiger.

Why Kazi? Why steal something you had no use for?

There was only one reason I could share with her.

I wanted to let it go. I knew eventually the animal would die, and the butcher would watch it happen, slowly, for it would have taken all of the butcher's precious meats displayed in his shop to properly feed such a beast and he would never sacrifice his livelihood for an animal, nor would he care day by day as he watched the tiger's ribs protrude, its cheeks hollow, and its flesh sag. He already saw that every day among his human patrons, and their suffering didn't sway him. Besides, he would profit from the tiger's death too, selling its tough meat as magical, pulling its enormous teeth from its jaws for trade with other merchants, selling patches of its striped hide to the *chievdars*, and its clawed paws to governors who loved exotic trophies from the land beyond the Great River. When the last roar of the tiger was gone, death would be a bonus, bringing more rewards to the butcher. He paid a hefty sum to the Previzi driver but knew he would triple his investment in a few short months, and in the meantime he would derive his ultimate pleasure from the fear he would sow, and he'd have yet another way to chase the undesirables from his stall.

I had already experienced the fear he liked to spread four years earlier. My mother had been gone for only a handful of days. I was lost without her, and my eyes itched with hunger. I had stumbled upon his shop, his skinned lambs hanging from hooks, a flurry of flies buzzing and tasting their slick pink flesh, his caged doves pecking at one another's bald heads, his mysterious pearlescent meats showing the rainbows of age, and I had stopped to stare, wondering how I might make such treasures mine, when I felt a sharp snap across my face. I hadn't even had time to reach up to touch my bleeding cheek, when it slashed across my calves. And then I saw him laughing, watching my confusion. He lifted his willow switch and snapped it again, the lithe green branches cutting across my brow. I ran, but he yelled after me, warning me to stay away. Street rats with no money were less welcome than the flies that swarmed his meats.

But the prize was something that could have easily turned and killed you. Was it worth risking your life?

She had looked at me thoughtfully then. I knew the queen had the gift, but I didn't think she could read minds. Even so, she saw the answer in mine. *Yes, it was worth it.* Every missed meal was worth it. The grueling new depths of patience I had to learn were worth it. Every groveling favor I had to pay off was worth it.

But there was more I couldn't tell her. A reason that hooked into my heart as sharply as a claw. It was the tiger's eyes. Their beauty. Their shine. Their amber glow that had wrapped me so tightly with memory that I couldn't breathe. I saw the desperate brokenness in them that was masked behind a defiant roar. *Shhh, Kazi. Don't move.*

In the flash of that moment, I already saw myself leading him across a rickety chain bridge, setting him free in a forest where he would roar, fierce, loud, and unbroken. At least that was my hope for him, to be restored and free.

The animal you steal for me will be even more dangerous, Kazimyrah. You must be every bit as careful and cunning, and above all, you must use every ounce of patience you possess. You must not be reckless with your own life nor with those who are with you. This beast will turn and kill you.

Cunning. Careful.

Patient.

I had always been patient. Even the simple stealing of a turnip or a mutton bone required waiting for opportunity to cooperate. It might take an hour or more. And when opportunity didn't present itself, more patience to create opportunity, or learning to juggle to distract a merchant, or telling them a puzzling riddle to make their minds tumble in different directions, abandoning their guard. The brass-button theft alone had taken a week of planning and patience. The theft of the tiger, over a month, testing my limits, always unsure if the tiger would survive long enough for me to follow through with my plan, wanting to rush, but then holding back, my patience gnawed and eaten away, like a worried bone. I thought nothing could be harder.

But this theft of a traitor had complications I hadn't foreseen, namely Jase Ballenger. And now something else had gone wrong, something worse than a complication. I could hear it in Mason's deliberate footsteps and the long silence between us. I could taste it in the air, the foreboding tang of blood and anger. In Venda, when I sensed things going wrong, I could back out, silently walk away, and disappear into a crowd. Move on to a different mark. Here, I couldn't do that.

Patience, Kazi. Patience. There is always more to draw from.

It was a lie I told myself.

So far I believed it and that was all that mattered.

I eyed the blood on Mason's sleeve. What business had suddenly taken them all by storm? Did they find Wren and Synové? What if the blood was—

"Why didn't Jase come and get me?" I asked.

Mason grinned. "Am I really such a bad escort? Don't believe the rumors."

"I always believe rumors."

"Relax. There's nothing to be worried about."

When someone said that, it was precisely the time to be worried. "I was only wondering—"

"Jase had to go clean up."

Clean up? He was spotlessly clean just a few hours ago. "It must have been some very messy business you were taking care of."

"It was."

I knew I wasn't going to get anything more out of him. Mason was tight in the inner circle, family, one of many keystones firmly wedged and committed, and nothing could make his lips slip free for anyone outside that circle. I understood and admired that because one loose stone could make a whole bridge collapse, but unfortunately, his loyalty did nothing to help me.

We reached the end of a long hall. Tiago and Drake stood on either side of the doors.

"They're inside," Drake said. "Waiting."

Who? A salty taste swelled on my tongue. *Patience, Kazi. The tiger is not yet yours.* And I knew patience was the dividing line between success and failure.

Mason opened the door and we walked in.

It was a small room, windowless, with dark paneled walls, but a candelabra in the corner provided soft golden light. Jase sat slumped in a chair, his boots propped up on the end of a long table, and Gunner and Titus sat on either side of him. Gunner reviewed scattered papers and carefully wrote on another.

Jase jumped to his feet when I walked in. He had a new shirt on. He stared at me. His brown eyes that had once swallowed me whole with their warmth were cold and distant. The anger and blood I tasted in the air was not imagined.

"Hello, Kazi," he said formally.

A fist pounded my sternum. It was death, fierce and strong, and I couldn't breathe. "Who have you killed?" I asked immediately, not waiting for any more formalities.

"Who says—"

"I want to see Wren and Synové! *Now!*"

Jase walked to my side and took my elbow, trying to guide me to a seat. "Sit down. Your friends are fine, but we can't bring them here—"

I yanked free. "You don't really have them. Is that it?" I asked, praying I was right. Praying he would confess this one truth to me. "That's why you won't let me see them."

Gunner stood and retrieved something from a leather case on the floor. He threw two items onto the table. Wren's *ziethe* clattered and spun on the polished wood. Synové's leather archer glove slid as smooth and golden as warm butter toward me.

Gunner grunted. "We thought you might need some proof."

I let out a shuddering breath, letting them think it was fear instead of relief. I maintained my distressed expression, but inwardly I calmed. Now I knew, with little doubt, that they didn't have them. Each of Wren's blades had dyed leather wrapping the hilt. The red one was the spare she kept carefully wrapped and buried deep in her saddlebag. The blue and violet *ziethes* were her blades of choice and the ones she wore at her sides. Synové's monogrammed archer glove was a gift from the queen, a spare she had not yet worn. She was too much in awe of it. The leather was still pristine and unblemished. Gunner had only gotten hold of their saddlebags, perhaps taken by the magistrate at the livery while we were in town. If they actually had Wren and Synové, they wouldn't have had to dig deep through their belongings. They could have taken items in plain sight at their sides.

"This doesn't mean they're alive. I saw the blood on Mason's shirt," I said, keeping up the charade.

Titus shook his head. "She's a hard one to convince, Jase. I don't know how you spent all that time with her." He threw a loosely wrapped packet on the table in front of me.

I pulled a corner of the paper aside and choked back a gag.

"Those look like your friends' ears?" Titus asked.

"No," I answered quietly.

"Put them away, Titus," Jase snapped.

Titus wrapped the ears back in the bloodstained paper and set it aside. I tried to sort out how severed human ears played into this.

"We've had more trouble in Hell's Mouth," Jase said. "We need your help."

I looked down at the damson stain that Jase had carelessly overlooked on the toe of his boot. He saw me staring and drew my attention away, taking my arm and leading me to a seat at the table. They all took seats around me. They were sober as they laid it all out. They had found more labor hunters in town. That was the coldness I had seen in Jase's eyes—and now heard in his voice—his utter hatred for the scavenging predators. It was a hatred we shared and was an especially fresh horror for both of us.

I listened without interrupting, still wondering where "my help" came into play. They explained they were under attack by someone conspiring to oust them in a moment that the Ballengers appeared weakened. Jase said they were increasing defense and protections around the town, which would take care of the short term, but knowing a powerful sovereign was recognizing their authority with a visit would help calm nerves, support their right to rule, and might make whoever was orchestrating these attacks back off. They suspected it could be two or more leagues working in a concerted effort.

I sat back, knowing where this was going. The appearance of more labor hunters had made Gunner's impulsive outburst rear its ugly head again.

"Then ask the King of Eislandia to come here," I said. "He has jurisdiction over Hell's Mouth."

They all laughed, but it held no genuine mirth. I remembered Griz rolling his eyes when he described the king. Apparently the brothers held a similar opinion of him.

Mason pushed back from the table. "The king is barely a king at all."

"He's a joke is what he is," Titus added.

Gunner's expression held similar contempt. "Except for drawing his two percent tax, he wouldn't know Hell's Mouth from a swamp in the Cam Lanteux. Last time he was here, he only came looking for breeding stock for his farm, and then he was gone."

Mason sneered. "And the breeding stock he chose was more like a laughingstock. He's not even good at being a farmer."

"Like I said," Jase repeated, "we need a *powerful* sovereign recognizing our authority. We need—"

"She won't come," I said flatly, cutting him off before he went any further.

Gunner leaned forward. "She will if you write a letter requesting her to come to Tor's Watch. In fact, we've already written it. You just need to copy it in your hand and sign it." He pushed a blank piece of paper toward me.

I ignored Gunner and turned to Jase. "They already believe she's coming," I said. "Isn't that enough? I'm sure Gunner can weave more of his ridiculous lies when she doesn't show." Gunner's lips pulled tight against his teeth, his eyes smoldering with anger.

"It would cost you nothing." The coldness in Jase's voice receded. His gaze penetrated mine, as if searching for a way to reach me. He knew it was a long shot. Still, among all the other things he could do, this mattered to him. It mattered to his family. Why? "What can a simple letter hurt?" he added.

It couldn't hurt, and in some ways I sympathized with them. I hated labor hunters too, but this was about more than just turning Gunner's lie to truth. About more than labor hunters and attacks on Hell's Mouth. It ran deeper. The Ballenger weakness was showing, a thread pulled loose, a seam unraveling, their enormous pride exposed. They truly believed they were the first kingdom, and they wanted it recognized.

I pulled the letter closer and read it slowly. I shook my head at the audacity. "This is not how these things work."

Titus tapped the table impatiently. "It's the way they work here."

"It sounds more like a veiled threat."

"Only because you choose to read it that way," Jase said.

"It could take weeks for this to reach her and then—"

"We have Valsprey."

I paused, wondering how that was possible. The swift birds were from Dalbreck, trained by handlers and only gifted to the kingdoms in the last few years as a speedy form of communication between them.

"The merchants in the arena offer a surprising array of goods," Jase explained.

Stolen goods. I wasn't terribly surprised. Valsprey were only trained to fly between certain cities. Hell's Mouth was not one of them. He said that the queen's reply via another Valsprey would go to Parsuss but would be relayed back here by messenger in only a few days.

They had it all figured out. Almost.

And the almost was huge.

The queen would not come. She would never give them what they wanted—legitimacy—because they were thieves. That much the King of Eislandia had voiced clearly—the Ballengers collected taxes from the citizens and then kept half the proceeds for themselves before sending the rest on. They had the gall to take a cut of everything in Hell's Mouth— even the king's purse. Even the air that Vendans breathed. The king had told Griz that the family had a stranglehold on the northern region and he was at a loss for how to control them. Recognizing their right to rule was the furthest thing from any monarch's mind. But a letter could buy me a few more weeks here to search their compound for a traitor, find Wren and Synové, connect with Natiya and the others, and be on our way with our prisoner—and best of all—I might be able to address another problem in the process. The queen would be more than pleased. *Make a wish, Kazi.* It seemed mine were coming true.

The brothers anxiously stared at me, waiting. I'd let them taste victory for a few minutes, let its claws sink in good and deep—before I snatched it away again.

I reached for the parchment and began copying it. "I'll need to change some of the wording, and include Wren and Synové, or the queen will know I didn't write this."

"Small changes only," Gunner said.

They hovered like duped merchants stepping close to watch me juggle, watching every letter fall neatly into place, their anticipation building.

Your Majesty, Queen of Venda,

I'm writing to report that our investigations have gone well, but they did reveal some surprising revelations. The Ballenger Dynasty is a vast and well-managed one, which is astonishing since it is not an easy world to rule.

There are many threats to the citizens from outsiders, but the Ballengers are experienced and have protected them for untold centuries, long before any of the kingdoms were established. Their ways may not be like ours, but in this wild and untamed territory they do what is necessary and the citizens of Hell's Mouth are grateful to them for their leadership and the protection they provide.

We strongly request your presence here, acknowledging the work of the Ballengers and their authority to rule this region. We're settled in at Tor's Watch, taking in every aspect of their hospitality, and until you arrive, Wren, Synové, and I will be staying on here. We're learning much—

I set my pen down.

"Why are you stopping?" Jase asked.

I chewed on my nail as if thinking it over. "Before I finish and sign, I do have one simple condition of my own."

Jase's chest rose in a deep breath. He knew it would be anything but simple. "And that would be?"

"No conditions," Titus argued.

Gunner's eyes bulged. "Is she blackmailing *us*?"

Mason huffed out a disbelieving growl. "I think that's exactly what she's doing."

"Only because you *choose to read it that way*," I said and smiled. "I prefer to call it payment for services rendered. A simple business transaction. You Ballengers understand that, don't you?"

Jase's voice turned flat and to the point. "What do you want?"

"Reparations," I answered. "I want everything that was stolen from the Vendan settlement restored—*with interest*—and all their destroyed structures, pens, and fences rebuilt."

Tempers exploded. A host of angry objections whirled between them. Jase jumped to his feet. "Are you out of your mind? Haven't you gotten the message? We *want* them to leave."

"It is their right to be there. Venda has gone to great expense and effort in establishing this settlement, and the King of Eislandia specifically approved the site."

Jase growled. "The king who doesn't know Hell's Mouth from his own ass?"

I shrugged. "No reparations. No letter."

"No!" Jase went off on a rant, walking around the room, his hands waving, punching the air, reiterating that his family hadn't destroyed anything and helping the Vendans would be the same as posting a welcome sign for anyone to come and take what they wanted. All of his objections were punctuated and reinforced by the others. They fed off each other like a pack of jackals. "They are half the cause of our troubles in the first place! You let one encroach on your territory, and then everyone thinks you're weak and they want a piece too!"

I sighed. "They are seven families. Twenty-five people. It's not even land that you use. Are the Ballengers so very small that a few families are a big threat? Can you not see them as an asset instead? A way to grow your dynasty?"

They looked at me like I was speaking a foreign language.

I leaned back, crossing my arms. "Those are my terms."

Angry glances bounced between them, but no words. I watched their frustration mount, jaws growing rigid, nostrils flaring, chests rising with furious indignation. The silence ticked.

"We'll move them," Jase finally said. "And rebuild in another location."

A heated chorus of grunts erupted. The others objected to this concession.

"But it has to be fair and equitable," I answered, "water, good land, and still within a day's ride of Hell's Mouth."

"It will be."

"I have one other stipulation."

Gunner's hands flew into the air. "Can I wring her neck right now?"

"The Ballengers must do the work," I said. "Specifically, the *Patrei*. You, Jase. You personally must physically help rebuild their settlement. It shouldn't take long. A few weeks at most. They had so very little to begin with. I will stay on here—of my own free will—to make sure the work is done, and you will remove the guards at my door, so I will be a true guest, just as your letter so poorly tried to imply."

Jase's hands curled into fists. His gaze was deadly. "Sign the letter."

"Does this mean we have an agreement?"

His chin dipped in a stiff affirmation.

Titus groaned.

A hiss burned through Gunner's teeth.

Mason shook his head.

"Sign it," Jase repeated and pushed the letter back in front of me.

I looked at him, knowing I had chipped away a large piece of the Ballenger pride, but knowing something else about Jase, too—or hoping I did. I saw it when he whispered stories to me late into the night, when he pressed a wish stalk to my blistered foot. I saw it when he held Nash in his arms then wiped away his tears.

"Thank you," I whispered. I dipped my pen back into the inkwell and signed with flourish.

All is going well. In fact, after an unfortunate fire that destroyed some settlement structures, the Ballengers have generously agreed to rebuild them on a new site that will be even more productive. I know you've been busy with travel but I hope this news will hasten your arrival here. Please bring golden thannis as a gift of goodwill—our kind hosts deserve this honor. We look forward to seeing you soon.

Your ever faithful servant,

Kazi of Brightmist

Jase picked up the letter and examined it, looking for some sort of betrayal. "Thannis?" he asked.

"The thorny vine you saw embossed on my vest that the hunters took. It's on the Vendan shield too. It's a wild plant that's native to our land—we take great pride in it. It's our traditional gift we give to all visitors—unless, of course, you think a weed is beneath you?"

"I remember seeing it on her vest," Titus said.

"A goodwill gift is fine," Gunner interjected.

Jase nodded. "We'll be sure to have a nice gift for her too."

———————

With the letter signed, I was returned to my room. Drake and Tiago escorted me to my door but then left, as per my agreement with Jase. When I went inside, I found a small bowl of fruit on the dressing table. Oranges. Three perfect oranges.

Had he already known I would sign the letter? Was this his thank-you?

I picked one up, my fingernail drawing a spray across its skin, and held it to my nose, breathing in its magic.

Or maybe this was the thank-you I never got for giving him the ring?

No, I thought as I peeled it.

This was just Jase remembering I loved oranges.

CHAPTER TWENTY-TWO

JASE

EVEN WITH BOTH WINDOWS OPEN, THE AIR WAS HOT, STILL, AS if the world had stopped breathing. My back was damp against the sheets. It seemed impossible that only this morning when I woke I was lying on a bed of grass with Kazi nestled against my chest, a chain still connecting us.

It was well after midnight and I should have been passed out in my bed with exhaustion by now, but instead I tossed and turned and paced—in one of the guest rooms. Oleez had been afraid to tell me. I was finally back at Tor's Watch and shut out of my own room.

I could have easily had Kazi moved, but there were other battles ahead and this one wasn't worth fighting—and strangely, some part of me liked the idea of her being in my room. I wasn't sure why. This room was larger, more comfortable, meant to impress guests, and I knew by now she had probably explored every *thing* in my room. What did she think? Had she gone through my books searching for the stories I shared with her? Rummaged through my clothes? The forgotten clutter in the bottom of my wardrobe? There were three knives that I could remember. I suspected she already had one on her. I wasn't worried. Had she taken another bath? I saw the revulsion in her face when Titus threw the ears on the table. After she left, I grabbed him by the collar and threw him up against the wall. *Don't ever do that again*, I had told him. *We may have dirty work to do, but everyone doesn't need to see it.* Especially not her. I had seen her expression—the fear—when she thought I had harmed her friends. Killed them. The terror in her eyes had whittled through me like a dull knife. She had seen something in my face, maybe all of our faces. She knew death when she saw it.

The harm I actually did do hadn't been hard for me, and I would do it again.

Foley had come to tell me what had happened.

When Mason, Gunner, Titus, and I walked into the warehouse, Lothar and Rancell already had them on their knees. Tiago and Drake hovered nearby.

"We spotted their wagon in an alley," Rancell said. "When we lifted the tarp we saw the brewer's boy gagged and chained. The other chains were still empty. They hadn't gotten the rest of their cargo yet."

I stepped closer to the three men. Two of them began crying, begging for mercy. The third said nothing, but sweat beaded on his forehead. They were a more ragged crew than the ones who had taken Kazi and me. Their tattered clothing was ripe with stench, their knuckles creased with filth, but their story was the same. They'd been paid up front, but they didn't know by whom. The fellow who approached them with a fat purse wore a wide-brimmed hat pulled low, and they weren't even sure what color his hair was.

"Which of you took the money?" I asked.

"He did," the two sniveling ones cried.

I looked at the silent one, his sweat the only indication he knew the gravity of his situation. My hatred for him rose to a different level. It was personal. The brewer's boy was fourteen.

"So you're in charge?"

He nodded.

"Have you done this before?"

"Not here. Other places. It's good money. But he said it had to be Hell's Mouth and—"

"You know whose town this is?" I asked.

He swallowed, his expression suddenly crackling with eagerness. "I'll give you a cut," he said. "We can make a deal. Half. You want half? Half for doing nothing."

"You know what would have happened to the boy you grabbed?"

"A mine. He would have worked in a mine. That's all. Good hard work."

There was nothing good about dying in a mine. Nothing good about being shackled and hauled in the back of a wagon against your will. He couldn't conceive that the brewer's boy had a life, a future. He only saw him as an article of profit. I drew my knife.

"All. You can have it all," he pleaded. "The money's in my vest. Take it."

"All of it?" I stepped closer and knelt so we were eye to eye. "That's quite a deal you're offering, but I'm in a hurry, so here's a better one. I'll kill you quickly instead of letting my dogs tear you to pieces—which is what you deserve." I wasn't sure the words had even registered before I plunged my knife into his throat. Blood sprayed my shirt and face, and he was dead before I had pulled my knife free.

I stood and my attention turned to the other two. They began wailing, trying to back away on their knees, but Mason and Titus stood behind them, preventing them from going anywhere.

"Want me to do those two?" Tiago asked.

I walked over, as if studying them. "Maybe not," I said. "Maybe they'd be more useful to us as messengers. Would you two rather be dead or deliver a message?"

"A message!" they both agreed. "Please, any message! We'll deliver it."

I motioned to Mason and Titus. They jerked their heads back by their hair and in a swift second, an ear from each man was on the ground in front of them. Their screams bounced off the walls of the warehouse, but when I told them to shut up, they did. They had already witnessed what else could happen to them.

"Better. Now here's the message. You go back to whatever hole you crawled out of, and you let everyone get a good long look at your ears, and you let them know who did it—the Ballengers—and you tell them that this is the kind of trouble they'll find in Hell's Mouth, and no amount of money that anyone offers them is worth it. The citizens of this city are off-limits. And if I ever see either of you here again, even for a sip of water, we'll be cutting off something much more valuable to you than your ears. My word is good. You can count on it. Understand?"

They both nodded.

"Good. Our business is done, then."

I looked at Lothar and Rancell. "Get them bandaged up. I don't want them bleeding out before they deliver our message."

It was on our way back to the main house that Gunner said it was time for other messages to be sent too, the one my whole family was pushing for, and now I finally agreed. We had nothing to lose. Or so I thought.

I still couldn't quite believe that to make good on my promise to my father, I had also agreed to rebuild a Vendan settlement. If the gods had carried that news to his ears, he was probably beating on his tomb walls, demanding to be let out, demanding to name someone else as *Patrei*.

I rolled out of bed and went to the window. It was dark, the work yard below quiet, a dim bluish light in the gate tower the only sign that anyone was awake, and then I saw a shadow moving through the blackness. Or I thought I did. It was just as quickly gone. Maybe one of the dogs patrolling. Barking erupted but quickly quieted again. Yes, only the dogs.

I stepped away from the window, paced, and wondered if she was having as hard a time sleeping as I was. I remembered her face when I came to her chamber, at first soft, happy to see me, but then it turned sharp.

What do you want, Jase?

I knew what I wanted.

She did too.

———

My hand hovered as I debated whether I should knock. It was late. The middle of the night. If she was asleep, I would wake her.

She's not asleep. I knew it was impossible, but I sensed it. I could feel her eyes open, scanning the walls, pulling the drapes shut, opening them again, watchful, unable to rest, needing a story, a riddle, something to ease her into a dreamworld. I rested my hand against the door wanting to go in, knowing I shouldn't.

What is this, Kazi?

What do you feel?

She couldn't answer me before when I had asked. Or she wouldn't. Maybe it was best not to know. Her loyalties were clear.

And so were mine.

I pushed away from the door and walked back to my room.

———◦◦◦◦———

Candles glowed in red glass globes in the apse of the temple, and the heavy scent of amber hung in the air. I was the only one inside. The priests were asleep in the manse. They would find my offering in the morning. I took out my knife and nicked my thumb, squeezed it, letting the blood drip onto the plate of coins below me. *A coin for every child in the city. This is only between you and the gods, Jase. Not the priests. Nor anyone else. This is your promise to protect them with your blood, just as Aaron gave with his blood to save the Remnant. Gold pleases men, but blood serves the gods, because in the end, your life is all you have to give.*

The drops of blood trickled down the pile of coins and they shifted, a bare clink, echoing through the silent temple. My father's last desperate words were ones he had heard from his own father, words every *Patrei* heard. I had read them in the histories and transcribed them at an early age.

The candlelight caught the glint of my gold ring. *I gave it to you when it mattered.* She had stepped forward willingly and helped me, and instead of thanking her, I questioned why she hadn't given it to me sooner. Everything was more complicated now, even something as simple as gratitude.

Footsteps scuffled behind me. "You ready?"

Mason had caught me on my way out and insisted on coming with me. *You lost your mind? Leaving without straza?* And then he laughed. *Let's go.*

He walked down the center aisle toward me and whispered, "The town will be waking soon. We should go while it's still dark."

We left, the streets silent, the roads dark. Halfway home he asked about Kazi. "How did you two end up being . . ."

He knew something had happened between us, but he stumbled with the rest of his question, as if he didn't know how to craft it—as if he was still not quite believing it himself. He had seen her slam me up against the wall, threaten to cut me. He hadn't taken it any better than I had.

"It was different out there," I said. "She was different. So was I."

"What about now?"

"I don't know."

"I've never seen you like this. I know you're not asking for advice, but I'm offering it anyway. She might have been nice to curl up with out there, but back here she's not someone you want to get tangled up with. She can't be trusted."

I hated to hear him say it, but it was true. Kazi had secrets. She performed a skillful dance around everything we said. Last night I had seen genuine fear in her eyes when she thought I had hurt her friends, but then I saw how she played us too, the fear dissolving and being replaced by something skilled and calculating. It was the same look I had seen in her face when she had studied the driver, like in her head she was constructing something solid, stone by stone. Her shrewdness managed to get reparations we didn't owe out of the deal. Even with her letter we had no guarantee the queen would come, but there was hope and that was a short-term bandage we needed. I'd use it to my advantage for now. Soon we wouldn't need anyone tossing us crumbs of respect. Soon we'd have a greater share of trade on the continent, and it would be the kingdoms begging for a place at the table with the Ballengers.

We reached Tor's Watch, but before Mason left to go back to his room and catch what little sleep was left of the dark morning hours, I said, "Tomorrow when we go into town, pull Garvin from tower security and put him on her watch. She doesn't know him, and he melts into the background. Add Yursan as a decoy too."

Mason's brows rose. A decoy tail, especially for someone like Garvin who was good at what he did, was a grand admission of my doubts.

I hoped Mason was wrong. I hoped I was wrong. Because I was still tangled up with her and I didn't want to be cut loose.

Miandre is our storyteller. She tells us stories of before.
It was a world of princesses and monsters, and castles and
courage. She learned the stories from her friend's mother.
Someday I will tell the stories too, but my stories will be
about different monsters, the ones that visit us every day.

—Gina, 8

CHAPTER TWENTY-THREE

KAZI

BOOKS WERE PILED ON THE BED AROUND ME, GHOSTS PEEKING from their pages, a whisper here, there . . . *Hold on no matter what you have to do.* The Ballenger ghosts sounded as desperate as those I had known. *Survive, no matter who you have to kill.* Maybe more desperate.

I spent a good portion of the night reading the books from Jase's shelves. After thumbing through several, I realized that nearly all of them were handwritten—and most by Jase. Some of the first books on the top shelf were in a more childish scrawl. It seemed to be a part of his schooling, having to record the family history and stories in his own hand. Maybe that was another reason he knew it so well. Many of the histories were curious, not long stories but hundreds, maybe thousands of short journal entries, some of them bare sentences, beginning with the first one from Greyson Ballenger: *Write it down, write down every word once you get there, before the truth is forgotten.*

It was one of the ways Pauline had taught Wren, Synové, and me to read, copying some of the ancient histories of Gaudrel, though I hadn't begun to fill even a single book with words, much less shelves of them. This wall of books wasn't just a matter of a reading lesson, this was the Ballenger code, a passion, never forgetting where they had come from. Whereas some of us tried to do just the opposite.

I found myself touching the words, imagining Jase as he wrote them, imagining him as a child like Nash, imagining him growing up in this large, close-knit, powerful family, imagining his concentration as he wrote every word.

I startled awake to the sound of rapping at the door and found my hand still lying across the middle of an open book. It felt like I had barely dozed off. I had just thrown back the sheet when Vairlyn, Priya, and Jalaine burst through the door. Vairlyn carried a breakfast tray; Priya, a folded pile of clothes; and Jalaine plopped a pair or riding boots down on the floor, then made herself comfortable at the foot of my bed.

They breezed in like they knew me, like I wasn't just a grudging guest, but someone else. Priya whisked open drapes, letting light flood in, and Vairlyn set the tray on the side table by the armchair and poured a warm drink into a cup from a small pewter pot. They all seemed in a cheerful mood, even the sullen Priya. She shook out a folded riding skirt, eyeing it for size. "This should fit. I'm taller, but this is one of my shorter skirts. It hits me just below my knees. It should be fine on you. I don't know what Jase was thinking when he sent for one of Jalaine's dresses."

"He wasn't thinking," Jalaine said. "He was—"

"Sorry to wake you," Vairlyn said, "but we're heading out soon."

She handed me the cup she had poured and then a bowl of some sort of eggish pudding.

Jalaine's gaze swept across the room. She had a broad grin pasted across her face. "You kicked out Jase?" She was clearly amused, seeing Jase only as her big brother and not as *Patrei*.

"I didn't exactly—"

"Let the girl eat," Vairlyn scolded. "It's too early for questions."

"Where are we going?" I asked.

They explained that we were on our way to Hell's Mouth. Apparently, the whole family was making a show there today so the Ballenger presence was strongly seen and felt. They didn't only want to erase doubts among the townsfolk, but also wanted to reinforce among the leagues that the passing of power hadn't weakened the family. I was to be part of that show—a premier soldier of the Vendan queen walking side-by-side with the family.

"And Jase? Will I see him?"

Priya laughed, and she exchanged a glance with Jalaine. "I think she still doesn't get it."

"Yes," Jalaine answered. "You will definitely see Jase."

⚬⚬⚬⚬

We stepped out the front door of the main house, and Priya noted with a grumble that our horses still weren't here. I asked if there was time for a little tour before we left, and I was surprised when Vairlyn readily agreed.

"Why not," she answered. "It looks like we have a few minutes until they bring the horses around."

Maybe getting the lay of the land at Tor's Watch wasn't going to be as hard as I thought—at least now that I was an insider. Getting around last night had been impossible. Eluding the guards wasn't hard, but unlike a very willing tiger, the dogs were trained not to take food from anyone, so the meat I had taken from the kitchen to cozy up to the beasts went to waste. And hissing *vaster itza* did nothing to calm them— apparently they only liked hearing the order from Jase. But with a little patience, I was sure I'd find a way into their dark, snarling hearts. Even

the most hardened lords and merchants had chinks in their cruel armor.
"Where are the dogs?" I asked hesitantly as we walked down the front
steps.

"You heard them last night?" Priya asked.

"Only a little snarling."

"Probably just chasing a rabbit," Jalaine interjected.

Vairlyn patted my shoulder. "Don't worry. The night dogs are ken-
neled during the day. The only ones about now are the gate dogs, and
they're likely resting in a nice shady spot. The days are getting so hot."
She brushed back a thick lock of hair, and I was struck again with how
young she seemed—and yet a widow already. This way," she said, pointing to a path that ran between the towering main house and another
large building. As we walked past it, she told me that each of the houses
had a name. "This one here is Raehouse. It was named for the first child
of Greyson and Miandre. It holds the offices for the Ballenger businesses.
Priya manages it."

"How many businesses do you have?"

Priya blew out a puff of air. "Dozens. Farms. A lumber mill. The
Ballenger Inn. But the main ones are managing the arena and Hell's
Mouth."

Dozens. What were the others she hadn't mentioned? It was those I
was curious about, particularly the purpose of housing a cold-blooded
killer. What was his business here? According to the queen, the former
Watch Captain at the Morrighese citadelle wasn't notably skilled at any
one thing. *He's an average swordsman, an average commander, but he's an
above average deceiver. His skill is in his patience.* The betrayal of her family
burned in the queen as much as the betrayal of the kingdoms. She would
never forgive nor forget it. Besides poisoning her father, the Watch
Captain planned a massacre that killed her eldest brother, and he insti-
gated another attack where her youngest brother lost his leg and her

third brother was gravely wounded. He never fully recovered and died a year later. When the whole plot was uncovered, she found out that the captain's stake in all this, besides a fortune, was one of the many kingdoms the Komizar had planned to conquer. Gastineux was to be his. Captain Illarion never got his prize. All the outside world held for him now was a noose—or perhaps he thought there was a second chance to regain what had slipped through his fingers. Is that what he hoped to gain here? His lost wealth and power? And why would the Ballengers be willing to give it to him? Did their ambitions match his?

"The records for all the businesses are kept here in Raehouse. Priya is good with numbers," Vairlyn said with obvious pride.

Priya shrugged. "Numbers don't lie. They're far more reliable than people."

"Really?" I questioned. "Numbers can be manipulated."

Priya shot me a long sideways glance. "Not as much as people."

A skeptical murmur rumbled from Jalaine. "What Priya really likes is the solitude. Numbers don't talk back. She enjoys peace and quiet here, whereas *I* have to deal with a lot of griping mouths at the arena."

"And that, my sister, is your specialty—a griping mouth."

Jalaine gave Priya a playful shove. The elder sister took it in stride. Their digs went no deeper than marketplace banter where the cost was already assured. Their devotion was as certain as a firm price.

"Watch your head here," Vairlyn said, pushing back a branch. "These need to be cut back, but I rather like the wildness of it."

The path had narrowed and we walked through a long, tunneled arbor that was thick with yellow climbing roses. The ground below it was littered with a rainfall of petals. It was a striking contrast to the foreboding spiked structures that towered on either side—one was meant to invite, the other to turn away. We emerged from the arbor onto the back side of the main house, where there was a sprawling garden with raked walkways, low hedges, and tall rows of shrubs. A large fountain bubbled at its center. Beyond the gardens were three more stone buildings with more sharp turrets. Homes, Vairlyn called them.

"That's Riverbend at the far end," Jalaine said. "It houses our employees. Next to it, set back in the middle, is Greycastle, where more family lives."

"My sister Dolise and her family—and a few cousins who are not overly social—live there. More family live down in Hell's Mouth."

"There are seventy-eight of us Ballengers altogether," Priya said, "and that's not counting third cousins."

"Third cousins like Paxton?" I asked.

An icy wall fell over Priya.

"Yes," Vairlyn answered, "like him."

"Of course, we are hoping for more little Ballengers soon," Jalaine quipped. Priya jabbed her elbow into her sister's side.

Vairlyn jumped in quickly as if trying to sweep past Jalaine's suggestion. "And the one next to Greycastle is Darkcottage."

Darkcottage was not a cottage at all. It rose two stories above us with four spiraling turrets that went even higher. The cottage was made from glistening black granite.

"Who lives there?" I asked.

"It's empty right now," Vairlyn answered. "Only filled with memories and stories." Her gaze was wistful. "Sometimes guests stay there. And that's the tour, except for a few outbuildings, and the stables down that path over there."

"What about the vault? May I see it?"

Priya's brows arched. "Down in the tunnel? You know about that?"

"Jase told me."

"It's a bit dank and dusty," Vairlyn said doubtfully.

"Still, I'm curious after all the stories he told me."

Jalaine and Priya exchanged a knowing smile as if I had confessed something important.

"I'll have Jase show you the vault when we come back from town," Vairlyn said. "The horses are probably ready for us by now, and the others will be waiting."

With those words said, Jalaine and Priya left, walking back down the path eager to be on their way, but Vairlyn didn't move, her attention still fixed on Darkcottage. I waited, unsure if I should go or stay. When they were out of earshot, she said, "Thank you for your letter to the queen."

"I'm not sure thanks are in order. It was Gunner's letter. I only copied it. And you do know it came with a price? I didn't give the letter freely."

"The settlement. Yes. I'm aware. I do know something about compromise. Sometimes we must give something up in order to gain something else that is more important to us. I see it as a win for both of us."

"The queen coming here is that important to you?"

"It was important to my husband, and that makes it important to me. Keeping promises is important. Soothing fears is important. Protecting Hell's Mouth is important."

Yes, I thought, *I understand about promises. Mine are important too.*

As we walked back through the arbor, she paused, lightly touching my arm. "I was wondering, by any chance is Kazi short for Kazimyrah?"

I stared at her, her simple question squeezing the air from my lungs. I tried to figure out how she knew. Did she suspect something about how I signed the letter? "You've heard the name before?"

"Yes. In Candora. It's not an uncommon name up there among fletchers, especially for first daughters. In their old tongue it means 'sweet arrow,' which is the . . ."

She continued to explain, but I already knew what the sweet arrow was, that rare arrow among a dozen quivers that flies truer and farther than the rest, the one in which a fletcher's craft is elevated by something as intangible as the spirit within the wood.

"No," I answered. "My name is just Kazi."

But as we walked back to the front gate, my mind whirled with this new knowledge that even my own mother hadn't known. Had my father been a fletcher from Candora? Had he named me? Old wounds split open again, every answer that should have been mine stolen like it was only a cheap trinket to be traded away at market. Thousands of years of history were revered by the Ballengers. My own brief history had been ripped from my grasp. There were a hundred questions I would never be able to ask my mother.

When we got back to the front gate, everyone was waiting for us, the army of Ballengers, *straza*, and other hands, ready to head into Hell's Mouth.

Everyone but Jase.

All eyes fell on me. I might have been on the inside of the gate, but I was still a foreign object, a stone caught in a horse's shoe and dragged into their inner sanctum. Priya smirked. She had seen me scanning the group.

"Don't worry. He's coming," she said, as if to let me know nothing slipped by her.

"Come ride by me!" Nash called.

"Not just yet, Nash. I'm going to ride with Kazi first." Heat raced between my ribs. I turned to see Jase approaching from another path, guiding two horses. One was coal black—*mine*. I ran to him, checking his tack, all in place but now dust free and freshly oiled. His coat gleamed, and his mane was carefully groomed and braided.

The others headed out through the gate, leaving Jase and me alone.

I nuzzled my horse's neck and scratched his forelock. "*Mije, gutra hezo,*

Mije," I whispered, and he blew out a robust snort of appreciative air, his expression of excitement, and a signal that he was ready for a gallop through open fields. He was high energy and meant for speed, a venerable breed of Vendan stock specifically bred for Rahtan and not used to the long confines of a stable.

"His name is Mije?" Jase asked.

My focus remained fixed on Mije's neck and I nodded, unable to look at Jase, caught off guard by the sudden tightness in my throat. *Stupid horse*, I thought, *don't do this to me*, but I couldn't hide that I was glad to see him.

"The mane was Jalaine's idea. I hope you don't mind. She kind of fell in love with him."

"It's a bit fancy for him, but I don't think he minds. He'll probably expect extra treats from me now too." I looked up. Jase's eyes were trained on me.

"Tiago found him at the livery when they were searching for you and the other Rahtan." He straightened, his shoulders stiff and uncomfortable, and he frowned. "We don't have the others, Kazi. We never did. I want you to know."

This wasn't about horses. He was talking about Wren and Synové.

"Why tell me now?"

"Because of last night. I saw the look in your face. The fear. I don't want you to think of me that way. I would never harm them. You know that, don't you?"

I thought about my reaction. I had been afraid. I had felt death in the room. It had rushed over my skin, like a stampeding army of ghosts, and then I saw Jase. He had killed someone—I had known it—and dread had gripped me. My first thoughts had jumped to Wren and Synové, and I realized that what I knew about Jase and what I knew about the *Patrei* were two different things. The *Patrei* ruled a different world than the one where Jase and I had roamed. I was still getting to know this other person.

"Why did you lie and say you had them?"

"They had disappeared, and we've had trouble in town. I have to consider all possibilities."

"And if I believed that you had them in custody you thought I might confess something. They became leverage."

A crease formed between his brows. "Yes."

"Jase, I had vanished into thin air—just like you. Maybe they feared they were next. Did it ever occur to you they might have disappeared because they were trying to keep their own necks safe?"

"It occurred to me. But where are they now? Everyone knows you're here and safe."

"I don't know where they are."

"Kazi—"

"I don't know, Jase. I swear."

He studied me. Whatever he saw, it had to be truth, because I didn't know where they were now. Not exactly. I guessed they were on the move, probably from one crumbled ruin to another on the outskirts of town. And whenever I did make contact with them, they needed to remain out of the Ballengers' sights. I might be inside Tor's Watch, but I needed them on the outside and not under scrutiny.

He finally moved past the subject of missing Rahtan and said we needed to catch up with his family. He checked my cinch and handed the reins over to me. He looked at my boots as if still taking in the changes—our long days of walking barefoot together were over. "This time yesterday—"

"I know," I said. "We were still chained together."

"A day can change everything, can't it?"

"Less than a day," I answered. "A spare minute can send us careening down a new path and turn our lives upside down."

He stepped closer. "Is that what your life is right now, Kazi?" he asked. "Upside down?"

Utterly and completely, but I answered the way I should. "Not at all. I'm a soldier who is now a guest in a very comfortable home, and we have struck up an agreement that will be advantageous to my kingdom— if you plan to keep your word."

Distaste sparked in his eyes at the reminder of the reparations and resettling of the Vendans. "My word is good," he grumbled, and he got up on his horse.

"I can't promise when or if she will come, you know?"

He nodded. "I know. But you've made a good-faith effort. We can't ask for more than that."

Good faith.

I slipped my foot into Mije's stirrup, settled into the saddle, then nudged him forward with a touch from my knee. The *straza* who had hung back waiting for us followed behind. We were just past the gates when Jase asked how I had slept last night. Polite talk. Something I supposed people who lived in fine houses asked guests.

I guessed that a polite response was required even though I had barely slept at all. I couldn't reveal to Jase the reason why his comfortable room gave me no rest. It seemed that having his lovely cave of a bed wasn't enough after all. It was still missing something. *Him.* He had become a bad habit. Too quickly, I'd become accustomed to the weight of his arm around me, the feel of his chest at my back, his whispers in my ear as I dozed off to sleep. *Tell me another riddle, Kazi . . .* If not for his books, I might not have dozed at all.

"Fine," I answered, "and you?"

"I slept well. It was good to finally sleep in a soft bed instead of on hard ground."

It wasn't so hard. I remembered him commenting on the thick grass or the beds of leaves that rustled beneath us. He had liked it then. I was strangely disappointed by his answer. It was all so quickly left behind. Leaves. Grass. Us. And yet, that was exactly what I had counted on. I had told myself over and over again that it would soon be behind us, that everything we said and did was all right, because it was only temporary. It was our way to make the best of it. My own feelings had become a thorny riddle for which I had no answer.

The road traversing back and forth down to Hell's Mouth was steep. I couldn't let Mije break into a gallop until we hit level ground, but when I finally gave him free lead, he was a black specter not tied to this earth, his gait so swift and steady, he became a dark wind flying down the road and I was part of that wind. Jase worked to keep up, and the pounding, the noise, the strain in my thighs and calves as I lifted in the stirrups, the thump in my heart and bones made me feel alive, and the moment was all there was, and the answers to riddles were forgotten in the trail of dust behind us.

CHAPTER TWENTY-FOUR

KAZI

As soon as we arrived in Hell's Mouth, I was whisked away by Vairlyn, Priya, Jalaine, Nash, and Lydia—a whole troop of us heading toward the dressmaker.

"Don't keep her long," Jase had called after us, an exasperated expression darkening his face. It was obvious this was not part of his plan, but apparently a *Patrei's* mother and sisters could override even him in some matters.

Vairlyn said it would be best to get the visit out of the way first thing so there would be time for the dressmaker to get some alterations done. She thought it necessary for me to have a few clothes of my own for my stay in Hell's Mouth—instead of just borrowed ones. I had to agree, especially in regard to underclothes. I promised to pay her back, but she waved me off saying it was the least she could do after I had helped her son escape the labor hunters.

Guilt riddled through me. She had no idea that I'd been forced to help him and that my intent was to use him for my own purposes. My goals and loyalties hadn't changed. Ever since the queen had asked me to find this fugitive, I had imagined the grand moment I would hand the elusive traitor over. *You can make some things right.* The moment had grown in my thoughts. It became a color that gleamed behind my eyes, a silver stitch in a wound that would close a gash that had been open for too long or a golden stone in a tall wall that would finally erase my mistakes. I needed to believe that maybe even a worthless little crap-cake like me could make a difference that mattered in this world. It became a deep need and I worried—what if the Watch Captain had already vanished? What if he wasn't here at all? Sometimes people vanished and no matter how badly you wanted to find them, they were never seen again.

It was disquieting to be drawn into their family circle. I was certainly good enough at conversation—it was one of the tools of my trade. When I was forced to engage a merchant instead of just slipping away with my pilfered goods, I had to redirect their thoughts, make them so transfixed by something that they could perceive nothing else—like the labor hunter who was so intent on the answer to the riddle I withheld, he forgot he even had keys at his side.

But this was different. It felt far more intimate, their chatter, their laughter, the touching and nudging. It didn't seem right that I should be in the middle of it, and yet it intrigued me the way listening to a foreign language might, trying to understand the nuances behind their words. They held fabric up to my face and asked me what I thought. I didn't know. I left the decisions to them.

The dressmaker quickly took measurements, and fabrics were chosen. The only other time I had been fitted for clothes was as a Rahtan soldier. We didn't have uniforms. We chose our own clothing, and I chose carefully. I missed my boots and the shirt I had been forced to shred in order to cross Bone Channel, but most of all I missed my leather waistcoat the hunters had ripped from my possession while I was unconscious. It wasn't exactly like Jase's ring, but it was symbolic of something—the revered thannis of Venda was gracefully embossed across the deep bronze leather. It was the most beautiful item of clothing I had ever owned. Growing up, I had only known layers of rags covering my back, and I was lucky to have those. Vairlyn spoke quietly with the dressmaker for a few moments while I entertained Lydia and Nash with a shell game using the dressmaker's thimbles.

In a short time, as promised, I was delivered back to Jase and our tour of Hell's Mouth continued. He walked closely beside me, his shoulder occasionally brushing mine, his hand sometimes at the small of my back, directing me down one avenue or another. His close proximity was orchestrated, a subtle signal to all who watched and a confirmation that the rumors were true. Everyone could plainly see that it was, after all, the Rahtan soldier from Venda who had ended up being arrested—by the charm of the *Patrei*.

I noticed Jase's ease when he spoke with the townspeople, how he knew the details of their lives and they knew his, how an old shopkeeper pinched his chin because he was one of the untamable Ballenger boys she had chased or chastised multiple times.

"So you were trouble as a child too?" I said.

"Probably less trouble than you."

I didn't admit to him that he was probably right.

But even with the pinching of his chin, the playful wagging of a finger, or the ruffling of hair, which he was far too old for but endured with a strained smile, there was an undeniable regard for his position too. Patrei, *good to see you*. Patrei, *taste my powdered srynka*. Patrei, *meet my new son*, and a baby would be shoved into Jase's arms. He was new to this part of his role, and he would awkwardly hold the squalling child, dutifully kiss its forehead, and hand it back. I learned it was a custom here for the *Patrei* to pledge to protect and care for every child in the city—the same way the first Ballenger leader had.

I had seen the merchants and citizens at Sanctum City nervously pander to the Komizar when he walked the narrow lanes of Venda. What I saw here wasn't fear—except when they spoke of recent troubles. After mentioning the recent spate of fires, a store clerk said he had heard rumors of caravan raids and wondered about the flow of supplies to the city. Jase assured him they were only false reports and nothing more. All was well and under control.

I studied every avenue we passed out of habit. You never knew when one of them could become an escape route. I also scanned the shadows for Wren and Synové.

"You might try to smile once in a while," Jase said, nodding back at someone we had just passed.

"Of course," I answered. "But I'm afraid that will cost you, Jase Ballenger. Everything comes with a price, you know? The Vendan settlement could use a few more short horns. Or maybe a root cellar? Do you like to dig, *Patrei*?"

"I'm afraid that by the end of the day you will be costing me far more than a root cellar."

I smiled, wide and deliberate. "You can count on it. Dig deep in your pockets. I have many more of these smiles to toss about."

His hand slid around my waist, drawing me closer, and my pulse raced in an uneven beat when his lips brushed my ear. "Be careful," he whispered, "I just might cost you something too."

A breath skipped through my chest. *You already have. More than you know.*

The truth was, it was easy to smile, and it was more work not to. I drank in the smells, sights, and sounds of the city like I'd been offered a sweet nectar. If the brisk ride had made me feel alive and above this world, the streets here made me feel grounded. They were busy and familiar.

Jase told me the story of the tembris, the great trees that were like none I had ever seen. Legend said they sprouted from a shattered star that plummeted to the earth during the devastation. The stars carried magic from another world, which is why the trees reached back toward the heavens. It was a tall Ballenger story I could almost believe, and I loved that the giant trees created a shadowy maze that made the city itself blink with magic. Every corner came alive, ever changing, exhilarating, and I memorized these details, too. Attention to detail was another sort of magic. It had helped me survived on the streets of Venda, and as I walked, I heard a familiar ghost tutoring me, *watch, my chiadrah.*

My beloved.

My everything.

Chiadrah, the crooning name she called me as often as she had Kazi. I had been her world. *Watch and you will find the magic.*

It had been her lesson to me after I heard other children talking about the great gift of the lady Venda. They said that her magical sight that helped the early Vendans was from a time past. They said that the gods had abandoned us and now magic was dead.

My mother shook her head furiously, denying it. *There is magic in everything, only you must watch for it. It does not come from spells or potions or the sky, nor by special delivery of the gods. It is all around you.*

She had taken my shivering hands and clasped them between hers.

You must find the magic that warms your skin in winter, the magic that perceives what cannot be seen, the magic that curls in your gut with fierce power and will not let you give up, no matter how long or cold the days.

She had taken me to the *jehendra* and told me to watch carefully.

Hear the language that isn't spoken, Kazi, the breaths, the pauses, the fisted hands, the vacant stares, the twitches and tears, for everyone can hear spoken words, but only a few can hear the heart that beats behind them.

Like wish stalks, my mother would not let me stop believing in magic—the hope it held. She was the one who taught me to discern, in a glimpse, the danger or opportunity that was not just in my path, but well beyond it. It almost became a game. *Where is the anger? Do you feel the air? Who is coming?* Every day, she made me see in a deeper way, as if she knew one day she wouldn't be there for me, as if she knew something as precious as her love for me would not go unnoticed by the gods, and they would snatch it away like a jealous merchant.

Make a wish, Kazi, one for tomorrow, for the next day, and the next. One will always come true.

Because if I could believe in tomorrow or the next day, maybe that would give the magic time to come true. Or better, maybe by then I wouldn't need the magic at all.

"This way," Jase said, guiding me down another avenue. I saw him eye some men at the far end of the street. His demeanor changed and his pace slowed. I asked who they were.

"Truko and Rybart, leaders of other leagues." He said they controlled trade in smaller towns in distant regions and would love nothing more than to control Hell's Mouth. They all wanted a larger share of the Ballenger power—if not all of it. That made them suspect in the fires and appearance of labor hunters, but they brought business to the arena. It created a rocky sense of partnership—as long as everyone remembered their place.

"Like Paxton? What happened between his branch of the family and yours?"

He hissed out a disgusted breath. "Too many run-ins to count." He explained that it began three generations ago. Control of Hell's Mouth had fallen out of Ballenger hands several times in their history, but never for long. Most recently was when Paxton's great-grandfather had sold it off for a handful of coins in a drunken card game with a farmer from Parsuss staying at the inn. It turned out the farmer was the King of Eislandia. Hell's Mouth was isolated and small, and the king had no interest in it, other than collecting a tax. The kingdom's borders were redrawn, reaching high to include Hell's Mouth, which explained the odd tear-shaped kingdom. All offers to buy it back were rejected, but it was still left to the Ballengers to maintain order. After that, Jase's great-grandfather took control at Tor's Watch and banished his older brother who had gambled away the town. The brother went south, sobered up, and he and now his spawn had schemed to get back control of Tor's Watch ever since.

"So Gunner or Titus could oust you?"

"If I did something stupid enough. Or Priya or Jalaine. Even Nash or Lydia for that matter. And that's the way it should be. It's not about a single *Patrei*, but the family and those we owe loyalty to. When you swear protection, you don't go gambling it away for another round of drinks."

"You Ballengers hold grudges for a long time. You never forgive?"

"Just as the gods gave us mercy, we do too. *Once.* Turn us into a fool a second time, and you pay."

By *pay*, I didn't think he meant a fine.

"What about the arena that you've mentioned? Is that part of Eislandia too?"

"No," he answered emphatically. He said the arena was nestled below Tor's Watch on its western side. It began centuries ago in the ruins of a huge complex where the Ancients had once held sporting matches. The family had repaired and expanded it over the years, and even more so since the new treaties were established and trade had increased. What used to be a place just for farmers was now a principal trading site for merchandise of every kind, and also for negotiations and future deals to be made. Luxurious rooms were provided to ambassadors, well-to-do farmers—anyone who could pay the price. Four of the Lesser Kingdoms had permanent apartments there, and more were showing interest.

"What about those two?" I asked, nodding toward Truko and Rybart, who were almost upon us.

"No apartments, but they have space on the arena floor like other merchants."

The two league leaders eyed us briefly as they passed. While others we had encountered had offered condolences to the *Patrei*, these league leaders only returned a stiff but respectful nod to Jase and continued on their way.

We turned another corner, which brought us to the wide plaza in the center of town. For all of Jase's nods, smiles, and slow, easy strides, the tension gripping the town was most noticeable here. Wagons were stopped without warning and inspected, tarps thrown aside. Perhaps citizens thought something had been stolen because news of the labor hunters seemed to have been effectively quashed. As far as I knew, none of the wagons had revealed anything suspicious, but I saw Jase's eyes turn sharp every time one lumbered past, as if he was memorizing every unfamiliar face.

Besides the *straza* walking both before and behind us, guards stood watch on the elevated skywalks that connected the tembris. More guards stood on corners. There was nothing to distinguish them from anyone else in town, but I saw the knowing glances between them and Jase as we passed. They were waiting for a war to erupt—or maybe this was their way of making sure that it didn't.

We were just nearing the temple when Jase grumbled under his breath. Paxton was approaching us. Several large men who were well-armed walked behind him. Today, Jase was armed too. A dagger on one side, his sword on the other. I hadn't seen him use either weapon yet—just his fist in the hunter's throat, which had proved deadly. I wondered about his skill with these other weapons.

I only had the small knife in my boot, but as Natiya taught me, a small, well-thrust knife was as lethal to a heart as a large one, and much easier to conceal. The air changed to something more deadly as the two cousins locked gazes. I surveyed the men behind Paxton, already choosing which to take down first if circumstances took a turn for the worse.

"Good to see you out and about, cousin," Paxton called.

"You still in town?" Jase replied, as if he had spotted something smelly on the bottom of his boot he couldn't quite scrape free.

Paxton stopped in front us, and though today his dress was more casual, he was still impeccably groomed, his white shirt and tan trousers wrinkle free, his face gleaming with a close shave. "I have a caravan on its way to the arena," he said. "I thought I might as well stay and settle a few things myself."

"So your hawker can't be trusted?"

"I've hired a new one. I'm breaking him in. And the times have changed."

"Not as much as you might think, cousin."

Paxton turned his attention to me. "A pleasure to see you again— forgive me—I'm afraid I didn't catch your name yesterday."

With rumors flying through town, I was sure he knew, but I played his game anyway, hoping he would move along quickly. I had just spotted something that interested me far more than Jase's boorish cousin— something I had been looking for all morning—Wren and Synové. They waited in the shadows of the tembris on the other side of the plaza, their Rahtan garments exchanged for clothes with local flavor. Large hats shadowed their faces.

"Kazi of Brightmist," I answered.

Paxton reached out to take my hand in greeting, and Jase and the *straza* all moved imperceptibly, their hands just a bit closer to their weapons, making me wonder again about the bad blood between the Ballengers and Paxton's branch of the family. This wasn't just an old grudge. What were those run-ins Jase had mentioned? It was perplexing that they were still compelled to do business together, but I supposed much could be tolerated in the name of profit. Paxton squeezed my fingers and kissed the back of my hand, which I found to be an overly familiar custom. I pulled my hand away.

"Welcome to the family," he said and looked back at Jase. "She's quite lovely. I'm sorry I missed the wedding. I—"

"There's been no wedding," I corrected.

"What? Still no wedding? I got the impression yesterday that—" He dismissed his thought with a wave of his hand then asked, "What are you two waiting for? The temple is right here." His theatrics were maddening and I wished he would just get on with his point, but I wasn't sure he had one. Maybe simply annoying Jase was his goal. "Oh—it's the queen, isn't it? Waiting for her imminent arrival?"

"Yes," I answered. "The queen is my sovereign. I am a soldier in her army, and I require her blessing."

Paxton grinned, his eyes leisurely roaming over me. "For your sake, Jase, I hope the queen comes soon—or someone just might come steal away your *prize*."

The way he said it, I knew he considered a Vendan soldier anything but a prize, but it pushed Jase's patience to its limit. "Move along," Jase ordered. "We're done here."

The mood changed in an instant, and Paxton's flippant attitude vanished. This was not an order from one cousin to another, but from *Patrei* to underling, and it cut through the air with as much menace as a sword. There was no question that one more word from Paxton, and Jase would do something unpleasant. Paxton stiffened, his Ballenger pride evident, but he wasn't stupid. He silently left without a good-bye, his crew following close behind him.

Jase's eyes remained fixed on them as they walked away, a vein at his temple raised and hot.

"Is there nothing you won't steal, Jase Ballenger?"

He looked at me, confused.

"Move along?" I said, trying to prick his memory. "My phrase to you? At least you didn't threaten to cut his pretty neck. Or maybe you only said it because you were swept away with a nostalgic moment?"

A gleam lit his eyes, warmth replacing the rage that had been there seconds ago. "I guess your words suit me. Will borrowing them cost me something else?"

His gaze settled into me, touching me in intimate ways. I needed to throw the wall back up between us, but instead my blood raced warmer. I pulled in a shaky breath. "Not this time," I answered. "Consider it a gift."

His lips had barely parted, a reply imminent, when his attention was turned away by Priya and Mason, heckling his name as they laughed and strolled toward us, talking about the hour being well past noon, the hot sun, a cool tavern, a cold ale, roast venison, and—I didn't hear what else. Timing was everything, and theirs was perfect. The noise rose, the shadows swirled, sun dappled shade swayed with the breeze, and the arms of the city reached out to spirit me away.

And even the eyes that had been quietly watching us from afar were bewildered when I disappeared.

Wren meant to be angry. I saw it in her eyes, but once we were far from everyone else, in a quiet little alley, she blew out a fierce relieved breath and hugged me. Hugs were rare from Wren. In fact, the only time I could remember one before was when she clutched me after her family died.

"By the gods, where have you been?" she demanded, her face flushed with heat.

"You didn't lose faith in me, did you?"

Synové's eyes narrowed in the shadows of her hat, their blue ice sparking, a wicked smile curling her mouth. "Who cares where she's been? What has she been *doing*? Tell us *everything*."

I told them about the labor hunters and our escape—and about the chain that kept us together. I skipped the parts of our journey that I knew Synové was hoping for. "But the best part is I'm inside Tor's Watch now and have a reason to stay for a while." I explained further about the letter to the queen, and the conditions I had laid down. "My little business agreement with the *Patrei* will not only give me access and time to search the compound, but will also provide reparations to the settlers in the process. They're going to get everything back that they lost." They stared at me, not looking as pleased as I had expected. "It really couldn't have worked out better," I added. "Any sign of Natiya yet?"

"Hold on just a minute," Synové balked. "You think we're going to let you breeze over the main item? *Him.* You were both out for blood last we saw you, but just now, the sparks flying between you two could have singed my hair. What's going on?"

I looked to Wren for help. She shrugged. "Might as well tell us. You know she won't stop."

I confessed that there had been a moment or two between us when we were out in the wilderness, but now it was over.

Synové snorted. "As over as an old man's grudge. Did you do it? You know, *it*?"

"No!"

"Don't be so touchy, Kazi. Whatever you had to do to occupy your time is fine with me. And he does clean up well. So does his friend. That tall, dark, handsome one. What's his name?"

I looked at her in disbelief.

"Just playing with you," she said and shoved my shoulder. "Sort of." She leaned against the wall of the shop we were hiding behind and folded her arms, ready to get down to business. "There's no sign of Natiya and Eben yet. We've been watching for them in town. Nothing."

It was a worry. It wasn't like Natiya to be late, but our plan had cushions in it for the unexpected, like weather or lame horses. We discussed the possibilities—even bandits on the road—but between Eben and Natiya, we were sure bandits would be on the losing end of any encounter. Eben had been trained to become the next Assassin of Venda, but after the war that position was eliminated. The queen disapproved of stealth murders, especially since she had narrowly escaped one herself. But his skills were still there. His mastery of a knife was awe-inspiring.

"We know they'll show up," Wren said. "They're just delayed for a good reason. That will give us plenty of time to lie low, like she ordered."

"And for you to milk as much as you can out of the Ballengers for the settlement," Synové added.

I smiled. "Yes, that."

Wren's brow lifted with skepticism. "You really think they'll keep their word?"

Jase loathed the idea. His brothers were furious. But yes, I did believe they would keep their word—that lofty Ballenger pride. It was a business transaction they had agreed to. "They'll not only keep their word—they're doing the work themselves. It was all part of our deal. The *Ballengers* will be digging fence posts."

Wren grinned. "You're evil," she said. "You could steal the nose off a man's face, and he wouldn't know it was gone for a week."

"It's genius, I admit," Synové said. "Even Natiya would crack a satisfied smile at that one. Any sign of our man yet?"

Our man. The reason we were here. I heard the tension in her voice.

I shook my head and explained that it was a large, sprawling compound with multiple homes and offices that were as big as palaces. "And there's the tunnel too, though I'm not sure it leads to much. To search everything is going to take a while, plus there's a lot of people who work there that I—"

"And dogs!" Wren interjected. "They have crazed dogs! Did you know that? Dozens of them!"

Dozens? I had only seen two. Becoming friends with that many might be more of a challenge than I thought. Wren said their efforts to look for me inside the walls of Tor's Watch were thwarted by the nasty beasts.

"A few arrows could have taken them down," Synové replied.

Wren frowned. "And a dozen dead dogs just might rouse the guards' suspicions."

Synové shrugged. "Could have taken them down too."

"And killing everyone in sight just might go against the queen's orders," I reminded her.

Synové knew that. We were ordered not to kill anyone in order to catch our game—unless our own lives were threatened. There was still some distrust when it came to Venda—we weren't to make it worse for Vendans who were trying to settle in new areas. *Get him and get out.* That was our task, and that was it. Like plucking a rotten apple from a crate.

I told them that we also had the bad timing of being plummeted into the middle of a power war spawned by Karsen Ballenger's death. Other factions wanted control of Hell's Mouth and its riches. "And these other factions were the ones who sent in the labor hunters. They paid them up front with no other expectation than to scare the citizenry and create a mutiny of sorts in order to gain control. It could be they were the ones who really attacked and burned the Vendan settlement too."

"No," Wren argued. "Caemus said—"

"Caemus said the Ballengers took a short horn as payment. That is all."

"That's enough. It's still stealing."

"I'm not disagreeing with that, but it was too dark to see who attacked and pillaged the settlement that night. Maybe someone else is trying to stir the wrath of the Vendan queen. Jase denies it was them."

"And you believe him?"

I shrugged. "It's possible."

Wren and Synové exchanged a long knowing look.

"I know what you're thinking but—"

"He's duped you, Kaz," Wren moaned. "You of all people. I can't believe you've fallen for—"

"I haven't fallen for anything, Wren. I just want you to know there are other risks here besides the Ballengers, and we have to watch out for them. Someone's been setting fires too. Six so far. Have you seen anything?"

"We set one of them," Wren answered.

"Maybe two," Synové added.

"You what?"

"I had no choice!" she said. "It was the middle of the night, and we were still hiding from corner to corner trying to get out of town. I shot a burning arrow into an oil lamp and another into a woodpile. I had to create a distraction so we could get our horses out of the livery. You know that bastard stable master stole our saddles and gear?"

Dear gods, if Jase finds out that they set even one of those fires—

"Did you burn a house?" I asked, afraid to hear the answer.

"A woodpile, Kazi. And a wagon of hay. Why are you so jumpy?"

"Because the Ballengers are jumpy and determined to find who is attacking the city. I don't want you mixed up in that battle." I thought about the severed ears. "They wouldn't understand, and it could get ugly."

"No one knows we're here."

Yet. Jase memorized details. Their changed clothes and hats wouldn't hide them for long. They needed something more permanent to protect them. They needed Jase's word.

CHAPTER TWENTY-FIVE

JASE

"WHERE IS SHE?"

My back had only been turned for seconds. She'd been right next to me. Drake and Tiago jumped, embarrassment flooding their faces, their eyes shooting across the plaza, down avenues, wondering how she could have disappeared so fast.

She was gone.

I didn't think someone could have taken her. She was gone because she wanted to be.

I scanned the plaza, looking for Yursan, and spotted him outside the pub. He shrugged. He had lost her too. But there was no sign of Garvin—which was a good omen. We moved to the center of the plaza, watching for him, waiting.

And then a whistle pealed out.

His signal.

"Hello, Kazi."

She was walking on the boardwalk in front of the apothecary when I intercepted her. "Where'd you rush off to?"

Her steps faltered, then stopped. "Me?" she answered innocently. "I didn't rush anywhere. Just taking in the sights. I guess I must have wandered off."

"Meeting friends?"

She whirled and saw her cohorts at the end of the walk. Mason held the one with long red braids by the arm. Samuel and Aram stood on either side of the other one. The rest of our crew stood behind them, including Garvin, who had done his job well. There would be no more slipping away. Her fellow soldiers had been here the whole time, and I was certain Kazi knew it.

She looked back at me, her eyes narrowing to slits. Her tongue slid slowly over her teeth, and then she walked toward me. "Look here, Jase," she said, patting the wall. "The place of our first meeting. I bet this is no accident, is it?"

I looked at the apothecary sign over our heads, surprised. "Actually, it is."

She stepped closer and her hands slid upward around my neck, her face drawing near, her lips inches from mine. It was an unusual moment for an embrace. I wasn't expecting it, but I wasn't opposed to it either. My arms slid around her waist and I pulled her closer.

Her cheek touched mine. "Think again," she whispered into my ear. "This is no accident. I led you here. This is a grand moment I'm offering you—*if* you do the right thing. Imagine, the mouthy Rahtan captivated by your charm and leadership while everyone watches—playing with your hair, laughing, smiling, maybe even kissing you. What a perfect way to erase the shocking image of me slamming you up against this very wall and holding a knife to your throat. Everyone would have a

new image to remember and whisper about. It would cement your claim
that I, and by proxy, the queen, am on your side."

She smiled, her fingers playing with my hair as she had just described,
playfully pulling a strand over my eye. "Release them," she ordered quietly. "Now."

No doubt everyone who was watching was imagining a very different conversation playing out behind our whispers. "Keep your word and
our agreement," she said, "and acknowledge Wren and Synové as guests
of the Ballengers, free to come and go as they please. In fact, they prefer
to stay here in town. I'm sure you can put them up at one of your inns.
Free of charge. No questions asked. And they keep their weapons."

"And if I don't?"

"The alternative is I slam you up against this wall again and make the
image of the *Patrei* on his knees permanent." She shrugged. "I imagine
that would only add to your troubles. It might even be written in your
history books. The Fall of the Ballengers."

"So this is another one of your blackmailing schemes?"

"A business proposition."

I laughed and tightened my hold on her back, squeezing her against
me. "You? Take me down again? Things have changed a little since that
last time."

"Think so? You don't even know half of my tricks yet. Do you really
want to take that chance? Everyone's watching. I think I even spotted
Paxton across the way."

"Why are you doing this?"

"I'm helping you, Jase. I'm giving you a chance to do the right thing.
My friends are not your problem. Let them go."

"I don't need an outsider, much less a Vendan, to tell me the right
thing to do."

"Maybe you do. You promised me you would never harm them.

Holding them against their will when they've done nothing is harm. Your word means nothing?"

Neither of us were smiling now.

"A large dinner out in the gardens is planned tonight for family and friends. It would be better if your friends came along quietly with us. As our new guests, their absence would be both suspicious and insulting."

She rolled her eyes. "Is there anything that you Ballengers don't find insulting?"

"Plenty. It's just that you Vendans are so accomplished at dishing insults out."

"Fine. They'll come to your little festivity, but they're free to leave when it's over."

Her gaze was steady, unrelenting.

Rahtan as guests and in possession of their weapons, which included quivers of arrows, when we still didn't know who had started the fires?

Kazi's gaze held, as unblinking as a statue, her loyalty to them fierce. I finally looked away, calling to Samuel. "Show our guests to the Ballenger Inn. Make sure they have the best rooms and everything they need."

Her finger gently pushed on my jaw, turning my attention back to her. "One last thing, *Patrei*. No more tails. Call them both off. I am either your honored guest with whom you have an agreement. Or I am not."

How did she know? The decoy, I understood, but Garvin was damn near invisible.

"No more tails," I agreed, and I brought my mouth to hers before she could say one more thing. I was through with conditions.

I thought the kiss would be awkward, strained, but she relaxed in my arms, creating the show that she promised. I pressed her against the wall—the image that would burn in everyone's memory and erase the last one—but that was the last of the show, at least for me. I felt her tongue on mine, the warmth of her lips, breathed in the scent of her skin and hair, and we were in the wilderness again, and nothing else mattered.

———∞∞∞———

We sat in a dark corner of the tavern sipping a cool ale. Priya fanned herself with a tattered menu, and Mason absently spun a spoon on the table. After seeing Wren and Synové escorted to the inn, Kazi had gone back to Tor's Watch with Jalaine and my mother.

"She made you," I said.

Garvin swilled back the last drips of his ale. "No. She never looked my way," he answered. "But when you stopped her outside the apothecary, she did spot me in the crowd."

"She's seen you before?"

He bit the corner of his lip, still chewing on some memory. "I didn't place her when Mason first pointed her out to me. I was too far away. But seeing her up close—I know her, somehow, from somewhere, but I'm not sure where." He told me that when he used to run wagons sometimes he went into Venda, mostly for the Komizar, sometimes for merchants in the *jehendra*, but the last time he was there was about seven years ago. "How old is she?"

"Seventeen."

He rubbed his bristled cheek, trying to recall where he had seen her. "That would make her just a kid the last time I saw her. What about her name?"

"Only Kazi. No surname. But she goes by Kazi of Brightmist. I guess that's the—"

"It's one of the poorest quarters in Sanctum City. Well, truth is, they're all poor, but Brightmist is an especially bad one. Don't let the name fool you. Nothing bright about it. Never sold any goods there. No one in those parts has two coins to rub together. Her name doesn't sound familiar though."

"There must be a few well-to-do families. She said her father's a governor and her mother a general."

He shrugged doubtfully. "It's possible, I guess."

I asked why a ten-year-old among thousands would stand out for him. He shook his head. "Don't know. But I'll place her eventually. Faces are what I'm good at—even if she was just a kid at the time."

"Seven years, seven inches, and"—Priya gestured toward her chest—"plenty of new curves tend to transform a girl."

Garvin nodded in agreement. "But the eyes—those don't change. Something about hers sticks. The fire in them. That girl has burned people." He pushed his chair back from the table. "I'll see you tonight. Maybe it will come to me by then." He tipped his hat and left.

Priya circled her finger in the air to the barkeep for another round of ale then leaned forward with a warning glare at Mason, clapping her hand over the spoon he kept spinning to keep him quiet. She looked back at me. "Up until her little disappearance, she did well today. We were following in your trail, and everyone we talked to mentioned her. Apparently she pulled a coin out of the ear of the baker's daughter? They were both impressed."

I laughed. "Yes, so was I. The girl tripped and was crying over a scraped knee, but Kazi was able to captivate her with a shiny coin she magically found hiding in her ear. The tears were forgotten." I thought about how Kazi didn't hesitate, how she shed her tough exterior, and knelt down to eye level with the girl. Kindness was a default for Kazi, even if she wouldn't admit it, especially when it came to children.

"Well, Nash and Lydia both think she's better than a holiday trifle. All I heard this morning was Kazi this and Kazi that. When we popped in to the tailor today, she juggled brass thimbles for them and gave them a lesson on how to do it too. Get ready for some broken dishes at home."

Her eyes suddenly widened. "And speaking of dishes, you hired a cook? What were you thinking? Aunt Dolise was grumbling around this morning. That's her domain, you know?"

"The *Patrei* can't hire a cook? We needed another one. She's always grumbling about that too. There are a lot of people to feed at Tor's Watch, not just the family. I happened to be there just as the guards at the gate were turning a cook away this morning—a vagabond woman looking for work, along with her husband. They'll start tomorrow at Riverbend. Aunt Dolise will still have her kitchen, but some extra help too, when she needs it." What I didn't tell Priya was that I asked the woman if she knew how to make sage cakes—the vagabond food that Kazi had said could bring her to her knees. When the woman said it was her specialty, I hired her on the spot. Her husband too. She said he was handy with a knife in the kitchen.

"Well, you should have run it by Aunt Dolise first," Priya complained. "Being *Patrei* doesn't win you any kind of points with her, and there are two kinds of people you don't want on your bad side—those who guard your back, and those who fill your stomach"

"I'll smooth it over with her."

Priya shot me a smirk. "Sure you will." Priya knew Aunt Dolise turned to a pat of butter when any of us boys wandered into the kitchen looking for something to eat.

"The dressmaker was impressed with Kazi too," she said. "Good job on whatever you did today to keep her in line. It worked."

I frowned. "She's not a trained dog, Priya. She doesn't jump at my bidding."

"Everyone in this town jumps at your bidding now, Jase. Get used to it. The important thing is, after seeing her walk so compliantly beside you, everyone we passed thinks we've now achieved the upper hand with Venda."

"Maybe not everyone," I said.

"You saw Rybart and Truko?" Mason asked.

I nodded. "And I didn't like that they were walking together."

"I saw them talking to Paxton too," Priya said. "When did they all get so cozy?"

It was a question that didn't need answering. We knew. They became cozy the day our father died. They might all hate each other in the end, but for now they'd use whomever they could to oust the Ballengers.

"I don't like that they're still here," Priya added. "Paying respects is one thing. Don't they have businesses to run?"

"I think that's exactly what they're doing," I answered. "Attending to a new kind of business. Getting rid of us."

"At least we have the Rahtan in custody. We don't have to worry about them anymore," Mason said.

"Technically, we don't have them in custody," I reminded him. "They're guests. Remember that."

Mason raised a dubious brow. I had him place guards in the tembris skywalks above the inn. They weren't exactly tails, but they were watching for suspicious activity. As long as Wren and Synové did nothing suspicious, we had no problems.

"What did you think of them?" I asked. Mason had escorted and questioned them along the way to the inn.

Mason snorted. "They're a strange pair. Wren, the skinny one, didn't have much to say, but Samuel and Aram were way too preoccupied with her scowls. We need to get those boys out more often. And the other one—" Mason shook his head. "She never stops talking, but not a word she said amounted to anything important, even when I asked her questions." He leaned forward, a mystified expression on his face. "She talked about my *shirt*. She knew everything about how the fabric was woven and where the buttons were made—and then she played a game guessing my height the whole way there. I think she was trying to make me smile. I didn't like any of it. Like I said, an odd pair of soldiers, but I doubt they had anything to do with the fires. I'm guessing they were just hiding out because Kazi disappeared. And now of course, they're eager to hang around and see the settlement rebuilt. They mentioned that several times too."

Priya huffed out a disapproving sigh. "Are you really going to do that?"

"We gave our word," I said. "And I've already ordered the supplies."

"It will—"

"It will be a compromise, Priya. And it's going to cost us very little in comparison to what we gain. Laying out a single copper for trespassers wasn't high on my list of things I wanted to do, either—until Gunner shot off his big mouth and said the queen was coming. What choice did I have? At least now there is some measure of truth to our claim, and with the letter Kazi wrote, the queen may actually come. It's what our father wanted. If it takes rebuilding a few shacks far from our territory, I will swallow the gall in my throat and do it—and so will you and everyone else."

"But what right do we have to move them, Jase? The king may have something to say about that."

"The king can go yatter to his chickens as far I'm concerned," I answered. "He'll never know they've been moved, and we'll have our land back."

It was true, what Kazi said, that we had no defined borders. It was a hard thing to explain to an outsider. It had to do with comfort, and what felt intrusive, and too close. *As far as you can see.* We knew we didn't own the land all the way to the horizon.

"So what was with that kiss? I'm pretty sure that even Paxton had to have his jaw rehinged after that display. Kazi told me you didn't care a rat's whisker for her."

My fingers tightened on my mug. "When did she tell you that?"

"Last night."

After lying to her about where we were going, threatening to throw her off the horse, and then her suspecting I had harmed her friends—I suppose those were all grounds to believe I didn't care about her—and I had failed miserably at conveying how I really felt, or maybe I just kept hoping my feelings would go away. Instead, they only grew larger, like a rock in my path that I couldn't maneuver around. That rock was the size of a mountain now, and I couldn't get past it.

Priya looked down and shook her head. "Oh damn, Jase. She's got you by the throat."

"I'm the *Patrei*, remember?" I answered, trying to sound more sure than I was. "No one has me by anything."

She didn't look convinced.

The barkeep came and set down the new round of ales Priya ordered.

When he left, she reached out and squeezed my hand. "I love you, brother. You know I'm behind you in whatever you do. Just be careful."

Mason cleared his throat and tapped the spoon on the table. Priya reached out and squeezed his hand too, but much more violently than she had mine. "I love you too, brother," she said to him. "But if you make any more clatter with that spoon, I'll dig both of your eyes out with it."

Mason deliberately dropped the spoon on the floor to irritate her, and they began wrestling like they were twelve years old again. The ales suffered the brunt of the tussle, all three sliding from the table. Some habits didn't die and I was glad. Mason finally called surrender when Priya dug her nails into his ear.

"All right, I've had all the fun I can stand here," she said, letting go and giving the fallen ales a cursory glance. "We should get home anyway.

There's a party in the garden tonight with our new special guests. Let's see if these Vendans know how to dance."

I already knew.

Kazi was an expert dancer—but not the kind Priya was talking about.

Mason rubbed his ear and stood. "I'm taking those other two back to the house now. They can cool their heels there until the party starts. I'm not making another trip down here in a few hours."

"Be careful, Mason. Last time I said I was going to make a Rahtan cool her heels, it cost me more than I bargained for."

"Those two?" Mason answered. "I'm not worried."

That's what I had said too.

"Coming?" Priya asked, gathering some packages she had purchased.

"I'll be along. I have a late meeting at the arena."

Priya rolled her eyes. "The ambassador?"

I nodded.

"Give him hell, Jase. I'm tired of that asshole."

The asshole who was responsible for a good portion of our revenue. I smiled. "I'll be sure and give him your regards."

"Be careful," she added as she left some coins on the bar to cover our tab. "Those Candorans are crazy."

Give him hell and be careful.

Walk the razor's edge.

That summed up the role of *Patrei*.

Winter has come. The walls are frozen.

The floors are frozen. The beds are frozen.

There is no wood, no more oil, so we burn ledgers and books instead.

When those are gone, I will have to go back outside to where the scavengers wait.

—Greyson Ballenger, 14

CHAPTER TWENTY-SIX

KAZI

"Dear gods, Kazi. We've got to call a healer. *Fikatande dragnos!*"

It wasn't just surprise I heard in Wren's voice. It was fear.

"No. I'll be fine." Wren and Synové helped me over to the tub so I wouldn't get more blood on the floor. "Just help me rewrap it."

"Not until it's clean," Synové argued. She remembered something about that in our training. The truth was, none of us had ever had a major injury, and that was because what we did, we did well—only others came away injured. The problem was, none of us were sure how to clean it and I wasn't sure I wanted to. The pain was already making it hard for me to focus. It took all my control to keep my hands from shaking, which made no sense because they weren't injured. I curled my fingers into my palms to keep them still.

Wren took a closer look and let loose with another long string of curses against the black toothy beasts.

I had barely made it back to my room when Wren and Synové had arrived for tonight's dinner party. Mason had delivered them to my door early to await the evening with me, but he hadn't seen me. I called from the bath chamber for them to come in.

A shudder of air escaped my throat as I lifted my foot into the tub. I should have worn my boots, but the slippers were quieter.

It mostly got my ankle, but the bites went to the bone. The puncture wounds burned like hot pokers were stabbing my flesh, and there was a one-inch jagged tear on the inside of my calf. That's where most of the blood was coming from.

"What if it punctured an artery?" Synové wailed. "You could bleed to death!"

"Keep your voice down," I warned. "If it had punctured anything vital, I'd be dead already. It was a long way back here from the tunnel." My greatest worry was if I had left a trail of blood behind—evidence of where I'd been.

It had seemed like the perfect timing to do a little poking around. Jase and the others weren't back, and the night dogs hadn't been released yet. I searched Darkcottage first. It had been a simple enough task, because it was so clearly empty—the larder bare, the oven cold, and there were no signs of personal belongings in any of the rooms.

Riverbend had been fairly easy to navigate too. With so much activity in the gardens, preparing for tonight's dinner party, the domicile of the Ballenger employees was mostly empty. That left Greycastle. I was nearly spotted as I crept down a hallway, peeking into rooms, but I heard the floor creak just before Uncle Cazwin came around a corner. I slipped into an alcove and he passed without a suspicion. The captain didn't turn up in any of the rooms there either.

I made Greyson Tunnel my next target. I had slipped effortlessly through it. There weren't many workers in it like the first time I had passed, perhaps because they'd been called to the gardens to help with those preparations, and it seemed every passing wagon and dark shadow was conspiring with me to cover my steps. In minutes, I made it to the intersecting tunnel marked with the faded Ballenger crest. I discovered there were three more tunnels that branched off from it that got progressively smaller. I chose the farthest one and walked to the end, using the same logic of searching for valuables in a chest—the best things were always hidden in the bottom.

Except for the eerie echo of dripping water, I hadn't heard a sound. And then I rounded a corner. I had peeked first to make sure no one was there. The small dark tunnel only extended another twenty feet and appeared empty, a wide metal door blocking the end. A dim line of light shone at the bottom. I walked forward to investigate and test the lock. I hadn't seen the black dogs chained in dark alcoves on either side of the door.

But they saw me.

They were silent devils, knowing exactly what they were doing, waiting for me to step into range, and then they lunged. I kicked them off fast but not before the damage was done. I was lucky they only got my leg. As soon as I was out of their reach, I ripped off my shirt and wrapped my ankle, carefully wiping the drips of blood from the floor as they snarled and lunged at the end of their chains. If someone had been alerted by the noise, they'd be there in seconds. In those first few frantic moments, I felt no pain, but I knew it was bad. I knew I was in trouble. My fingertips tingled wildly like needles were shooting from them. All I could think in that shocked moment was, I had to get back before someone discovered me.

Synové poured water over my ankle in an effort to clean it. A groan trembled between my clenched teeth. "I'm sorry, Kaz," she cried as she dabbed it. "Damn, there's another gash back here that you didn't see."

I didn't need to see that one too. There were more than a dozen puncture marks dotted around my ankle like a macabre lace stocking.

"Wrap it," I said between gritted teeth. "Just wrap it. That's enough cleaning."

They both tried to convince me again that a healer was necessary. "And how will I explain how I got these? Tell Jase I was just taking a quick sneak around?" I drew a deep breath and told Wren to go down to the kitchen.

Her gaze was fixed on the bloody water trickling down the tub toward the drain. "I don't know the way!"

"Don't worry, you won't get far before someone stops you—say you have a terrible headache and need something for pain. Ask for serpent's claw, capsain—anything. I need to be back on my feet before the party." If the captain was indeed holed up at Tor's Watch, we were hoping he would be among the guests.

"There's one other thing," I said, grabbing Wren's arm before she left. "The man who tailed me today? He hasn't always worked for the Ballengers. He used to be a Previzi driver."

Wren shook her head. "Are you sure? I didn't recognize him."

"I'm sure," I said, and told them he was the driver who had brought the tiger to the *jehendra* all those years ago. "I think he recognized me too."

"That's impossible," Synové said. "No one even knew you stole it."

Wren blew out a worried sigh. "But she did have a reputation. She was always suspect."

"But she has breasts now! Hips! She doesn't even look the same."

I kept telling myself that too. I had changed. I had meat on me now. My cheeks were no longer hollow caves. I was barely the same person at all. But his eyes had been anchored onto mine, and in that moment I had seen something flicker in his memory. "If he's here at Tor's Watch, or at the party tonight, avoid him. And if he says anything, tell him I was a barrow runner for Sanctum Hall. Steer him in that direction. Deny anything else."

Wren nodded and left. While she was gone, Synové carefully wrapped my leg. Just the pressure of the cloth pressing against the wounds made the throb worse.

"They need sewing, Kazi," Synové said apologetically. I didn't answer. Sewing was out of the question. A one inch tear could heal without being sewn up. Her eyes became watery. "I had a dream the night you disappeared. I saw you tumbling in water and you were drowning, but I never saw this. These damn dreams! They're worthless." She wiped angrily at her lashes.

I reached out and grabbed her hand. "I did tumble in water, Syn. And I did almost drown. Your dreams were right."

Her brow shot up. "Was it him who saved you?"

"Yes. More than once. He protected me against a bear, and he carried me across blistering sand. Have you had any other dreams?"

She bit her lip, hesitant. "I dreamed you were chained in a prison cell."

"That's not so surprising. I have been before. Sometimes dreams are only dreams, Synové. You were worried about me."

"But in my dream you were soaked in blood. I wasn't sure if you were alive."

"I promise, I have no intention of spending time in a prison cell ever again. It was only a dream." I hoped.

Wren returned with a tiny vial of crystals. It looked like simple salt. I sniffed skeptically, but there was no scent. She said Mason had intercepted her at the end of a hallway just as I had predicted. He led her to the kitchen and then searched through a storage room for the crystals. He poured some from a large canister into the vial for her. "He called it birchwings and said to mix it with water and drink it to ease pain."

Synové snorted. "Mason? I should have gone for the medicine."

"How much do I take?" I asked.

"I don't know," Wren answered. "Half of it? Maybe just a spoonful?" Her face twisted with worry. "I'm not sure he said."

At this point, I didn't care. I just wanted the pain to stop. Synové poured a quarter of it into a cup of water. The glass shivered in my hand as I downed the flavorless potion. They helped me to the bed and I lay down, my foot elevated on a pillow. Wren smoothed the hair from my face and lay beside me. Synové crawled onto the end of the bed, her hand rubbing my uninjured foot, and she began commenting on the accommodations to fill the silence. I smiled as she assessed the heavy blue drapes that surrounded Jase's bed. *Oh, the stories I bet these could tell . . .*

They told me I slept solid for two hours.

When I sat up, my leg was stiff and oddly heavy like it wasn't my own, but the pain was gone. There was only a mild throb when I swung my foot over the side of the bed and put weight on it. I held up the birchwings vial with supreme admiration. "I'll be sure to bring this along tonight in case I need more."

"Nope," Wren said, snatching it from my hand. "It's also what knocked you out cold for the last two hours." I eyed the deceivingly benign vial in Wren's hand. Powerful crystals like that could be useful. "Unless, of course," Wren added, "you want that Ballenger boy carrying you back to your room?"

Synové winked. "Of course she does." She turned, waving to the
side. "Look what came while you were out."

Laid out across the armchair were three dresses.

"The yellow one is mine," Synové beamed. "I already tried it on. It
fits in all the right places—if you know what I mean."

We knew. Synové had a lot of right places, and she knew it. Everyone always thought she was older than she was.

"I have to applaud Madame Ballenger," she added, "very perceptive
of her in light of the short notice. She barely got a glimpse of me in town.
The violet one's yours."

That left the one in the middle for Wren. She stared at it like it had
gills and claws. "I am not wearing *that* thing. I don't even know what
color that is."

"Pink," I said.

"Like a tongue?"

Synové squinted one eye. "A cold, pale tongue. Wouldn't you like
to feel *that* on your skin?"

I shot Synové a warning glare. Sometimes I had to use my thieving
skills even with my friends and right now something needed to be stolen
back—Wren's confidence. Nothing was going quite as planned, and she
demanded that everything follow an ordained path. She liked to be prepared and for a strategy to play out as, well, as *planned*. She would have
made a terrible thief, because being ready to pivot and change the plan
in the flutter of an eyelash was what had kept all my fingers intact. Pivot
was practically one of my rules. Our plan had gone awry, and this latest
misstep, seeing me on the floor of the bath chamber with blood spatter-
ing the tiles, had pricked memories that for her would never be shaken.
And nowhere in our carefully wrought plan was Wren supposed to attend
a party at Tor's Watch in a pink gown. She was supposed to gather
supplies, get me whatever I needed, keep her *ziethe* sharp and her eyes

sharper, and be ready to move when the signal was sent. Now, as she looked at the dress, I knew she was already wondering where her *ziethe* would go.

But tonight a party was ordered, and it was essential that we appear relaxed, as true guests with nothing to worry about—so the Ballengers would relax too. Not to mention the guests who might be there.

I tested my foot, and when it appeared stable, I crossed the room and touched Wren's dress. I knew how to entice her. "Oh, this is unexpected," I said, gathering it up in my hands. I lightly passed the hem over my cheek.

"What?" she asked.

"The fabric. I'm not sure I've ever felt anything so soft. It feels like it's woven from clouds. Feel," I said, holding it out to her.

She shook her head, refusing, her curls bobbing, but she stepped forward anyway, and gave it a cursory swipe with her fingers.

Wren was sharp, calculating, seeing every move I made, and knowing on some deep level why I made them. *Trust me, Wren.* As tough as she was, she knew her weaknesses, too—and the things that brought her comfort. I had never known why she was so drawn to soft things, why she was drawn to that fleece in the marketplace that I stole for her, or the downy duckling she had cupped in her hands at a pond and been reluctant to let go. I was sure it was tangled up in something from her past, all of those things that none of us talked about, the secrets that we stuffed down deep in a dark broken part of us. Maybe it was something that even she didn't understand. It might be something as simple as the memory of her mother's cheek touching her own.

"It's soft," she admitted, still noncommittal, "but that color."

"The violet one might fit you. We could trade."

She grabbed the pink dress from me, already knowing all the reasons why she needed to wear it, why she needed to smile and pretend we were there for no other reason than what everyone believed, that we were honored guests of the Ballengers.

"But I'm still wearing my *ziethe*," she said.

CHAPTER TWENTY-SEVEN

JASE

THE AMBASSADOR'S BELLY PRESSED OVER THE LOW TABLE LIKE A rising loaf of bread, and his buckles, belts, and jeweled chains rattled against it every time he coughed or pulled in a deep, wheezing breath. He inhaled another long pull from his water pipe. The sickeningly sweet tobacco smoke hung in the stale air.

The apartments at the arena that the Ballengers provided—for a price—had been remade in the Candoran style. Heavy tapestries darkened the walls, and fur rugs covered the floors. The shutters were pulled tight and the only light came from a bronze oil lamp glowing on the table between us. The flickering flame cast shadows on his bodyguards standing behind him, enormous men with shimmering sabers hanging at their sides. It was all for effect. Our *straza* stood behind us for the same reason.

The ambassador's upper lip twisted in discontent. "You are not your father's son. He would have met with me last week. He knew—"

"I'm here now," I said. "State your business. I have other meetings besides yours."

I had no more meetings, and my harsh reply was part of the game. I had warned Gunner to keep his mouth shut before we entered the room. He didn't like long silences. Like the one we were having now. I grinned, cool and calm, and leaned back in my chair, but inside I was as tense as Gunner and Titus.

The ambassador stared at me, rolling his pink puffy lips back and forth, the corners of his mouth glistening with saliva. I stared back.

"There are other places to trade," he said.

"But not as profitable as here. You make a killing at this arena, and we both know it. We process the orders, you know?"

"Profit is only good when there's no loss. Your father made promises about protection, and yet we still have none. We have ears and eyes. We know what's been going on. Our caravans will be the next to be hit. There's the trading center at Shiramar and the one at Ráj Nivad. We could take our business there. Rents and cuts are smaller, and the routes less dangerous." He took a long easy drag on his pipe. "And if we pull out . . . others will follow."

Gunner's fingers coiled into a fist. I nudged him with my boot beneath the table.

"My father's promises are good," I said. "The weapons we're developing—"

"Developing!" he spit out, his lip lifted in disgust. "What does that mean?"

"It means that your goods will be protected from door to door. That's all you need to know."

"That's a grandiose claim for someone—"

"Grandiose!" I answered with the same level of disgust he had just thrown at me. "What does that mean? An idea too big for your small Candoran head?"

His wiry brows twitched and a grin lit his beady black eyes. "Your father always sweetened the pot for us when we had to wait for something."

I paused, even though I already knew what I would give him. If I gave in too easily, he would balk and argue for more, and I wanted to get out of here as soon as I could with what we needed—and what we needed were the Candorans. They were our largest trader, and they had legitimate complaints.

We had patrols on the major routes to conduct raids on those who came under the guise of trading at the arena, but then, just short of it, only sent a lead man in to make contacts and lure buyers away to where their caravans waited, offering them better deals and avoiding our cuts. No one used us as a storefront without paying the lease. The same patrols who guarded our interests offered a degree of safety to our legitimate traders too, but we didn't have enough manpower to escort every caravan once they left our territory—and that's where the other caravans had been hit. A hundred miles out. Even with their own security, drivers died and goods were lost. If there were even rumblings of them pulling out because of raids, it would hurt our business. That's what other leagues counted on, but it was about to change. Soon, just one of our hands could single-handedly guard a whole caravan. Protection was what the Ballengers had always been good at. Now we would be able to extend it beyond our borders.

"Nothing?" the ambassador pushed, revealing his eagerness to still work with us. Our location was ultimately more central and far more comfortable—we made sure of that. Shiramar was a hot, dirty pit, and Ráj Nivad out of the way. Not to mention we looked the other way on the ambassador's little side trades that his king knew nothing about—as long as we got our cut on those too.

"A free lease on these apartments until we deliver on our promise. That sweet enough for you?"

The ambassador nodded, his stubby fingers happily tapping his chest. "I was wrong. You are your father's son."

I stood. Gunner and Titus rose beside me.

"The Ballengers keep their word," I said. "Now don't bother me with any more of your demands."

He huffed to his feet, a greasy smile wrinkling his face. "*Patrei*. Always good to do business with you."

Once we were out of the apartment, Titus whispered, "Free lease is going to cost us a fortune. And if the other tenants get a whiff of the deal we gave him—"

"It will only cost us a fortune if we don't deliver on our promise."

From the arena, we went straight to see Beaufort, prepared to pressure him. For us to deliver on our promise, he and his cohorts had to deliver too, and we were tired of waiting. His promises had worn thin. But as soon as we came through the gates, he greeted us as if he anticipated our visit and ushered us over to the testing range, saying they had worked out a major stumbling block. "It was all a problem of translation," he said, then gave us a demonstration of the arms they had promised. It was half the scale of the final firepower, but still impressive. It looked like it was everything we had hoped for—and more.

"Another couple of weeks. A month at the most to refine," he promised. "But we do need more supplies." Gunner and Titus gawked at the destroyed target that was more than a hundred yards away, then erupted in hoots. "Just tell us what you need," Gunner said. "We'll have Zane get it to you right away."

"And the fever cure?" I asked.

Beaufort's brows pinched together and he shook his head. "That's a bit harder to rush along. Phineas is testing it. Don't worry, every day brings him closer."

Closer. I had been giving my mother that same update for months. It was a thread of hope that seemed to appease her, and for the time being, it appeased me too. The weapons we needed now, and I'd just seen evidence of that success.

Back in my room, I bathed, washing away the heavy stench of the ambassador's apartment. I felt hopeful as I dressed, thinking about the weapons. There had been no more fires last night, and today, no evidence of more labor hunters. Things appeared to be returning to normal. I hoped the ambassador was wrong about caravan attacks, but if there were any, our patrols were instructed to come down hard—hunt down the attackers no matter what it took and find out who was ordering the hits.

Gunner whistled low. "Now that's a sight you don't see every day."

Wren, Kazi, and Synové emerged from the arbor, shoulder to shoulder.

I stared at Kazi. She hadn't spotted me yet. Her black hair was braided in an elegant crown around her head—no doubt a creation of Jalaine's. A dusting of fallen yellow petals from the arbor clung to her hair, and her violet dress floated in light waves past her ankles. Her shoulders were nearly bare except for the smallest wisp of sleeve draped over them. Her eyes skimmed another part of the garden, searching for something, and I couldn't help but wonder—or maybe hope—that she searched for me.

Titus elbowed me. "Close your mouth, *Patrei*. You look too eager."

I was eager.

"What's going on with the one in pink?" Gunner asked.

"That's Wren," Aram and Samuel said simultaneously.

Wren was transformed too, barely looking like the cutthroat we had seen in the alley earlier today—except for the curved sword at her side.

"No one told her she could leave it at home?" Gunner said.

My attention went back to Kazi. Disconnected words flooded my head, and I heard my father's long-ago warning, *Choose your words carefully, even the words you think, because they become seeds, and seeds become history.*

There were words I had avoided even thinking ever since I met Kazi. When my mother asked about her, I only said she was resourceful—a safe, stable word. But now others flowed freely, sown recklessly in my head. I wanted them all to take root, grow, become history—part of my history. *Clever, smart, ruthless, determined, brave, devious, loyal, caring.* She turned, her eyes grazing the tops of heads, the breeze lifting loose strands of hair at her neck, and another word came, *beautiful,* and it was the only word I could think of, until another one bloomed on its heels, *future,* and I wondered if it was too dangerous a word to entertain. But I already felt it taking root.

More guests arrived, sweeping Kazi and her friends from our view, and Aram and Samuel took off in Wren's direction. Mason was right— they were a little too preoccupied with someone who could likely break both of their necks in unison while smiling. I'd have to talk to them.

Last night had been the small family dinner, but tonight all the family was invited to celebrate the new *Patrei,* along with close friends and colleagues. The priestess, seer, and healer who had tended my father would be here too.

Beaufort had broached the idea of coming too, hanging back in the shadows, but I said no. He was getting itchy from so many years of hiding, and maybe a little cocky too, having eluded the kingdoms for so long, but he wasn't going to get caught on my watch, at least not while he still had goods to deliver. We had too much invested at this point. He had joined us for dinners in the past, but there would be too many here tonight outside of the family—especially Kazi and her crew. He said his appearance had changed and he wasn't likely to be recognized, but it was too much of a risk. He was still wanted by the kingdoms. We had seen the occasional warrant brought into the arena by traders and had mostly become numb to them. They named people we were unlikely to ever see, but Beaufort had been different. He had come to us with the wanted bill in hand, not trying to hide who he was. He was tired of running. He said the reason he was really wanted was because he had escaped with valuable information and he would prefer to share it with us than with people he didn't trust.

According to him, he'd been an officer in the war between the Greater Kingdoms and there was bad blood between him and the Morrighese king. Beaufort claimed the king was corrupt and in turn, the king charged him with treason for switching sides. After the war, the kingdoms had signed new treaties, so now he was wanted by all of them. We had doubted that this was entirely true, but neither did we care about the political collusions and grudges of distant kingdoms, except as they affected Tor's Watch. Still, my father had sent a discreet message to the king's magistrate in Parsuss regarding "a warrant floating through the arena" to check out Beaufort's story. The magistrate had no details to offer on Beaufort and could neither confirm nor refute the charges.

It could be that we're actually doing the kingdoms a favor—keeping him out of further trouble, my father had said, but it was mostly the promise of the fever cure that made us look the other way. And, of course, the weapons were simply a benefit that made our arrangement all the sweeter. Whatever it took to keep the family—and that included everyone in Hell's Mouth—safe was all that mattered.

"*Patrei.*"

I turned toward the graveled voice. It was the seer. She was suddenly at my side, her azure eyes looking up into mine, a crooked smile twisting her lips. Her hood was pushed back, which was rare, but her wild black hair still circled her face, casting her features in shadow. She kissed my hand, and paused, looking at the ring, then shook her head sadly and crooned, "They found you, *Patrei*. I am sorry."

For the first time, it occurred to me that maybe her warning that they were coming for me had been about the labor hunters and not the leagues.

"What news have you?" I asked.

"I taste new blood. They circle near."

"It's been taken care of. We killed those who came after me."

Her eyes glowed with worry. "Not them," she whispered. "*Others*. Guard your heart, *Patrei*. I see a knife hovering, ready to cut it out."

I smiled. "Don't worry. I'll keep my *straza* near. Go, enjoy some food and drink. My mother has a seat of honor for you. Titus will show you." I grabbed Titus by the back of his shirt, pulling him away from another conversation, telling him to get the seer a drink and help her to her seat. I wondered sometimes if her warnings were prompted by my mother's concerns. They spoke each day at the temple, and my mother generously contributed to her keep. There were few in Hell's Mouth who had the gift. The Vendan queen was rumored to be strong in it, and I wondered about Kazi and the way she slipped away so quietly, almost like magic. Our Ballenger histories mentioned the gift, but it seemed to have faded with the generations.

Titus left with the seer, and I strained to see through the crowd. I spotted Garvin. He stood alone, staring. I followed the line of his gaze, and it led to Kazi.

Brightmist. It's one of the poorest quarters. Don't let the name fool you. Nothing bright about it.

Garvin was wrong.

There was at least one bright thing about it.

CHAPTER TWENTY-EIGHT

KAZI

WE WERE OUT OF PLACE HERE, FRAUDS IN EVERY WAY, PLAYING roles, wearing fine dresses as if it was something we had done hundreds of times when we never had. Not even once.

Wren kept hitching her shoulder up like the whole thing was going to fall off of her, saying its flimsy construction made no sense at all, while her fingers absently made small circles on her abdomen, feeling the pink softness over and over again. Synové held a goblet out, trying to catch her own reflection, watching the yellow fabric dance in the crystal before her eyes, then she would smooth her hands over her silky curves, pressing the dress there like it might vanish. I was no different. I had always thought my vest an extravagance, but it served a purpose. Its hidden pockets held weapons and maps. The sturdy leather protected me from the weather. The dress I wore now served no purpose at all except to feel beautiful. It didn't belong on me. I had never felt beautiful in my life. I was only the dirty street rat no one wanted to see coming.

And then there was the food.

"Do you smell that?" Synové whispered.

It was impossible not to smell. The scent of marinated roasting meats was a glorious complex tapestry hanging over our heads, swelling our cheeks and awakening our stomachs like a song. Tables overflowed with first courses of cheese, savory breads, and an abundance of food that filled us with both wonder and guilt. There were still shortages in Venda, which was what made the settlements so vital. It felt traitorous to nibble on one tiny delicacy after another.

But we played our roles. We ate. We smiled. We improvised. We were Rahtan, and we could chisel what made us uncomfortable and awkward into an ice sculpture in hell if we had to.

I searched for Jase. I couldn't see him, but I knew he was probably occupied with other guests. There were so many. I guessed about two hundred.

Lydia and Nash ran between tables and shrubs with their young cousins, laughing and playing tag. Surely if the captain was here he'd be among the guests, perhaps going by a different name to hide his identity. Maybe the Ballengers didn't even know they had a wanted criminal in their midst? Was that possible? It was a hope that suddenly sprang in me.

And then, against my will, my eyes searched again for the pale, bloodless face, but I came to another one instead. The man who had followed me today. I alerted Wren and Synové. He obviously wasn't tailing me anymore, so why was he so intently keeping an eye on me?

"He's still watching," Wren whispered to me a few minutes later.

"He knows who I am," I said.

"If he knew, he wouldn't still be watching," Synové answered. "He's still trying to figure it out. Even if he makes the connection, you can deny it. You don't look anything like that girl anymore."

"But her name," Wren replied.

"No Previzi driver ever knew the name of a street rat."

"Not Kazi. Her other name. Ten. Everyone knew that one."

"She simply denies the name too."

The name that would make doors close for me. No one let their guard down around an accomplished thief.

I turned and looked directly at him and smiled as if surprised. He nodded and walked away.

"Taste *this*," Synové said, already forgetting the driver, shoving a small crisp of bread slathered with a thick tangy relish into my hand. She rolled her eyes like she was tasting a fruit of the gods.

I groaned with pleasure. Wren licked every crumb from her fingers.

Synové grinned and put her hands on her hips. "Look at us. Being fed and clothed like royalty."

Wren smacked her lips. "Enjoy it while you can."

We all knew this was a short-lived indulgence.

"Oh, trust me," Synové answered, "I am. But not as much as Kazi's enjoying it." Her eyes narrowed, and I knew what she was implying. I waited for a lecture but instead I saw unexpected worry. "I like him too," she said, "but you know that can't last either. Not once we—"

Her brows lifted and she left the last thought hanging for me to complete. Not once we steal away his secret guest? Not once he finds out why I'm really here?

"I'm not expecting anything to last," I replied with disdain. "I'm only doing my job the best I can."

"Admirable," Wren answered and exchanged a dubious glance with Synové.

The thing that still puzzled me was, why? What did a traitorous, on-the-run captain who had no army to command have to offer the Ballengers? He had barely escaped a battlefield with the clothes on his back. He had never gotten his promised fortune from the Komizar, and yet, he had *something*. Something worth their risks. *If* he was here. But the queen was certain her informant was reliable, or she wouldn't have sent us.

As we nibbled more food, I told them about the layout of the compound, pointing only with eyes to the various buildings. "Behind Greycastle and Riverbend are the stables and outbuildings. Darkcottage is empty, so he's not staying there."

Music started up and a group of women began dancing, Vairlyn among them.

Wren grimaced. "How's your foot?"

"Throbbing," I answered. "The birchwings is beginning to wear off. You two will have to do twice the dancing to cover for me. The Ballengers are insulted easily and if none of us dance—"

Wren's brows pulled down in a disturbed V. "I don't know a thing about dancing."

"Sure you do, Wren," Synové said, nudging her with her elbow. "We used to dance to the flutes in the *jehendra* on market days."

"That was twirling, falling on our backsides, and laughing."

Synové shrugged. "It's all about the same. Add a little swaying. Just watch what everyone else does. Damn, with that dress on, no one will be watching where your feet go anyway. We—"

Lydia came running our way, her eyes wild as she squealed, "Hide me! Hide me, quick!"

Wren's hand immediately shot to her *ziethe*.

I reached out and stopped her. "It's a game, Wren," I said quietly. "Only a game." But my heart beat a wicked dash too.

Hide me. Please, hide me.

The screams were as vivid now as the day I had heard them, the tearful pleas as crowds ran from Blackstone Square, beating on doors, trying to hide in dark corners when the slaughter began. *Hide me.* It was no game. We were only eleven years old. I hid three people in my hovel. There was no door to lock. The only weapon I had was the same small stick my mother hadn't been able to reach in time—useless against the guards' swords and long halberds. No one came inside, but we heard the pounding of footsteps as guards hunted people down. We heard the screams. The clans had made the mistake of cheering for the princess after she stabbed the Komizar. The princess attacked him because he had killed a child—Aster, a girl who worked as a barrow runner in Sanctum Hall. Unfortunately, he didn't die from his wound, and he sought immediate revenge on the clans for their disloyalty

"Quick!" Lydia pleaded again.

I shoved her behind us, and then Wren, Synové, and I moved shoulder to shoulder, creating an armored wall of silk and satin. Lydia giggled behind us as Nash came running up, asking if we had seen her.

"Seen who?" Wren asked, her breath still rushed.

"We haven't seen anyone," Synové confirmed.

Lydia squealed and tore out between us, racing past Nash. He chased after her, and we all stared, still shoulder to shoulder, watching them run away.

"Only a game," Synové repeated and swallowed. She had been one of those who had hidden in my hovel.

Tor's Watch was a different world from our own.

The games were different.

"We were talking about dancing," I said, trying to refocus our thoughts.

"Right," Synové answered. Her chest swelled against the yellow silk in a deep cleansing breath. She rose on her toes, and her eyes skimmed the far reaches of the gardens. "I'm already on it. If I can just find one very tall, dark, and . . ." She walked away, but there was little doubt who she was on the hunt for. Eben had been temporarily displaced by Mason.

I looked to my right and saw Jase's twin brothers walking toward us, their gazes focused on Wren. I elbowed her. "Aram and Samuel approaching," I whispered. "Jase's younger brothers. I think they have a thing for you. Be nice."

"What makes you think I don't know how to be nice," she grumbled. She hitched up her shoulder, smoothing her scalloped pink sleeve into place, then twisted her scowl into a smile. "There. Now which is which?" she whispered.

"That's for you to figure out—but don't leave permanent marks."

"You're no fun at all," she said and walked off to meet them.

It was my opportunity to slip into Raehouse—the only house I hadn't yet searched. The offices were closed now, and Priya would be at the party. The front door was in shadows and as it turned out, unlocked—and tonight because of the party there were no dogs roaming, only a few guards patrolling who were easy to slip past. The dim glow from the party lanterns filtered through the windows, giving me enough light to maneuver. The offices were sparsely furnished, most of the rooms on the first floor looking like sitting rooms, perhaps for business discussions, and though there were three floors of rooms, the majority filled with storage, there appeared to be only one office—Priya's.

This explained the quiet and solitude that Jalaine had talked about. Priya's office took up most of the second floor and was the opposite of the rest of the house. What she lacked in companionship here, she made up for in décor. It was neat and excessively ordered, but overflowed with color and detail, as if the sum of her twenty-three years was laid out in this room. Whenever I had broken into a quarterlord's or merchant's home, I always took a few minutes to study their belongings. What they filled their houses with was revealing. Spiked strips beneath windows, caged rats with chopped off tails, silky underclothing in bright colors, and always knives under their pillows. They trusted no one.

In Priya's office there were, of course, ledgers and books, quills and ink, maps and stacks of paper waiting her attention, but the collection of small polished pebbles laid out in a neat row across the top of her desk caught the light and my notice. Just below them was a tiny spotted quail feather laying precisely in the middle of her blotter. To the side were small charcoal sketches of butterflies, which revealed a softer side she didn't readily radiate.

On the other side of her desk, a note caught my eye.

For Jase's approval:
Supply request from BI

BI? The Ballenger Inn?

I surveyed the list—Morrighese wine, Gitos olives, Gastineux fish eggs, Cruvas tobacco, large quantities of charcoal, and several powders that I'd never heard of before. Herbs?

At the bottom of the page was Jase's signature. Priya's list had been approved. It was the only approval request I saw on her desk, but it was a costly one—maybe that was why it required Jase's approval.

I heard a door click, and then a light glowed in the downstairs hallway. By the time Priya stepped into her office, I had already stepped out and found my way down a back staircase. Maybe she had remembered another supply request that couldn't wait until morning, or maybe she simply needed a break from the party and a dose of her solitude again. She would find that here. The captain wasn't a guest in Raehouse either.

When I rejoined the party, I finally caught a glimpse of Jase. He was on the far side of the garden near Darkcottage, immersed in a conversation with two older men. His black shirt made his blond hair brighter, and his cheekbones still bore the warm polish of our long trek in the sun. I watched him as I walked closer and noted what I had seen already today, the way he commanded attention. It wasn't just because he carried the title of *Patrei*. There was a presence about him, an intensity that was both sobering and alluring. He was tall and his shoulders wide, but it wasn't his stature that stopped people. It was more about the angle of his head when he looked at you, the lift of his chin, the awareness in his eyes, the way you could see thoughts spinning behind them, like a tailor measuring before he cut the cloth. There was precision in his stare, and that precision could slice right through you like diamond shears.

I don't need an outsider, much less a Vendan, to tell me the right thing to do.

His head turned as if he sensed someone watching him. From far across the garden, his eyes met mine. He didn't smile—he offered no expression at all—but his gaze lingered, and then he said a few quick words and left the man at his side, making his way toward me.

A flutter skipped through my ribs. I was still uncertain about our parting today. He had left abruptly, and the kiss I had meant to control had felt like anything but a show.

"Jase," I said when he stopped in front of me.

He stared at me, his jaw tight, a vein raised at his temple, and then he reached out and grabbed my hand. "We need to talk. Alone."

He pulled me along, his pace feverish, and I felt the increased pressure on my ankle as I worked to keep up. Had he found out something about me? Discovered the drops of blood in the tunnel? We hurried along the shadowed side of Darkcottage.

"Jase, what are—"

But then he suddenly pulled me into a dark arched alcove. He swung around, his arms braced against the wall on either side of me.

"What is it?" I asked.

Even with darkness concealing us, I saw the dampness that glistened on his brow. A storm gusted through his eyes that I didn't understand. He swallowed and leaned closer. "I want to kiss you, Kazi," he finally said, his voice a whisper. "And I want you to kiss me back. But this time

I don't want it to be because we're only making the best of it. And I don't want a kiss that's for show or has any conditions. I want you to kiss me just because you want to. Because you deeply want to. No one's watching now. You can walk away, and I won't say a thing. I promise, I won't ever bring it up again."

My breaths stopped up in my chest. He knew I had kissed him willingly today, but there had been conditions. Everything about us was so confused. It wasn't a kiss he was looking for, no matter how true and heartfelt. He was searching for a clarity that couldn't be ours. "Jase, I'm a soldier in the Vendan army. I—"

"I'm not asking you to be anything else."

"In a few weeks, I'll be leaving. When the settlement—"

"The settlement may take more than a few weeks. And I could make the rebuilding last a very long time."

His eyes drilled into mine, searching for something clear, sure, and simply delaying the rebuilding wouldn't give it to him.

What is this, Kazi? What is this between us?

The question was still there, but its *thrum* had grown louder. Coals burned in my stomach. I still had no answer, or maybe I simply didn't want one. "I have to go back, Jase. We only have a short time—"

"A lot can change in a few weeks, Kazi. Plans can change. There are no guarantees. We could all be dead."

I was intimate with destinies being yanked and pummeled and turned inside out. I knew about being thrown down unexpected paths. But Jase dead? Not him. His presence was too full, too felt, too—I shook my head, rejecting the possibility. It was just his father's unexpected death weighing on him.

His shoulders pulled back and his hands slid from the wall back to his sides, releasing me as if he had received his answer. An angry tic pulsed in his neck.

I have no answers, Jase! I screamed silently. *Not for this!*

He started to turn away, but I hooked my finger onto his belt, stopping him.

He paused, his nostrils flared, waiting and wary.

"A kiss will not make all of our differences go away, Jase. It won't—"

"I'm not expecting our differences to disappear!" he hissed. "I'm just asking you to be honest about this one thing! Would you stop thinking about tomorrow or a thousand days from now! In this moment, what do you *want*, dammit!"

I looked at him, unable to speak.

My heart hammered wildly. *Pivot! Steady! Blink last!* My rules tumbled in a freefall. I felt him pulling away again, and I gave his belt a harsh tug, drawing him to a standstill. My gaze locked onto his, and everything inside me split in different directions. "Yes, I want to kiss you, Jase Ballenger. Not for show or to make the best of it. I want to kiss you because I want *you*, every part of you, even the parts that infuriate me beyond telling, because you've infected me with a poison that I don't want to flush out, because you're a mad viper twisting around my middle, cutting off my breath, yet I want you more than I want to breathe. Yes, Jase, I *want* to kiss you, just because I do, but the one thing I cannot do is promise you any tomorrows."

He stared at me, and I could see every word I had spoken passing through his eyes. He measured them, turned them over, rejected and absorbed them. Finally his shoulders eased down a fraction of an inch.

"Poison?" His mouth pulled in a smirk. "Here, let me infect you some more."

Was it possible to live two lives side-by-side? To serve two goals that were destined to collide? To weave lies with one hand and unravel them with the other?

It was his kindness that had seduced me, and now everything else about him captivated me. I was dancing with fire and hoping not to get burned.

We returned to the party, our hands woven together, the music brighter, the food more sumptuous, invisible wish stalks tucked in our pockets. *Be honest about this one thing.* And I was.

Even though tables were set, dinner was an ongoing loose affair, meats brought from smoking pits, and more fare set out on long tables as the night wore on. Jase introduced me to nearly everyone there, and more than one guest mentioned their gratitude that the queen was coming for a visit and tour. The story had already evolved.

When we finally had a moment alone, Jase swooped to the side and his lips met mine, easy, and a warm flush spread across my chest. "Do you see who your friend is dancing with?" he asked.

I looked over his shoulder. It was Mason, and he didn't look too happy with the situation. It wasn't a dance that required much touching, a simple country jig that was common in many regions. But Synové was making plenty of missteps, and the Ballenger version had an extra hop or two. Synové playfully jabbed Mason's ribs as they spun around. He offered a polite strained smile in return, acting like the cordial host, probably on Jase's orders. She was radiant, her cheeks glowing with heat, her long locks shimmering in the lantern light like golden marmalade, swinging in rhythm with the zitaraes and flutes. I wished I could be her sometimes, jumping into every moment fully, her cheer covering the darkness that still lurked deep inside her.

I spotted Wren too. "I'd worry more about Aram and Samuel," I answered. I saw them farther away on either side of Wren, one of them trying to maneuver around her *ziethe* every time she turned.

"They're not safe with her?" Jase asked.

"Of course not, but they probably think that's half the fun."

Jase smiled and nodded in agreement.

"What about us?" he asked. "Should we join them? We haven't danced yet."

I had already deflected his question twice. A third time would be obvious. I couldn't pretend that I hated to dance. I still remembered hooking my hands around his neck one night in the middle of the Jessop plain, dancing with him beneath a moonlit sky, the grass waving at our ankles, crickets accompanying the tune he hummed into my ear. I had told him I didn't want the night to end.

Now it seemed this night never would. My ankle had grown steadily worse. It was stiff and hot and, I was certain, swollen, but I didn't dare peek at it beneath my dress. The medicine had worn off and the pain was circling around my leg like a spiked iron, every movement taking a bite out of my flesh. Even my thigh burned now. A thin line of sweat beaded at my hairline. When Jase commented on my damp back, I responded that the evening was warm.

"All right," I answered. "Let's join them." Maybe a short dance would be bearable and the subject would be dropped. No hopping, only swaying.

We had only taken a few steps toward the brightly lit square strung with lanterns when Jase stopped. "What's wrong?"

"What do you mean?" I asked.

"You're limping."

I looked at him and wiped some damp strands of hair from my brow. I forced a smile. "It's only these slippers. They don't fit well—"

"Then take them off. Here, let me help you—" He started to bend down.

"No!" I said, far too loudly. Sweat trickled down my back and pain was squeezing my skull now, and it occurred to me that maybe the dogs were diseased. What if—

"Kazi." Jase's gaze was sober. He knew.

Pivot, Kazi. He sees your lies.

My foot gave way beneath me, and I stumbled forward but Jase caught my arm before I hit the ground. He muttered under his breath as he scooped me up—then spotted the bandage.

I stared at it in horror. It was bloody.

The wounds were seeping.

"What the hell—"

"Jase, please—"

My face flashed with sickening heat, and Jase called for Tiago and Drake. He carried me down a dark path, away from the guests, ordering Drake to find the healer and Oleez. Doors slammed open against walls and a long hallway bobbed and weaved around me. Jase laid me down on a couch, then found a pillow to prop behind my head.

"What happened?" he demanded. He was already unwrapping my ankle.

I deliberated taking a chance with the truth—at least some version of it. Chills suddenly overtook me and then a violent cramp in my stomach doubled me over. Diseased. The dogs had to be diseased.

Vairlyn, Jalaine, and two other women rushed in on Drake's heels, and the room became a swirling chaos of questions.

"It was the dogs," I answered. "I was afraid to tell you. I'm sorry."

"Which dogs?"

"Lower your voice, Jase!" Vairlyn ordered.

"In the tunnels," I said. "I—"

"What were you doing in the tunnels?"

Jalaine pushed Jase's shoulder. "Mother said to stop yelling!"

"This is my fault," Vairlyn said. "I promised her you'd show her the vault this afternoon."

"It's Jase's fault," Jalaine snapped. "I told him she wanted a tour."

"Get out, Jalaine!" Jase shouted. "We have enough in here without you—"

"I'm not going—"

"Move aside. Give me some room." A tall, thin woman elbowed her way in and pulled my dress higher, looking at my leg. "Yes, she's definitely been bit by the ashti. Look at the spidering moving up her thigh. A servant is bringing my bag."

Jase's attention jumped from the healer back to me. "The ashti are stationed well past the vault entrance. What made you go way out there?"

"I was turned around. I—"

"There aren't signs that say *vault*, Jase!" Jalaine interrupted. "How would she know?"

Another spasm gripped my abdomen and Jase was yelling again, this time at the healer, it seemed. At least I think he was. I couldn't be sure. His lips moved out of sync with the sound I was hearing, echoing in long garbled ribbons.

I writhed in pain, my fingers digging into my stomach. And then I saw Death squeeze into the crowded room, grinning, waiting in the corner, his bony finger pointing at me. *You, you are next.*

"No," I cried. "Not yet! Not today!"

The spasm finally passed and I saw a hand swipe the air, hitting the side of Jase's head. His mother. "You heard her! Move aside! Give the healer room to work."

The healer lifted a glass to my lips, encouraging me to sip a bitter blue liquid. I gagged as I choked it down.

"This will help. There now, keep it down. Another sip. That's right."

She used more of the blue powder to make a paste and applied it to the wounds on my leg. I heard her groan. "This one will have to be stitched. Eh, here's another one. What were you thinking, girl? Here, take a sip of this now. It will put you out while I sew these up. The antidote should take effect soon. You'll be fine by morning."

"Antidote?"

"The dogs that bit you are poisonous," Jase said. "Without the anti-dote, you would have been dead by week's end. It's a long and agonizing death."

Poisonous dogs?

The thought became lost in a cloud of others, my lids growing heavy. The last thing I saw was a thin glint of steel and a thread being pushed through its eye.

CHAPTER TWENTY-NINE

JASE

KAZI'S HEAD RESTED AGAINST MY CHEST, DEEP IN SLEEP AS I carried her back to her room, but troubled words tumbled from her lips, *Don't hurt me . . . I have nothing . . . Please . . . don't.* She had mumbled similar words in the drawing room as the healer sewed her up. *Please don't hurt me.* Her words had brought a crashing hush to the room.

"*Shhh*," I whispered as we turned down the last hallway, "no one's going to hurt you." By the time we reached her room, her expression had relaxed and she was silent, drawn into a deep, oblivious sleep. I still didn't know how she hid the wounds from me for half the night. The bites alone had to be unbearable, but the poison—

My mother walked ahead of me and threw open the bedroom door. I carried Kazi inside and laid her on the bed. She didn't stir an eyelash. I looked for a pulse at her neck. It was the only thing that told me she was alive at all.

"It's the sleep elixir," my mother said, as if she could read my mind.

We both stood there for long, quiet minutes, staring at her.

I knew what my mother was thinking too. *Sylvey.*

Their coloring wasn't the same, but in sleep, Kazi still looked like her in many ways. Small, vulnerable, swallowed up in a sea of rumpled bedclothes. Sylvey was eleven when she died. I was the one who carried her from the ice bath back to her bed. She died in my arms.

Hold my hand, Jase. Promise me you won't let go, she had cried with the last of her strength. *Don't let them put me in the tomb. I'm afraid.* I had thought it was only delirious words brought on by her fever.

Stop talking like that, sister. You're going to be fine.

Promise me, Jase, don't put me there. Not the tomb. Please, promise me.

But I didn't promise her. Her lips were peeling and pale, her eyes sunken, her skin clammy, her voice already a ghost, all signs that she was leaving this world. But I had refused to see. I wouldn't accept that a Ballenger could die. Especially not Sylvey.

Go to sleep, sister. Sleep. You'll be fine in the morning.

She had relaxed in my arms then. I thought she was sleeping. My mother had stepped out of the room for only a few minutes to check on my brothers and sister who were sick too. When she came back, Sylvey was dead in my arms.

My mother wiped Kazi's brow with a cloth. "You were harsh with her," she said.

"I was only trying to get answers."

"I know." She pulled a stool closer to the bed. "And you were frightened. I'll sit with her. Go find your answers."

―――――

The air was dank, as it always was here, as if the chilly breaths of the dead still hung here in the darkness, unable to escape. The tunnels were both sanctuary and prison, stuffy like the tombs that Sylvey had begged me to save her from. I listened to the silence, the solitary sound of my boots scuffling on the cobbles, and I imagined Kazi slipping through here undetected. The tunnel was deserted now except for guards at the entrance, but today when she had passed there had to have been dozens of workers passing through—and none had stopped her?

Still, I looked at the wagons parked along the perimeter, the pallets, the shadows, all providing places to hide if you were careful, and it was only a spare number of paces from the workyard to the *T* where another set of tunnel systems branched off the main one. I stopped at the faded crest that marked the entrance, barely illuminated with lantern light, the only thing that indicated the vault was down this way.

You were harsh with her.

I remembered shouting, feeling out of control. One minute I had been thinking about dancing, and the next I was unwrapping a bloody cloth from her leg as she doubled over in pain. Right beneath my nose something was going on, and I hadn't seen it. *I was afraid to tell you.* Had I refused to see it? I thought about her damp back. I had noticed the beaded line of sweat on her brow too. *It's the warm night.* It wasn't that warm, and there was a breeze. But I had accepted her explanation and let myself be distracted by other details.

I went past the entrance to the vault and walked to the end where she had gone—so much farther out of the way. I turned the final corner and barked a command to dogs I couldn't see. They came out of their alcoves to greet me, moaning and cooing, with their hind ends wagging, hoping for a scratch behind their ears. The *ashti* looked just like any other dogs, though closer to the size of a timber wolf—and sly. They could have killed her. They had killed before. Her reflexes had to be fast to escape them.

The dogs kept intruders away, but most would-be trespassers were far more terrified of dying from their poisonous bite than from being torn apart. It was an unpleasant way to die, and not many had the antidote.

It came from the far north where the dogs were from. Kbaaki traders had gifted them to us generations ago after we gave them refuge during a late winter storm. The milksap antidote didn't grow here, and the Kbaaki still brought us a supply once a year when they made their pilgrimage to the south.

I bent down, holding the torch closer to the floor. A stain had been smeared. She had taken the time to clean up the blood, trying to cover her tracks. Why?

Mason's words stung me over and over again, like a wasp that wouldn't die.

She can't be trusted.

I stepped up to the door and checked the lock. It was secure and appeared to be undisturbed. I turned and scratched each dog behind the ear, and they whined their appreciation.

It was true—the vault wasn't marked. You had to know where to turn, but what made her pass up two other passages and come all the way out here? Only curiosity? I had told her about the vault in the first few days we were together. She'd been fascinated by it, the idea of a shelter carved into a granite mountain and the history and stories that began there. Even though I knew she didn't believe it all, I'd been happy she had taken a genuine interest. It wasn't surprising that she wanted to visit the source of my claims, and I should have known by now that Kazi didn't wait for permission for anything.

Be sure to save time for a tour, Jase. Kazi wants to see the vault. Jalaine had tried to say it offhandedly as she left for the arena this afternoon, but her tone had been thick with pride. Kazi was Vendan, an outsider, and she wanted to see the vault. It was an acknowledgment that for us was a sign of respect. And for Jalaine, I guessed, it brought Kazi deeper into our inner circle—the vault was our beginnings, where our schooling began, the source of much of our history.

Without the vault, none of us would be here. It was nothing but a dusty, mostly abandoned relic now. Nash and Lydia still did some transcribing there, as we all had once done, but I hadn't been inside in months. In spite of the broken, decayed furnishings, it was still remarkable in many ways, the natural filtration of the mountain still providing fresh air and water, but beyond that it was uninhabitable, partly by design. It was meant to be remembered as it once was.

It's Jase's fault.

I returned to the main house. Servants were still clearing the gardens after the party, all the guests now gone or retired to Greycastle. Wren and Synové had all but ripped Kazi from my arms when they burst into the drawing room and saw her. There was no trust there, and they assumed the worst until they saw the healer and Kazi's stitched wounds. Then an expression of guilt washed over them. They knew she had been bitten, but they too had said nothing. Of course, they had no way of knowing that the dogs' bites were deadly. Once assured she would be fine, they allowed a crew to escort them back to the inn.

I opened the door to Kazi's room. My mother still sat on the stool, and Oleez was in the chair on the other side of the bed. I noted that Kazi's dress had been removed and replaced with a nightgown, and her hair had been unbraided from the top of her head, falling in loose waves across her pillow.

"I'll sit with her now," I said. "You can go."

Once they were gone, I walked over and looked down at Kazi, still lost in her drugged dream world, her chest rising in reassuring soft breaths.

You were watching my chest?

I remembered when she caught me in this confession, how I had tripped over my words trying to explain, as if I was twelve years old. We had both distrusted each other then. That day already seemed like a hundred years ago.

I kicked off my boots and eased down on the bed beside her, pulling her close. She nestled in with a gentle murmur, her arm locking around mine.

You've infected me with a poison that I don't want to flush out.

I lay there next to her, and even though the healer assured me she would be fine, I pressed my fingers to her wrist, feeling the thrum of her pulse.

I can't promise you any tomorrows.

And that was all I wanted.

CHAPTER THIRTY

KAZI

WHEN I HAD STIRRED IN THE PREDAWN HOURS THIS MORNING, it was to a memory, a scent, a touch. *Jase.* He was kissing my neck; we danced beneath the moon; he pressed a wish stalk to my ankle; he was whispering about tomorrows. But when I opened my eyes to reach out for him, he wasn't there, and the nightmare of the night before flooded back in. Had I dreamed it all?

The horrible, cramping pain was gone, but when I wiggled my toes there was a stiff ache. I remembered Jase's anger and his accusing questions, and when he walked through the door with a breakfast tray a few minutes later I braced myself for the worst. Instead, he set the tray on a side table and didn't mention the last part of the night at all, but the strain of what he wasn't saying showed in his stiff movements.

"Jase, about last night . . ."

"I'm sorry for shouting," he said, "especially since you were in so much pain. I should have warned you about the dogs. Maybe then you wouldn't have slipped past the guards."

Ah, there it was. An accusation couched in an apology. "I didn't slip past the guards, Jase. I walked past them, and they didn't stop me. I guess with all the activity they didn't notice me. I didn't know I needed permission to visit the vault. Do I?"

A thousand questions swirled behind his eyes. He looked back at the tray, pouring me hot tea. "I plan to take you right now. Are you up to it?"

Now? I knew my answer had to be yes. I quickly wolfed down my breakfast, and we left for the vault. I still had a limp, but it looked worse than it felt. Jase slowed his pace as we walked.

We turned down the first passageway and stopped about twenty yards in when we reached an enormous steel door. He spun the wheel in the middle of it, and it seemed forever before a loud *thunk, chink,* and *whoosh* sounded, like a hundred locks had slipped out of place.

"Stand back," he advised.

The door appeared far too large for him to pull back on his own—it was twice his height and wide enough for two wagons to pass through—but it moved easily at his touch. It swung open and open, like the endless maw of some ancient hungry beast, and revealed a dark cavern behind it. The musty age of the world behind the door reached out, gripping me with anticipation. If ghosts walked anywhere, it was here.

"Hold on," Jase said, and he slipped inside. I heard some stirring, and then a flicker of light was followed by a burst of illumination that lit the entire cavern with an eerie yellow glow.

He waved me in, explaining that there was a lighting system in here that used thousands of mirrors. A single lantern could light an entire room.

A hall lay before us that was roughly hewn from the granite mountain, and either side of it was lined with empty steel shelves. At least half of them were collapsed into heaps. Rusty girders jutted upward like broken bones.

"The family quarters are in better shape. This way," he said.

"What about that?" I asked, pointing to another steel door.

"We call it the greenhouse," he said, "but it's just a cave. The only other way in is through a hole about a hundred feet up, but it lets in enough water and sunlight to keep the rest green." He said it was overgrown and a few animals like snakes, badgers, and squirrels that survived the fall through the hole lived inside. Once they encountered an injured Candok bear. The first Ballengers foraged in there and actually grew a few things to survive. "I'll show you that another time. We don't go in unless we're armed with spears and nets."

We turned down another passageway and came to a smaller, more ordinary door. Jase opened it and lit another lantern.

It wasn't what I expected. A chill crawled down my spine. The thick metal frames of hundreds of bunks lined the walls like an army barracks. A few were collapsed, but most stood at attention like they were still waiting for occupants. The mattresses were long eaten away, and wispy filaments hung from the frames like ghostly skirts. The smooth walls were an eerie mottled gray. "What is this place?" I finally asked.

"This is where it began," he answered. "It was a shelter meant for hundreds. Only twenty-three made it."

"But the writing?" I said as I walked down the aisle between the beds. Scrawled over every inch of the walls were words. Thousands of words written in a language I didn't know. Jase said it was the earliest version of Landese, which had changed over the centuries, but I did recognize names—those hadn't changed. I saw Miandre and Greyson. More names, Leesha, Reyn, Cameron, James, Theo, Fujiko, Gina, Razim.

"It was the last order of Aaron Ballenger—to write it all down as well as they could remember. They did. There was no paper, so they used the walls. There's more. This way."

He took me into another room, and another. A kitchen, a study, a sick room, all of it covered with words. There was no reason to where or how they wrote. Some sentences stretched the length of the room in large block letters. Others were tiny balls of sentences, barely readable.

"All of these rooms? Supplies? And there was no paper?"

"They burned it for fuel." He pointed to the empty shelves in the study. "These were probably filled with books. They were trapped inside for a long time. Scavengers waited for them outside."

"You know what all these say?"

He nodded and looked at a group of words next to him. "This is one of my favorites." He translated it for me.

I hate Greyson. He looks over my shoulder as I write this. I want him to know. I hate him with the heat of a thousand fiery coals. He is cruel and savage and deserves to die.
—Miandre, age 13

"But weren't they—"

Jase smirked. "Years later. I guess she changed her mind."

"It still doesn't say much for your revered leader."

"He was fourteen. He kept them all alive. That says everything."

"Why do they write their ages, after every entry?" I asked.

"This might explain it." He crossed the room to the opposite wall and crouched to read an entry near the floor.

Today is Fujiko's birthday. Miandre made a cake from a ration of cornmeal. She says birthdays used to be celebrated and we must do the same because we don't know how many more we will have. Every year is a victory, she says.

After we eat the cake, I write all of our ages after our writings.

Someday we will all write 20, 30, or 40, I say to everyone.

By then we will run out of walls, Miandre says.

By then we will have new walls, I answer.

It is the first time I have thought of a future in a world that has always been about After. Tor's Watch is our new Beginning.

—Greyson Ballenger, 15

"Don't you think it's strange that they wrote their thoughts on the walls for everyone to see?"

"I think everything about their lives was strange. Living in here was strange. Maybe when you're fighting to survive, you need to share things with other people—even your deepest secrets."

I knew it was no accident that his eyes landed back on me with his last few words. Digging. Did he still suspect something about my encounter with the dogs?

"Maybe," I answered.

"We can't always judge a world by our own. I try to see it through their eyes, not mine."

He walked to another wall and read more to me. Only six of those who lived in here were witness to the stars that fell. The rest were born later. Of the six, only a few—Greyson, Miandre, Leesha, and Razim—had any memory of the world of the Ancients. They saw the ruins before they were ruins. They lived in the shining towers that reached into the sky, flew in winged carriages, and remembered all manner of magic the Ancients controlled with their fingertips—the light, the voices, bending the laws of the earth, and soaring above it. One thing was certain, these were children leading and protecting other children from predators.

It explained a lot about the Ballengers.

It made me wonder if their claim was true—that they were the first kingdom. Tor's Watch appeared to have begun less than a decade after the devastation. Morrighan was established six decades after that. The other kingdoms, centuries later. When Pauline had first told us histories that were different from the ones that Vendans knew, I remembered we had all been skeptical.

Jase crossed the room to read more entries on the wall.

They promised they would leave if we gave them supplies. Instead they stabbed Razim and tried to take more. We do not know if he will live. I cannot stand the weeping any longer. The vault is full of beds, but no weapons. I use tools to rip one apart and hoist the metal upward, testing it with my arm. If it were sharp, it would make a good spear, and hundreds of beds could make hundreds of spears.

—Greyson, 15

Razim has recovered. He is an angrier and tougher Razim. He sharpens spears all day long now. I help him. There will never be enough, because more scavengers always come.

—Fujiko, 12

My grandfather was a great man and he ruled a great land. He has been dead for a year now. If we ever get out of here, I will go back to where he died and give him a proper

*burial. I will pile rocks high in his honor. I am not a savage
as Miandre thinks, but sometimes I'm forced to make savage
choices. There is a difference.*

—Greyson, 15

I looked up to see Jase studying me. He wasn't reading the passages
to me, but reciting them from memory. His shoulders were leveled, his
chin lifted, his stance like a wall that couldn't be moved.

"Why did you bring me here, Jase?"

"I want you to know our history and understand a little bit more
about who we are before we head out."

"Head out? What do you mean?"

He laid it out quickly. The supplies had come in, and we were leaving
this morning for the settlement site. The timing was good. Things were
quiet here for now, but still, he couldn't be gone for more than a day.

"But you said—"

"No more than a day, Kazi. I agreed to help. I will. I'll dig a fence post
or two and make sure the plans are set, but tomorrow morning I have to
return to Tor's Watch. My greater responsibilities are here. I've already been
gone for too long. I can't turn right around and disappear for days again."

"And who will make sure the work gets done?"

"One of my brothers or someone else I trust will always be there
supervising."

I rolled my eyes. "Not Gunner, I hope."

"He'll do as I ask."

"That's right. You're *Patrei*. Just so you know, the Vendans aren't
impressed by titles."

"Then we have something in common."

As we left the vault, I paused and looked down the opposite way—somewhere at the end of this long, dark tunnel was a locked door, poisonous dogs, and maybe poisonous secrets.

"Go ahead," Jase said. "Ask."

"What's behind the door?"

"Us, Kazi. We are behind the door. There's nothing on the other side. It's only another portal into and out of Tor's Watch. Every good stronghold has more than one way out. Otherwise you could be trapped. It leads to a path that goes down the back side of Tor's Watch. It's narrow and more treacherous, but it's a way out. Or in. We have to keep it guarded."

An exit? I had imagined something far more sinister on the other side of the door, like a large dark room with Illarion sitting in the center of it hiding from the world. I thought back to the ambassador I had mistakenly stabbed, and the face I had searched for over and over again that never materialized. I wondered if the captain could be an elusive ghost too, not hiding behind any doors, as far from this world as the face that haunted me.

The thin line of light I saw could have been from sunlight shining behind it. And I had felt a draft coming from beneath it. Maybe it added up. Maybe it was a simple portal, guarded by dogs just as the front gates were.

"When we get back, I'll show you. There isn't time now."

I nodded. Pushing the point would reveal I had been searching for something and not just lost, and since he was open to showing me, it didn't appear that he was hiding anything.

But when we reached the main tunnel, I noticed there was a guard stationed at the entrance who hadn't been there before.

"A new guard?" I asked.

"There's always been a guard posted here. He must have just stepped away when you passed by yesterday."

With every mile we traveled, the tension grew thicker. Jase rode ahead with his brothers. More followed behind us—*straza* and drivers with empty wagons to haul Vendans and their belongings to the new site. Jalaine and Priya had wanted to come too, but Jase said he needed their muscle keeping an eye on the books and trades at the arena more than he needed them stringing together chicken coops or digging fence posts.

Even Aram and Samuel, who were by far the most convivial of the boys, were stiff-backed and mostly silent. They had only looked back at Wren once. It was clear now that what Jase wanted me to understand this morning was that though the Ballengers would fulfill their end of the agreement, they weren't going to pretend to be happy about it.

"It should be quite a jolly time when we dish up dinner tonight," Synové quipped. Jase had insisted Wren and Synové come too, as additional buffers between the Ballengers and settlers.

It was difficult for the three of us to talk freely as we rode. A brisk wind at our backs carried our words forward.

"Looks like you've lost some admirers," I whispered.

Wren snorted like she didn't care.

"Did you ever figure out who was who?" I asked.

"Easy," Wren answered. "Samuel has longer lashes than Aram. From the back, it's all about hair curl." She motioned to the boys riding on either side of Mason. "Samuel on right. Aram on left."

Both of them had straight hair.

Synové and I looked at each other, mystified, then laughed.

As disgruntled as the Ballenger boys were about the day, Synové was ebullient. She didn't worry about her voice being carried, and in fact, that was sometimes entirely her point. She talked about the extreme foolishness of keeping poisonous dogs, the superiority of Vendan steel, and how perfectly well her dress fit last night, as smooth as butter. Most of her taunts were aimed at Mason. He completely ignored her, but his reactions could still be seen in the tilt of his head, as if he was working to get a kink out of his neck. She talked about his finesse as a dancer, that he would be good if it wasn't for his four feet. They were quite large and always getting in the way.

"And look at that," Synové said loudly. "I wish someone would make him stop. He can't keep his eyes off me!"

Mason predictably shook his head in frustration, certainly counting the miles until we reached the settlement. We all silently giggled.

As we neared the Vendan settlement midmorning, Jase galloped back to where I rode. It was agreed that he should approach the settlement with me at his side, while his brothers and the rest hung back—including his *straza*—so we didn't look like a hostile army descending upon them.

"It's time. We're getting close," he said, and I rode forward with him.

His jaw was clenched. This went against everything he believed. He saw it as rewarding people who had trespassed.

"Remember, Jase. It's not officially your land. It's part of the Cam Lanteux and was granted to them by the King of Eislandia. They have a reason to be angry too."

I knew it was a sore spot for him, but it had to be said. Just as he had wanted me to understand the mindset of his family this morning, I needed him to understand the mindset of Caemus and the others. He was not going to be greeted with open arms or gratitude.

He was silent and his eyes remained fixed on the rolling hills, waiting for the settlement to emerge from behind one of them.

"How's your ankle?" he finally asked.

"Better than your jaw."

He turned and looked at me. "What?"

"Stop clenching it."

His eyes were ice, and his jaw remained rigid.

At last, the settlement came into view. Our long line of horses and wagons had to be a formidable sight. One by one, settlers gathered in front of their homes carrying hoes, shovels, and pikes. When we were still a good distance off, Jase raised his hand to the line of those behind us as a signal to stop and wait.

As we neared, Jase stopped to look at the barn, burned down to the timbers, a hulking skeleton ready to fall over in a stiff wind. His eyes swept the charred sheds next, and then the pens that were noticeably empty. Only a few chickens pecked and scratched near a trough. The scorched grass reached all the way to the homes. The only thing that was green was the small vegetable garden we had seen Caemus hoeing the last time we were here. The settlers looked like they were ready to defend it to the death.

"*Watavo, kadravés!*" I called. "*Sava Kazi vi Brightmist. Le ne porchio kege Patrei Jase Ballenger ashea te terrema. Oso tor—*"

Caemus glared at Jase. "*Riz liet fikatande chaba vi daka renad!*"

I looked at Jase but didn't dare translate. "He's happy to see you," I said.

Jase scowled and got down from his horse, bypassing my mediation. "You understand Landese?" he asked Caemus.

"We understand," Caemus answered.

"Good. And I know enough Vendan to know when I've been called a horse's ass. Let's get this straight right now, Caemus. I'm going to offer you a deal, and it's a helluva one. But it's only good for this minute, right now, right here, and it will never happen again because I hope to never lay eyes on you again after today. We're going to move you. Everything. And we're going to rebuild your settlement on a better piece of land that's far away from us." Jase spit the terms and details out firmly, then took another long, scrutinizing scan of the burned buildings. "We took your shorthorn as payment for trespassing, but we didn't do this and don't know who did. We'll try to make sure it doesn't happen again, but if you ever wrongly accuse us again, it's going to be more than a barn that you lose. Accept or not?"

Before Caemus could answer, a small boy who'd been standing behind him ran forward wielding a stick and swung it into Jase's knee with a loud *smack*.

Jase bent over, wincing, cursing, grabbing his knee with one hand and yanking the boy by the collar with the other. "You little—"

"Don't hurt him!" Caemus said, stepping forward.

Jase looked puzzled by Caemus's command but turned his attention back to the boy. "What's your name?" he growled.

The boy was smaller than Nash, and even though an angry man held him by his collar, his large brown eyes were still full of defiance. "Kerry of Fogswallow!" he snapped back.

"Well, Kerry of Fogswallow, you are personally going to help me dig fence posts. A lot of them. Understand?"

"I'm not afraid of you!"

Jase's eyes narrowed. "Then I guess I'll have to work harder on that."

The boy's eyes grew just a little bit wider. Jase released him, and the boy ran back behind Caemus.

"We accept," Caemus said.

I heaved out a controlled sigh. As Synové might say, this was off to a jolly start.

The next hour was spent walking the property, taking inventory, assessing what was salvageable, loading up tools and chickens, grains and crates, dishes and people. As the brothers surveyed the grounds, I sensed there was a sobering awareness of how little time it took to collect all the Vendans' worldly goods. At times, Jase simply stared, as if he was trying to figure out why they were here at all. He eyed the tethers of bones hanging from their hips too. Vendans didn't wear them into town because of the attention they drew, but here the bones clattered at their sides as a remembrance of sacrifice.

Wren, Synové, and I quickly helped a few women pluck ripe beans from the garden, dig up root vegetables, and then layer them into barrels with straw. We pulled up the herbs, root balls and all, and placed them in crates for replanting later. Anything that could go would go. As we worked, I spotted Jase, Gunner, and Mason walking up a hill some distance away. It seemed odd because there was nothing out there—no outbuildings or livestock. They carried rocks in their hands, and when they reached the crest they placed them on a mound of rocks that I hadn't noticed before.

When they returned from the hill, I asked Jase about it. He said it was a memorial marking the spot where Greyson Ballenger had covered his dead grandfather with rocks to keep animals from dragging away the body.

<hr />

The new site was fifteen miles south, but with so many wagons, supplies, and horses, it took the whole afternoon to get there. On the long ride, Jase and I rode at the head of the caravan together. He was mostly quiet, still stewing over something.

"So you understand some Vendan after all?" I asked.

He shook his head and smirked. "No, but some words don't need interpretation. It's all in the delivery."

"Well, you were astonishingly accurate. I guess it's not hard to interpret a club to the knee either. How's it doing?"

"I have a decent knot. I'm lucky the little demon didn't crack my kneecap."

"I guess he's the lucky one, getting off with digging fence posts."

"It'll be good for him. We'll feed everyone first. They can't dig on empty stomachs." He reached around behind him and began rummaging through his pack. "I almost forgot. I meant to give this to you earlier." He handed me a small lidded basket. "Go ahead. Open it."

I pulled the lid off and gawked at the small square. "Is this what I think . . ." I put my nose close to take a deep whiff.

"Sage cake," Jase confirmed.

"You remembered!" I broke off a corner and shoved it in my mouth. I moaned with pleasure. It was every bit as heavenly as I recalled. I licked the crumbs from my fingers. "Here," I said, leaning over and popping a piece into his mouth. He nodded approval, swallowing, but clearly not loving it as much as I did. "How?" I asked. "Did Dolise—"

"No. I hired a new cook. You can thank her yourself when we get back to Tor's Watch."

We entered a wide, gentle valley. Low, forest-covered hills were on one side, a meandering river on the other, and dark lush grass not yet brown with summer waved beneath us. When I spotted the supply wagons in the distance, I knew this was the site. By now Caemus was riding at our sides, and we all paused, taking it in. It was breathtaking. Caemus got down from his horse and grabbed a spade from a wagon. He shoved it into the earth and turned it over, revealing a chunk of dark, rich, loamy soil. It crumbled easily as he passed the spade over it. I remembered him hoeing the hard clay ground at the other site.

He looked up at Jase, his expression stern. "Good soil."

"I know," Jase answered.

The rest of the Vendans poured out of the wagons, walking the rest of the way. I watched them stoop, feeling the ground, running their hands over the grass. The scent here was fresh and full of promise.

I got down from my horse too and walked in circles, taking in every view. A nearby forest for hunting and wood. A close abundant water source. Good soil and level land. Some stately oaks in the center to provide shade. I looked back at Jase, still in his saddle, my throat swelling. Caemus and I had both doubted him.

"It's perfect, Jase. Perfect."

"Not perfect. But they'll get better production. And it's a tucked-away valley. They won't be bothered here."

Like they were at the last site. I believed Jase, and I think maybe Caemus did too. It wasn't the Ballengers who had attacked the settlers. But whoever did wanted it to look like them.

I watched the Vendans continuing to walk down the valley. I saw the wonder in their footsteps, and a different kind of wonder crept into me. This site was far superior to the last one. Was the Eislandian king really so inept and uninformed about the northern reaches that he randomly chose the old site? Was it only coincidence that it happened to be close to Tor's Watch and in clear view of the Ballenger rock memorial? Or was it a deliberate choice, meant to stir trouble? To be a burr in the saddle of the family? Was that his revenge for not getting the full bounty of the taxes the Ballengers collected?

Jase surveyed the valley, calculations already spinning behind his eyes. He was far more invested in this than he would admit. The emotion that had swelled in my throat now crept to my chest.

What is this?

The answer was never as close to my lips as it was now.

"We should catch up," he said. "There's only a few good hours of daylight left, and I want to get some of the settlement layout established with Caemus. I have some ideas where the barn should go. And I promised you a fence post. I want to dig that much before I leave in the morning."

"You have Kerry to help you now too."

He rubbed his knee and his mouth twisted with a malevolent grin. "Yes, I'll keep the little urchin busy."

CHAPTER THIRTY-ONE

JASE

THE LAST TIME WE WERE THERE I HAD BARELY GLANCED AT THE settlement. When we'd rounded up the shorthorn in an outer pasture, my father had yelled, "We already warned you—our land, our air, our water. You trespass; you pay! We'll be back for more if you stay." We didn't go back, and if we had, we would have taken only one more shorthorn. But someone did go back and took more. They took everything.

"Who did it? Find out!" I growled to Mason. He was the one who supervised the magistrates. One of them had to have seen or heard something.

The Ballengers were being attacked from all angles. Even if I disliked the Vendans, this was not their battle. They didn't even know what they were being used for.

We had been struck silent when we first saw the destruction, but then rage had taken hold. As we walked up the hill to the rock monument, out of range of others who might hear us, everyone threw out possibilities of who had ravaged the settlement.

"Rybart and Truko," Mason said. "They'd steal socks off a baby. This has their hands all over it."

"Four Ravians were taken," Gunner added. "They'd be easy enough to spot in their stables."

Titus shook his head. "No, they would have sold them off by now. I can check with the Previzi when we get back. See if they had any questionable trades."

"Half their trades are questionable," I reminded him. The Previzi unloaded merchandise that was better left untraced—like the Candoran ambassador's side deals. Like the Valsprey that had come into our hands. We took advantage of what they offered just like everyone else. *Some goods need to be bought and sold discreetly*, my father had explained when I was twelve and questioned why we used them. *And some questions are better left unasked*, he added.

"What about the dozen short horns?" Gunner asked. "It wouldn't be easy to herd them, especially in a midnight raid. Where did they take them?"

"Dead in a gully somewhere," I answered. "Maybe the Ravians too. Starling Gorge isn't far from here and has some good forest cover. This wasn't about acquiring merchandise. It was a message."

"To make us look bad."

The fires and labor hunters were meant to scare the citizenry, the caravan attacks to hurt business and frighten off traders from the arena, but this attack was meant to bring the kingdoms down upon us.

When we loaded up the last of the meager Vendan belongings, it felt like our questions had been wrung out of us and we were struck silent again. Kazi's words jabbed me like a bony elbow in my ribs. *They had so very little to begin with. It shouldn't take long to rebuild.*

The words stuck with me as Caemus and I walked the length of the valley floor hammering stakes into place to mark foundations. The two of us had gotten off to a bad start, and things hadn't improved much from there. He was a bullheaded ox. Good soil? *It was damn fine soil.* Maybe being an obstinate block of wood with a perpetual frown was what was necessary for someone to lead a settlement out here in the middle of nowhere.

I had already known the soil was good. I'd been to this valley many times before, camping here with my father and older siblings. The towering oak still spread out in the middle of the valley, and a rope with a stout stick tied to the end still swung from it too. I fell from that rope more times than I could count. Somehow, I never broke anything.

When I was nine, I told my father that one day I would build a house and live here. He said no, this valley was only a place to visit, that my home and destiny was back at Tor's Watch. This valley was for somebody else yet to come. I had always wondered who that would be.

The shouts of the children turned both of our heads. They had already found the rope and were taking turns swinging from the tree.

"Another house, here?" I asked.

"We've already staked out four. That was all we had. Some of us share."

Kazi had told me there were seven families so I had sent enough timber for seven homes.

"We may end up with extra lumber. If you were to build more houses, where would you want them?" I had been careful to leave the choices up to him. I didn't want to be accused later of sabotaging their settlement.

He looked at me warily. He still suspected a trick.

To hell with it.

I was tired and I was hungry. I staked out the last three myself.

Kerry worked silently, not complaining, but stabbing his small garden spade into the soil like it was my kneecap.

"How old are you?" I asked.

"Old enough."

"What kind of answer is that?"

"Old enough to know I don't like you."

"Four," I said. "You must be about four."

His eyes flashed with indignation. "Seven!" he shouted.

"Then you should know the proper way to dig a post hole."

"Nothing wrong with my—"

"Come over here. I'll show you."

He grudgingly walked over, dragging his spade behind him. I marked a small circle in the soil, and we began a new hole together. He twisted his face into a scowl but followed my directions.

"You go to school?" I asked.

"Jurga teaches me letters, but she doesn't know them all."

"Is Jurga your mother?"

"Sort of. She took me in."

I learned there were eight children at the settlement. Three were orphans, and Kerry was one of them. He only had a faint memory of his parents. They had died in a fire back in Venda. It explained the pink scarring that crept up his arm.

"Would you like to learn all the letters?"

He shrugged. "Maybe. Don't see what use it is."

"You like stories?"

His eyes brightened, but then he remembered he was supposed to be scowling and his brows pulled down. "Sometimes."

"If you learn all your letters, then you can read stories on your own."

"Still no use. Don't have no books."

I thought about the belongings gathered from the homes and loaded in wagons. There was crockery, barrels of dried food, cookware, tools, clothing, some basic furniture, and nothing more.

"This hole's finished," I said. "That's enough digging for today. Go get some dinner."

I pulled off my shirt and washed up at the river's edge. There were several Vendans down there doing the same. I felt their stares, scrutinizing the tattoo across my shoulder and chest, trying to make sense of it. Or maybe just trying to make sense of me.

Heavy footsteps tromped behind me. "Canvas is up," Mason said, then stooped beside me to wash up too. I'd had several large open air tents brought in to protect against the sun and possible rain until the homes were finished. He leaned closer. "Friendly bunch, aren't they?"

"At least one of them is."

He knew who I was talking about and frowned. "She has it out for me. I don't know why."

"Maybe because you were the one who relieved her of her weapons back in Hell's Mouth."

"I gave them back—which I still think was a big mistake."

"It was my agreement with Kazi. I don't think you need to worry about Synové stabbing you."

"She's an expert archer, you know?"

"Most of those on our patrols are expert archers. She's Rahtan. It doesn't surprise me."

"No, when I say expert, I mean, *expert*. She could shoot the shadow off a fly at a hundred paces."

He told me that when he gave her weapons back as I ordered, she drew an arrow with hardly a thought and shot a loose chain on a passing wagon, pinning it into silence, saying the jingle annoyed her.

"I think she was trying to impress you more than threaten you. Nervous?"

He shook his head. "Her mouth is what's going to do me in."

"Speaking of mouths, Gunner behaving himself?"

"Whatever you said to him must have sunk in. He hasn't said a single word." I didn't think I really needed to warn Gunner to keep his temper in check. He'd been notably quiet ever since we left the old site. He was probably thinking the same thing as the rest of us. The Vendans had been caught in the crossfire of a battle that wasn't theirs.

A shadow passed over us, and I looked up. It was Caemus. He washed up silently near us, but with a long riverbank in both directions, I knew he could have chosen a spot farther away. There was something on his mind.

He scooped up a handful of sand and rubbed it in around his fingernails, trying to scrub away the embedded dirt. "Kerry do a good job?" he finally asked.

"He's learning."

Caemus finished his hands, scrubbed his face, then stood, wiping his hands on his trousers. He looked at me, his weathered face still shining with water.

"I didn't know you had kin buried there."

I was silent for a moment, old angers rising again, not feeling I had to justify any of the reasons why we wanted them off our land.

"We don't," I finally answered. "It's a spot to mark where an ancestor died." I stood so we were eye to eye. "We don't know for sure if it even happened there, but it's a traditional spot we've recognized for generations. And we Ballengers are big on tradition."

His head cocked to the side, his chin dipping once in acknowledgement. "We have traditions too."

I looked down at the tether of bones hanging from his belt. "That one of them?"

He nodded. "If you have a minute, I'll tell you about them."

I sat back on the bank and pulled Mason down beside me.

"We have a minute."

CHAPTER THIRTY-TWO

KAZI

THE COOK DISHED OUT HEARTY STEW INTO BOWLS AND PLOPPED
a thick slice of black rye bread on top. Jase had brought in field cooks
from the Ballenger lumber camps. If you included Wren, Synové, and
me, there were about an equal amount of Vendans and Ballengers. Thirty
of them, thirty of us, and as each person got their dinner they filed off to
sit with their own.

The Ballenger crew sat on one side of an oak, and the Vendans on
the other, which prevented any conversation between them, but maybe
that was the goal. This was going to be a long, dreary evening, maybe
even a contentious one if someone took a sharp word too personally. A
small fire burned in a ring in the center, ready to stave off darkness as
dusk rolled in. There were some benches and chairs from among the
Vendan belongings, but not enough for everyone, and so they perched
on the sides of empty wagons or on stacked lumber as they ate their meal.

Jase was the last to arrive at the cook wagon. As he got his meal,
Titus called to him, offering a seat on a crate beside him—on their side.

He didn't even look for me, and I wondered if my encounter with the dogs in the tunnel had created a permanent distance between us.

I noted that the Vendans still watched Jase closely. When we had unloaded wagons, I heard their sentiments, ranging from disbelief to continued wariness, but knew they all felt cautious gratitude. Mostly, they were still puzzled by this new development. Many eyes glistened with tears as they unloaded their goods to a designated spot beneath a strung canvas. There was no question that this was a site that held more promise than the last. One woman had openly wept, but now, as we sat eating, they kept their words quiet and emotions in check, as they had learned to do around outsiders.

But there was a curiosity, too—on both sides. I saw the glances. Even the camp cook had regarded them with something that wavered between worry and compassion. He was generous with their portions.

"Well, would you look at that," Synové said. Her eyes directed us to Gunner across the way. "The nasty one keeps looking at Jurga."

She'd been the one weeping earlier today.

"How can you be sure he's looking at her?" I asked. There were several Vendans huddled close to her.

"Because she's looking back."

I watched more closely and it was true, but Jurga was careful, only looking sideways at him through lowered lashes when he looked away.

Maybe the divide wasn't as great as I thought. If the nasty one could catch softhearted Jurga's eye, maybe the divide only needed a little help to narrow.

"I'll be right back," I said. I strolled across the empty expanse, and several pairs of eyes followed me, like I was a plow churning up a furrow of soil in my wake. Gunner didn't like me. He'd made that clear, but the feeling was mutual so I didn't hold it against him. Once I signed the letter to the queen, my purpose was done, and I was dead to him.

When I stopped in front of him, he looked at me like I was a swarm of flies blocking his view. "She won't bite, you know? You could go over and say hello."

"I'm just eating my dinner. Don't know what you're talking about."

"Your bowl is empty, Gunner. Your dinner is gone. Would it be the end of the world to get to know some of the people you're building shelters for?"

I reached down and took the bowl from his lap and set it aside, then grabbed his hand and pulled him to his feet. "Her name is Jurga. Did you see her weeping today? It was with gratitude for what you Ballengers have done."

He yanked his hand loose. "I already told you, I don't know what you're talking about. Let me finish my dinner in peace."

We both looked at his empty bowl.

"Hello."

Jurga had come up behind us.

Perhaps seeing me talking to Gunner had given her courage to do the same. I wasn't sure, but Gunner calmed, shifting awkwardly on his feet, and I stepped away, leaving the finer points of introduction to the two of them.

Now I turned my attention to another Ballenger.

I walked over to one of the older Vendan boys testing notes on a flute. I asked him if he knew "Wolf Moon," a common Fenlander song that Synové sometimes hummed. He did, and when he started playing the first tentative notes, I ambled over to Jase, still deep in conversation with Mason and Titus, and I curtsied in front of him, quickly getting their attention. "We never got to dance last night, *Patrei*. Would now be a good time?"

He looked at me uncertainly. "What about your ankle?"

"I've ridden for hours, dug up a barrel of parsnips and potatoes, and helped unload two wagons today, and now you're worried about my ankle? Maybe it is *your* delicate feet that are too weary? Are you trying to get out of this dance, *Patrei*? Just say so and I'll find someone else to—"

Jase was on his feet, his arm sliding around me, pulling me to the center of the Ballenger-Vendan divide. The truth was my ankle was still tender, but Jase seemed to sense this in spite of my protest, and he limited our dancing to gentle swaying.

"I think this is the least we can do to warm the chill between these two camps," I said.

"So this is all for show?"

"What do you think?"

"I think I don't care anymore, as long as you're in my arms."

The tune was slow and dreamy, the notes gliding through the air like birds heading home through a dusky sky to roost. Jase pulled me closer, his lips resting against my temple. "Everyone's watching," he whispered.

"That is entirely the point."

"Not entirely." His mouth edged closer to my lips.

The question of whether it was a show was swept aside, forgotten. There may have been other secrets between us, but this much was true and honest—I wanted to be in his arms, and he wanted to be in mine.

Maybe that was enough.

Maybe moments like this were all the truth we could expect to get from the world. I held on to it as if it were.

"Last time we danced we were knee deep in grass," I said.

"And now there's not even a chain between us," Jase whispered.

"Maybe we don't need one anymore." We were in the wilderness again, and it felt easy and natural to allow ourselves to slip through a hole that was familiar.

I had an awareness of others joining us, but my eyes were locked on

Jase's and his on mine, and as I heard more feet shuffling, others dancing around us, I wondered if they had fallen through that same hole with us, and I wondered if, this time, we would be able to make it last.

———◦◦◦◦———

Tell me a riddle, Kazi.

Jase had seen me, restless, walking, organizing supplies that were already ordered. Everyone else was asleep on their bedrolls. He came up behind me, his hands circling my waist. "I can't sleep either," he said. His lips grazed my neck, and he whispered, "Tell me a riddle, Kazi."

We laid out a blanket on a bed of grass, the stars of Hetisha's Chariot, Eagle's Nest, and Thieves' Gold lighting our way, far from everyone else.

I settled in next to him, laying my head in the crook of his shoulder, his arm wrapping around me, pulling me close.

"Listen carefully now, Jase Ballenger. I won't repeat myself."

"I'm a good listener."

I know you are. I've known that since our first night together. That's what makes you dangerous. You make me want to share everything with you. I cleared my throat, signaling I was ready to begin.

> *"If I were a color, I'd be red as a rose,*
> *I make your blood rush, and tingle your toes,*
> *I taste of honey and spring, and a good bit of trouble,*
> *But I make the birds sing, and all the stars double.*
> *I can be quick, a mere peck, or slow and divine,*
> *And that is probably, the very best kind."*

"Hmm . . ." he said, as if stumped. "Let me think for a minute . . ." He rolled up on one elbow, looking down at me, the stars dusting his cheekbones. "Honey?" He kissed my forehead. "Spring?" He kissed my chin. "You are a good bit of trouble, Kazi of Brightmist."

"I try my best."

"I may have to take this one slowly . . ." His hand traveled leisurely from my waist, across my ribs, to my neck, until he was cupping my cheek. My blood rushed; the stars blurred. "Very slowly . . . to figure it all out." And then his lips pressed, warm and demanding onto to mine, and I hoped it would take him an eternity to solve the riddle.

Wren, Synové, and I sat on a stack of lumber, fanning ourselves in the shade and taking a break from leveling a foundation. It was midmorning but already sweltering with the height of summer.

I thought Jase would be gone by now, that all the family would be on their way back home this morning, along with us, but Jase got caught up in discussions with Caemus about the barn and then with Lothar, one of his hired workers he was leaving to supervise the crews, and then when he watched stonemasons moving in to lay the foundation for one of the sheds, he decided it needed to be a bit larger first, and then he paused, eyeing the whole valley, the children swinging from the oak tree, and his gaze fell on the future shed again. He turned to Mason and said, "I'm thinking they need a root cellar too. Why bother with a bigger garden if they have no cool storage? If we put our backs behind it, we should be able to dig it in a few hours."

A root cellar?

I wasn't sure I could believe what I was hearing.

It became a competition between Jase, Mason, and Samuel digging on one side, and Aram, Gunner, and Titus on the other. A slow competition. They were feeling the heat too, their shirts long shed. Sweat glistened on their backs. They stopped to wipe their brows often and drink long gulps of water from buckets brought from the river. Sometimes they just poured the water over their heads.

Synové was mostly silent, her eyes wide, forgetting to blink. "I swear, I've never seen so much beautiful artwork on skin in all my life."

"We should probably get back to work," I said.

"Hell's bells we shouldn't," she said firmly. "I'm certain we need to rest a bit longer."

We didn't need much encouragement. None of us moved.

Wren took a long sip of water. "It looks like a whole flock of beautiful, muscled birds taking flight."

Their tattoos were all different—some on chests, some on shoulders, backs, or arms—but they all had some form of the Ballenger crest on them, the wings of eagles fluttering in front of us. I stared at Jase's, as taken with it now as the first time I had seen it. Synové was right; it was a work of art, one that I happily gazed upon.

He looked up, catching me watching him. He smiled and flames shot through my belly. "Halfway done," he called.

Halfway.

That's what I felt like. I was halfway between worlds, trying to find a story that fit neatly into both. When the root cellar was finished, he moved onto the barn, and then the waterwheel and a sluice from the river. A day passed, and then another. Four days, four nights. The valley was alive with banging, hammering, and sawing. Gunner went back to Tor's Watch. Titus went back. Aram and Drake went back. There was business to tend to. But Jase stayed. He was giving up tomorrows he didn't have to spare, tomorrows I had been unable to promise to him.

I began to wonder if I'd been wrong about everything, wrong about the way they ruled Hell's Mouth, wrong about their history and place among the kingdoms, wrong about their right to govern. Their work here wasn't just a grudging gift to fulfill an agreement. It felt like far more. It felt like a wish stalk pressed to a blistered foot, like words spoken under a midnight moon to lull me to sleep.

⚬⚬⚬

We stood together at the cookwagon, waiting in line for our food. Jase was close behind me, his hip brushing mine, a reminder that he was there, and I suddenly thought there were things I was hungrier for than dinner.

"Ten?"

A whisper.

My shoulders went rigid. The question came from somewhere behind me. I didn't dare turn with recognition, but it came again, louder this time.

"Ten?"

A girl circled in front of me. "I'm sorry, but aren't you Ten? I've been trying to place you ever since the first day, and I just remembered. My family was in Sanctum City for a year when—"

I shook my head. "I'm sorry. You've mistaken me for someone else."

"But—"

"My name's Kazi," I said firmly. *"Bogeve ya."* Move on.

Her eyes shifted to Jase and then she quickly looked down, as if she realized her mistake. "Of course. I'm sorry to bother you."

"No bother."

"Ten?" Jase said as she walked away. "What kind of name is that?"

I shrugged. "I think it's a highland name—short for Tenashe."

"I'm surprised she didn't already know that your name was Kazi."

"There are a lot of new names to learn. She probably just got confused."

I was grateful that Jase's attention turned back to food as the cook cut off a slab of venison for our plates, and I decided I was glad that we were returning to Tor's Watch in the morning after all.

Just before dusk, Aleski rode in with news that made our return more urgent. It was a message from Gunner. *Come home. A letter has arrived from Venda. The queen is on her way.*

CHAPTER THIRTY-THREE

JASE

MIJE SNORTED. THE BRAIDS JALAINE HAD WOVEN INTO HIS MANE were brushed out, and I think he and I both preferred it that way. He was a magnificent beast, muscled but balanced, with a gleaming black coat. The Vendans knew something about breeding. Kazi finished brushing him then slid his saddle blanket down his withers. I picked up his saddle.

"I can do that," Kazi said, reaching for it. She was on edge. Maybe because we were going back to Tor's Watch the unspoken words between us simmered closer to the surface.

I held it firm. "Please, let me help, Kazi. Besides, I think he likes me."

She rolled her eyes. "It's because you feed him treats. Don't think that I don't see."

I shrugged and lifted the saddle onto him. "Only a few snap peas."

"And parsnips."

The traitorous Mije nudged my arm, exposing me.

"See? You've spoiled him." She patted his side. "And he's getting thick around the middle."

He wasn't, and I knew she didn't really mind. She reached down and tightened his cinch. "We'll catch up soon," she said.

"Our horses won't be moving fast," I said, rubbing Mije's neck. "Take your time."

She spotted where I had nicked my thumb this morning. "What happened?"

The cut was business between me and the gods. Blood vows weren't only made in temples, but sometimes in meadows. "Nothing," I answered. "Just a scratch." I turned back to the wagon I'd be driving, double-checking the hitch and then the tack on my horses.

Mason, Samuel, and I were each driving teams of horses back to the arena. Tiago would go with us. The long timber wagons that had brought in supplies were specially equipped for heavy loads, and they'd be needed soon back at the lumber camps. They were empty now except for a few rocks loaded on the back to keep them from bouncing. The drivers who had brought them in would stay and help with the work.

I'd only intended to stay one night. I had a lot of work to take care of back home, but wagons had come each morning with more supplies—and with reports that all was well at home and at the arena. Gunner had everything under control. With the momentum here, it seemed important to keep the progress rolling. The animal pens were done, and we had raised the barn in one day. But now, for the next several days, most of the work was left to the stonemasons, bricking up the root cellar, finishing up the ovens, and laying the stones for the foundation lines before walls went up on the homes. Maybe there were other reasons I wanted to stay too. Things were different between Kazi and me out here. In some ways, I never wanted to go back.

Kazi finished strapping on her saddlebag and turned to face me. "I've been wondering, what will the king do if he finds out you moved them?"

"He'll never find out, and if he does, he won't care. This world up here means nothing to him. One piece of land is the same as the next as far as he's concerned."

"Are you sure, Jase? What if he deliberately chose the other site to aggravate you—a site that was in clear view of your memorial?"

"He'd have no idea about that. It's just a pile of rocks to him and the rest of the world—not to mention, he's never been there. He left it to scouts to find a suitable site."

"What about his tax money you keep? Could he be angry about that?"

"We only keep half. Who do you think pays the magistrates, the patrols, the teachers? Repairs the cisterns and skywalks? It takes a lot to keep a town running. There was never a single coin of his tax money put into this town until we started holding back. The Ballengers made a big mistake when we sold it for a round of drinks. It doesn't mean everyone in Hell's Mouth has to pay the price. The one percent we keep doesn't begin to cover the expenses. He knows that. We cover the rest. He's getting a deal—and even he isn't stupid enough to walk away from it."

She nodded, as if still not convinced, then her attention was drawn away to the children playing beneath the oak. We'd strung a fresh rope because the old one was frayed.

"Caemus says you're sending a teacher. They can't afford that, Jase. They barely—"

"You ordered reparations with interest. This is the interest. The teacher will be on the Ballenger tab. Maybe that way Kerry will have other things to interest him besides bashing in my kneecaps the next time I come."

"Next time?"

"When we come back out to see the finished work. It could be as early as another week. It's moving along fast."

"So you've decided not to drag it out after all?"

"I'm not going to play games with you, Kazi. You know how I feel. You know what I want. But sometimes we don't get what we want."

"What happens to us when we get back?"

"I guess once the settlement is finished, and the queen leaves, that will be up to you."

———————

The trail was wide and we rode in a staggered line to avoid eating each other's dust. Driving alone gave my mind time to wander back to the settlement. I was still pondering something I'd seen last night. It was late and I was walking through the oak grove to meet Kazi, trying not to make noise. A sliver of moon shone through the boughs, and I spotted Mason leaning forward against a tree. I thought he was sick. I heard moans. But then I saw there was something between him and the tree.

Synové.

She had spotted me and silently waved me on. More like a *scat, get out of here.*

And I did, as fast and as quietly as I could.

Mason and Synové? After all his protests?

I guessed he had either succumbed to her advances or had been charmed by them all along but didn't want to admit it to me. He was the one, after all, who told me Kazi couldn't be trusted. I wondered if he still felt that way.

The pace was slow and as we plodded along I made a mental list of more supplies the settlement would need. *Sheep,* I thought. *Send some sheep too*. One of the women said she used to spin wool back in Venda. What they didn't use for themselves they could sell. Yarn was always in demand. They needed more lanterns too. Oil. Paper. Writing tools.

Fruit trees.

Fruit would grow well in the valley. Kerry had given me the idea.

I had worked with him each day, either digging a hole, shoring up the sluice, or showing him how to sharpen the edge of an ax. He did his best not to smile through any of it, but one day he spotted Kazi walking by and he grinned. I thought maybe I had competition.

"What's the smile for?" I asked.

"I like her better than I like you."

I couldn't blame him. "Why's that?" I asked.

"She's the one who snuck oranges into our sack. We didn't even know they were there till we got home."

I had turned then and watched as Kazi helped a Vendan woman lift a tub of water. I thought back to the first time I had ever seen her.

I paid for those oranges. You and your bunch of thugs were too drunk to see beyond your own inebriated noses.

Maybe she did pay for them. Maybe she didn't. She was right; I'd been too fuzzy-headed to be sure of what I saw. But I'd never stopped to wonder what happened to those oranges.

Orange trees would grow well in the valley too.

For when the Dragon strikes,
It is without mercy,
And his teeth sink in,
With hungry delight.

—Song of Venda

CHAPTER THIRTY-FOUR

"Hurry up, Synové!"

She was still scrubbing her face and hair in the river. She'd had an unfortunate incident with horse dung. She'd fallen face-first into a large warm pile, and everyone in camp heard her screams. While we were sympathetic, Wren and I were ready to go, and an unwritten rule of the Rahtan was to be on time. Always. Eben and Natiya had made us pay for it dearly when we were late for drills. We were supposed to leave at dawn with the others. I felt like Griz, impatiently shuffling from foot to foot.

"Next time keep your eyes on where you're going, not on the artwork," Wren said. We didn't know for sure what had distracted her—she refused to say—but we had a good idea.

She stomped out of the river, dripping with water, indignation, and utter nakedness, far beyond caring who gazed upon her beautiful curves. She jerked on her clothes, the fabric sticking to her wet skin, and then proceeded to comb and tightly braid her long hair, checking it often, making sure no trace of horse dung was left.

When we were finally on the trail, a good half-hour behind Jase and the others, we talked about the surprising progress made at the settlement.

"Caemus told me Jase was sending a teacher," Wren said. "He already gave him the money for it. A big bag of gold coins, but there was blood on them. Caemus wondered—"

Synové wrinkled her nose. "Blood?"

"Jase nicked his thumb this morning," I said. "Maybe he was still bleeding when he counted out the coins."

Of all the unexpected things the Ballengers had done—the root cellar, the extra homes, the supplies—the teacher probably filled us with the most wonder. Our schooling had started late, not until we came to the Sanctum. We were eleven. Before that none of us could read a single word. Most Vendans couldn't. In six years of training, we had learned to read and write in two languages—Vendan and Morrighese. It was grueling, as much of our time spent with a pen and a book as with a sword. At times, we had railed against it. Pauline and the Royal Scholar were demanding teachers, but it was the queen who were made fluency a requirement of the Rahtan—and Rahtan was something we were all determined to be. I had struggled with the studies, my frustration often bubbling over. Until I learned to appreciate the quiet, puzzling world of words, I couldn't see the point, but never did I see the point more than when I composed the letter to the queen, carefully molding the words Gunner had already written into ones that would send a different message to the queen: Ignore this letter.

I know you've been busy with travel.

The queen hadn't traveled in months. She was *unable* to travel and knew I didn't expect her to.

Bring golden thannis as a gift of goodwill.

We only gave the bitter purple thannis as gifts. The sweet golden thannis was deadly. It had nearly killed her father.

Our kind hosts deserve this honor.

Confirmation that they were not to be trusted.

We're settled in at Tor's Watch, taking in every aspect.

We've made it inside and have begun our search.

Your ever faithful servant, Kazi

The queen only called me by my full name, Kazimyrah. Signing off with *Kazi* would clang like a warning bell in a graveyard.

She was not coming as I knew she wouldn't. Whatever letter she had sent would have its own hidden message just for me. All Gunner saw were the words she wanted him to see.

"Look there," Wren said. "Straight ahead. We caught up sooner than we thought."

In the distance, a dust cloud churned up behind a wagon.

"Maybe I can get Mason to teach me how to drive a team of horses someday," Synové mused. "If we come back."

Wren shook her head. "One—first you need to get Mason to talk to you at all, and two—I don't think we'll be welcomed back."

Synové shrugged. "Depends. Kazi's searched the grounds, and we haven't seen any sign of the captain. If he's not here after all, we'll be leaving under friendlier terms."

Friendlier terms? Synové was weaving a scenario I hadn't considered.

"It's possible the coward's gone already," Wren agreed. "He deserted a battlefield. He's run before. Running is what he's good at."

Yes, he was a coward in some ways, but he wasn't afraid to kill on a grand scale. I saw the worry in Wren's face, the way she chewed on the corner of her lip. It weighed on us all. Wherever the Watch Captain was, he was a danger. It was like having a poisonous snake loose in a dark room. Anywhere you stepped could be deadly. The queen's lead had been at least a little bit of light shed on the corner where he lurked.

Synové blew out a dramatic sigh and batted her lashes. "But if he should turn up at Tor's Watch, we'll have our monster . . . and I suppose poor Mason will just have to learn to live without me."

Wren chuckled. "Kind of the way Eben does?"

Synové shot her a frown, then studied me. "What about you, Kazi? Is it going to be hard for you to leave?"

I knew she would dig in this direction eventually. "In some ways," I admitted, trying to tiptoe around the obvious, foolishly hoping she would drop it. "I'm entranced with every square inch of Hell's Mouth. I've never seen a town like it. The tembris and skywalks are—"

"You know what I'm talking about," Synové said. "That other item you're entranced with."

I was silent for a long while. "No," I finally answered. "It won't be hard for me to leave." Staying was never an option.

I watched the wagons ahead of us, the dust billowing to the side, when something else caught my eye. "What's that? Way over there?" My stomach squeezed with dread.

"Riders," Wren confirmed.

A lot of them—and my instincts told me they weren't friendly.

"They're stalking the wagons," Synové said.

"Like wolves," Wren added.

I didn't need to say a word to Mije. The nudge of my knee and my weight lifting in my stirrups were all he needed to send him flying, and together we became a dark wind racing across the landscape.

My thoughts galloped as fast as Mije, and somewhere in my head I heard desperate words that couldn't be mine. *I do want tomorrows with you, Jase. I want a lifetime of tomorrows.*

CHAPTER THIRTY-FIVE

JASE

"YOU SEE THAT?" I YELLED, MOVING MY TEAM CLOSER TO Samuel's. Tiago sat beside him.

Samuel nodded. "I've been keeping an eye on them."

I had too. They were a good distance away but had been riding parallel to us for a while, riding out of a copse of trees we'd passed a quarter mile back. We were on a little-used trail. We hadn't expected to see anyone out here. Mason had moved far ahead of us, out of earshot, and the riders were staying just out of his line of vision. I was certain he hadn't seen them or he'd have slowed down and fallen back with us.

"I count ten," Samuel said.

"Eleven," Tiago countered.

It was hard to count. They were far away and bunched close together. However many there were, it was too many to be riding without a wagon. And they weren't herding stock. They had no purpose out here, and I didn't like the way they stayed in a tight pack. They were conferring. Planning. Raiders.

I took a deep breath, put two fingers in my mouth, and let out a shrill whistle, trying to get Mason's attention. He didn't hear it. The wind blew the sound back at us.

"They're going for him first," I yelled to Samuel. Take out the stray before they hit the rest of the pack. We were closer to Mason than they were, but draft horses pulling a wagon couldn't move as fast as lone riders. "Toward Mason's right," I said. "Ready?"

"Let's go," Samuel answered.

"*Ha!*" We snapped our reins. "*Ha!*" As soon as our teams took flight, so did the riders, heading for Mason.

"Ha!" I yelled, over and over again. The teams pounded across the plain, the wagon beds bouncing, the rocks we put on the back for weight flying off behind us. Samuel yelled for all he was worth too. But being upwind and with the noise of his own wagon and horses, Mason still couldn't hear us. Even if he turned around and spotted them, he'd be one against ten. Or eleven.

And then a shadow flew past on the other side of me. I drew my knife, but it was already a black blur far ahead of me. Two more shadows followed, and I thought it was an ambush from all sides—until I realized it was Kazi, Wren, and Synové. They raced toward the raiders to shake them off Mason. As they neared, half of the riders split from the pack and came for us.

We kept our wagons thundering forward, but in seconds they were upon us. Two headed for my wagon, one racing beside me. He jumped onto the back, coming toward me, and I had no choice but to let go of the reins and draw my sword. I jumped over the seat onto the bed, a weapon in each hand, the wagon still racing ahead. We were both jostled, our aim off as the wagon bumped over ruts, but my steel still met his, our edges slicing, juddering against each other. The clangs reverberated with all the other noise and shouting surrounding us. His swings were vicious and strong, someone trained and determined to overcome at all costs.

I caught a glimpse of Samuel and Tiago, in fights of their own, over-run with riders surrounding them. A bump threw me to my knees, and then the whole wagon lurched as the other raider jumped on board. I was caught between them, turning, meeting their blows, and then a third rider approached. I couldn't hold off three. I lunged, knocking the first attacker off balance, then swung my other hand, plunging my knife into his thigh. He screamed and fell from the moving wagon. I spun again, ready to meet the other raider, and now the third one was on the wagon too, trying to pull the spooked horses to a halt.

The second man jumped forward before I could get to my feet. I swung, knocking his sword from his grip, but he had momentum and sprang toward me, throwing me backward, his knee jamming into my ribs. My head hung over the side of the wagon, perched precariously close to the spinning wheel. Dust flew into my eyes, and our arms strained and shook against each other as he pressed a knife downward toward my chest. The knife tip pricked my skin again and again as the wagon bumped on the terrain. My eyes watered with grit. I could barely see, but behind him I glimpsed the blurred hulk of third man coming toward us, and then a fourth—

I blinked, trying to clear my vision. It was Kazi. When she jumped onto the wagon, the other raider spun toward her and advanced, their swords crashing, but he was twice her size and his attacks sent her backward. I jammed my leg upward, trying to unbalance the man over me, trying to get to her, but when he tumbled he dragged me with him, and both of us fell from the back of the wagon, rolling in the dirt. When I finally came to a rest, I spotted his knife lying between us. We both lunged. He was closer and got to it first—but he was still stretched out on his belly, and I wasn't. He rolled, but my fist was already flying, knocking him senseless, and I hit him again, and again, until his face was a broken, bloody pulp, and the knife in his hand no longer mattered. I took the knife and ran for one of their abandoned horses.

The wagon had already gone far ahead, and even from atop my galloping horse I couldn't see Kazi or the raider on it. As I rode I saw blurred glimpses of the others, Wren fighting by Samuel's side, her *ziethes* flashing, blood spurting from a raider's neck, Tiago and Samuel bringing their attackers down. In the distance, more riders circled Mason's wagon and Synové was letting loose with a volley of arrows. I saw one raider fall and another, and Mason engaged with a third. Up ahead my wagon had finally come to a stop, the horses still prancing nervously, but neither Kazi nor her attacker was on it. I rubbed my eyes, grit still making them water. My lungs seared with fire, and then the last of my breath was squeezed from them. I spotted her on the ground, almost buried beneath him. I jumped from my horse, the knife tight in my fist, praying to the gods I wasn't too late, a thousand prayers and pleas uttered in a few frantic seconds—*Not her, please not her*—the knife ready to slice the raider's throat, when I heard Kazi say, "He's dead. Get him off me."

I dropped to my knees and shoved him off. She was drenched in blood and my fingers instantly searched for wounds.

"His blood. Not mine." I saw the knife clutched in her hand. She was still gasping for air, hardly able to speak, her lungs as drained as mine. I brought my lips to her skin, her forehead, her cheek, choking breaths coming from my throat. "You're all right?"

She nodded. "The others?"

"Still standing. We got them all."

* * *

There were twelve of them altogether. Kazi and Wren had each killed two, Synové, three. Mason, Samuel, Tiago, and I had killed the remaining five. We were all spattered with blood and had nicks, cuts, scrapes, and bruises, but Samuel was the only one who had received a serious injury, a deep cut across the palm of his hand. It would require stitching when we got home. Wren was tending it and had commandeered Samuel's shirt for a bandage. A knife thrown by one of the attackers had grazed Synové's scalp, and while it didn't seem to be a serious cut, it bled profusely, and her head needed to be wrapped. Kazi ripped Samuel's shirt into strips. My own shirt had a small stain of blood over my heart where the raider's knife had pricked me. I thought about the seer's warning, *Guard your heart*, Patrei. *I see a knife hovering, ready to cut it out.*

He nearly had.

As Mason and I loaded bodies onto the back of one of the wagons, we looked at each other, still in wonder. We'd never seen anything like it. The raiders had numbers and surprise on their side. We had Rahtan watching our backs.

"I'd be dead if not for them," Mason said.

"All of us might be. I bet you're glad you gave Synové her weapons back now. You're right; she could shoot the shadow off a fly."

He glanced over at her. She was holding a rag to her head. "But she needs to learn how to duck."

He told me Kazi had killed one of the men who was about to split his skull in two with an ax. "What she lacks in stature, she makes up for in speed. She's fast."

I'd been on the receiving end of that the first day I met her.

All of them had flown into that valley with no thought for themselves, driven like furious demons. I knew Rahtan were well-trained and disciplined soldiers, but until I saw the aftermath of all the bodies, I didn't quite appreciate how skilled they were.

How many have you killed?

Two. I try to avoid it if I can.

Now she had killed four. There was no avoiding death today. This was no ragtag group of bandits who attacked us. They'd been a team on a mission. We'd already gathered their horses and gone through their bags looking for some clue about who they were. They were suspiciously clean. Even their saddle blankets gave no clue as to where they were from.

Kazi walked over, bruises on her neck beginning to darken. The last attacker had choked her before she stabbed him. She grabbed a skin of water to take back to Samuel, who was still being cleaned up by Wren. "You should flush out your eyes again," she said. "They're still red."

"I will. After this."

She paused and looked at the bodies we were stacking. "Why would they attack empty wagons? There was nothing to steal."

"Large empty wagons are sometimes the greater prize," Mason answered. "They're headed to market to buy goods, and that means they're carrying fat purses."

When she walked back to where Wren nursed Samuel's wound, Tiago said what we were all thinking. "Or it was another staged attack to discredit the Ballengers."

Possibly.

We made a point to look at each face as we loaded bodies to see if we recognized any league hands. Was this a chance raid by bandits, or an attack to stir fear—or was there another motive? An attack to specifically kill the *Patrei* and his brothers?

Whatever the motive was, we had to take the bodies and dump them in a gorge. We didn't want other traders who might pass this way to see the bloodbath. News would spread through the arena like wildfire. Every trader there wanted to earn a profit, but like the Candoran ambassador, they valued staying alive more and didn't want to be caught in the middle of a power war.

Mason shook his head. "Something about them is strange," he said. "Something—"

"They're shaven and clean," I said. "Their clothes don't stink. These aren't men who've been lurking on the trail for a long time waiting for prey to come along. They came here for this purpose. They knew we'd be here."

But how? And who sent them?

We moved the wagon ahead to pick up the last body—the one I had shoved off Kazi. He was facedown. Mason and Tiago grabbed him and threw him up on the wagon. I rolled him over and his head lolled to the side, his eyes still open.

The three of us recognized him.

Tiago hissed through his teeth.

"Son of a bitch," Mason said.

It was Fertig—Jalaine's beau.

We threw Fertig's body into the gorge first. It disappeared into the rocky ravine. No one would ever spot it. I told Mason and Tiago not to say anything to the others, including Samuel, about what we had discovered.

As far as we knew, Fertig didn't work with any of the leagues. He was a groom at one of the arena stables. Tiago said Fertig liked the gaming tables and had a weakness for dice. Maybe someone had taken advantage of that and paid him to keep his ear to the ground. Was that what his interest in Jalaine had been all along? She managed the arena office and was usually discreet, but there was no better source of news than her.

We pieced it together. She had bragged about the queen's letter, and then mentioned Gunner's message telling us to come home.

That was how Fertig and his gang knew we would be here.

Jalaine had told him.

Strangely, racing side-by-side with my rage was a sense of relief. I already knew there were conspirators, but at least now we had a clue. And one clue always unveiled more. They had a habit of leaving messy trails. Now, we had one to follow.

CHAPTER THIRTY-SIX

KAZI

THIS TIME, I THOUGHT.

This time I am going to die.

My knife was gone, lost in the tumble from the wagon.

His weight had crushed me, his hands crazed steel rings around my neck. My nails scratched at flesh, face, arms. Sound blurred. I had no more air, the deckled edges of the world ruffled away, disappearing, my fingers doing a last desperate dance.

I saw Death standing behind him, smiling. *You are next.*

My fingers pulled, searched.

Make a wish, Kazi, make a wish for tomorrow.

No breaths.

Make a wish for the next day, and the next.

No air.

One will always come true.

And then my hand knocked against something hard. His knife. His knife was still sheathed at his side.

I sat on the wagon seat beside Jase, his arm around me, and everything about it seemed right and easy and blessedly calm. My clothes were still drenched in blood, and his knuckles were bruised and swollen. Mije followed behind, tethered to the back. The raiders' horses were tethered behind other wagons. I leaned into Jase, sometimes closing my eyes. Sometimes dreaming. Sometimes feeling his lips brush my temple.

Tomorrow.

The next day and the next.

The ghosts, they never go away. They call to you in unexpected moments.

Because if I could believe in tomorrow or the next day, maybe that would give the magic time to come true.

There was a time when I wondered if it was all a dream. A nightmare. That she had never existed at all. That I was sprung from a fevered sleep and had always been a hungry shadow on the street. Her face faded, her touch faded, the same way a dream does no matter how hard you try to hold on to all its parts. But her voice remained clear as if she had never left me. The memory was bittersweet, saving me, when she couldn't save herself.

You must find the magic, my chiadrah.

I nestled closer to Jase.

Maybe I had.

Maybe there could be tomorrows.

It didn't seem like such a dangerous thought anymore.

The main house exploded with activity. We had rolled in the back way through Greyson Tunnel so we wouldn't parade our injuries and bloodstained clothes through town and create a panic. The news raced through the tunnel, and by the time we reached the front steps of the main house, Vairlyn was already out there shouting orders. *Fetch the healer! Call Gunner and Jalaine home! More bandages from the stockroom! Set out supplies in the dining room! Buckets of ice from the icehouse!* She walked from Tiago to Samuel to Wren, examining them for injuries, grabbing chins and turning heads from side to side. *Go to the dining room! Inside!* Though Synové tried to flinch away, she couldn't escape Vairlyn's clutches, and Vairlyn examined her bloody, bandaged head. More orders were shouted. *Draw baths! Prepare guest rooms!* It was clear she had done this before. Maybe too many times.

At the bottom of the steps, Jase pulled me aside before she made her way down to us.

His fingers gently skimmed the bruises on my neck, and he shook his head. "I don't want to say you shouldn't have come, but if you hadn't—"

"No thanks necessary, Jase Ballenger. I did it for an entirely selfish reason."

His brows lifted. "Which is?"

"You still owe me a riddle. A *good* one. You're not getting out of it that easy."

He smiled. "I always make good on my word, Kazi of Brightmist. You'll get your riddle." He bent to kiss me, but a hand suddenly pushed him away.

"Time for that later," Vairlyn said. She looked at my neck. "Dear gods, I hope the animal who did this is dead." She touched the welts gently. "We'll ice it. Inside."

She looked at Jase's cut cheekbone first, then grabbed his hand and looked at his knuckles. "Broken."

Jase pulled his hand free. "They're not broken—"

"I know broken when I see it! Go to the dining room with the others."

"Not now," Jase said firmly, his tone changed in an instant. "I have to talk to Jalaine first. Send her to the study as soon as she gets here."

Vairlyn slowed, her eyes studying him, a wordless exchange between them, and she nodded. "Come when you're finished." And then I understood. This was not her son. This was the *Patrei*.

Sounds of healing—bandages being cut, hot water being wrung from rags, winces and moans as scrapes, cuts, and wounds were cleaned—filled the dining room. Tiago had the stature of a bull but was the most vocal as Vairlyn tweezed splinters from his arm. He mewed like a forlorn cat.

At the other end of the long dining table, Oleez applied a tincture to Wren's elbow, scraped and bloody from a roll, and then she washed and examined my neck. She gave me a bag of ice to apply to the bruises. While Priya dabbed Mason's cut lip with ointment, he watched Synové squirm as the healer examined the cut on her scalp. It had stopped bleeding, but her hair was caked with blood. The healer gave her a balm and new bandage to apply once she had bathed. Then we were free to leave.

Wren glanced back at Samuel as we left. His arm was tensed, the muscles and veins bulging and his eyes were squeezed shut while the healer stitched his palm. He didn't say a word, but his chest rose in careful measured breaths. "He'll have a scar," Wren said. "Now I won't be the only one who can tell him apart from Aram."

We had almost reached our rooms, all of us eager to bathe and change, when a breathless servant hurried after us. She held out a plate that was topped with a delicate napkin. "From the new cook," she said. "She wanted you to have this."

I took the dish from her and she hurried away again, the house still busy with new chores. Before I even lifted the napkin, the aromatic smell bloomed around us. *Sage.* Synové snatched the cloth away. Three small sage cakes lay snug together in the middle of the plate. A message was tucked to the side.

The Patrei *informed me about your love of sage cake. I have other vagabond specialties if you'd like to come sample them in the kitchen. I'll be there throughout the evening as the regular cook has taken ill. I even have a bit of thannis tea you might enjoy.*

"Thannis?" Synové squeaked.

"Holy demons," Wren whispered, "do you think . . ." But she didn't dare say the thought aloud.

We walked back down the stairs, nibbling our cakes, nodding at servants, *straza*, no one concerned about our passing anymore. We had fought side-by-side with the *Patrei* and his brothers. We were bandaged and bruised, and our stained clothes bore the evidence of our battle. We were above suspicion.

When we turned a corner, we were hit with more glorious scents wafting from the kitchen. Vagabond scents. While Aunt Dolise was an excellent cook, these smells were familiar—garlic, dill, rosemary, thyme, and, of course, sage.

"You here to see the cook?" a servant asked as she walked out the swinging door with a stack of plates. "She thought you'd come. She has treats set out for you. She and her husband are inside."

Our casual steps vanished, and we all squeezed through the door at once, stumbling to the center of the room. The cook turned away from a steaming pot on the stove, her face stern, her hands wedged on her hips. Her partner walked out of the pantry, and she motioned to the door. He nudged it open a crack. "All clear."

I knew she wouldn't hug us. Neither would he. But her rigid stone face that tried to hold back emotion failed miserably, and relief shone in Natiya's eyes. Maybe Eben's too.

"Cooks?" I said. "You got in as *cooks?*"

"You doubt my skills?" Natiya wiped her hands on her apron. "Cooking is still in my blood, you know? But I think we only got in because the *Patrei* wanted to please *you.* Something about sage cakes?" She lifted a condemning brow. "Explain that."

I gave her the short version, a brief account of our being chained to each other and the aftermath. She listened quietly, her eyes registering amusement when I told her about blackmailing the Ballengers.

"Well done," she said. "What about our rabbit? Any signs of him yet?"

I shook my head. "I've searched everywhere except for the stables and a few outbuildings. Nothing."

"We haven't seen anything but the inside of a kitchen," Eben muttered.

"They're a suspicious bunch," Natiya explained. "They watch our every move."

"But then, we can't disappear like the Shadowmaker," Eben said, still keeping watch at the door.

Which had done me little good so far. The secret places of Tor's Watch hadn't produced anything.

"He has to be here somewhere. What about the arena?" Natiya asked. "Have you checked there?"

From what Jase had told me, the arena bustled with people. It didn't seem a likely place for someone to hide out, but it was worth looking into. "Jase is going to the arena tomorrow. I'll ask to go along—"

"Incoming!" Eben whispered.

Natiya pointed to the counter, and we all quickly grabbed a delicacy laid out on the plates, chattering with delight as the servant came through the door. She gathered pewter mugs from a cabinet.

"Heavenly!" Synové said. "Try this one, Kazi."

"Exquisite!"

"Delicious!"

"May I have another?"

Natiya beamed on cue, but as soon as the servant left again, her smile vanished and we returned to less tasty questions.

"And how did all . . ." She waved her hand at our bloodstained clothes. "*This* come about? No permanent damage?" she asked, peeking under Synové's bandage.

"We're fine," I answered. "There are other troubles here that have nothing to do with us. With Jase becoming the new *Patrei*, we're caught in the middle of a power war."

"So I heard. I also heard they got a letter from the queen. They really believe she's coming?"

"They do. It was part of our agreement—in return for the settlement reparations that are already under way."

"Good job, *kadravés*," Eben said, but his eyes landed on me and he nodded. He understood the compromise, the things you finally had to let go.

"What about Dolise?" I asked. "What did you two do to her?"

Natiya wrinkled her nose. "Just a little coralweed. She'll be sticking close to her chamber pot for a few days."

"We had to get over to the main house kitchen to talk to you somehow," Eben added as he slivered open the door again.

"Just a good *cleansing*, as Aunt Reena used to call it," Natiya said and held out a dish of treats to us. "Now go. Clean up. Rest. We'll see you tonight at dinner."

"What if he's not at the arena either?" Wren asked.

Natiya frowned, unhappy with this possibility. "If we have to, then we move on. We search elsewhere until we find him."

Move on.

That wasn't the queen's directive. We were only to come here, then home. It was impossible to search an entire continent for one person without a clue. I already knew that intimately. Maybe it was more of a desperate hope Natiya held on to—that the man who helped orchestrate the deaths of so many would be found before he killed again.

I took the dish from her. "The sage cakes are perfection, by the way."

"Even better than her aunt's," Eben replied.

Natiya grinned. "You better never say that in front of her."

Eben smiled. "I'm not stupid." His gaze lingered on Natiya as if he forgot for a moment that we were all there.

We gathered up another plate of the vagabond delicacies to take back to our rooms, and Eben and Natiya returned to their work. They still had to continue their charade as cooks and prepare the evening meal. As we walked to the door to leave, Synové turned. "Just so we know we have the story straight, you two are posing as husband and wife?"

Eben set down the pot of water he had just filled, and Natiya paused from mincing scallions, the silence long and full.

"No," Eben answered. "We're not posing." And then he went back to his work.

CHAPTER THIRTY-SEVEN

JASE

MY FATHER'S STUDY WAS NOW MY STUDY. I HADN'T BEEN IN here since he died. It was a room for both contemplation and condemnation—a place of privacy. When he wanted to speak alone with one of us, this is where we were invited. Two overstuffed leather chairs faced each other in a dark corner of the room.

Jalaine sat across from me in one of them, trembling, screaming, still not understanding.

I jumped to my feet. "Look at me, Jalaine! I'm covered in blood! And I got the best of it! Samuel may never be able to use his hand again!"

"But Jase—"

"That's it! My decision is made! I'm pulling you from the arena!"

"It was one time! One mistake—"

"But it was a huge one! They nearly killed us all!"

"Are you sure it wasn't *your* mistake?" she yelled, trying to fling the blame back at me. "Did you even ask him before you killed him?"

"Let me see, when should I have done that? Right before he came at me with his sword? Or while he was choking Kazi?"

"It wasn't just me! Gunner was telling everyone about the queen coming!"

"But Gunner didn't tell everyone about the message he sent for me to come home, or the trail I'd be riding on! They knew exactly when we would be there!"

A new thought hit me—were they the same group that had posed as Ballengers in the attack on the Vendan settlement?

"What about the shorthorn? Did you mention to Fertig about us going out to the settlement for payment?"

Her eyes grew wide and then she sobbed, "I didn't know, Jase. He loved me. He swore he loved me."

I threw my hands into the air. "When did you become so stupid, Jalaine?"

She lunged at me, striking out with her fists, her nails catching my jaw. I grabbed her, pinning her arms to her sides, and held her tight against my chest. She shook with sobs.

When she finally calmed I whispered, "Did you know he was fond of dice?"

She nodded.

"You're going to give me a list now, of everyone you ever saw him talking to. I don't care if he was talking to his horse, I want to know."

I stood over her, watching, as she wrote at the desk. Her tears fell on the paper. When she was finished, I looked it over, then folded it in half.

"You'll be at dinner tonight," I said, "and you won't say a word. You'll sit there and take a good long look at everyone at that table. You'll look at every scratch, bruise, and bandage, and at the faces of those who could have been hurt next, like Nash and Lydia. You'll reflect on all the things that might have been lost, just because you didn't think."

Only pieces of Before are left, scant memories that don't add up to anything whole. Before doesn't matter anymore but I tell the pieces to the crying children, anything to make them quiet.

Once upon a time . . .

Gaudrel's mother told me the stories because my mother was already dead. Sometimes I was too afraid to listen to her. I wish she was here. I fill in the empty spaces with my own words now.

A great fortress stood on a hill . . .

The scavengers bang loudly on the gate demanding entrance. They say they will kill us, maim us, torture us, but we do not let them in. Greyson springs a lever and we hear screams. The pikes he set have done their job.

I look over the gate and signal him as the rest run away. He pulls another lever, and there are more screams. The few who still live will not bother us again. We outnumber them now.

—Miandre, 16

CHAPTER THIRTY-EIGHT

KAZI

I PERCHED IN THE WINDOW NOOK OF SYNOVÉ'S ROOM, HOLDING a bag of ice to my neck as the healer had ordered, my knees drawn to my chest. From here I had a clear view of the gardens below and the massive houses that sat behind them like heavy kings on thrones, their spired crowns piercing a tangerine sky.

Thin, gauzy clouds tinged with the same color flowed in lazy stripes above them, making the great fortress seem less like a fierce stone warrior and more like a warm refuge. I was tired. I ached. A refuge was all I wanted it to be.

The beauty suddenly turned magical when a dark beating cloud streamed across the sky. Bats. Thousands, maybe millions, a thick swirling, undulating line all set on the same course. Twilight glanced off their wings like sparks in a wind storm. Jase had told me the Moro mountains were riddled with caves, some so large they could hold all of Tor's Watch. Now I knew they held bats too.

Come watch, I was going to say, but Wren sat snugly in a chair with her eyes closed, her fingers strumming the soft robe she wore. Synové still lingered in her bath, marveling at the hot water available with just the turn of a handle.

"How do you think they do it?" she asked.

I told her what Oleez had told me. There were heated cisterns on the roof. The mountains that loomed behind the fortress provided ample water and pressure. Synové leaned forward, adding more hot water, cooing with its luxury, then lay back again.

I studied her, wondering at her silence. Her arms were folded behind her head, and her toe played with a drip from the faucet. It was curious that she hadn't mentioned Eben yet. Not once. His last words as we left the kitchen should have spawned hours of speculation from her. Just a few weeks ago, she was mooning over him. Now she seemed more entranced with her hot bath than the surprising news—Eben and Natiya were not posing as husband and wife. They were married.

As I mused about Synové, it was Wren who surprised me with her thoughts instead. "I understand why Natiya despises the captain so much. I think he might be more contemptible than the Komizar."

"How's that?" I asked. I couldn't imagine anyone more despicable than him.

"The Komizar had been poor like us and knew what having nothing was like, but the captain—he had everything—a prestigious position in Morrighan, a seat on the cabinet, wealth, power, but it wasn't enough for him. And with all he had, he was cruel too. When the queen was shot—"

"No," Synové said.

Wren and I both startled. We turned to look at her, uncertain what she meant. She was still immersed in the tub, her eyes distant, staring up at the ceiling. I wasn't even sure she had been listening to us.

"It was the governors and guards who turned on us that day at Blackstone Square," she continued. "They were the most contemptible ones." Her gaze seemed fixed on a distant memory, and then she blinked, as if surprised she had said the words aloud. We all had our own horrors, but we didn't talk about them. We circled the edges, mended one another's outer cracks, and helped each other jump the breaches, but we didn't step into the middle of them.

She blinked again and smiled as if that could sweep away the last few seconds from our memories, then sat up in the tub. "So neither of you are going to say a word about Eben and Natiya?"

Wren stumbled over her words. "We—I didn't know—"

"It came as a surprise," I added.

Synové blew out a puff of air. "Oh, I saw it coming. How could you *not*? But I guess we know the answer to the *it* question now, don't we?"

I guessed we did.

Wren sighed. "So we don't need to bring it up again."

Synové stood and stepped from the tub, wrapping herself in a towel. She walked to the wardrobe, surveying the fresh clothes Vairlyn had sent her, commenting on each piece, wondering if we would all be eating in the dining room together, if Mason would be there, what we would have for dinner, how strange the large Ballenger family was, did anyone mind if she ate the last goat cheese ball, Synové being Synové again.

"Vairlyn thanked me, you know? For helping her son. I set her straight. I didn't just help Mason. I saved his ass. But it—"

"Balm," I said, pointing to the jar the healer had sent up for Synové's head.

Wren stood and grabbed the jar from the table. "I'll do it."

I leaned back against the nook wall again, mesmerized by the glowing gardens, listening to Wren chastise Synové, ordering her to hold still, her admonishments making me smile, thankful that we were all alive. Thankful that Jase was alive. All I could think as I galloped forward on Mije today was that seconds mattered. Seconds could change everything. Seconds could erase one path and send you reeling down another.

"What's that?" Synové asked, her hand feeling the back of her head.

"Nothing," Wren answered, swatting her hand away. Nothing but a bald spot. Neither of us had told Synové that a small chunk of her lovely copper locks had been a casualty of the knife slicing over her scalp. Careful combing would camouflage it until it grew back, and Wren already seemed to have that part managed.

My eyelids were heavy as I watched the bubbling fountain in the center of the garden—but then something disturbed my dreamy calm—a sharp movement in the corner of my eye. I turned and glimpsed a figure hurry up the steps of Darkcottage and disappear inside. I sat up, not sure of what I had just seen, it happened so fast.

He was tall and square-shouldered, but from here I could discern no features. It was more the way he hurried, then looked back out at the garden before he slipped inside that unsettled me. Maybe he was afraid the dogs would be loosed soon. Or maybe he was afraid of something else.

"What is it?" Wren asked, my slight movement catching her attention.

"Someone just went into Darkcottage," I answered.

"An employee?"

"Maybe. But he was tall and square-shouldered." Those had been the queen's exact words to describe the captain.

Synové jumped up from her chair and peeked out the window. "What color was his hair?"

"White, I think, but it was hard to tell. Everything is cast with an orange light."

"The captain's hair is black," she said.

Wren joined us at the window, surveying the grounds with her sharp eye. "It's been six years. Hair can change."

———◦◦◦———

It felt like a trapped bird banged around in my chest as I hurried up the steps of Darkcottage. The clouds above had grown thicker and more threatening. I didn't have much time before night fell and the dogs were loosed. I listened at the door before I eased it open a crack. I was met with silence, but as I stepped inside, I smelled something. A scent.

The whiff of wine? Sweat? Maybe with the house closed up, it was just stale air.

But it was something I hadn't smelled the last time I was here.

A thin beam of light peeped through a draped window. It was all I had to navigate through near darkness. I stayed to the edges of the wooden floor to avoid creaks that might reveal my presence. I crept, room by room, through the kitchen, the drawing room, the pantry, the cellar, and the many chambers on the upper floors that I had searched the last time I was here. Again, they were empty, unchanged. I found no one.

I checked the door at the back side of the house. When I opened it, the grounds were empty, still as only twilight is. Through hedges and trees, I saw a glimpse of the stables. Had he been on his way there? But why go through Darkcottage? There were more direct paths. I closed the door. It was getting late. I needed to get back.

But when I turned a chill caressed me—*Go*—a voice crawled up my spine—*Leave*—a finger turned my jaw—*Hurry*—and then there was a rushed blur of voices, hands, faces, running through the hall—*Shhh, this way, run, don't say a word.* Death strode among them, glanced at me, but this time he didn't smile. He wept. His arms were full and he could carry no more.

⸺≫✦≪⸻

My chamber door was ajar when I returned to the main house. I cautiously opened it to find Jase looking in my wardrobe, pulling open drawers and ruffling through them. He wore only trousers—no shirt, no shoes, his hair still wet—as if he'd rushed in to search for something.

I shut the door firmly behind me.

He turned, startled. "Sorry, I knocked but you didn't answer. I was getting ready for dinner and I realized I was out of shirts. And socks. I only had a few in the guest room and those are dirty in my saddlebag now."

My shoulders relaxed. It was *his* wardrobe he was searching. Not mine.

I had almost forgotten I had commandeered his room.

"I moved your things to the bottom drawers," I said. "Take your time. I'm enjoying the view." And I was. He held up his hand. His fingers were bandaged. A grin lit his face. "I'm injured. Maybe you can help me?"

I rolled my eyes. "Poor baby. As injured as a spider spinning a web, and you're luring me into yours."

"But it's a very nice web?"

"I'll be the judge of that."

I strolled over and he drew me into his arms, his kiss a bare whisper against my lips as though he feared he might hurt me. "My neck is fine," I said. "Only bruised—no lasting damage. But your knuckles—" I pulled away and lifted his hand, examining his two bandaged fingers. "Your mother was right? Broken?"

He shrugged sheepishly as if reluctant to admit it. "Maybe a little cracked. At least according to the healer."

"You should always listen to your mother."

"So she tells me."

I knelt to rummage through the bottom drawer for a shirt. "White? Gray?"

"What about you, Kazi?" he asked. "Do you always listen to your mother?"

I paused, gripping the socks in my hands, kneading them between my fingers. "It's different for us, Jase. I already told you. She's a general and has a lot of responsibilities. We don't see each other often."

"But she must still worry about you. And today—" I heard him sigh. I heard the guilt. "This isn't your battle. First the labor hunters, and now this. Does your mother even know you're here?"

Does she? Loss flooded my throat. It had gripped me today with a fresh, cruel hand, reaching into my heart, tugging, reminding me of what I had lost. When I saw the concern in Vairlyn's eyes as she looked at my neck, when she shooed me into the house like one of her children to have my injuries tended, I saw the lost moments with my own mother, all the memories I never got the chance to make. That was something else the Previzi driver had stolen from me. Six short years was all I had with her. My mother's absence hit me in a new, bitter way, because sometimes you can't begin to know everything you've lost until someone shows you what you might have had.

I rummaged through another drawer. "How about this cream one?"

"Kazi—"

I stood and faced him. "Stop. You don't have to feel guilty. My mother raised me from a very young age to be a soldier. And apparently I do it well. I'll take my reward now."

I drew his mouth to mine and I kissed him, long and hard, working to create a memory I could hold on to. When I pulled away, I began buttoning up his shirt. His chest rose in a deep quivering breath. "I guess there are some advantages to having bandaged fingers."

"I think you can do your socks yourself. I have to get ready too." I shoved him back in the armchair then threw him three pairs to choose from. "How'd your talk with Jalaine go?"

He was quiet, as if thinking it over. "It went well," he finally said. "I'm all caught up on arena business now."

"That much to catch up on in just a few days?"

"The arena is a busy place. A lot can happen in a short time."

I asked if I could go along with him tomorrow and he seemed pleased, but warned me he would have a full day and I might be left to my own devices at times. His being busy was convenient for me—it would give me time to look around unfettered, maybe just to find more of nothing. Is that what I hoped to find? Nothing? I wasn't sure anymore. For months, I had thought that finding the captain would close a door in my life. Many doors. It would not only erase present dangers but erase past failures too. It would make something right. It would bring justice to many where it couldn't be found for one.

Jase noticed my silence. "What is it?"

Secrets I still can't tell you, Jase. Oaths I can't break. Truths I want to share but can't. What is this? I knew the answer now as certainly as I knew the exact shade of Jase's brown eyes. "Turn around," I said. "I need to change."

His mouth pulled in a smirk. "You forget that I've already seen you half naked?"

The intimacies of being chained together and my thin wet chemise had left little to the imagination when we were in the wilderness. "But only half. Turn."

As he pulled on his socks, I threw on fresh clothes and began brushing my hair. I casually asked, "Will there be guests at dinner tonight?"

"No, just the family."

"What about the guest staying at Darkcottage? When I was in Synové's room, I saw someone go in there."

He pulled on a boot and a puzzled expression filled his face, but he didn't miss a beat. "No guests. It was probably just one of the groundsmen checking to make sure the windows were all shut. It looks like there's a storm moving in."

A storm. It made sense. I had seen the thickening clouds. And every window and shutter was pulled tight.

"He had white hair," I added.

Jase stood, thinking for a moment. "Tall?"

I nodded.

"Yes. That's Erdsaff. Good man. He's been with us for years. Summer storms can be the worst."

I thought about the sudden violent storm that had hit when Jase and I crossed Bone Channel, and as I did the room flashed with light and a crack of thunder shook the windows—as if on cue to confirm it was only a groundsman I had seen.

<hr />

Jase's fingers laced with mine. We walked through the halls, a rhythm to our steps that announced we were *together*, a rhythm that felt powerful, unstoppable. Inevitable. We paused, kissed, lingered, like the world wasn't waiting for us, like the secrets between us didn't matter, like the entire house was ours and ours alone, every wall, every corner, every landing. We had escaped death today, and a second chance was ours.

"You're a good bit of trouble, Kazi," he said, pinning me against the foyer wall, "the kind of trouble that I—" Words burned in his eyes, words he wanted to say, but held back, a silent bargain between us. His thighs were hard against mine, and breath rippled through my chest like a fitful breeze. His thumb lightly traced my lower lip. "We could skip dinner," he said, his voice husky. He had never pressured me, but I knew what was on his mind. It was on mine too.

"Dinner, pretty boy," I whispered against his jaw. "Your family's waiting."

Everyone was already seated when we arrived in the dining room. Notably absent were Aunt Dolise and her family.

"Nice of you to finally join us," Mason said.

"Beware the gods—you missed prayers," Titus added.

Priya clucked her tongue. "At least the cold soup won't get cold."

Their greetings were sarcastic, but a smile hid behind each one. They were happy to see their brother. Maybe even me.

"I'm sorry we're late," I said. "Time got away from us. We—"

"No need to apologize," Vairlyn said. "It's been an eventful day."

Bowls filled with cold mint soup were already placed in front of everyone. Vairlyn and Gunner sat at one end of the long table and the two seats at the head remained empty. Jase pulled one chair out for me, and then he took the other.

"Hmm," Priya said quietly, noting my spot at the head of the table.

Wren and Synové sat near the middle, and I noticed that Mason was seated next to Synové. I wondered how she had orchestrated that. Samuel sat across from Wren, his right hand heavily bandaged and his arm elevated in a sling. Between his injury, Synové's bandaged head, and the scrapes and cuts on Wren, Mason, and Jase, we were a sorry looking lot, though decidedly less bloody than earlier today.

"Did you see it?"

"Did you see it?"

Lydia and Nash bounced in their seats, echoing each other's excitement.

"Open it! Read it!" Lydia said.

Lying beside my bowl was the letter from the queen. The seal had already been broken. I looked down at the other end of the table and Gunner shrugged. "You weren't here. I wasn't sure if it was urgent."

I unfolded the letter and saw immediately that it was written in Morrighese, not Vendan. As I expected, the queen intended for them to read it. I read it aloud, though I was certain most of those present had already viewed it.

"Dear Kazi, Faithful Rahtan in valued service to the crown,"

Wren choked on her water and I sent her a warning look. The queen was more of a casual note writer. She wasn't one for pomp and circumstance, and her formal greeting made it clear that none of her words were what they seemed. She had understood my letter to her to its core.

"I read your letter with delight and gratitude that the Ballenger family is extending its warm hospitality to you, and to my other esteemed guards."

Delight meant the whole Vendan Council had a good laugh over it.

"Your revelations are indeed astonishing."

I don't believe a word.

"This wild and untamed territory you've described is intriguing, and I trust you are using your time wisely to learn all you can about it."

I hope you've found our man by now.

"Lord Falgriz—

I stifled a snort of my own. Griz was no lord, and he hated the teasing title the queen sometimes called him.

"Lord Falgriz," I continued, *"is escorting my brother to the palace at Merencia where I intended to meet with him."*

Griz is waiting at the rendezvous point, along with troops.

"But I can put some of my longer-term plans on hold and make a short stop at Hell's Mouth."

Even a queen could not put some plans on hold.

"I accept the Ballenger invitation to visit. I look forward to seeing you at month's end."

If you have still not found your quarry by then, he is not there. Come home.

"Your faithful service is a gift to me and all the kingdoms. It will never be forgotten."

She signed off with all four of her given names, which I knew she never used.

The letter held no surprises except for the last line. It was a reminder—*I believe in you.*

Pleased chatter erupted around the table, all of it polite because Wren, Synové, and I were present, but I heard the crisp ring of entitlement. This was something they felt they had coming, and it was long overdue, but I noticed Jase said nothing, his eyes focused on Jalaine instead. She'd said nothing ever since we arrived, her back stiff against her chair, her eyes cast downward at her lap.

While still looking at Jalaine, Jase asked, "Samuel, how is your hand?"

The mirth of the room dulled.

Samuel struggled to master his spoon with his left hand, the green soup spilling over the sides with his clumsy movements. "I'll live," he answered.

"Jalaine, look up from your lap," Jase said. "Look around. You have nothing to add?"

"Jase," Priya said, warning in her tone.

He shot her an icy stare to quiet her.

Jalaine's attention rose from her lap. Her eyes were swollen and red. Her gaze circled the table, as if seeing everyone for the first time, until her eyes landed back on Jase. "Nothing to add, brother. Not a word."

Wondering glances ricocheted around the table. Surprisingly, it was the nasty one who tried to bring a measure of cheer back to the room. "I have more good news," Gunner said. "While you were away, another kingdom signed a lease for apartments. Cruvas will now make us a base for trading too. And that shipment we promised the Candorans? I have confirmation it will be here in two weeks."

Now Gunner had Jase's full attention. "Two weeks? That's excellent news." He leaned forward, eager to discuss it more, but then sat back. "We'll talk more later."

Vairlyn's eyes nervously swept the table. "That's enough about business," she said. "Let's enjoy our soup."

Conversation erupted as everyone dug in. Nash asked Wren question after question, mostly about her *ziethes*, which I had persuaded her to leave behind in her room tonight, though she still wore a dagger. I was surprised to see Mason talking quietly to Synové, asking about her head, whispering something else I couldn't hear. Priya questioned Samuel about the settlement, but I noticed Jalaine remained quiet.

"What's wrong with your sister?" I whispered to Jase.

"I'll explain later," he answered and his hand reached under the table and squeezed my thigh. His expression was taut, and he looked like he wanted to be anywhere but here right now.

A loud clatter stopped the conversation and everyone looked at Samuel. His spoon had tumbled from his fingers and green soup splattered the table. "Sorry," he said. "It may take me a while to get the hang of using my left hand." He blotted the green spots with his napkin. Wren pushed her seat back and circled around to his side of the table, grabbing a mug from the sideboard as she walked. She placed the mug in front of him and poured the soup from the bowl into it. "There," she said. "Drink. Problem solved." She returned to her seat.

Samuel smiled and lifted the mug to his lips, but Jalaine's eyes pinched with horror as she watched him. She pushed back her chair and fled the room.

"What's wrong with Jalaine?" Lydia asked.

Nash looked at Wren. "Can I drink my soup from a mug too?"

"Should one of us go after her?" Aram asked.

"Jalaine will be fine," Jase said firmly. "She's just tired. I'm giving her some time off from the arena."

Gunner leaned back and moaned. "Why would—"

"Gunner," Jase said, stopping his brother mid-sentence with a sharp glance. I saw how quickly Jase could be two different people, the brother and the *Patrei*. That was the strain I had seen in his face earlier, the weight of it pressing on him.

His focus turned and I watched him eyeing Lydia and Nash, choosing his next words carefully. He stood and walked to the sideboard. He grabbed two mugs and set them in front of Nash and Lydia, then emptied their bowls of soup into them as he explained. "One of the crew we encountered today was a friend of Jalaine's."

Priya's mouth fell open. Titus sat forward in his seat. Vairlyn's lips pressed tight. Everyone but Nash and Lydia knew that the "crew" we encountered were dead at the bottom of a gully now.

"Who was it?" Aram asked.

Jase sighed. "Fertig."

A hush fell at the same time Lydia shouted, "I know Fertig! He's Jalaine's beau."

She and Nash began happily slurping their soup from the mugs.

Jase walked around the table, returning to his seat. "There's more. Jalaine had mentioned Gunner's message to Fertig—the one calling us home. That's how he knew where to find us."

Vairlyn leaned forward, her fingers pressing on her forehead.

"Fertig?" Priya said, as if she still couldn't quite believe it.

"Why didn't you say something when we were out there?" Samuel asked.

"I wanted to get information from Jalaine first."

"Which one was he?" I asked.

Jase eyed my neck, my question answered.

Fertig was the one who had choked me—the one I had killed.

CHAPTER THIRTY-NINE

JASE

TODAY WAS EVERY HELL MY FATHER HAD EVER DESCRIBED. I stumbled from one fire to the next. A raid. A betrayal. Kazi pinned beneath the body of a raider, soaked in a pool of blood. The memory punched me again and again. And I still had more business to address.

There will be times you won't sleep, Jase.

Times you won't eat.

Times you'll have a hundred decisions to make and not enough time to make just one. Times a choice will make you feel like your flesh is being peeled from your bones. Times you'll be hated for the decisions you've made. Times you will hate yourself.

You'll be torn a hundred ways. You'll doubt your decisions and whom you trust, but above it all, you must always remember that you have a family, a history, and a town to protect. It is both your legacy and your duty. If the job of Patrei *were easy, I would have given it to someone else.*

Now I understood my father's anguish as he lay on his deathbed passing his duties on to me. It was as much a burden as it was an honor.

I burst into Cave's End, and Beaufort jumped up from the divan to welcome me, a full goblet in one hand and a bottle in the other.

"What the hell did you think you were doing?" I said.

"Well, this wasn't the greeting I expected. Especially not when—"

"We had an agreement that you'd stay out of sight. One of the Rahtan soldiers staying with us spotted you going into Darkcottage. I had to make up a story about you being a groundsman."

Beaufort sneered. "Why are they still here? I feel like a caged animal! I thought I told you to get rid of them!"

I looked at him. Looked through an arched doorway at the rest of them sprawled around the "cage" as he called it, stocked with fine wines, tobaccos, ridiculous amounts of imported Gitos olives and Gastineux fish eggs, and *he* was giving the *Patrei* orders now? I already saw myself throwing the whole lot of them out the gates of Tor's Watch in the middle of the night, weapons be damned.

He realized his mistake. "*Patrei, Patrei,* I'm forgetting myself. Forgive me. Come in. Can I pour you a drink?"

He explained that with so many of us away and Tor's Watch so quiet, he had thought it was safe to go to Raehouse and speak to Priya about more supplies, but then our caravan rolled into Greyson Tunnel, creating a flurry of activity. He waited until dusk when things quieted to return to Cave's End.

More supplies? "We just filled a large order for you."

"There's a lot of waste with experimentation I'm afraid, but now with the formula and craft perfected, we're ready to go into production."

I couldn't deny I was happy to finally hear this news. Whoever was behind Fertig and his gang would crawl back to their hole and never bother Hell's Mouth again.

"And the fever cure?"

He shrugged. "Getting closer."

The same answer. Three children in Hell's Mouth had died last winter with fever. Three children too many. Beaufort had shown me the scholars' stacks of notes and the strange flasks and dishes that they experimented with, but the calculations meant nothing to me.

"Find it," I said. "Before winter comes."

"Of course," Beaufort answered. "I'm sure we'll have it by then."

He set his goblet down and yelled toward the other room. "Sarva! Kardos! Bahr! All of you! Get out here and help me show the *Patrei* what his money has bought!" He put his arm over my shoulder, the rest of his sordid crew following after us, including the scholars, Torback and Phineas. "This way," he said. "Let's look at the final product."

We stood in the shelter of the sky cap, the part of the cave that extended over the house and a good portion of the grounds, but the winds were fierce and we were still pelted with rain. At least the storm and thunder would disguise the sound.

"Like this?" I said, holding the launcher to my shoulder the way Kardos had shown me. He, Bahr, and Sarva were former soldiers. Sarva had once been a metalsmith, and he fashioned the launcher based on the scholars' designs.

"Keep it snug," Bahr warned. "The mount will absorb a lot, but be prepared for kickback. Eye your target as if you were shooting an arrow. Now keep it steady while you pull the lever back."

A loud crack sounded and a flash lit up the end of the launcher, punching it into my shoulder and sending me back a step, but the noise was nothing compared to the explosion when it hit the target two hundred yards away. The surrounding mountains reverberated with the concussion.

There were cheers all around.

"That going to take care of your problems?" Bahr asked.

"Yes," I answered. "And then some." I couldn't wait to see the Candoran ambassador's reaction to it. He wouldn't be yammering about development anymore, and no one would be touching arena caravans again.

"You can get four shots out of each load," Sarva said. "Though I doubt you'll have anything to shoot at after the first."

"You have all the specs written down?" I asked. "Carefully documented?"

"Of course we do," Beaufort answered.

"What about storage?" I asked. "Any dangers there? We're close to the family homes."

"None," Kardos said. "Though I wouldn't throw the loads into the kitchen oven." They laughed like they were schooling a boy on the basics of safety.

"You don't need to worry about those details now," Sarva said. "We'll go over it all when we deliver your first shipment."

I smiled, like *shipment* was the only word he needed to utter to send me on my way. "In two weeks?"

Beaufort nodded. "That's right."

"Good," I said. I turned the weapon over in my hands, examining it again. "I'll take this one in the meantime." I slung the launcher strap over my shoulder.

"Hold on," Sarva ordered. "You can't take that." He reached out for me to hand it over.

I stared at him. I had almost been expecting his response but was still surprised. "Why not, Sarva? It's mine, remember? I paid for it. For almost a year, I've been paying for it. And you have all the specs written down to make more."

He and Kardos exchanged glances, uncertain what to do.

Beaufort stepped forward, smiling, a forced chuckle in his throat, trying to tamp down the tension. "Yes, of course we do, but—"

"Then there's no problem here. I want to start training some of my men up in the lumber camps to work as caravan escorts. They always need the winter work." I reached over and swept the stacks of loads from the table into a canvas bag. "And I'll take these too."

Sarva's mouth hung open as I turned away. There was still plenty more he wanted to say. As I left, Zane strolled out of the main drawing room into the foyer, eating a chicken leg. He was as surprised to see me as I was to see him. "What are you doing here?" I asked. "It's late for a delivery."

He hissed out a frustrated breath and shook his head. "I know. I came up the back way to drop off goods." He rolled his eyes. "More wine and olives. The storm hit and now I'm stuck."

"We can put you up at Riverbend if you'd rather?"

"That's all right. I've already got my stuff stowed. Hopefully, the storm will pass by morning."

He eyed the launcher on my shoulder. "You taking that with you?"

"That's right."

He shrugged. "Want me to deliver it somewhere for you? As long as I'm here? I can—" He reached out to take it from me.

"No," I said, walking away, "I've got this one."

<hr />

My hand rested on the door, just as it had several nights ago, debating whether to knock. I was soaked through, and my hair dripped onto the floor. *Kazi.* I still wasn't sure how this happened. When we were alone, when the world wasn't looking over our shoulders, everything was easy. All I wanted was to be with her, hold her, listen to her voice, listen to her laugh, *You don't even know half of my tricks yet.* I wanted to know them all. She might not commit to tomorrows, but I knew she wanted them as much as I did. It was late, probably too late—

The door swung open as if she had sensed I was out there.

"Look at you! You're drenched," she said and grabbed my hand, pulling me inside. "You need a dry shirt and—"

"I only need you, Kazi, that's all I need."

CHAPTER FORTY

KAZI

OUR PATH GLISTENED WITH WATER AND SMALL RIVULETS streamed across the trail as last night's storm drained down the mountain. Blinding blue sky winked back at me from puddles and swollen ruts, and bands of jays squawked as we passed.

The back side of Tor's Watch was green, the trees thick, and enormous colorful lichen taller than a man fanned out on the ancient ruins that lined our path like gaily clad spectators. Everything in this part of the world seemed to grow large.

We were taking the back way that Jase had mentioned to get to the arena. Priya, Titus, Gunner, and *straza* rode with us.

Jase seemed more like himself now, his eyes focused, already simmering with the work ahead of him. But last night when he came to my room he was a different Jase. He held me, soaking me in his grasp. *I only need you, Kazi.* After dinner he said he'd had to take care of some business matters. "Business out in the rain?" I had asked doubtfully. The storm had been raging, the windows rattling with thunder so loud I thought they might break. He said the business was out in Greyson Tunnel, and he was caught in the downpour. I wanted to ask about Jalaine. I knew she had to be one of those matters—but I saw his weariness so I said nothing.

We had changed into dry clothes and lay on a thick rug in front of the fire. *Tell me a story, Jase,* I said, because this time I sensed that it was he who needed to be rescued from his own thoughts, just as he had rescued me so many times. His shoulders relaxed and his gaze softened, melting into a part of me that only wanted more. More of Jase, more of us. He told me about Moro Forest, and the legend of a creature that lived there. His head rested in my lap, the fire crackling, my fingers raking through his hair, until his lids grew heavy and they closed, his story unfinished, his face peaceful. *My chiadrah,* I whispered somewhere deep inside me where no one could hear, and then I nestled down beside him and we had both slept.

A loud *squawk* sounded and we both ducked. We had turned on a switchback and loud jays darted close over our heads. "Easy, Mije," I said, and I rubbed his neck to soothe him.

Jase looked at Mije's mane and frowned. It was braided again. I suspected Jalaine had escaped to the stables last night and shared secrets with Mije that she could share with no one else.

When Jase rode ahead, to speak with Gunner about something, Priya fell back with me.

"How's your neck?" she asked.

I had worn a high-collared shirt and left my hair loose around my shoulders to help hide the bruises.

"Fine," I answered.

She huffed out an amused breath. "Not much flusters you, does it?"

I wondered if she knew I was the one who had killed Fertig. I wondered if Jalaine knew.

"Did you see your sister this morning? How is she doing?"

Priya shook her head. "Still holed up in her room. She won't come out."

I kept thinking about her red and swollen eyes. Her silence. "Did she love him?" I asked.

"It doesn't matter now," Priya answered. "The minute he plotted against the family, Fertig became dead to us."

"But—"

"Jalaine will get over it. She understands the cost of betrayal. She would have run him through herself if she had known. Fertig's aim was to kill her brothers. And maybe the rest of us too. It wouldn't be the first time the *Patrei* and his family were all slaughtered."

"What?"

She grinned. "I guess that's one story Jase didn't tell you. But I can assure you Jalaine knows it quite well. Centuries ago, a *Patrei* and his whole family were slaughtered at—"

"But I thought the Ballenger line had never ended."

"All killed, *except* for the baby daughter." Priya told me that an uncle had succumbed to the flirtations of a lover. He let her in through a bolted entrance in the middle of the night. A flood of attackers followed behind her. As the family fled, they were cut down by rival powers, but a servant scooped up the baby, and they escaped down another path, making it to the vault. The servant eventually made it out through one of the caves and raised the daughter among cousins in the mountains. When the girl turned twenty, she returned with those cousins in tow and there was another slaughter in the very same house—but this time it was the daughter avenging her family's death, and a new reign of Ballengers began with her. "Some swear they can still hear the dead walking through the rooms. That's why many guests aren't fond of staying there."

"There?"

"Darkcottage. It was the first Ballenger house." She shrugged. "I've never heard anything in there."

But I have.

"Are you afraid of spirits?" she asked.

Was I? I wondered. They whispered to you in unexpected moments, and sometimes crossed the boundaries of life and death and touched you with cool fingers, and sometimes they warned you, but that was all.

"No," I answered. "The dead can't harm you. It's the living I fear."

Priya cast me a long sideways glance. "I doubted you when you first came. I thought you were going to be a big load of trouble, but I admit, I was wrong—even if you lied to me."

"I'm not sure I know what you mean."

"It never was a show. You always cared for my brother. I just don't know why you tried to hide it. Is it against your Vendan laws for a soldier to fall in—"

"No," I said quietly, cutting her off before she could utter the word I had avoided. Saying *love* aloud seemed dangerous. It made it tangible, easier to grasp and break. Or maybe I was just afraid the gods would take notice and steal it away.

"The Ballengers will never forget what you did for my brother."

Yes you will, I thought. *If you ever find out why I really came here, that I have searched every room of your house and rifled through your private belongings, that I combed through your desk and touched your neatly ordered pebbles, that I was an invader instead of an ally, you will only remember me for that.*

The whole family would remember.

We rode silently and my thoughts returned to Priya's story. A whole family slaughtered was a horror beyond imagination. No wonder the Ballengers were so protective, so diligent about teaching their history. But something Priya said niggled at me, *A servant scooped up the baby, and they escaped down another path.*

What path?

There were no direct paths to the vault from Darkcottage. She would have had to run out in the open, through the work yard, making her an easy target—though the attack did come at night. As long as the baby didn't cry, she might have hid in the shadows and made her way there. *If* the baby didn't cry. I remembered everything I'd had to do to keep a tiger quiet when I smuggled it out of Sanctum City, and that escape was extremely well planned, not a panicked flight from intruders.

"Just a mile to go," Jase called. He circled back to ride with me again, his business with Gunner finished, and Priya rode ahead.

"I'll give you a quick lay of the land when we get there, but while I go over leases and other business, you can explore the rest on your own."

"Other business? Like Fertig?"

"That too. Whomever Fertig plotted with took a substantial hit with twelve men dead in a gully. There will be rumblings."

"They were twelve well-trained men, Jase. There won't be rumblings. I saw how they operated, signaled each other, ticked off their moves as smooth as a timepiece. Wren, Synové, and I have never been injured before. Those were no common bandits. They were as cool as ice—even Fertig. He was soulless when he choked me, and then when I stabbed him . . . he smiled."

Jase was quiet, soberly taking in my assessment.

"Who's the one you least suspect?" I asked. "That's your guilty party."

"I suspect them all," he answered. He told me there were five league leaders, Rybart, Truko, and Paxton the most powerful among them, but the other leaders had raided caravans and stirred trouble before too. "Twelve dead crew will put a halt to any of their plans for a while. A dozen dead men would hurt our operations. It will cripple theirs. Still, I want to know who's behind it."

So they'll pay a greater price. The unsaid words simmered in his eyes.

We turned at the switchback and Jase pointed. "Look there." I got my first glimpse of the arena through a clearing in the trees. It looked like a city in itself. The jagged oval structure rose six stories into the sky. Eight towers around its circumference looked like the fangs of some heavy-toothed beast rising up out of the earth. Its mouth was open and alive with activity. Behind the arena were more structures—warehouses, barns, silos, and fenced pastureland.

Jase told me about the traders at the arena, some of whom sold actual goods, and others who displayed items to be sold and delivered on contract. On the center ground floor were local merchants selling food, small goods, and trinkets. On the perimeter were the larger traders.

"Reux Lau sells exotic leather goods that aren't found anywhere else on the continent, and Azentil sells every flavor of honey you could imagine."

I didn't know there was even more than one kind.

"And the Quiassé lace from Civica draws an exorbitant price, but there's always plenty of buyers and not enough lace."

It seemed the whole world out there was far richer than the one I knew.

"And you get a cut of it all?"

"We're fair. We negotiate cuts, but if it weren't for the arena, they'd only sell a fraction of what they do now. They make a considerable profit too. That's why they come."

No wonder the leagues ached for control of the arena, even to the point of trying to kill the *Patrei* who controlled it. I'd seen people kill for less.

The toothy towers I had seen from afar were actually long, circular ramps that led to the upper floors and to apartments on the highest level. The

Ballenger apartments were surprising—far more elegant and luxurious than Tor's Watch. This was where they entertained ambassadors, wealthy merchants, and sometimes royalty who traded at the arena. This was where deals were made. The rooms were deep and dark, windowless on three sides except for the walls that faced out on the arena, so there were glittering ornate chandeliers to light the interior.

"Who else do you entertain here?" I teased, peeking into one of the elaborate bedchambers.

"I'd be happy to entertain you here," Jase said, sneaking up behind me and sweeping my hair to the side. He nibbled on my nape as his arms circled around my waist.

"*Patrei,*" Gunner called impatiently from the foyer.

Jase growled. "I have a meeting with Candora. I'll find you in an hour."

I turned to face him. "And how will you find me in this enormous maze?"

"You're not the only one with tricks up your sleeve."

He kissed me and left, but just before he reached the foyer he turned. "You can get oranges on the floor too. I hear if you mention that you know the *Patrei* you'll get a good price—maybe even one for free."

"Really?" I said, pulling my brows down in disbelief. "And I heard just the opposite—mentioning the *Patrei* could get me into a good deal of trouble."

He smiled. "That too. Live dangerously—take your chances."

He left me alone in the apartment, free to explore the entire arena—not the sign of someone who had anything to hide. Still, I did an obligatory sweep through the rooms, finding nothing suspicious. One worry rolled off me and another took its place. *Move on.* I pushed away the thought and left to finish my job—to search any hidden corners of this world.

My fingers itched the minute I hit the floor of the arena. The noise, the bustle, the hawkers—it was like I was in the *jehendra* again, staking out my next meal. I kept reminding myself I had a full stomach and coins in my pocket now, but playful banter with the hawkers could do no harm.

In the outer ring on the ground floor, I saw some of the traders and goods that Jase had mentioned—the flowered carpets of Cortenai, the linens of Cruvas, the honeys of Azentil. And more. Everything that could be sold was sold here—furniture, gems, metalwork, wheat, barley, spices, animals for breeding stock, lumber, fine writing papers, minerals, intricate weights and measures, crystals—the finest products of a dozen kingdoms all converging in an irresistible stew of sounds, smells, and flavors. I breathed in the delicious fingers of woodsmoke that floated in the air. The hum of voices, the clatter of wares, and the distant, delicate warble of a flute wove together in a seductive welcome. Some merchandise ran loose. A bevy of keepers ran after a silky llama who escaped their lariats. He ran between stalls, always a step ahead of the keepers. I admired his technique.

I kept my distance from most of the shops, perusing them from a distance, but then I paused to eye the trinkets in one of the center stalls of a local merchant, focusing on a ring that reminded me of home—a delicate silver vine winding around a circle of gold. My mother used to weave a crown of vines through my hair on holy days. The merchant immediately spied me looking at it and out of habit I braced myself for a litany of jeers. *Scat! Filthy vermin! Shoo!* I ran through my mental bag of tricks—a riddle, a sleight of hand—to soothe his temper, but instead of a jeer he began a pitch that I was all too familiar with—the pitch that was always reserved for *others*. On the outside, I appeared to be one of those others now, but on the inside I would always be that girl who was ready to run.

"You have a discerning eye!" he said, his hands moving with enthusiasm as he spoke. "This ring is a rare find! A singular and scarce, splendiferous spangle! Pure gold and the finest of silver!"

I doubted that it was real silver and gold at all.

"You deserve such a treasure! A dazzling delectation for a delightful lady!" he went on with exaggerated flourish, his tongue twisting with glee over his descriptions. "For you, today, I will cut the price in half. Ten gralos!"

I smiled and shook my head. "Not today—"

"But wait!" he said, grabbing my hand. "You must try it on! It was made for your exquisite hand." He was a short, stout man, his face cheerful and round-cheeked with lines etched around his eyes.

"Your tongue is golden sir, and your words alluring, but I cannot afford to spend coin on a luxury like this."

He slipped the ring on my finger. "There. It's yours! Surely you have something to offer me in return?"

His methods were certainly different from merchants in the *jehendra*. He seemed as eager to engage as he was to sell. I smiled, thinking for a moment. "I can only offer you this as a testament to your mastery of persuasion. A riddle crafted just for you."

His eyes lit up and his long wiry brows twitched with delight. He waited with anticipation. I added extra theatrics as a bonus just for him.

"I have no fingers, but can pick you apart,

"I'm not a healer, but can mend a heart,

"I amuse and hush, deceive and astound,

"And there's no sword forged that can cut me down.

"With rosy enticement, and pouty appeal,

"I can twist and shape and pour forth zeal,

"I am made of snare, and wit, and gold,

"And you, kind sir," I said as I held the ring back out to him, "add a touch of bold."

With my last phrase, he clapped his hands with jubilation. "Words?" he cackled. "Yes, words!" he said, spouting the answer again. "The joy of my trade!" He curled my fingers back around the ring in my palm. "A fair payment, bought and paid for."

The more I refused the more he insisted, and I finally thanked him for his generosity and moved on. I hadn't gotten far when someone fell into step beside me, someone as welcome as a flea on a scalp.

"I've never seen that old curd quite so enamored with anything besides his own wares."

It was Paxton.

"He's a logophile."

Paxton clucked and wrinkled his nose. "That sounds nasty."

I was pleased that, courtesy of the Royal Scholar, I knew a word that the very polished Paxton didn't know.

"What do you want, Paxton?" I asked, hoping to be rid of him as quickly as possible.

He started to link his arm with mine. "Ah. Careful there. Only if you wish to lose it," I said, eyeing his arm.

He glanced at the dagger at my side, then grinned. "We're practically cousins. I thought it would be a good idea for us to get to know each other. Be friends."

"I think I know enough about you already. I got quite an eyeful the first time I saw you."

"At the funeral? Emotions were high. In runs in the Ballenger blood."

"Not Jase's."

Paxton tweaked his head slightly forward, eyeing my bruised neck. "Yes, maybe especially his."

I pulled my hair forward to hide his view. He turned and looked up at the towers above us, shaking his head. "No doubt he's spotted me strolling with you by now, so it's time for me to take my leave. Just remember, I'm a Ballenger too, and not an unpleasant one most of the time. I hardly ever break wind at the table anymore." When I didn't smile he took my hand, at risk of losing his, and squeezed it gently. "If you're ever in need of assistance, I'm here for you. Tread carefully, cousin. Remember, everyone is not always what they seem to be, and crossing the wrong person can get you into more trouble than you bargained for."

Was he threatening me? "Sage advice I didn't ask for," I replied, "but I'll keep that in mind—"

"Paxton?" a voice called. "I thought it was you!"

Paxton spun, his composure shaken for a moment, when a man in dusty, rumpled clothes clapped him on the shoulder. He quickly regrouped, and his worry sprang into a wide smile. "This is an unexpected pleasure!"

The man was tall, lean, his cheekbones sharp, and his attention turned to me. His dark, windblown hair swayed perilously to the side like a cresting wave, as if he had just gotten off a horse and hadn't bothered to rake it back into place.

"And who would this delightful creature be?" he asked. "Are you forgetting your manners, Paxton?" The man grinned and his fingers tapped together like an eager child.

"Uh, yes, of course," Paxton muttered, glancing up at the towers again. "Your Majesty, this is Kazi of Brightmist, a visiting soldier sent by the Queen of Venda."

I stared at the man, from his lopsided mane of hair, to his smudged boots, to his foolish grin. "Your Majesty?"

"King Monte of Eislandia," Paxton clarified.

The king clasped his hands in front of him, his brows and shoulders rising with expectation. "Do I get even a small bow?"

A buffoon just as Jase had described. A buffoon with an ego. "Yes, of course, Your Majesty." I bowed low and deep, and when I rose his dark eyes danced with amusement. And maybe something else. Expectation? Was he hoping for just a little groveling? "Forgive me for my lapse," I said. "I meant no disrespect. I just didn't expect to see you here. It's a great honor to meet you."

His grin wavered. "Yes, I suppose it is."

I looked at his hands. They were uncalloused and his nails were neat and manicured, not the hands of a working farmer. A silent moment passed, his gaze resting on me for an extra beat, just long enough for me to see unease behind his jolly banter. "What brings you to the arena?" I asked.

"Llama. Suri, to be precise," he answered. "Such is the life of a farmer king—always trying to make ends meet. I hear the Candorans have some fine breeding stock to offer. *If* I can afford it, that is." He chuckled and raised his shoulders again like everything was a jest. "And how are your investigations of treaty violations going?" he asked, at last making the connection between Natiya visiting him and why I was here.

"Quite well, Your Majesty." I wasn't about to tell him that the settlement had been moved. The less said, the better.

Paxton stared at me, his expression hungry for more information, but I left my answer short and vague.

"Is it now?" the king answered. "That's good to hear." He turned to Paxton, already bored with the subject. "Walk with me to the Candoran stables, will you? We're preparing to forge more plows and farm equipment, and I have a question about your next shipment of pig iron. I have a supplier who claims he can give me a better deal." They said their good-byes to me and I watched them walk away, *straza* and the king's small contingent following close behind, but between the mass of bodies I caught sight of the king as he turned to Paxton, glancing back over his shoulder, his clownish grin gone, his eyes sharp and alert. A *straza* suddenly blocked my view, but when he stepped away again I saw the king fingering something in his vest pocket. Had Paxton just given him something? Or was the king about to give it to Paxton?

I took my newly acquired ring and placed it on my little finger, where it was loose, and then cut through the stalls to the other side of the arena. I circled around on the main path and walked, looking down, admiring my ring, carefully sidestepping other shoppers until I spotted smudged boots in my small line of vision and plowed headlong into their owner, nearly knocking both of us down. The king caught me in his arms as we stumbled together, my hands gripping his sides.

I looked up. "Oh, Your Majesty! I am so very sorry. What an oaf I am! I wasn't paying attention. My ring—"

His hands lingered on my arms, pulling me a bit closer than necessary, as if I still needed to be steadied, and he smiled—not with his inane grin this time, but one that hinted at a different kind of interest. "We meet again so soon. No harm done," he replied, suddenly gallant. "There, I see your ring. Let me." He bent, picking it up, then blew the dust away, before placing it back in my hand.

"Thank you," I said, smiling demurely.

Paxton's eyes glowed with suspicion. "Watch your step," he warned. "You might run into something more dangerous next time."

We tear the pages out and burn another book. Miandre cries as she holds her shivering hands to the fire. She wants to go outside and gather wood instead, but Greyson won't let her. We hear the howls. We don't know if it is wolves, monsters, or men.

—Fujiko, 11

CHAPTER FORTY-ONE

KAZI

MY BLOOD STILL RACED WITH EXHILARATION. STEALING FROM
a king was a first for me, especially with a contingent of guards and
straza standing nearby, though the prize turned out to be less exciting
than what I had anticipated, merely a piece of paper with a name scrib-
bled on it—*Devereux 72*—perhaps the trader who had promised a better
deal on pig iron? Or maybe Paxton had slipped the king the name of his
new hawker who would meet the deal? I didn't know exactly what compelled me to go after it. Maybe it was the sly glance the king tossed over
his shoulder, his eyes suddenly sharp, a hint that something more pressing was on his mind than bidding on Suri.

Or maybe it was just seeing him walk beside Paxton. Everything
about Jase's cousin was suspect—and his arrogant warning words, *Tread
carefully*, didn't help to instill trust.

"Enjoying yourself?"

Another arena patron fell into step beside me, but this one was
welcome.

"Immensely," I answered. "It's been two hours. I've toured every floor, eaten at least a dozen oranges, and I've had my eye on a very clever and handsome llama."

"I have competition?" Jase asked. "Must be that long neck of his."

I laughed. "And his soulful eyes. Be worried. What delayed you?"

"My meetings ran long. So you met the king?"

I stopped and faced him. "How did you know?"

He shrugged deviously. "I told you, I have tricks too." But then he glanced up at the towers. "Every one of those is manned with my men and each has a spyglass. It helps keep trouble to a minimum."

So, they were watching me? How much did they see? But there was no hint of suspicion in Jase's tone or expression.

"What kind of trouble?" I asked.

"Pickpockets, petty thieves. Or sometimes a squabble breaks out and fists are involved."

"Then I suppose everyone must feel very safe here."

"That's the goal. When people relax, they spend money. What did you think of the king?" he asked.

"A buffoon just as you said. And not much of a farmer. His hands look like they've never wrestled anything more dangerous than a tea-cup. Did you know he'd be here?"

Jase nodded. "Gunner told me he was spotted coming in early this morning. Something about Suri breeding stock this time. It's always something new. The man doesn't know how to manage his own farm, much less an entire kingdom."

"Maybe he just needs more practice. How long has he been king?"

"Three or four years. That should be enough time to figure it out." He explained that Montegue became king at twenty when his father was crushed against a wall by a draft horse. "What about Paxton? What'd he want?" Every time Jase uttered Paxton's name there was a lethal edge to it.

"He wanted to be my *friend*," I answered. "And to warn me not to get mixed up with certain people. I wonder who he could mean?"

A vein twitched in Jase's neck. "If he comes near you again—"

"Then I will handle him again, pretty boy. Relax."

"*I'll* handle him, Kazi," Jase said firmly. "I've had my fill of his snide innuendo. Next time, he'll be swallowing a mouthful of teeth."

I wove my fingers into his, feeling his calluses, remembering him swinging axes and digging cellars, and I was grateful for the roughness of his hands. "Enough about Paxton. Show me the rest of your arena."

We headed toward the rear tunnel exit that led to the sprawling warehouses and stable grounds behind the arena—and to a livery. It was where Fertig used to work, and Jase wanted to ask a few questions. As we walked, Jase's mood lightened. Merchants greeted him with smiles and lighthearted humor, much of it directed at the lovely jewel gracing his very plain arm. Jase was pleased to see that Gunner had everything running smoothly in his absence—which eased my mind as well. I didn't want him to regret his time rebuilding the settlement. As we walked, I saw the relief and maybe even the pride in his face. There were hundreds of years of Ballenger history here, a legacy to keep secure, and it had all fallen on his shoulders so very recently. He was eager to point out every detail, drawing me deeper into another part of his world, and I happily fell into it.

We were halfway through the tunnel exit when a chill brushed my arms. It wasn't a breeze. I felt it circle. Cool fingers grazed my shoulders. My neck tingled. Then a quiet voice, *Go back.* A faint cold warning and then more followed in a rush. *Stop. Go back.* Glints of light spread in a line across the end of the tunnel, linked hands blocking our passage. *Do not pass this way.*

"What's wrong?" Jase asked. I hadn't realized I had stopped. People walked around us, continuing on through the tunnel.

A breeze lifted my hair. *Not this way.*

"Kazi?"

I felt for my dagger at my side, though the voices had now fallen silent. There were centuries of history here. I was bound to hear some of it. Death had passed this way many times. "Nothing, " I said, and we continued forward.

We emerged into a large square, the sun warming my skin again, the scent of pine easing my mood, everything in order and as calm as a bustling arena can be. Tall trees cut striped shadows across a plaza that was bordered by large warehouses and barns. I saw the livery ahead, but as we walked toward it I spotted something else tucked back in a dark shady corner. Wagons inside another warehouse were being loaded and covered with tarps. Something about them—

I stopped. "What is that, Jase?"

He hardly gave it a glance. "Just another warehouse," he answered, grabbing my elbow to urge me forward.

I pulled free. "What kind of warehouse?" I didn't wait for his answer. I was already walking toward it. I stopped just inside the gaping entrance. It was dark. Cool. My stomach hovered near my heart, everything inside of me light and airless, something taking hold of me, my steps moving all out of order. I was numb, part of me soaring above it all, watching. Three wagons were being loaded. Rope was woven over the tarps—tarps with black stripes. It was the stripes that stopped me. They were sharp nails dragging across my throat.

"Previzi," Jase said, coming up alongside me. "They operate out of this warehouse."

An enormous warehouse. I could see rows of other empty wagons stored along the side, waiting to be loaded. By now, several of the workers had noticed us standing at the entrance. I scanned their faces, none the one I searched for.

My skin. My eyes. Floating. Not part of me. My voice, barely mine, sounding like someone I didn't know. Young, fragile, breakable. A girl too afraid to run.

"But Previzi are illegal," I said. "They've been illegal for years. They're not allowed in the kingdoms." My voice still soft. Lost.

Jase hovered in a different world, strong, confident. "Maybe officially, but trust me, merchants in every kingdom eagerly buy from them. They provide—"

I spun, my voice stronger. "Provide what? Stolen merchandise?"

"Sometimes there's merchandise that—it doesn't quite—"

"What did you mean by 'operate'?" I asked.

He looked at me, confused, finally understanding that something was very wrong. "This is their base," he answered.

Base? "For how long? How long have they been based here?"

"Kazi, what difference—"

"How long?" My voice was loud now, a scream. The air shattered in fragments, every sound sharp in my ears.

"I'm not really sure."

"Eleven years, Jase? Have they been here for eleven years?"

He nodded. "At least."

Everything that had been weightless inside me was now molten, rushing in my head, burning my skin. "They're thieves! You're harboring thieves! They sell nothing but—"

"Kazi, lower your voice," Jase ordered between gritted teeth. Workers had stopped loading wagons and were listening. A crowd gathered just outside the door, watching. Jase leaned close. "The Previzi drivers are—"

"Predators!" I yelled. "Scum! And I will not lower my voice! How can you just look the other way—"

"Stop!" Jase ordered. He grabbed my arm and began pulling me away. I twisted free and my other arm swung, hitting him in the jaw. He stumbled back, incredulous, his eyes locked on mine, and then I ran. I was a girl running through the *jehendra*, through stalls, through shadows and mud and nightmares, a girl running with nowhere to go.

CHAPTER FORTY-TWO

JASE

I TOOK A FEW STEPS, WATCHING HER RUN AWAY, THEN TASTED the blood in my mouth. I touched my hand to my jaw.

"Should we go after her?" Titus asked. He and Gunner had been nearby when the shouting broke out.

I shook my head. "No, let her go." I already knew they'd never find her if she didn't want to be found. I was still trying to understand what had happened. I looked at the people who had stopped to watch. All the people who saw the *Patrei* get smacked in the chops by a Vendan soldier half his size.

And then a voice from behind me.

The wrong voice.

Clucking. Sighing. "Oh dear. A lover's quarrel? Affection is so fleeting, isn't it?"

When I turned, Paxton took a step back, his *straza* a step forward, maybe seeing something in my face.

It didn't do them any good. My fist shot out, sending Paxton flying to the ground.

"If they weren't broken before, they are now," Mason said. I winced as he pulled on my fingers and rewrapped my knuckles.

Gunner had brought some ice for my jaw. The inside of my mouth was raw where my teeth had sliced into it.

"She's got a helluva swing," Titus mused with admiration, ignoring that it was my mouth that was her target.

"What's going on?" Priya asked, walking through the foyer of the apartment.

"Apparently, Jase's favorite Vendan soldier doesn't approve of Previzi," Mason answered. "She gave him a stinging lecture about them in front of everyone."

"And she hit you?"

"She wasn't herself," I answered. But who was she? I didn't think she heard half of the things I said to her. She was transformed the minute she saw the Previzi warehouse. Their goods were sometimes questionable—but dammit, every kingdom dealt with them. Yes, we looked the other way. So did everyone else. They had merchandise people wanted. And they bought plenty of goods to trade here at the arena at a fair price too.

Priya's brows rose. "So Vendans are sticklers for the letter of the law?"

No. Kazi skirted too many edges to be a stickler. Something else bothered her. She had acted strange from the minute she stepped into the tunnel. Her eyes had been glazed.

"We'll go do damage control out in the arena," Priya said. "Say you two are cozy again and having a good laugh about it. Just a lover's spat. Enough saw you two all kissy and hand in hand today that they'll buy it." She paused, her hands on her hips. "And it's true, Jase, isn't it? Just a spat?"

I nodded. Maybe. I was still retracing all our steps and words.

"Well?" Gunner grumbled as he, Priya, and Titus walked out the door. "Go find her and actually get cozy again. We've got a queen on her way."

Mason stayed behind. He tied off the bandage and eyed the door waiting for it to shut. "I didn't want to bring this up in front of the others, but I thought I should mention it. Something a little peculiar."

I slid my tongue along the swollen flesh in my mouth. "Say it."

He told me the apothecary in town had approached him today and asked when we would be getting another shipment of birchwings in. He was out of stock and had a request from a patron.

"You know how often we get it, Mason. Once a year, twice if we're lucky." It was made from a fungus that grew like wings on birch limbs in the north. The Kbaaki brought it along with other potions they concocted. I didn't care about fungus right now. "He'll get it when he—"

"It's not about the birchwings. It's about who asked for it. Wren. And she asked for enough to knock out half the town."

"Maybe she just doesn't understand dosage."

He shook his head. "I gave her a small vial from the storeroom on the night of the party. She said she had a headache. I told her it was four doses' worth."

I remembered seeing the half-empty vial when I rummaged through Kazi's wardrobe for a shirt.

"Why do you suppose she'd want so much?" Mason asked.

I shrugged. "I don't know. Maybe to take back to Venda with them. They may not have medicine like that there." I stood. I had to go find Kazi. She was probably back at Tor's Watch by now. "Just keep an eye on our stockroom. Make sure it stays locked."

I was just stepping out the door when I ran into Garvin. I waved him off, saying we'd have to talk later. "I think you'll want to hear this now. It's about that girl from Brightmist."

My pulse raced a little faster. "Go ahead."

"I finally figured it out. I was in the tower, keeping an eye on her in the arena when it came to me. I saw her stumble into the king—deliberately. I think she nicked him."

"She *stole* from the king?"

"I can't be sure," he answered. "Not from way up in the tower. She was smooth. But she meant to run into him, I know that much. I watched her run between the stalls, circling around right into his path—and then her hands were all over him."

I ran my fingers through my hair, blowing out a frustrated breath. She didn't mention taking anything from the king. I looked back at Garvin. "You said you figured something out?"

"Her name. Ten. She was a petty thief in Venda. Probably the best."

CHAPTER FORTY-THREE

KAZI

My breath came in gulps. Eben's arms clamped around me. "Breathe, Kazi. Take it slow," he whispered in my ear.

Water steamed in a kettle. Hot bread lay on a rack. Half-chopped turnips were abandoned on the cutting board. Their voices were details, like the bread and steam and the stab in my throat, all of them splintering through me, as if I had stepped into a world that was exploding apart. Eben had seen me storm through the hallway and pulled me into the kitchen. Natiya's eyes loomed in and out of my vision. Wren bit her nail. Synové pulled on her braid. I closed my eyes.

As I hurried up the mountain, all I could think was, *Eleven years.* For eleven years, the driver had been coming and going with the Ballengers' blessing. He was here all along. This was where his journey began, where he slept and ate and bathed, where his life went on, when mine had stopped.

"Are you all right?"

All right? I made a vow. I had no choice but to be all right.

But my insides bled.

Drained through my pores.

Every part of me hollow again.

I remembered the brokenness.

The hunger.

The years vanished, and I was hiding under a bed again.

Where is the brat? Where is she?

In the warehouse, I had reached for my knife. I was ready to kill them all, just as I had been when I'd gone after the ambassador. It was only the flash of the prison I had landed my whole crew in that made me stop.

The man who took my mother was here. Somewhere. And if he wasn't here today, he'd roll in on a wagon tomorrow, or the next day, and when he did I would do something that would jeopardize everyone in this room because he mattered to me more than a thousand valleys piled with dead. I craved justice for one.

I need you, Kazimyrah. I believe in you.

I floated between worlds, between oaths and fear, promises and justice—between love and loathing.

"Drink this," Natiya ordered.

Eben loosened his hold, and I took the water Natiya held out to me. I finished the glass and asked for more, turning away, leaning against the counter, molding composure the way I did when my next meal depended on it. A hundred tricks, one piled on another, fooling myself that I could do it, digging my nails into my palms until one pain masked another that I couldn't bear.

I downed the second glass of water and finally turned back to face them. I told them about the Previzi warehouse.

Anger pinched Wren's face. "Previzi? *Based here?*"

"And the welcome mat is rolled out for them," I confirmed. "Something else happened too. I punched the *Patrei* in the face."

A deep silence fell in the room.

"Did you knock any teeth out?" Synové finally asked, a certain desperation in her wink and smile.

"If I did, it wasn't enough."

Natiya sighed. "You'll have to smooth it over with him until we leave. An apology—"

I would not apologize. Ever. "We leave tomorrow," I said.

"But—"

"*With* our quarry," I added. "I know where the captain is—at least I think I do."

I told them my hunch. It was Jase who had given me the answer. And Priya. And my own forgotten wishes that my mother and I had had a second way out.

As I had escaped from the arena, as Mije gave me all he was worth racing up the back trail to Tor's Watch, I heard Priya speaking again, *They escaped down another path*, and then Jase, *Every good stronghold has more than one way out. Otherwise you could be trapped.*

Another way out.

<hr/>

Wren and Synové came with me.

"You might hear voices," I warned Synové. "They're harmless. You'll be fine. Just stay close."

We casually sauntered through the gardens, smiling in case anyone watched, turning, pointing at butterflies that didn't exist, and when each of us had scanned the grounds and the windows that looked down on us and had given the all clear, we walked down the path that led to the rear entrance of Darkcottage. We quietly slipped inside and I eased open a shutter in the kitchen, just a crack to give us some light. We only used hand signals. I pointed to the stairs that led to the cellar. I went first, made sure the room was empty, then signaled for them to follow. Except for a circle of dim light at the base of the stairs, the room was completely black.

I had already told them to feel the walls for hinges, handholds, loose stones, anything that could be moved, to look for cracks of light, and feel for drafts. We moved silently and slowly, careful not to make any sound that might reveal us. The cellar was large, and it was slow work moving in the dark. I reached the end of one solid wall and started on another, meeting Synové in the middle. Nothing. I was still certain—

And then Wren ticked a soft sound, one that could be mistaken for a creak in an old house. She found it—on the wall that supported the stairs—a draft between panels. We listened, and when we were sure there was nothing immediately behind the panel, I pressed on it. It sprang open a crack, and we stepped into the end of a very long tunnel. At the other end was a door with a thin line of light streaming from the bottom of it. Once we started down, we'd have no cover. We'd be open targets if someone should enter from the other end. The only weapons we had were the daggers at our sides. Carrying a bow and a quiver of arrows through the gardens would have been too conspicuous.

"Ready?" I whispered.

They nodded. We crept down the tunnel, the only sound my pulse drumming in my ears as we neared the door. I put my hand out to have them wait while I carefully eased forward to make sure there were no alcoves for dogs to hide in. It was clear and I put my ear to the door, then gently squeezed the latch. Our breaths caught at the faint *click*. I eased it open a hair's width at a time and cool fresh air rushed in, green with the scent of soil and grass. The other side of the door was stone that matched its surrounding walls, impossible to see unless you knew it was there. I peeked out on a large empty terrace, almost like a foyer, that had several arched passageways intersecting it. The one straight ahead emptied out onto rolling empty grounds covered with grass, still lit by the fading light of dusk. But something in the distance at the far end of the grounds caught my eye—a wide curved double door set into a stone wall—a door that was strangely familiar.

Stand watch, I signaled to Wren and Synové as I stepped out onto the terrace, carefully hugging the walls and shadows. At the end of the terrace, I looked across the grassy grounds at the distant door, and I realized I was looking at a door I had already seen—but I had seen it from the other side. Jase had claimed it was only another exit. *There's nothing on the other side.*

Except all of this.

A cold fist gripped my spine.

All of this.

I looked up at the roof of a cave that seemed as high as the sky. It swept out over half the grounds like a wave poised to crash. Tendrils of vines hung from its ceiling. Tucked below it against its wall was a long house, shallow in depth, with multiple staggered terraces. Only steps away was another outbuilding. Where the wall of cave ended, more of the fortress wall began, obstructing it all from view. It was a hidden enclave right within Tor's Watch.

I skulked along the outside wall of the house, just another shadow creeping across its porches, hiding behind pillars, peeking in windows. I passed room after room of bedchambers and sitting rooms.

And then I heard a low rumble of voices. I stopped and sweat flashed over my skin. I was both eager and afraid of what I would find. I listened, but the words were indiscernible. I moved closer to the sound, then ducked behind a pillar when I saw someone cross a room with doors that opened onto the broad terrace.

"Save some for me. We're almost out."

Another voice.

"More comes in the morning."

"Morning is not now."

And still another voice.

"It will be a shame when this party is all over."

"This party won't end. Thanks to the Ballengers, our riches will only become greater."

Laughter erupted.

"The Great Battle will look like a spring picnic."

"Soon all the kingdoms will be under our thumb. We'll say jump, and they'll ask how high."

"Especially that bitch in Venda."

"She'll be in for a surprise when she arrives, and it won't be a royal welcome."

"She'll finally get what's coming to her."

"A noose."

There was a murmur of agreement.

"I still don't like that he took our only working weapon."

"Within a week, we'll have an arsenal. One small weapon won't matter. He's probably already used up all the loads practicing on trees."

There was a hearty round of guffaws.

A noose? An arsenal of weapons?

"I'm going to need more supplies."

"No worries. The Ballengers are generous. They'll give us more. They're as eager for this as we are."

More laughter.

Eager for what? What were Jase and his family planning? All the kingdoms under their thumbs? Was inviting the queen here only a trap?

"To the Ballengers, our generous patrons."

I heard the clink of glasses lifted in a toast, a chuckle, and then a long unapologetic belch, followed by a stumble, a curse, and a wail as a shin or knee met an immovable object. I used that moment to peek around the pillar.

It was the first thing I saw—a clear view of a moon-shaped scar on a wide forehead. My attention jumped to a deep cleft in a stubbled chin, and the man who wore both so infamously had white hair. It wasn't Erdsaff but Captain Illarion.

Jase's manipulations piled on. He had fed me one lie after another.

Then the captain and two other men I didn't recognize stepped aside and my throat went dry.

Sitting on a divan behind them was Governor Sarva of Balwood. He was the one who had led the attack against the clans in Blackstone Square. After the Great Battle, all that was found of him was part of his charred breastplate with the Balwood insignia. He was believed dead. Sitting beside him was Chievdar Kardos, swigging back a mug of ale, another member of the Komizar's Council who was unaccounted for but believed dead. And seated at a table near them, picking at meat on a trencher and licking his fingers, was Bahr, one of the Sanctum guards in the clan attack—

I pushed back behind the pillar, pressing against it.

How would I tell Synové?

Everything had just gotten more complicated. These men were as vile as the captain, maybe worse, hated criminals of Venda. My mind whirled. Jase was harboring them all. A sour taste swelled on my tongue. *This beast will turn and kill you.* Now we had many beasts.

Take them all back? We had to. But was that even possible?

Maybe, I thought. Maybe there was one way.

I was going to need a hay wagon.

When we were safely back in the kitchen at Darkcottage, I told them.

"Yes, the captain's there. It was him with the white hair just as I thought."

Wren blew out a long slow breath. We had done it. We had finally found him.

"But that's not all," I added cautiously. "There are five others." I looked at Synové and pressed her shoulders against the wall, trying to stave off her reaction. "One of them is Bahr."

Synové shook her head. "But he's dead. In the battle. He—"

"No," I said.

Her mouth opened, and I clapped my hand over it before she could scream. Muffled noises leaked between my fingers. Wren helped me hold her back, both of us using all our weight to keep her pinned in place. Tears streamed down her cheeks.

"We'll take him back," I whispered, "just like the others."

She moaned a violent muffled objection.

"He will pay," Wren promised. "But he goes back to face justice, like the queen wanted. The long ride will be the best torture we could inflict." The *chievdar* who had killed Wren's parents had died in battle, but her lip trembled and her eyes brimmed with tears too, knowing Synové's pain as her own.

We stayed in our tense knot, holding back and holding on, Synové's heaving breaths the only sounds in the room. Her shoulders finally went limp beneath our hands. Her breathing calmed, and she nodded, resigned to her vows and duty.

Evening was quickly falling, and we returned to the main house with our plan still forming, my hands still salty with Synové's tears. We were just inside the door when I heard the dogs loosed.

My legs ached as I walked the final steps back to my room, as if every bit of strength had finally been wrung from them. I was already raw with pain of my own, and Synové's agony had only deepened it.

I dreaded dinner tonight. I dreaded seeing Jase. How could I pretend I didn't know?

How could he have hidden all this from me? Doors guarded by poisonous dogs that he claimed led nowhere? An invitation to the queen that was really a trap? A groundsman who was really a murderous fugitive? Weapons to dominate all the kingdoms?

His little enclave was a dragon's dark den.

Fool me once, Jase.

My thoughts jumped, my own words taunting me. *The thing about a mark is they've created lies in their head, a story they've invented that they desperately want to believe, a fantasy that merely needs to be fed.*

But this time it was I who had been that round-mouthed fish breaking the surface of the water, following crumb after crumb, swallowing each one whole.

I was the mark, the witless dupe of my own game.

And Jase had played me expertly.

CHAPTER FORTY-FOUR

KAZI

"WHERE HAVE YOU BEEN, KAZI?"

I gasped, whirling toward the voice.

Jase sat in the chair in the corner of my room. In the dark.

"Here, let me." He reached out and turned the wheel on the bedside lantern just until I could see him, the rest of the room still cast in shadows.

His face and voice were frighteningly void of any expression. "You didn't answer me," he said. "I've been waiting quite a while. Where have you been?"

You'll have to smooth it over with him.

Apologize.

Juggle, Kazi. Juggle as you always do.

"None of your business," I answered. "Get out."

I had no juggling left in me. Not in this moment. Not for him.

His expression barely flinched. Just the slightest lift of his chin. Cold. Detached.

He stood.

"I think I see the problem here. I didn't address you properly. I apologize. I should have called you *Ten*."

He took a step closer, his shoulders pulled back. He knew. My stomach squeezed. "I—"

"*Don't*," he warned, his gaze as sharp as a razor, his cool veneer vanished. "Don't even try to deny it. It's all obvious now, palming the keys, my ring, disappearing right beneath our noses, the girl at the settlement calling you *Ten* and you shutting her up." His nostrils flared. "It's ironic, don't you think, all that self-righteous indignation you flung at me when we were in the wilderness because *I* was a thieving Ballenger. I should be laughing, shouldn't I?"

He strained to keep his fury in check, but even in the dim light I saw his temples burning with fire. "And then today?" He stroked the bruise on his jaw where I had struck him. "In front of *everyone* at the arena, you screamed and lectured me on the Previzi, when you were nothing but a common thief yourself! Is that why you hate them so much, because they remind you of *you*?"

My hands trembled. I swallowed, trying to maintain control. "Get out of my room, Jase, before I hurt you."

He stepped toward me. "I expect an answer, dammit!"

"You mean you demand it, *Patrei*, don't you?" I spit back at him. "Because you get whatever you want! You take whatever you want! You do whatever you want!"

His eyes sparked, dissecting me, judging, blazing. The bruise on the side of his face was an angry purple. "I'm not leaving," he growled. "Not until I get an answer."

My nails dug into my palms.

He didn't blink. He would wait here until morning if he had to, fueling his own self-righteousness. My own rage suddenly tipped beyond a point I recognized, seams coming loose, ripping, popping, everything tearing free. "All right, Jase," I yelled, "here's your answer! Yes, I was a thief! But don't you dare call me a common one!"

I flung my hands up in front of me. "Look at my fingers, Jase! Take a good long look at every single one, because I'm not missing any. *That's* how I got my name! And I'm proud of it! In Venda, before the queen came, the Komizar's punishment for stealing was cutting off a fingertip—even if you were a child! Even if you only stole a handful of bread!

"I was alone on the streets from the time I was six. Completely on my own. No one cared if I lived or died. Can you imagine that, Jase? I didn't grow up like *you*." I heard my voice getting louder, more heated, more poisonous, more out of control. I didn't pace, didn't move. I was a stone rooted to the floor. "I stole to survive! I had no family. No dining room table to sit at and pass pretty dishes. No carpets under my feet or chandeliers over my head. No servant to bring me food. No parties in the garden. I had to scavenge for every rotten mouthful I ever ate. I had no coats made by tailors. I wore rags upon rags to stay warm in winter. I lived in a hovel carved out of fallen ruins. No heat! No hot baths! No soap! If I did bathe at all, it was in icy water in the public washbasins. Sometimes I cut my hair off with a knife, because it was so infested with vermin I couldn't feel my own scalp!"

I stepped over to his bookshelf and swiped an armful of books to the floor. "And I had no tutors, no books, no pens or paper! If it couldn't be eaten, it had no use for me. My whole life revolved around my next meal and how to get it. I lived on the edge of death every day of my life until I became good at thieving, and I won't apologize for it!"

His face had changed, the hardness gone, probably trying to imagine the filthy urchin I had once been. "What about your parents?" he asked.

The poison racing through me pooled to ice in my veins. I shook my head. "I never knew my father. I don't know if he's alive, dead, or the emperor of the moon! I don't care!"

I looked down. I knew what was coming next. The thing that always hung between us. Every other question was hinged to this one, a thousand doors opening a single doorway.

"And your mother? What happened to her?"

I had never told anyone. Shame and fear perched in my gut, ready to spring. My jaws ached, the words wedged behind them. I turned away and walked toward the door.

"Fine!" he yelled. "Run away! Shut yourself off like you always do! Go live in whatever prison you've created for yourself!"

I stopped at the door, shaking with rage. *The prison that I created?* A furious cloud swirled in my vision. I whipped back to face him, and his eyes latched onto mine.

"Tell me, Kazi."

Clamminess crept over my skin, and I leaned against the door to steady myself. I felt some part of me splitting in two, one part still cowering, the other watching from a thousand miles away like an uncertain observer. "I was six when my mother was taken," I said. "It was the middle of the night, and we were lying together on a raised pallet in our hovel. I was asleep when I felt her finger on my lips and heard her whisper. *Shhh, Kazi, don't say a word.* Those were the last words she ever said to me. She shoved me to the floor to hide me beneath the bed. And then—"

I looked up at the ceiling, my eyes stinging.

"And then what, Kazi?"

My shoulders twitched, everything inside me shrinking, resisting. "I watched. From beneath the bed, I watched a man come into our home. We had no weapons, only a stick propped in the corner. My mother tried to get to it. She didn't make it in time. I wanted to run to her, but we had signals, and she signaled me to be quiet and not move. So I didn't. I just lay there cowering beneath the bed while the man drugged my mother and carried her away. He said he'd get a good price for her. She was merchandise. He wanted me too, but couldn't find me. *Come out, girl*, he yelled, but I didn't move. My mother lied and told him I wasn't there."

My vision blurred and Jase grew fuzzy. "I lay in my own waste for two days under that bed, shaking, crying, too afraid to move. I was terrified he'd come back. He didn't. Neither did she. It took me years to learn how to sleep on top of a bed again. You asked me why an open world frightens me, Jase? Because it gives me nowhere to hide. That's been my prison for eleven years, but trust me, I didn't create it."

I blinked, clearing my eyes, and I saw the dawning in his face. "Eleven years. That's why you wanted to know how long—"

"That's right, Jase. He was a Previzi driver. While I was starving and freezing and thieving on the streets of Venda, and my mother ended up the gods know where, you were providing him with a warm, safe home. How wonderful for him."

"That was eleven years ago. How can you be sure he was even Previzi? Your memory—"

"*Don't!* Don't you *dare* question my memory!" I growled. "I'm good at details, and I've had to live with those every day since I was six! Some days, I've prayed to the gods that I could forget! He drove in on a wagon that morning—four black stripes on his tarp!"

Jase was well aware that was a distinguishing mark of the Previzi.

"You were six years old! It was the middle of the night! It might not have even been the same man! He might—"

"He was tall, Jase—like you! But thin, bony. He had dead white skin and long strands of greasy black hair. His eyes were shiny beads of onyx. You know the new cook's husband? Except for the eyes, he looked remarkably like him. I'm guessing he's about thirty-five by now. And his hands—as he forced drugs down my mother's throat, I saw the dark hair on his knuckles and a large mole on his right wrist! How's *that* for details?"

He didn't answer, as if he was already digging through eleven years of memories.

"You may have been a child eleven years ago too, but you know them all by now," I said. "Is there a driver who fits that description?"

"No!" he shouted, throwing his hands in the air. He turned away and paced the room. "There are no drivers like that!"

"How can—"

There was a tap at the door.

I turned, swallowing my next words. We both stared at the door. Another light tap. I crossed the room and opened it.

Lydia and Nash stood side-by-side, their eyes wide and worried.

"Nash. Lydia." I didn't know what else to say.

"Were you two fighting?" Nash asked. His voice was small, delicate, and it stabbed me with its innocence. I stared into his frightened eyes. He looked like he had been punched in the stomach. I hated how easily innocence could be robbed—how quickly a child could go from plucking wish stalks at a pond's edge to clutching stolen bread beneath a coat.

I knelt so we were eye to eye. "No, of course not." I forced a smile. "Just a loud discussion."

"But . . . you were crying." Lydia reached out and wiped under my eye.

"Oh, that." I quickly swiped my hands over my cheeks. "Only dust in my eyes from a long, galloping ride," I said. "But what's this?" I reached behind both of their ears and frowned. "Did you two forget to wash today?"

They grinned with wonder as I pulled a coin from behind each of their ears and clucked with feigned dismay. I tucked the coins into their palms.

"What did you two want?" Jase asked.

"Mama wants Kazi to come down for supper early so she can talk about food."

"The kind the queen likes!" Lydia added.

Jase told them we'd be down shortly. I watched them race along the hallway, laughing, forgetting about the shouting they'd heard, the tears they saw, and I wished all memories could be erased so easily.

CHAPTER FORTY-FIVE

JASE

NASH SWIRLED HIS CREAMED SQUASH INTO THREE GREEN CIRCLES.
I looked at his small fingers gripping his spoon, playing with his food the
same way I had when I was six. Lydia arranged the pieces of meat that
Mother had cut for her into a sunburst around her plate.

I was on the streets from the time I was six.

I couldn't imagine either Nash or Lydia fending for themselves. I
couldn't imagine them being all alone and the terror they would feel. I
couldn't imagine that they would survive at all.

Look at my fingers, Jase! Take a good long look.

An image of Kazi's long beautiful fingers with missing tips kept seeping through my mind. Why didn't she tell me before? All the times in
the wilderness when I had asked—

I didn't grow up like you.

I had never seen a single tear in Kazi's eye. Not when she ran across
burning sands that blistered her feet. Not when a labor hunter hit her
across her face. Not when a raider nearly choked the life from her. But

this, a memory eleven years old, made her unravel. I watched her struggle to hold it back, like she was trying to dissect her feelings from the facts.

But when Lydia and Nash came to the door, she steeled herself and became someone else. *How do you do that?* I had asked as we walked to dinner, *How do you go from anguish to pulling coins out from behind ears?*

It's an acquired skill, Jase. Something all thieves learn.

I heard the sarcasm in her reply. I knew what she thought I had meant, that even her tears had been a shallow act. It was just the opposite. I watched her sacrifice part of herself for their sakes, like hiding a bleeding limb behind her back and pretending she wasn't in pain.

"Jase, you're picking at your food," Priya said, waving her fork at me. "You're not hungry?"

I looked at my plate, untouched.

I had no servant to bring me food.

No parties in the garden.

I wore rags upon rags to stay warm in winter.

I remembered in the wilderness when she was ready to eat minnows before we had cooked them. *I had to scavenge for every rotten mouthful I ever ate.* And now I knew—there were worse things than raw minnows, and she had eaten them.

My mother eyed my full plate. "I can ask Natiya to fix you something else if you like?"

"No," I replied. "This is fine." I stabbed a piece of meat and chewed.

I made more of an effort to concentrate on the multiple conversations running around the table. They seemed fuller and louder tonight. Maybe it was an effort to avoid any uncomfortable silences. An effort to cover Jalaine's absence. To avoid the obvious—Kazi's outburst at the arena—though the evidence on my jaw was a little harder to ignore. Lydia had asked me what happened. "A fall," I answered, and that wasn't far from the truth. I had told Garvin to keep his revelation just between us, so at least no one knew she had once been a thief.

And maybe, on occasion, she still was.

She nicked the king.

What did she take from him? And why?

There were still so many questions I hadn't asked. Things I wanted to know. How does an orphaned street thief become a premier guard of the queen? Where had she been in those hours I couldn't find her? But after Lydia and Nash left, she went into the bath chamber and closed the door. I heard her running water and splashing her face. When she came out, the redness in her eyes was gone, but it felt like she still teetered on an edge and I was afraid to push her over it. My questions retreated. At least for a little while.

"More ale, *Patrei?*" Natiya stood next to me, a pitcher poised in her hand over my drained tankard.

I nodded. "Thank you."

Apparently I was more thirsty than I was hungry.

Synové was always chatty, but tonight more so, hardly finishing one sentence before she began another. Even Wren, the quiet one with searing eyes who always filled me with some level of trepidation, was more talkative than usual. Aram and Samuel hung on every word as she explained the history of the *ziethe,* a weapon of the Meurasi clan that she hailed from.

Kazi spoke enthusiastically with my mother about foods the queen preferred, as if we hadn't just had a screaming conversation in her room. As if she hadn't just broken down and sobbed in front of me. As if none of it had happened at all.

"Maybe we can meet with the cook in the morning," Kazi said, "and discuss which dishes she would recommend. I know the queen has a fondness for vagabond food."

Something about it all was off.

It didn't feel right.

The cook and her husband had come in several times to replenish dishes or take them away. I stared at the husband each time. He was reserved, aloof, the opposite of his wife. Since they had been here, she had expressed her gratitude to me several times for giving them work. The first day, she had patted her abdomen and said their family would soon be expanding, so she was especially grateful. He had shown no emotion. He just kept going about his work in the kitchen, chopping vegetables with quick smooth movements. She was right about one thing; he was good with a knife.

And Kazi was right about another thing—his appearance. Now every time he walked through the kitchen door his appearance turned my stomach.

What I had told Kazi was true. There was no Previzi driver who looked like him.

But there used to be.

Now he worked for us.

My father had hired him a year ago.

———❦———

She's racked with guilt, Jase. I've tried talking to her. You have to speak to her.

My mother had intercepted me after dinner, pulled me aside. *Talk to her.*

I watched Kazi walk away to her room—our room. I wanted to go after her, but I saw the worry in my mother's eyes.

I tapped on Jalaine's door and called to her.

She didn't answer.

I knocked a little louder.

"Jalaine, open up. I need to talk to you."

A Patrei *never apologizes for decisions he's made.* And my father never did. This was one of his deathbed instructions—right after he had said I'd be faced with countless decisions. I didn't regret pulling Jalaine from the arena. I didn't regret our talk in the study or reprimanding her, but my anger was still loose and hot when we were in the dining room that night. When I had seen Kazi pinned beneath Fertig and soaked in blood, something furious and ugly had ripped through me. I wanted to tear something apart. Or someone. I shamed Jalaine in front of the family.

She was sixteen years old. She made a mistake. A serious one that nearly cost us our lives, but she was still my sister. She was family. And *Patreis* made mistakes too.

"I shouldn't have shamed you in front of the family," I whispered through the door. "I'm sorry."

There was no answer.

If the job of Patrei *were easy, I would have given it to someone else.*

Sometimes, I wished he had. I wasn't just having to live with my bad decisions, but his too, even decisions that seemed right at the time but now were all wrong, ones that had grown rotten over time, like forgotten eggs in the larder.

I stepped lightly through the hall, careful not to wake anyone. I had a new understanding of my father. There were decisions he had made that I had vehemently disagreed with. Decisions he put off that I railed against. And decisions he had made that I never blinked at. Like hiring Previzi drivers.

How can you look the other way?

And now I couldn't. Kazi had described Zane, our man who

coordinated deliveries at the arena, and the only one we trusted to make discreet deliveries to Beaufort. We didn't want it to become common knowledge that he and his men were here. Zane was thirty-three, an older version of the cook's husband.

"Mason," I whispered and pushed his shoulder to wake him.

He lunged from his sleep, knocking me to the floor, a knife in his hand.

He blinked, realizing it was me. "Are you crazy?" he asked, his eyes wild, still coming awake. "I could have killed you."

I should have known better than to push his shoulder to wake him. Mason always slept with a knife under his pillow. He was too young to remember details about his parents' deaths, but he still had vague haunting memories of the night they died. They were killed in their sleep— an attack by a league that no longer existed. My father had wiped them out. Mason's father was my father's closest friend. That was when he became part of our family.

"It's the middle of the night," he groaned, still annoyed. "What do you want?" He pushed off me and stood, giving me a hand up.

"I'm hungry."

"*Hungry?*"

"Let's go to the kitchen and find something to eat."

He hissed but grabbed a shirt from the end of his bed and pulled it over his head.

I lit an oil lamp and brought a pitcher of milk from the larder and two thick slabs of currant cake.

"We haven't done this in a while," Mason said, more of a question than a statement. Middle-of-the-night visits to the kitchen were reserved for disasters or planning for them. A few embers still glowed through the grill on the stove. The quiet of a midnight kitchen seemed quieter than anywhere else in the house, maybe because in a large family like ours it was usually filled with so much noise—the constant sounds of dough being punched, dishes clattering, meat being cleaved, the cutting, the stirring, the pouring, the chatter, and someone always coming in for a taste. It was the most comforting room of the house, its sole purpose to nurture. Maybe that's why I wanted to talk to Mason here.

He looked at me, waiting. "You should have eaten dinner." He knew this wasn't about being hungry.

"You know Zane?" I asked.

He grabbed forks from the sideboard drawer. "What kind of question is that? Of course I do."

I set the plates on the kitchen table, and we both pulled out chairs and sat. "What I mean is, do you know details about him? The routes he drove when he was a Previzi? Maybe most important, do you remember . . . does he have a mole on his wrist?"

Mason's brows pulled down. "What's going on?"

I explained why Kazi reacted the way she had when she saw the Previzi at the arena, and how she had described Zane to me right down to his greasy black hair.

Mason hissed, trying to absorb it. "On her own since she was six?"

I nodded but didn't tell him how she survived as an orphan.

He cut off a piece of his cake with the side of his fork. "I don't know about routes, maybe Zane went to Venda, but I do remember his wrist." He looked up at me and sighed. "There's a large mole."

If Kazi had remembered correctly, Mason and I both knew what it meant. Zane had a past with labor hunters. And that meant he probably had a present with them too. He wasn't just Kazi's problem. He might be ours too.

We agreed we were going to have to question him, carefully, so he wouldn't suspect anything. Previzi had the nose of a wolf and could sniff trouble before it arrived—and they were just as good at disappearing. If he thought we suspected him of being involved with the labor hunters who had come into Hell's Mouth, we'd never see him again. And if he was involved, we needed to know who he worked for—maybe the same person Fertig had taken orders from. We may have crippled their operations by killing twelve of their crew, but I wanted the rest of them too. I wanted them to pay for Samuel's hand, pay for torching the Vendan settlement, pay for burning homes in Hell's Mouth and stealing citizens off the street, pay for raiding caravans, pay for choking Kazi and nearly killing her. Their debt ran deep.

"It's hard to believe Zane's involved," Mason said. "He's a hard worker. Dependable."

"We'll find out. I have to make this right."

"Sorry, brother, but something like this can't be made right."

"But I can make sure it doesn't happen under our noses again." I told him I was calling a family meeting first thing in the morning— everyone's plans were on hold until we talked about ousting the Previzi or making them adhere to a new set of rules.

I rubbed my head. "There's something else," I said. And maybe it was my darker worry because I wasn't exactly sure what it was. It was something that didn't feel right. "Did you notice anything a little off at dinner tonight?"

He looked at me, surprised. "Yes . . . as a matter of fact, I did notice. Synové talked a lot, more than usual, but she was back to guessing my height, bringing up old conversations like she was distracted, like we had just met—"

"Like you hadn't already run your hands over every inch of her body?"

Mason lowered the forkful of cake he was about to shovel into his mouth.

"Yeah, I know about you two. Why'd you hide it from me?"

He moaned and leaned back in his chair. "I don't know. Embarrassed, I guess. After telling you not to get tangled up with Kazi—" He shook his head. "I don't know how I got mixed up with Synové, but she makes me laugh. And she is so damn . . ."

He didn't need to finish his sentence. His strong attraction to her was evident.

"What about you and Kazi?" he asked. "I thought we'd be getting a summons to the temple by now. What's holding you back?"

I looked down, mashing the crumbs on my plate with my fork. "She says she's bound by duty to go back to Venda. We avoid talking about the future, and I promised her I wouldn't bring it up again."

"But you—" He hesitated to use the word but finally said it anyway. "You love her?"

I looked up at him. Love didn't even seem like the right word to explain how I felt about her. The word seemed too small, too used, too simple, and everything I felt about her seemed complicated and rare and as wide as the world. I nodded.

He must have seen something in my expression. "She loves you too, brother. Don't worry. I'm sure of it. No one puts on an act that good."

I thought so too, but tonight I had seen hatred in her eyes. Even through tears, it was as pure and hot as molten glass. She and I never said the word *love*. It was a strange agreement between us and I wasn't sure why. Maybe it had started out in the wilderness. Everything about it was so temporary. But I had felt it growing then. *What is this, Kazi?* Because even then it felt like more, something lasting and sure. I know she felt it too. But there had been the secrets between us. I had lied about the settlement. She had lied to me about—

No one puts on an act that good. I looked back at Mason. "You didn't trust her when you first met her. What about now?"

He put his last forkful of cake into his mouth and washed it down with the rest of his milk. "It's hard not to trust someone when they've put their life on the line for you. They all did."

He stood, gathering his dishes and taking them to the sink. "Maybe tonight was off because Kazi was rattled by seeing the Previzi, and Synové and Wren were trying to fill all the gaps with talk. When Synové gets anxious, that's what she does. They're a close crew."

He was right. They were. And tonight, when I couldn't find Kazi, I couldn't find them either. I had gone to their rooms, trying to find her.

I stood and grabbed my dishes. "Go on to bed. I'll wash these. We'll talk more in the morning about Zane."

Mason left and I turned the tap, hot water splashing into the sink. Hot running water was a feature my grandfather had added to Tor's Watch. I had never thought much about it before. *I had no heat. No hot baths.* I saw everything through her eyes now. I had known Venda was poor, and Garvin had said Brightmist was the poorest quarter, and I had known her upbringing had been difficult but even my imagination hadn't plumbed the lonely depths she had to scrabble through. *No one cared if I lived or died.*

Maybe that was what was off. Me. Because every word she had said ate through me like a worm. I retraced our steps in the wilderness, seeing it differently, her feverish focus as we walked across an open plain, her dizzy steps when she looked up into a star-filled sky.

If Zane was responsible for this, he would pay.

After I put the dishes away, I paused, looking at the storage room just off the kitchen where the medicines were kept. I unlocked it and went inside. Vials and flasks, pouches and dried herbs were neatly ordered along the shelves. With so many at Tor's Watch—both family and workers—we kept a lot of remedies on hand. I found the canister labeled *Birchwings*—the one Wren had asked about. It was full. Enough to knock out half of Hell's Mouth. I thought about Mason's question again, *Why would she want that much?* My reply to him, that she wanted to take it back to Venda, seemed like a reasonable one. We had unusual merchandise from all over the continent here. There were probably a lot of wonders in Hell's Mouth that they would like to take back with them. Birchwings was only one of them.

When I left, I checked the lock on the door. It would be an easy five minutes for a common thief.

And less than that for an uncommon one.

CHAPTER FORTY-SIX

KAZI

IT WAS LATE MORNING, AND FRESH, SWEET HAY PERFUMED THE air. The groom whistled as he went about his work, and swallows darted through the rafters with morning meals for noisy hatchlings, a morning that at first glance was deceptively brushed with the perfect colors of a painting. But looking closer, I saw the frayed halter hanging from a nail, the rotten post on the first stall, the tail of a rat in the woodpile. I wondered if there were always things we didn't see, only because we chose not to look too closely. I had replayed yesterday over and over again in my mind.

The staggering lies.

The secrets.

Jase's angry face when he called me *Ten.*

But something else woke me from my sleep last night. *The laughter.* I heard the captain and the rest of them, *laughing.* The clink of their glasses. It needled through me, but I wasn't sure why. Maybe it was just the shock of seeing them altogether—seeing far more than what I bargained for.

When the groom finished pitching hay into the stall, I ambled over, sizing up the wagon. It was a small hay wagon, which was an advantage. It would still hold six men but it would be easier to maneuver around the back side of Tor's Watch over to the Greyson Tunnel trail. That path would draw the least attention. We couldn't traipse through town, and on the back trail the cover of night would swallow us up. We could only count on a few hours' lead time.

But hitching up a team of horses would be noisy. I looked at the groom's cottage at the far end of the stables. His supper would have to come via Eben too. It would be laced with birchwings, the same as with the keeper for the dog kennels. If he was passed out, no dogs would be loosed. The birchwings would also keep our quarry of six quiet on the trail.

I had slipped into the storage room in the kitchen during the middle of the night. The lock had been child's play. The small vial of birchwings that Wren had gotten for me still had two doses in it, which would take care of the groom and keeper, but I was going to need more. The full canister of birchwings was the solution but it was important that my theft wasn't noticed, at least not until long after we were gone, so I had poured the birchwings into a pouch and put salt in its place. No one would notice the difference immediately, though the salt wouldn't do much for a headache.

Wren and Synové rode in, dismounting and leading their horses into stalls. They'd been in town getting supplies together—spools of cording, more water skins, and dried food—presumably for our trip home in case anyone noticed. Though Synové was more than able to supply us with fresh game, it wouldn't be safe to build a campfire for a while—at least not until we met up with Griz and the troops.

"Have you spoken with Jase?" Wren asked.

I shook my head. Last night I had stayed awake for hours waiting for a tap at my door, a creak outside it, a sense that he leaned against it, but nothing came. I opened it twice, imagining he was there. He wasn't. He never did come. I had a dozen excuses to turn him away if he did, but I didn't need any of them.

"Are you going to be all right?" Synové's brows pulled low. There was concern in her voice but dogged anger also simmered in her eyes. Now that she knew Bahr was among the fugitives, this mission had become personal. Wren's promise that the ride back would be torture seemed to be a goal that calmed her.

"Of course she's all right," Wren answered, then looked at me, waiting for me to confirm it.

"Yes," I answered. And I was. I wasn't sure if it was a relief or not, but when Jase said there were no drivers like the one I had described to him, I at least knew I wouldn't turn a corner and run into him face-to-face. Not in the middle of all this, where I might jeopardize everything. I didn't want to come undone the way Synové had last night when Wren and I had to hold her back. Too much was at stake. Knowing he wasn't here allowed me to push thoughts of returning to the Previzi warehouse out of my mind and concentrate on what needed to be done.

I thought about Jase's question, *How do you go from anguish to pulling coins out from behind ears?* I had given him an angry answer, but the truth was, by shielding Nash and Lydia, it felt like I had reclaimed a small part of myself. And that was what I was doing now, reclaiming that part of me that believed I could still make some things right. It was all I had.

"Good morning, ladies!" Natiya rounded the corner, a tub of slop propped against her hip. "On my way with a present for the sow," she said loudly, in case the groom wondered why she was here.

She sidled close, and we smiled as we chatted, but our conversation wasn't about potato peels for the swine. We had already talked last night. I had told them about our additional fugitives and the Ballengers' motives for harboring them—weapons, domination, and a trap for the queen.

Eben was convinced that the two men I didn't know were scholars, more traitors lured away from Morrighan by the Komizar. He said it was never known just how many had lurked in the catacombs beneath Sanctum City, unlocking the mysteries of the Ancients, or just what they had escaped with. The captain must have hooked up with his crew of cronies, hoping for a second chance at the riches that had eluded them.

We set our plans in motion, fine-tuning the details to accommodate five more prisoners.

"Don't be late for dinner. Timing is critical," Natiya ordered. She said she was sending Eben with the stable dinners an hour before dusk to ensure the dogs weren't released. The family dinner had to coincide with the stable hands' dinnertime. "We might have more time, but we can only count on a two-hour window. What about the *Patrei*? He's complicit in this. Do we take him too?"

They all looked at me, waiting. They knew it was imperative that I feel right about this, and since I was lead, Natiya left it to me to call the final shots, but something nagged at me. Maybe it was Vairlyn's eagerness to talk about menus for the queen. Had Jase deceived his mother too? Or were they all masters at deceit? Or maybe I hadn't quite abandoned everything I believed about Jase yet—that there was a kindness deep in his core, that he wanted to do the right thing. I looked back at Natiya. Her gaze remained steady, waiting. Yes, Jase was complicit, but our mission had been to retrieve a single fugitive and now we had six, more than we could handle. "Not this time," I answered. "We already have a full load. Trust me, Jase isn't leaving Hell's Mouth. This is his home—he won't disappear. The matter of the *Patrei*'s guilt can be addressed later."

"What about Jalaine?" Wren asked. "She could be a problem if she doesn't come to dinner again."

"I'll talk to her," I said. "I'll make sure she—"

"Kazi, there you are!"

"Oh snakes, it's the nasty one," Synové rumbled under her breath.

Gunner walked toward us. "I've been looking for you." He slowed, noting Natiya's presence. "What are you all doing out here?"

"Morning, sir!" Natiya chirped, bobbing her head. "And it's a beautiful one, isn't it? Just on my way with slop for the sow. Her farrow should be here any day." She nodded at the heap of leavings in the tub. "A little planning ahead reaps great rewards—and pudgy piglets. Good day, ladies!" She bounced happily away, and Gunner's attention turned back to me.

"And I was just grooming Mije after a morning ride," I said. "What can I do for you, Gunner?"

"Jase wants to see you."

"He couldn't come himself?"

"He's wrapped up with something right now, but he wants to meet you by the fountain in the gardens in ten minutes. It's important."

By the fountain? It was more than odd, but I didn't want to upset Gunner's easily toppled applecart at this point with just hours left at Tor's Watch.

"All right," I answered. "Do you know what it's about?"

He shrugged. "Something about the queen coming." His poker face was pathetic. He obviously didn't share his brother's accomplished skill at lying.

"Sure. We'll be there."

"No," he said firmly. "Just you."

CHAPTER FORTY-SEVEN

JASE

We had the timing worked out so it would look like chance. Zane was just unlocking the back gate into Cave's End to make a delivery when I came riding down the road from the stables.

"*Patrei!*" he called. "Where are you off to?"

"Unexpected business that I need a quick answer for. What else is new, right?" I stopped my horse as if mulling something over. "Actually, I had a question for Garvin, but you might be able to save me a trip. It's about Venda. You ever run wagons there?"

"Sure. But it's been years. What's the question?"

"In Sanctum City, they have something called the jen-der, the ja—"

"The *jehendra*? Yes, that's their marketplace."

"So you delivered goods there?"

"Lots of times. Whatever the Komizar didn't want, we'd unload there. It's huge, but nothing like the arena."

I got down from my horse. "Here, let me help you." I opened the gate while he drove his cart in and then I explained I had a visitor, a merchant from the *jehendra* who had a deal that seemed too good to be true. I was skeptical but still intrigued. It might give us the first inroads into trade with Venda, and she offered me a very good deal I at least had to investigate. "She claims that she runs the largest textile shop in the *jehendra*—"

Zane nodded. "I might know her. I always had some fabrics in my load. The Komizar liked to keep certain friends well dressed."

"Good. I'd feel better if you'd eye her for me. Discreetly. Confirm she's really who she says she is."

I led him through the tunnel that ran to Darkcottage, saying that when I left she was walking in the gardens with Gunner and maybe she was still there. I watched him walk ahead of me on the cellar stairs, his steps heavy and confident, not the steps of a man who had anything to hide, his arms swinging as he walked. The detail I had ignored a hundred times was now all I could see—the mole on his wrist. When we reached the front drawing room, I opened the shutter and looked through the window. "There they are," I said. "Over by the fountain."

Her back was to us, but Gunner saw the signal of me opening the shutter and coaxed Kazi around to face us. The distance and reflection on the window would be enough to hide us from her view, but I was no longer watching Kazi. I only watched Zane. If he was really the one Kazi had seen, I doubted he could recognize her after all these years—but her mother was another matter, and I took a gamble that Kazi looked enough like her that she might spark some recognition.

He stared at Kazi, his head turning slightly to the side, as if he was confused. He studied her, and his expression went slack as though he were seeing a ghost. His mouth hung open, and he turned to me, his pupils pinpoints. He sensed a trick. "No, I don't know her."

But it was already too late. "You son of a bitch!" I grabbed him and slammed him up against the wall. Kazi had described him perfectly, right down to his onyx eyes. They were terrified now. *He wanted me too, but couldn't find me.* The room around me spun, dark and furious. Zane pushed back, fighting against me, but I slammed him back again. "You filthy flesh trader!" I yelled and swung, my fist colliding with his jaw. He fell over a table, but jumped to his feet quickly, drawing a knife from his boot, but then he saw Mason, Titus, Drake, and Tiago enter the room. He dropped the knife, knowing it was useless. His eyes grew wide. Blood ran from his nose.

"I swear! I don't know her!"

I shoved him toward Drake and Tiago. "I have to go meet Kazi. She's waiting for me. When it's clear, take him to the warehouse."

Screams couldn't be heard from there.

Zane would be answering our questions, if it took one fingernail—or fingertip—at a time.

CHAPTER FORTY-EIGHT

KAZI

GUNNER WAS CHATTY. NOT GUNNER AT ALL. HE APOLOGIZED for Jase being late and seemed distracted, like he didn't want to be there. He fidgeted, then circled around to the other side of the fountain. I turned to face him.

"I think it's clear that Jase isn't coming," I said. "I'll talk to him later."

"Give him five more minutes," he answered, but just a short time later he left, saying he would go look for him.

It wasn't that Jase and I didn't have plenty to talk about, but it seemed strange that he'd want to speak out here in the gardens where raised voices would be easily heard. *Smooth it over.* With only hours to go, I . knew Natiya's advice was prudent, but Jase wasn't an acquaintance like Gunner I could shrug off. Jase was—

I wasn't sure what he was anymore.

I stared at the bubbling fountain.

Setting traps for the queen? An arsenal of weapons to dominate the other kingdoms? That wasn't Jase. I still had a hard time reconciling it. Jase loved Hell's Mouth. This was his whole world. His history. It was all he wanted. All he wanted to protect. But the evidence was plain. His lies, hiding fugitives, an enclave guarded by poisonous dogs, the weapons. Is that what those stacks of paper were? Plans for weapons? Formulas? And the workshops filled with supplies? I remembered the strange list of ingredients on Priya's desk that Jase personally had to approve. *Supplies for BI*, not the Ballenger Inn but Captain *Beaufort* Illarion. What kind of weapons were they devising that could put all the kingdoms under their thumbs?

I looked around again. Where was he?

I dreaded speaking to him but found myself scanning the walkways between the houses, looking for a glimpse of his dark-blond hair, uncertain which direction he would come from. My anticipation grew and I finally turned away, frustration brimming inside. I was halfway through the long rose arbor when I heard footsteps. Running. I stopped and turned.

It was Jase.

He was at the end of the arbor. His steps slowed when he spotted me. He was breathless, as if he had run a long way. I didn't move as he walked closer, bracing myself for whatever he had to say. His hair was unkempt, strands falling over his brow. He stopped in front of me and raked them back. His gaze flooded mine, washed into every corner of my mind.

The silence stretched, and I heard a chain that was no longer there, jingling. I felt Jase holding me in a river, keeping my head above the water. For what? The throb in my chest deepened. If he had been cruel back then, his lies now would hurt me less.

"Kazi—"

His voice was more than I could bear and I began to turn away, but he stopped me, gently turning me back to face him.

"Please, Kazi, hear me out. There's so much we need to talk about. I'm sorry about losing my temper yesterday. I'm sorry for everything you've been through. My family's made mistakes, I know, and I'm going to try to fix them, but right now something else needs to be said. I know you've never wanted to hear this, but after yesterday I have to say it . . ." He paused, swallowed, as if afraid. "I love you. I love you with every breath, with every thought that's inside me. I've loved you from the first time I kissed you on that ledge. Even before that."

I shook my head, trying to pull away. "Jase, no—" But he pulled me closer and didn't stop.

"When I asked, *What is this?* I already knew. I knew what I felt, what I was certain you felt too, but I was afraid to say it, because it was all new to me. It seemed too soon, too impossible. But everything about us didn't just feel right, it felt like something rare, something delicate that I was afraid of breaking. Something that only comes along once in a lifetime."

He lifted my chin so I had to look at him.

Don't do this to me, Jase. It's too late. Pain knifed through me, my insides in pieces. All I wanted to do was believe every word, forget all his lies, feed my fantasy. A thousand wish stalks throwing pleas to the universe that we were lost and alone on a star-filled ledge again.

"I don't want to lose you, Kazi. I'm not asking for promises. I don't even want an answer now, but I want to ask you to at least think about staying here with me. Forever."

He cradled my face in his hands. "There. I've said it now, and I won't take it back. I love you, Kazi of Brightmist, and I will never stop saying it, not through a thousand tomorrows."

He slowly lowered his mouth to mine, and instead of turning away, I kissed him back. I tasted the sweetness of his tongue, and a wilderness swelled up around us, tall grass swaying at our ankles. I repeated my first glorious mistake again and again, but this time, I told myself, I was only smoothing it over.

Jalaine wasn't in her room. Oleez told me I could find her in the solarium on the top floor of the house. In the summertime, the solarium was mostly abandoned. Even with all the windows open, the air could be stifling. There was no breeze today, and I already felt the blast of heat as I trudged up the last few steps.

The wide double doors were pushed open. It was an expansive room with high vaulted ceilings, furnished with plain wooden furniture. I guessed that in wintertime they were covered with colorful cushions and coverlets. The scent of cut greenery hung in the heavy air. Jalaine was in the corner, her back to me, tending some sort of large potted shrub, but she was just staring at it, as if lost in thought. A pair of shears hung limply in her hand. A few cut leaves lay scattered at her feet.

"Either come in or go away," she called without turning.

Not as lost in thought as I had supposed. But then I realized she had seen me in the reflection of one of the many windows that were angled open. I entered and she returned to trimming the tiny leaves. Her thin white dress clung to her, damp with sweat. I eyed the shears in her hand. I still didn't know if she knew I was the one who had killed Fertig.

"We've missed you at dinner," I said.

She returned her attentions to the shrub. The quick furious *snip* of her shears cut the air. "I doubt that."

I decided it was best to get right to the heart of the matter. "I'm sorry about Fertig."

She turned to face me, the tiny leaves rustling under her feet. "Why would you be sorry? He almost killed you." She looked at my neck, the bruises new shades of purple today.

"I'm sorry because you cared for him."

"Fertig?" Her lip twisted with contempt. "I didn't love Fertig. Is that what you thought? You came to comfort me over poor Fertig?"

She laughed and her mouth pressed into a miserable smile. "I was flattered by his attentions. That's all. I enjoyed them." It was strange to hear the deep bitterness in her voice. It aged her. "It all seemed harmless. He was amusing. I even wondered if he might grow on me in a more permanent way. Eventually. I was drawing it out, playing with him, because he was a distraction from the dull routine of the arena office."

She tossed her shears onto the table and stared at them, her gaze lost in a distant world again. "But as it turned out, he was the one playing with me. Using me. He said he loved me, and I believed him. I was a gullible tool."

I swallowed. "Anyone can be duped. No one blames you."

"Jase does. That's why he pulled me from the arena. And he's right. I blame myself. I let the family down."

"We all make mistakes, Jalaine. But we have to move on. Come to dinner tonight. Please. Your family is still your family. They want you there."

She looked at me, brokenness filling her eyes. I saw her desire to be forgiven, but forgiving herself was another matter. Her pain riddled through me, something too familiar.

"I'll think about it," she said and turned away, still unconvinced. She grabbed a broom propped against the wall and began sweeping the cuttings into a pile.

I left to the *scritch, scritch, scritch* of the broom, Jalaine mindlessly sweeping, wandering in a world brimming with her own shame, and I was still uncertain if the problem of Jalaine coming to dinner was solved.

The stuffy staircase seemed like it circled around and down forever until I thought I would never take a deep breath again. *I let the family down.*

I raced to the last flight of stairs, wiping the sweat from my brow, and emerged on the cool landing at last. They are not my family, I reminded myself.

CHAPTER FORTY-NINE

JASE

"I SWEAR! I DON'T DEAL IN FLESH! I NEVER HAVE!"

After an hour of questioning, and with gardening shears clamped over his finger, he confessed to taking Kazi's mother. "She was a half-starved beggar! She was going to get a better life."

The way flesh traders always tried to justify their actions.

"That's why you had to drug her? Why you wanted her child too?"

His face went slack. It finally sank in, who he had seen in the garden. Not a ghost but the child of the woman he had taken. His eyes darted back and forth, looking around the warehouse, as if searching for an escape that he had overlooked. There were none. He was tied to a chair, surrounded by five of us. He looked back at me. "It was one time. I only did it once."

I could hear the squirming in his voice, the grasping, trying to find some way out of this. He had done it dozens of times, but even once was too many. Once changed Kazi's life, and her mother's, forever.

"And the better life she got? Who did you sell her to?"

His eyes grew wide. I saw the lie forming in them. "I never sold her. She died en route. I told you, she was weak and half starved." Right now he was more afraid of someone else than he was of me. That would change.

I was certain now that he was wrapped up with the labor hunters who had descended into Hell's Mouth, still working his old connections.

I leaned forward, my hands on the arm of his chair, my face all he could see. "Tell me, Zane, you know Fertig?"

He nodded.

"He's dead. He and his whole crew. They're not coming home. Whomever you're working for just took a big hit. But I want them out of business altogether. Tell me who they are, and you and I will work something out."

He shook his head. "I don't know anything!"

I stepped back and looked at Tiago. "The family's waiting. I have to go to dinner. If he has no fingertips when I return, that's fine. We'll move on to his toes next. Just make sure he doesn't bleed out. We're going to keep him alive until we have our answers."

I turned and walked toward the door, and Tiago picked up the gardening shears.

"Wait!" Zane cried, struggling against his ties, the chair wobbling beneath him. "I was given a satchel of money by someone named Devereux who told me to hire labor hunters! It was in an alley behind the pub. It was dark. I never saw his face. That's all I know! I swear! He didn't tell me who he worked for!"

I paused at the door without looking back. The smithy died because of Zane. Countless other lives were stolen. Kazi and I almost died. "That's a start. We'll talk more when I return. Tiago, you can go to dinner too. We'll hold off on his fingertips for now."

In a few hours, Zane would be tired, hungry, and crazed with fear.

He'd have time to reassess what he valued more, his fingers or the people he was protecting. There'd be no lies left in him. I was sure by then he'd even remember more names.

⚫

I rubbed my hair with a towel and paused in front of the mirror, looking at my tattoo like I was seeing it for the first time. I had just bathed, trying to wash away the disgust and slime of Zane. I ran my hand over my shoulder, my chest, the wings, the words, the scrutinizing eye of a bird staring back at me. We can become numb to things, so much so that we don't even see them anymore. I wasn't sure when the last time was that I had really looked at it. *Protect.*

My father had stood over me while I got every feather, every claw, every letter etched into my skin. *Protect and defend it all,* he told me. *This is who you are. It has always been in your blood, Jase. Now it is over your heart.*

Greyson Ballenger had had twenty-two to protect and a vault to defend. Tor's Watch had grown. The family had grown. There were hundreds, thousands to protect now. A whole city to defend. And because of the arena, the Ballenger world was still expanding. I had made a blood vow to protect the Vendan settlement. And it seemed that sometimes I would also have to protect people I'd never seen, people on the other side of a continent, people I'll never even know—people like Kazi and her mother.

I wondered about Garvin now too, the questions we didn't ask and should have. All this had come to a head in our family meeting this morning. I encountered loud resistance to creating new rules for the Previzi or ousting them—we could take a big hit in profits and anger some long-term traders who depended on them to peddle merchandise that had no bill of lading. I countered that when we crossed certain lines we invited others to be crossed too, and then I told them about my suspicions of Zane. I didn't get any more arguments.

Once we got all the information we needed from Zane, I was going to have to tell Kazi about him. But how, I wasn't sure.

Maybe that was why I had rushed to tell her how I felt today and asked her to stay. I was afraid. I needed her to know with certainty my feelings for her—before I told her that the man who took her mother worked for us.

CHAPTER FIFTY

KAZI

WE WALKED TO THE DINING ROOM, TRYING TO PRETEND IT WAS
a night like any other. Our weapons were stowed in our rooms, ready to
put on, riding leathers and boots laid out, other supplies already stuffed
into saddlebags. I listened to the gentle tap of our slippers on the wooden
floors, the *hush*, while my heart fluttered like a moth caught in a web.
This was not how it was supposed to be. It was not like me. When I
lifted a fleece, palmed an egg, juggled a fig into my pocket, even when I
took the tiger, a calmness always fell in the final moments of execution,
like every detail belonged to me and was mine to mold. For a few short
minutes, I was master of a small universe. I knew why that calm eluded
me now. Jase. My universe was tilting because of him.

"There they are," Mason said, his gaze lighting on Synové.

In the next moment, Jase's eyes met mine. They pierced me as if
searching for something. He finally smiled, and my stomach reacted
against my will.

No one was seated yet. All of them had been talking quietly at the far end of the room. Now everyone ambled toward their seats. Jase pulled out my chair for me and kissed my cheek. "Are you all right?' he whispered quietly.

"Of course." I knew I had to make more of an effort at acting normal, though I wasn't sure what that was anymore. His hand slid to my thigh beneath the table, and I reached down and cupped my hand around his.

"What's that?" he asked and lifted my hand to where he could see it. He looked at the ring on my finger.

"I got it at the arena yesterday," I explained.

He didn't ask the question, but it stewed in his eyes: *Did you pay for it?*

"It was a gift from a merchant," I said.

A slight pull at the corner of his mouth. *Sure it was.*

"It's nice," he replied with great effort, sliding our hands back beneath the table.

As usual, the busyness of a family dinner erupted, conversations intersecting one another across the table, pitchers of water and ale passed, goblets clinking as they were filled. Natiya brought in baskets of clover buns and carefully set first-course plates in front of everyone. They all admired the artistry of the elegant zucchini roulades shaped like roses, a black-bean paste between the thin petals. "You're spoiling us, Natiya," Vairlyn said.

"Hope you enjoy, ma'am." Natiya was doing twice the work tonight, covering for Eben while he was occupied with delivering special dinners to the gate guards and other tasks.

Vairlyn was about to offer thanks when Jalaine appeared at the doorway, and a quiet fell. She hesitated at the entrance. "I'm sorry I'm late."

Jase seemed surprised by her arrival and jumped up from his seat. He went to her place and pulled out her chair. "Not too late, sister," he said.

When she reached it, Jase pulled her into his arms and held her. He wasn't just a brother holding his sister, but a *Patrei*, holding her for the entire family, pulling her back into their circle. He whispered something into Jalaine's ear. Forgiveness? An apology? Vairlyn blinked, a faint smile curling her lips.

Once they were both seated again, Vairlyn bowed her head and offered thanks to the gods for our meal. When she finished, Lydia and Nash said, as they had every night since I taught them the words, "*Le'en chokabrez. Kez lo mati!*"

They looked to me for approval, and I nodded. "Me too." How quickly they had drawn me into the small routines of their lives. A lump grew in my throat.

Wren, Synové, and I dug in right away, hoping to set an example.

"It's my favorite vagabond dish," Synové said. "What do you think, Mason?"

He chewed and swallowed his first forkful. "Good," he agreed. "Very good."

Jase paused with his first bite, as if he didn't like it, but then swallowed. "You don't care for it?" I asked quietly. I held my breath. The Ballengers weren't picky eaters, and this was one of the most irresistible vagabond dishes. Aram's and Samuel's helpings were already gone.

"No," he answered. "It's very good. Just a different taste." He ate the rest, but it looked like he was only being polite.

When the last rose roulade was gone, Priya and Titus cleared the dishes, setting them on the sideboard, and soon Natiya came in with platters of roasted game hens and carrots. Vairlyn filled and passed the plates.

Wren and Synové both tried to eat their food with some degree of enthusiasm. I noticed Samuel scowling as he stabbed a carrot. He was usually the most cheerful of the Ballenger clan, and I wondered if he was growing impatient with his bandaged hand. In spite of Wren trying to engage him, he mostly looked down at his plate and uttered simple replies. Jalaine was quiet, but at least she was here.

Jase announced that he had gotten word this morning that the houses at the settlement were finished. Wren, Synové, and I voiced our appreciation. "Maybe we can all go out there next week and look over the progress," he suggested. He looked at me expectantly, waiting for my response. Our few days at the settlement had been a new beginning for us. Maybe he hoped it would happen again. "That would be wonderful," I answered, forcing just the right amount of smile, just the right amount of my gaze lingering in his, just the right amount of juggling.

"The teacher left for the settlement today," Gunner piped up. "I told her to enlist Jurga's help. She's going to have to teach the adults too." His eyes lit up when he mentioned Jurga.

Wren and I exchanged a glance, and I knew she was finding this conversation as difficult as I was. I was grateful when Titus brought up the new mare they'd acquired from Gastineux breeders. Still, each minute dragged by like an hour.

And then the first yawn came.

Vairlyn rubbed her eyes and shook her head. "I'm sorry, but I'm afraid I'm going to have excuse myself and turn in early tonight. I guess it's been a long day." She hurried Lydia and Nash along, in spite of their protests that they weren't tired, and took them with her. Priya and Jalaine agreed, both blinking and yawning, and they left too. Minute by minute, the dining room quieted as another Ballenger left, suddenly overwhelmed with fatigue. Except for Jase.

I finally said I was tired too and was going to bed. "I'll walk you," Jase offered, but as he stood I saw a slight stumble. He smiled. "I only had one ale. Promise." He tried to shake it off, but as we walked up the flight of stairs he stumbled again.

"I think Titus refilled your mug twice," I said. "Maybe you had more ale than you thought. Let's get you straight to your room."

He leaned heavily on me, and when we got to his room he fell against the door. "I don't know what—"

"It's all right, Jase. We're almost there." I opened the door, and he staggered inside. I eased his fall as he crumpled to the floor. I knelt down beside him and saw his eyes briefly trying to focus on me. And then they closed.

"Jase," I whispered. He didn't stir.

I raked his hair back and stared at him, touched the fading cut on his cheekbone, the bruise I put on his jaw yesterday. I felt his warm skin beneath my fingertips and the ache in my chest for all the tomorrows he stole, the ones he made me believe could be ours. *You lied to me, Jase. You've lied to me over and over again. You've conspired with fugitives against all the kingdoms.* But even as I stirred the embers of my anger, other treasonous feelings surfaced, feelings that I loathed but couldn't shake. A poison I couldn't flush out. My throat clamped tight.

I stood, looking down at him one last time before I left. "Damn you, Jase Ballenger," I whispered. *"Le pavi ena."*

And I'm afraid I will forever.

———◆———

We crept through the Darkcottage tunnel. Synové, Natiya, and Eben had arrows drawn, guarding us before and behind. We all wore bandoliers studded with throwing knives—small, silent, and deadly—a last resort. We wanted our game alive. Long swords were too risky because of the noise they could make, but Wren wore her *ziethes* and the rest of us had long daggers on our belts. I carried a smaller one in my hand and a pouch of birchwings hung from my hip. The rest of our gear was stowed on the hay wagon. Natiya carried a timepiece and signaled us each time ten minutes had passed. Since we left the dining room, twenty minutes were already gone.

I eased the door at the end of the tunnel open a crack. When I saw it was clear, I slipped out onto the terrace and hid behind a pillar. I paused, taking in every shadow, sound, and movement. One by one, I signaled the others out when I was sure it was safe, pointing to the position each should take.

The terraces of the long house were cloaked in darkness, but soft light streamed from a few of the rooms. Because of the summer heat, most of the doors were open, trying to catch a breeze. I made my way across the next section of terrace. When it was clear, I again signaled the rest to follow. I turned my head, listening, and heard the faint rumble of voices. I pointed to the room it was coming from and signaled the rest to wait while I got closer to see how many were there. The room was brightly lit with candles. Sarva and the captain were bent over a table playing some sort of game. Kardos, Bahr, and one of the scholars were lounging in overstuffed chairs around a cold hearth, drinking and throwing pits into the gray ashes as they ate olives, laughing and competing to hit some target. None of them were armed. One of the scholars, the younger one, was missing. I lifted my fingers to the others. Five. I went in search of the other one, looking into one room and then the next. I found him two rooms down, hunched at a desk, studying papers and writing notes in a ledger. I signaled Eben to come join me. When the time was right, he whined low in the perfect pitch of a wolf. The scholar's attention pricked upward. He stood to investigate, probably to shut the terrace door, but he was caught off guard by the unexpected sight of me, bending down on one knee on the terrace, pretending to tie my boot. When he stepped out, Eben grabbed him from behind, clapping one hand over his mouth and holding a knife to his throat with the other.

I stood. "Make any noise," I whispered, "and it will be your last. Understand?"

The white of the scholar's eyes shone in the darkness, and he nodded as much as he dared. Eben loosened his hold on his mouth just long enough for me to learn his name. Phineas.

I checked him for hidden weapons, but as expected there were none. These men were in a protected enclave—the only threat they had to fear was a drunken fall down the stairs.

"Interior," I whispered to Eben. He went in the house with the scholar still in his grip, and I went back with the others.

We got into position and waited. It was almost too easy. Unarmed, half-drunk men who suspected nothing. My greatest worry was Synové and the moment she saw Bahr face-to-face, though she had already assured me the shock had passed. She had latched onto the idea of the long journey home and the agony she was going to inflict. When I saw Eben's shadow in the hallway, I motioned to Wren and she whistled six notes of a night thrush. Eben burst in from the rear of the room, shoving the scholar into the center, and we entered from the other side. Synové, Natiya, and Eben had bows taut with arrows, their eyes cold beads on their targets. Wren's *ziethes* were drawn. I had cording in one hand and a dagger in the other.

A moment of confusion and disbelief erupted, all of them jumping to their feet, uncertain what was happening, the captain blustering about the intrusion like we were servants who had forgotten to knock. But even in the midst of the chaos, there was a splintered second when fullness engulfed me. The dragon was in our grasp at last.

The dawning truth came first to Chievdar Kardos. He knew Rahtan when he saw them. "*An ade fikatad.*"

"By order of the Queen of Venda, the King of Morrighan, and the Alliance of Kingdoms, you are all under arrest and will stand trial for treason and murder," I announced as a matter of necessity. "And now, gentlemen, do exactly as we order because we are not bound to bring you back alive."

Synové's arrow was trained on Bahr's head, and his eyes were trained on her. He knew all he had to do was make a sudden move for an arrow to fly.

The captain was still trying to dissuade us. "I'm afraid you've all made a terrible mistake. We're not—"

"No mistake, Captain Illarion." I motioned to the floor. "All of you, down on your stomachs. Now. We have some housekeeping to do before we go for a little ride."

No one moved, and Synové let an arrow fly, the *whoosh* sucking air from lungs. It grazed Bahr's ear and he howled, clapping his hand over the bloody flesh.

"Maybe the wax is out of your ear now," she said. "You were told to get down on your stomachs."

They all complied.

Wren and I tied their hands behind their backs while Governor Sarva tried to convince us we would never get away with it. "We do not recognize the queen's right to rule!"

"But the people of Venda do, and so does every kingdom on the continent," Eben said, hauling him back to his feet. "Now shut up."

I mixed the birchwings with a pitcher of water and poured each one a glass, ordering them to drink up. "It will make for a more pleasant ride."

The older scholar, Torback, wailed, refusing to drink what he thought was poison. Synové aimed her arrow at his chest, and he drank. I explained to them they would be asleep soon. In the meantime, we were going to gag them to ensure their silence, but we reminded them there were more permanent forms of silence and we wouldn't hesitate to use them.

Bahr spit and mumbled under his breath, "Filthy Rahtan."

I glanced at Synové, her hand hovering over her knife. A tremor ruffled her eyelids like a thousand barbed switches were shaking behind them, and I wondered if Bahr was better left here with his throat slit than facing the agonies she planned for him.

"Forty minutes," Natiya said. We were ahead of schedule. It was only a short walk down the covered terrace walkway to the back gate where the hay wagon and horses were waiting. I pulled the gag from Phineas. "The plans for the weapons, where are they?"

The captain moaned beneath his gag, furiously shaking his head. Sarva and the others had similar responses, still trying to preserve their treasures. Phineas hesitated, listening to their groans. I shrugged. "Who do you think you should listen to? Them or us?" Every one of our weapons was trained on him.

"The second outbuilding near the gate," he responded. "It's our workshop. All the formulas are there."

It was on our way. The gods were watching over us.

Before I stepped out onto the terrace, I pointed to the row of throwing knives on our chests in case they got any foolish ideas about fleeing in the darkness. "I wouldn't try to make a run for it. Tell them what Rahtan means, Kardos."

He mumbled beneath his gag.

"That's right. Never fail. Got that, Captain?"

He nodded, an angry line creasing the crescent scar on his forehead.

I stepped out onto the terrace. The grounds beyond were black with a moonless night. If there was a stray guard who wasn't in a birchwings sleep by now, he would not see us. The air was still, not so much as the ripple of a breeze, and the only sound was the warble of a thrush answering Wren's call.

We made our way down the stairs to the grassy grounds that led to the gate, the six men shuffling between the others, silent and afraid, as I walked ahead scouting our path. We were halfway to the gate when I heard a rustle. It was too dark here to signal so I whistled, a low warble to stop them.

Another rustle.

And then the sky lit up like dawn.

CHAPTER FIFTY-ONE

KAZI

"Positions!" I yelled.

In less than a second, we had our prisoners knocked to their knees. Synové, Eben, and Natiya stood behind them with arrows drawn, and Wren's *ziethe* circled around the captain's neck. I was a dozen feet in front of them all, with a dagger gripped in my hand.

The smell of sulfur burned the air, and my eyes adjusted to the sudden blinding flames of a hundred torches in the night.

And then I saw Jase.

He was standing in front of me, only steps away, blocking my path.

His family stood behind him—Vairlyn, Priya, Gunner, Titus, Mason, Aram, Samuel—even Jalaine. Their expressions were condemning, hurt, seething. The grounds were thick with guards, their arrows aimed, and *straza* with swords drawn.

Jase's eyes glistened, his head shaking, looking like he'd been kicked in the stomach. His mouth opened but he struggled to find words. "This?" he finally asked, holding up a canister of white crystals. "Is this what you meant to get?"

He switched the birchwings? His whole family had played along, even Jalaine. That was what Jase's last minute whisper in her ear was. "You knew," I said.

"Not for sure. I didn't want to believe it." He threw the canister, and it shattered somewhere in the darkness. He looked back at Eben and Natiya, the cook and her husband now revealed as Rahtan too.

"You were planning this all along." His eyes cut through me, accusing. "That's all this was ever about?"

By *this*, I knew he meant *we*. My anger flared. He had harbored ruthless killers, conspired with them, lied about them, used me to lure the queen here. I was the one who was betrayed. He had no right to reproach me.

My next words were sharp, trying to cut him loose. "That's right. That's *all* it was ever about. These men are under our arrest for murder and treason, and you're guilty of harboring them. Now step aside before we arrest you too."

He blew out a disbelieving breath. "Have you lost your mind? Look where you are! You're surrounded. Put your weapons down! Now!" he ordered.

We didn't move. Bows pulled tighter, stretching with more threat on both sides. Poised arms shook.

The tension grew more taut with every passing second. Shouting erupted.

"You're not taking them anywhere!" Titus bellowed. "You're trespassing in Ballenger territory!"

"You'll pay for this," Aram sneered.

"We're a sovereign domain," Priya yelled. "Your queen has no jurisdiction at Tor's Watch, and you definitely don't!"

"You're our prisoners now! Drop your weapons!" Mason shouted, his sword drawn.

Our captives screamed through their gags.

Save this, Kazi. Somehow save this.

"Move aside, Jase. Now." *Please. I don't want to hurt you.* I stepped forward, and more swords sliced free from scabbards.

Jase looked around at the growing tension. "Hold your weapons!" he yelled, and he held his hand up in a stopping motion toward me. "Don't move, Kazi. You're going to get yourself killed. You're going to get your friends killed."

"Let them shoot, Jase!" Titus yelled. "They're outnumbered!"

And we were. By far.

"Shut up!" Jase yelled over his shoulder and turned back to me. "Put it down, Kazi. There's nowhere for you to go. We need these men. We have an agreement with them for—"

"There's nothing that will make me give them back to you, Jase. Nothing. If we die, they die with us—and the scholars will die first." I was in the way of most of their shots. I would go down first, but there would be time for the others to slit our captives' throats.

The scholars moaned beneath their gags.

Jase's gaze locked on mine. There was no going back, but I still saw pleading in his eyes. For these men? He slowly edged closer as if I wouldn't notice.

"Give me your knife," he demanded.

"I'm asking you one last time, *step aside.*"

"I can't do that, Kazi. Everything we've said is true. We're the law here, not you or your queen." He took another step closer, his hand still outstretched. "There are thirty guards with their arrows aimed, and a lot of nervous *straza.* Someone's going to make a mistake and one of you will—"

And then there was a shout in the darkness. From Gunner. "This is what you really want, isn't it?" he called. "We'll trade."

Gunner stepped forward, his arm crooked around a man's neck. The man struggled beneath Gunner's grip, and our gazes met. Shiny onyx eyes looked back into mine.

My chest burned.

The air vanished.

My dagger shook in my hand.

I heard Jase shouting, *Gunner, no!*

More shouting. But it all seemed far away.

Kazi.

Kazi.

Where is the brat?

Time spun. Sweat trickled down my back.

Torches flickered and all I could see was golden light bouncing off walls. My mother reaching for a stick.

Come out, girl!

Here.

He was here.

How was that even possible?

It was as if no time had passed. He looked the same.

Fear swelled in my throat. My knees became hot liquid.

You're not powerless anymore.

He was mine. Mine for a simple trade. For a worthless captain and his cohorts.

Know what is at stake. Kazimyrah, I need you.

Justice for thousands, or justice for one. My feet were on two different paths, my insides splitting, tumbling in two directions.

The Previzi driver spotted the dagger in my hand and struggled to get away. I heard Mason call him Zane. They knew him. He had a name. *Zane.* Both Mason and Gunner were holding him now. He had seen the murder in my eyes. It fueled me, wanting him even more, a hungry, thirsty, ravenous need to spill his blood a drop at a time. "What happened to her?" I called. "What did you do to my mother?" The questions came out quiet, halting and unexpected. The sound turned my stomach to ice. I heard the voice of the child I used to be. The man called Zane looked at me as if he knew he had no chance.

He opened his mouth to speak, but Gunner clapped his hand over it and shoved him into someone else's arms behind him. "Trade first. Then you get your answers."

I stared at Gunner, wishing him dead, my rage so hot I could have torn him in two with my bare hands, but at the same time I was paralyzed. I might as well have had a sword slicing into my soul. The man who had haunted me for my whole life was here and Jase *knew. He knew his name.*

He had known all along.

I looked at him.

I didn't need to say it. I knew he could see it in my eyes.

This? You lied about this too?

He stepped closer. "Kazi, I was—"

Make a choice, Kazi. There was only one choice. I had to give one thing up to gain another.

Jase lunged toward me, but I was expecting it. I knew things too. Things like the moment a thief closes in on their mark—it's always when they are at their weakest.

I kicked him to his knees and yanked his hair, pulling his head back with one hand and pressing my knife snug against his throat with my other. A quick sleight of hand, a dance, a swift, practiced movement that had kept me alive for years, maybe just for this moment.

"I gave you a chance," I said between gritted teeth. I leaned close to his ear. "I gave you every chance." I pulled his hair back a little harder, pressed the knife a little closer. "Now tell them to move away."

"Step back," Jase said carefully. Even speaking was risky with the blade so tight against his skin. "She'll do it," he warned. "She'll cut my throat."

"You heard him!" I yelled. "The *Patrei* is going with us."

Everyone was shouting now, yelling for me to let go, telling me the horrible things they were going to do to me. I didn't know if Zane was among them anymore. *My throwing knife. Why didn't I throw it while I had the chance?*

Because too much was at stake. Too many crowded around him. A stray knife could have sent everything spinning out of control. My logic battled with my hunger.

I didn't throw the knife because Zane wasn't my mission and returning criminals to the queen was.

"Up," I ordered and moved my knife to the base of Jase's skull. "I know every vulnerable spot on your body. No more tricks. Lace your hands behind your head. Slowly."

He did as I instructed, and I began guiding him toward the gate with my crew following close behind. Jase's family, *straza*, and guards with their arrows still aimed followed on the sidelines, just waiting for an opportunity.

"You won't get away with this, Kazi," Jase said as we walked. "How long can you keep a knife pressed to my neck? The minute you drop your hand, they'll kill you."

"Eleven years, Jase. I can keep it here for eleven years if I have to."

"We can still work something out."

"Shut up. Save your stories for Zane."

As we passed an outbuilding, I ordered Synové to shoot a fire arrow through the window. It hit the rear wall and lit up the interior. Stacks of papers were scattered on a worktable.

The captain strained against Wren's grip, groaning and trying to work his gag free.

"What are you doing?" Gunner yelled.

"Kazi, don't!" Jase pleaded. "We have too much invested—"

"Do it," I ordered.

Synové shot another fire arrow, this one shattering a kerosene lamp on the table, and the room ignited in flames. I heard the groans, the cursing, damning us all to hell, and saw the furor in the captain's eyes. I felt the rage rolling off Jase.

"Open the gates," I said to Drake and Tiago.

They looked to Jase for confirmation. He nodded.

The hay wagon and horses were still there, not yet returned to the stables. They didn't expect us to get this far.

Natiya and Eben were methodical, chaining each man to the rail inside the wagon. More orders were being shouted, this time from Mason. He was calling for horses from the stables. They intended to follow us.

There wasn't room in the back of the wagon for both Jase and me, and I needed to stay with him. My knife at his neck was all that was keeping us alive. I ordered him up on the front seat. "Drive, *Patrei*. We're going to see the queen."

CHAPTER FIFTY-TWO

JASE

THE HORIZON TURNED FROM BLACK TO MISTY BLUE. THE STARS of Hetisha's Chariot retreated. The sun was coming up. "The horses need to rest," I said.

"I'll tell you when the horses need to rest."

"All right then, *I* need to rest." And I did. I ached—my shoulders, my back, my head, my eyes. I wasn't sure how much longer I could keep them open and focused.

"Tell your family to go home, and then we can all rest."

We had stopped for an hour during the night to water the horses, but there had been no rest for us. My family, *straza*, and guards circled around, torches blazing, waiting for Kazi to let up, make a mistake, succumb to fatigue or their taunts.

She didn't.

Not even when Sarva and the others started in. Once their gags were removed so they could drink, they were relentless. I knew what they were doing, trying to provoke her, trying to get her to lose her concentration and turn toward them so I could disarm her. But they went too far.

"Bet that Zane had a real fine time with your mother," Bahr sneered. Then Sarva began to describe the things he would have done to her. "Shut up, Sarva!" I yelled. He said things I wouldn't say to save my life. I felt Kazi's arm quiver against my back, but the blade stayed steady over my shoulder, her eyes frozen on the dark trail ahead.

I thought she'd waver or collapse by now—at least doze off as the wagon rumbled through the darkness and tedious miles. She wouldn't tell me where we were going. Her crew, who rode nearby, wouldn't tell me either. Right now, we were headed south, but I figured we were going to cut east soon.

"Are we going all the way to Venda?"

"None of your concern."

She had barely uttered a word to me, and the ones she had were hostile. I knew she must be exhausted too. She slumped beside me, but her knife was still in slashing range of my throat. I blinked, trying to shake off the fatigue. I heard snores from behind us. At least someone was getting sleep.

I tugged on the reins. "Whoa!"

Kazi sat up straight. "What do you think you're doing?"

"Telling them to go home."

Wren, Synové, Eben, and Natiya circled, defending the wagon as Mason, Gunner, and the others rode closer.

"Go home, Gunner!" I called. "Take everyone with you. Watch over the town until I return."

Mason rode his horse close to Synové's, trying to intimidate her, his eyes dark and angry. "We're not leaving without you," he called back.

"Yes, you are." I told them that somewhere ahead there would be troops waiting, and I couldn't afford for all of them to be taken into custody too. We were leaving the arena and everything else at risk. Mother, Nash, and Lydia couldn't manage it alone. The rest of them needed to be there to keep things going and safe until I got back.

My assertion that I'd be back rested in their eyes like a question.

Gunner grimaced but finally nodded. He knew I was right. "We'll keep it going." He signaled the rest to follow him as he turned back in the direction of home.

Priya rode up boldly to the wagon. Wren moved to block her path, but Priya still made eye contact with Kazi. "I warned you that I'd make you regret it if you hurt my brother. You will. This will never be forgotten. Ever. You'll pay for this."

Kazi didn't respond. She just met Priya's icy glare with a steady gaze. Priya looked at me, her expression filled with worry. "Be safe, brother."

"I will," I answered, and she turned and rode off.

When they were far enough away, Kazi lowered her knife and got down from the wagon. I followed and let myself collapse on the ground, my back pressing against the uneven earth, my muscles twitching.

Kazi and her crew took care of the horses and their captives in the back of the wagon, then took turns standing watch and sleeping themselves. Everyone was exhausted—except for maybe Beaufort and the rest, who I had heard snoring during the night. I dozed and slept in fits, and I wondered what hell I was in that for the second time since my father died I was a prisoner being hauled somewhere against my will.

We were given rations of water and dried beef, and when Bahr was unchained so he could go relieve himself, Synové taunted him, saying he should make a run for it while he could. I think he considered it for a moment, but he had no weapon and there was nowhere to run. The terrain was mostly flat now, with only a few distant groves to offer anywhere to hide.

I leaned up against the wagon wheel, chewing on my dry slice of beef, staring at Kazi, wondering what was going on in her head. She saw me watching her and looked away. I remembered what the seer had told me: *Guard your heart, Patrei. I see a knife hovering, ready to cut it out.*

I realized now it wasn't the raiders she had meant. She was warning me about Kazi.

She suddenly whipped around, her eyes blazing. "Stop it!" she ordered. "Stop looking at me!"

"Or what?" I answered. "What are you going to do, Kazi? What's left that you could possibly do to me?"

Since there was no room in the back of the wagon for me, I continued to drive it, but Kazi now rode alongside on Mije, apparently too repulsed to even sit on the wagon seat beside me. With my family and their threat gone, she could sufficiently guard me from a distance. Even that didn't last long. She traded positions with Wren and fell back with Eben and Natiya, our so-called cooks turned captors.

I shook my head, thinking about Darkcottage and its history, and the murderous lover who was brought into the fortress in the middle of the night by a Ballenger himself. *When did you become so stupid, Jalaine?* My own angry words flew back in my face like a well-aimed fist.

I gave you a chance. I gave you every chance.

She did. Why didn't I step aside? Why didn't I just let her go?

It wasn't only because I wanted to keep our investment safe. Tension was high, tempers higher, all of it about to spin out of control. I had been afraid. I was afraid she'd be killed.

When did you become so stupid, Jase?

She invaded my family, my home.

With every mile we traveled, my anger grew, not just at Kazi and her crew but also at the queen herself, for ordering soldiers into *my* realm, on my land, behind my walls. It was an invasion into my territory. If I had done the same, it would be considered an act of war, and I would be facing a noose.

"You were pretty slow-footed back there, weren't you *Patrei?*"

I looked at Wren. She eyed me with that lethal stare of hers. "Go torment someone else."

Surprisingly she did. She rode ahead with Synové. No doubt it was she who'd be keeping a close eye on me next. It wasn't as if I could go anywhere. My team of horses could never outrun them, and if I tried my back would be a sure target for one of Synové's arrows.

"We can take them," Beaufort said when he realized no one was there to hear.

I looked back at him over my shoulder. "No," I answered. "They're armed and they're Rahtan."

Sarva's lip lifted in a snarl. "But they still have soft skulls like anyone else."

Bahr lifted his shackled wrists. "Next time they unchain us to leak our lizards, we grab a rock and bash in their heads—"

"We're not bashing in heads," I said.

"Easy for you to say," Kardos jeered. "You don't know their queen. She'll have all our heads on pikes before we can say hello—including yours."

"He's right," Beaufort said. "She has a vicious streak, and a vendetta against anyone who defied her."

"You all fought against her?"

"Except for the scholars," Sarva answered. As usual, the scholars remained silent. They both seemed terrified.

"The rest of us fought with the Komizar," Bahr said. "Now, that man was a real leader."

The man who chopped off children's fingers?

I had heard rumors about him. That he was twelve feet tall. That his sword was made from the teeth of dragons. That he was an Ancient who had survived the centuries. That he wasn't really slain because it was impossible to slay a man who was part god. The stories surrounding him were as embellished as the ones that explained the stars in the sky. By the time information reached Hell's Mouth, it was hard to tell fact from myth. Even Bahr's firsthand account seemed more myth than truth. *No one disobeyed his commands. He could silence the devil with a whisper.*

His cruel punishment of children was the only story that didn't feel like myth. I remembered Kazi's eyes when she flung her fingers up in front of me. *Look at my fingers, Jase! Take a good long look.* In that moment, her eyes told me everything. I saw the desperate life she'd been forced to live.

Synové had caught some game—a small antelope—and its split carcass sizzled over a spit. We were camped in a copse of spirit trees that sprouted up among ruins. Trees walked up circular staircases and perched in windows like thin ghosts. Bahr didn't seem so brave about bashing in heads now. His head turned at every rustle, and I doubted he'd want to step alone into the dark to leak anything now.

I was chained to a tree. We all were. I had a shackle around my ankle once again.

Kazi was off tending Mije. She managed to avoid me all day, which took some effort since we were headed in the same direction.

Natiya reached over the fire and split the ribs of the antelope to help it cook faster.

"Hungry?" I asked. "Are you still eating for two? Or maybe it's eight by now? Your lies seem to multiply like maggots."

"Watch your mouth, *Patrei*," Eben warned, brandishing his knife. At least that much of what Natiya had said was true, he was good with a knife.

"Just eating for myself," she answered, cheerfully patting her flat stomach.

"Your queen never intended to come, did she? She's not just an invader but a liar too."

"I said, watch your mouth!" Eben snapped.

"Her letter was a farce," I snarled.

"My letter to her was a farce," Kazi answered. All our heads turned. She stepped out of the shadows into the light of the fire. "And the queen knew it. I gave her ample clues—ones you and your brothers didn't see. Golden thannis? It's poison. I asked her to bring you a gift of poison." Her tone was thick with sarcasm. "I would never have asked her to come to Tor's Watch."

She said it with scorn, like my home was beneath the queen. I stared at her. From the very beginning, everything was a lie. "Was there ever anything truthful about you?"

She met my gaze. "You will not lecture me about truth. Ever."

"I was under no obligation to tell you about family business."

"Business? That's what you call it? Stockpiling an arsenal of weapons?"

"Yes! That is our business! And we had every right—"

"To put all the kingdoms under your thumb? To put a rope around the queen's neck?"

"There you go with your Vendan embellishments again!"

"You were hiding known fugitives!"

"And you were—"

"Back, both of you!" Eben came between us, pushing us apart, our chests still heaving. I hadn't realized I had stood up or that she had stepped so close we were screaming inches from each other.

She glared at me, her breaths still coming in gasps. "The queen is not a liar. She couldn't submit to your thinly veiled demand to come to Tor's Watch because she's confined to her bed. She *can't* travel. Or I promise you she would be here to take this scum back to face justice herself!"

Her eyes glistened. "Don't ever talk to me about truth again." Her voice was broken, shaky. She turned on her heel and disappeared back into the shadows.

CHAPTER FIFTY-THREE

KAZI

I STOOPED AT THE CREEK'S EDGE, FILLING THE LAST WATER skin. Broken stone walls jutted up from the landscape around me. I had been grateful for the ruins last night and the dark cave they gave me to sleep in away from everyone else. It was likely the last shelter we would have for a while.

I corked the full water skin, and when I stood and turned Eben was there watching me.

"I'll help you with those," he said. He gathered five skins up in his arms, paused and looked at me again. "You all right?"

It wasn't like Eben to ask a question like that. You had to be all right, always. "What do you mean?"

He looked at me hesitantly. "That was him back there?"

Him. My blood rushed a little faster. Now I understood. Of all his secrets, how could Jase have not told me this? He knew what Zane had done. "Yes," I answered. "That was him."

Eben's lip lifted in disgust. "The bastard. But you did the right thing,

Kazi. I know it wasn't easy for you to leave him behind. There will be another chance. We'll go back."

I shook my head. "No, Eben. We both know he won't be there. By then he'll be long gone, hiding in some other faraway hole. I can't spend another eleven years looking for him."

"I'm sorry."

"No need to be sorry," I said, trying to force cheer into my voice. Instead my words came out wooden. "Look at the other bastards we caught. The one we set out for and a bonus of five."

"Six," he corrected. "What about the *Patrei?*"

I swallowed. "Yes. Six. The *Patrei* too."

But there was something I needed to tell Eben.

Something I had to tell them all, including Jase.

***

It was the laughter.

It had always been the laughter that needled through me, a repeated stitch that surfaced over and over again.

Laughter reveals in the same way a sigh or a glance does. It's an unintentional language. Worry, fear, deceit—they hide in the things unsaid.

Something about the laughter hadn't felt right that first night I discovered the captain and the others in the enclave, but the shock of their words had overshadowed it.

Last night when I had disappeared into the shadows I heard it again, all of them laughing, thinking Jase had gotten the better of me. That he had driven me away.

It wasn't laughter filled with merriment. It was filled with smug derision. The kind I remembered hearing from merchants when they tricked someone into paying more than they should, the kind of laughter that always came later, after their sucker was gone.

It was that kind of laughter I'd heard that first night when I heard them discussing the Ballengers. It wasn't a laughter of mirth but of mockery. The captain and his cohorts had been laughing *at* the Ballengers.

Was it a double-cross?

A betrayal?

Thanks to the Ballengers, our riches will only become greater.

Was Illarion using them?

The queen had said he was an average swordsman and commander, *but he's an above average deceiver. His skill is in his patience.*

Just as he had played two roles at the citadelle in Morrighan, had he played two roles at Tor's Watch? The role he wanted Jase's family to see, and his hidden role to benefit himself? I was certain the Ballengers had been duped.

"Let's be honest, Kazi," Natiya said when I gathered them at the creek's edge to tell them my suspicion. "Are you sure you're not just seeing the things you want to see because you still care for Jase?"

"That's over," I answered. "Some betrayals run too deep." His lie about Zane left me raw, and I saw the bitterness in his eyes too, when he caught me at the enclave. Our mutual betrayals had shattered anything we once had. I shook my head. "This isn't about Jase and me. It's about knowing the truth. Setting a trap for the queen? Jase's dismissal of the accusation was swift and genuine. I know that much about him."

"You thought other things about him were genuine too," Wren said.

I sat down on the tumbled wall at the creek's edge trying to sort it out, what was real and what was false, but I knew what I'd heard and the thirst for revenge against the queen had been thick in Illarion's voice. Jase would have nothing to gain from it. "Putting a noose around the queen's neck was the captain's agenda," I said. "For him, it's as much about revenge as riches. When he joined forces with the Komizar, he'd hoped to become a wealthy man, and instead the queen made him a hunted one. And putting all the kingdoms under his thumb? Jase's world is Hell's Mouth, Tor's Watch, the arena, and that's it. He doesn't want more than that." I looked to Wren, Synové for confirmation. "You both know."

They nodded.

"Even if it was a double cross, that still doesn't exonerate the Ballengers," Natiya countered.

Eben agreed. "They were hiding known fugitives for what they thought were their own purposes. Weapons."

And that was the crux of it, the one thing we couldn't ignore.

"To be accurate, the Ballengers only hid one fugitive," Wren corrected. "Even we didn't know the others were alive, and there was no warrant for them."

"Harboring just one fugitive is enough to charge him with conspiracy," Natiya said. "The Alliance of Kingdoms is very clear on that. It's in the treaties. We'll have to leave it to the queen to decide his fate."

Eben and Natiya left to start loading the prisoners back in the wagon. Today we would rendezvous with Griz and the troops who would escort us the rest of the way.

"When are you going to tell Jase?" Wren asked.

"Before we leave. I want him to know before we reach Sentinel Valley."

Synové frowned, swishing her bare feet through the shallow water. "You can't let him drive the wagon once he knows. He might drive the whole bunch of them off into a gorge. Bahr will not be going that way."

Wren and I both eyed her suspiciously. I had seen her watching Bahr, hunger in her expression. She had taunted him to make a run for it more than once. "How *will* he be going, Synové?" I asked.

She hopped out of the water, splashing us both. "However the queen chooses, of course," she answered and walked away, saying she was going to help with the prisoners.

"She's right about the wagon," Wren said. "He'll try something. The Ballengers don't take betrayal well."

How well I knew that. Priya had already pledged her revenge on me in multiple ugly ways. I was probably the number-one criminal listed on a warrant in Hell's Mouth by now.

"We'll chain his leg to the footbed," I said. "Jase takes his role of *Patrei* too seriously to take his own life." And that way he wouldn't be able to jump over the seat and attack them either. I had seen what his fist was capable of.

"He wouldn't be here at all if he'd stepped aside like you ordered. And then he all but let you take him down to use as a shield. I'm not sure we'd have gotten out of there otherwise. Every one of those Ballengers had blood in their eyes."

"What? That's crazy. I took him by surprise."

"He knows your tricks by now. I don't think he was surprised. And I saw him at the settlement, wrestling with his brothers. He's quick."

"Even so, I know what happened, and you were behind me where you couldn't see as well."

She shrugged. "Maybe so. But some things you can see better from a distance."

CHAPTER FIFTY-FOUR

JASE

"Is this the point where I'm supposed to plead for my life?"

While Eben and Natiya loaded the other prisoners into a wagon, Wren and Synové led me into the forest, then tied me to a tree.

"Could be," Wren said. "Just be quiet and listen."

Listen to what?

They turned and left, and I wondered if the plan was to leave me here to rot—or be eaten by a Candok. Minutes later, I heard rustling behind me. Human footsteps. Not Candok. I wasn't sure it worried me any less.

Kazi came into view. She stood in front of me and told me she wanted me to listen and not say a single word. There were things I needed to hear. She'd gag me if she had to.

"You can spare me another lecture on being a thief—"

"I said *not a word*."

I fumed. Strained against the rope that held me. "You have a true captive audience."

I didn't say another word. She paced in front of me as she spoke, trying to convince me I had been played by Beaufort. Her voice held no emotion, and her eyes were just as detached.

"Let me give you the particulars of his crimes." She told me Beaufort had been a trusted member of the Morrighese cabinet—a man of wealth and position, but he wanted more, and conspired with the Komizar to get it. She went into great detail, his crimes ranging from infiltrating the Morrighese citadelle with enemy soldiers, to poisoning the king, to planning an attack that killed the crown prince.

My mind ticked over the details she threw at me, taking in her version and Beaufort's, two scenarios, two possible lies, two possible truths. She continued to pace, her demeanor void of emotion—except for her hands tapping a tense dance against her thighs.

"Did I mention the thirty-two young soldiers who also died in the massacre he orchestrated? He was only warming up at that point. His crimes go on from there. You'll see soon enough.

"I realize you didn't know about the other men," she continued. "Torback and Phineas are Morrighese scholars who are able to decipher the secrets of the Ancients and bring them to life again. They're traitors too. They made vows to serve the gods, but instead they serve themselves."

She told me that Sarva, Kardos, and Bahr were Vendan. "Everyone thought they died on the battlefield. There were so many charred bodies it was hard to tell, but some of their personal effects were found. They obviously staged their deaths before they ran." She said Kardos was a general in the Komizar's army who used children as young as Lydia and Nash on his front lines. It was his method of unnerving enemy soldiers before he moved his cavalry forward.

"Sarva was the governor of a Vendan province, and Bahr a Sanctum guard." She said they led an attack against unarmed citizens, butchering them on the streets. Whole families died. Children, parents, grandparents.

One of those families was Wren's. She held her father as he died in her arms. "And Synové watched Bahr behead both of her parents. She had no choice but to run, because he came after her too. She was ten years old."

She turned to face me. "These are the men you gave sanctuary to, the ones who promised to make you weapons. What did you want them for, Jase? To protect Hell's Mouth? The arena? I can assure you, they had much bigger plans. You'll see just how big later today. I heard them reveling in the fact that they would have the kingdoms under their thumbs soon. That the Great Battle would look like a spring picnic. The captain's plans were for domination. The Ballengers were a lucky stepping stone for them, their means to an end.

"They laughed about it. They mocked you. I'm guessing they planned to kill your whole family once you gave them everything they needed—which apparently was supplies for weapons. Who better to acquire the raw materials than a wealthy family who has access to everything through the arena? I heard them laugh about the arsenal that they'd soon have. *Them*, not you. It wouldn't be the first time Captain Illarion has done something like this—but you knew when you hid a fugitive in order to get what you wanted that you were taking a risk."

She stopped pacing and stared at me as if she was waiting for something. "Well?"

"Oh? I have permission to speak now?"

She nodded.

My gaze locked onto hers and I spoke slowly, so each word had time to sink in. "Let me see if I have this straight. What you're telling me is they infiltrated Tor's Watch under false pretenses. They violated my family's trust. They put them at risk. Ate our food. Slept in our beds. They used us. They made promises they had no intention of keeping. They betrayed us."

She swallowed, my point made.

"So tell me, how are they different from you?"

She looked at me like I had slapped her face. "I wouldn't have killed you, Jase. I wouldn't have butchered your family. Can you say the same for them?"

"You intended to poison my family! You thought you were putting birchwings in our food!"

"It's not a poison and you know it! It's only a sedative."

"Nash and Lydia are children! I don't care what it is!"

"We didn't put it in their food!"

"And yet, Beaufort and his men never even did that much to us."

"Yet."

"We're an independent realm, the *first* country, and you violated our sovereignty. Who am I supposed to believe? A Rahtan soldier who dishonored my family's trust? Who mocked me? Or the word of a queen I've never met who seized land that was *ours*?"

"You have no borders, Jase. The land was in the Cam Lanteux. She chose it based on what the king told her. How was she to know?"

"So that excuse works for her, but not for me? I didn't know what Beaufort's crimes were beyond a tattered bill that he refuted."

"All you had to do was ask."

"We did! My father asked the king's magistrate, who said he had no information about him."

"Then you should have asked the queen!"

"The queen who doesn't answer our letters? The queen who doesn't even know we exist?"

"You hid him, Jase. That says everything." She paused, her eyes drilling into mine. "You hid a lot of things."

"Which crime am I really here for, Kazi? Hiding Beaufort, or hiding Zane?"

Her lip quivered. She turned and walked away, saying over her shoulder, "Wren and Synové will come back to get you." I strained against the ropes, crazy thoughts running through my head, thoughts that made no sense.

"Kazi, wait!" I called.

She stopped and for long seconds looked down at the ground.

"I was going to tell you about Zane," I said. "I swear I was."

She spun to face me. "When, Jase? When I took your ring, I gave it back to you when it mattered. When it helped you save everything you cared about. You had the chance to tell me about Zane—when it mattered to me. But you didn't."

She left, and I wished there had been anger in her voice or misery in her eyes or *something*. Instead, there was nothing, vast empty plains of nothing, and it hit me harder than if she had struck me in the jaw again.

The wind, time,
They circle, repeat,
Teaching us to be ever watchful,
For freedoms are never won,
Once and for all,
But must be won over and over again.

—Song of Jezelia

CHAPTER FIFTY-FIVE

KAZI

TAKE A GOOD, LONG LOOK AND REMEMBER THE LIVES LOST. REAL people that someone loved. Before you go about the task I have given you, see the devastation and remember what they did. What could happen again. Know what is at stake. Dragons eventually wake and crawl from their dark dens.

We stood at the mouth of Sentinel Valley, and I knew. I had done at least one right thing. Even justice couldn't erase scars—it only delivered on a promise to the living that evil would not go unpunished. And maybe it also delivered hope that evil could be stopped for good.

That promise bloomed now, in the sky, the soil, the wind. The spirits whispered to me. My mother whispered to me. *Shhh, Kazi. Listen. Hear the language that isn't spoken, for everyone can hear spoken words, but only a few can hear the heart that beats behind them.*

I heard the heart of the valley, the beat that still swelled through it.

"No!" Bahr cried. "I'm not going down there! No!" As soon as he spotted our destination, he began yanking against his chains.

Sarva and Kardos blustered similar protests. Some soldiers believed deserters could be sucked into the underworld, the dead recognizing their footfalls and reaching up through the earth to pull them under.

"You'll go and you'll walk the whole length—if you make it that far," Synové said, wanting to add to his suffering. It would slow us down, but we'd promised Synové that the long ride would be the best torture she could inflict, and this much agony Bahr was owed.

Even the captain, who had no such Vendan superstitions, seemed to pale at the prospect of returning to the site of the infamous battle he had helped orchestrate. Phineas bent over and puked, and he hadn't even seen anything yet.

Jase alone looked on with curiosity. He had never been here before. His eyes skimmed the towering cliffs, the ruins that sat upon them, and the peculiar green mounds of grass that rose up in the distance.

Eben drove the wagon behind us, and Natiya and Wren rode beside him, ready to shoot or cut down anyone who made an errant move other than walking straight ahead. Synové and I walked on either side of the prisoners.

For at least a mile in, no one spoke. For some of us, the valley demanded reverence, but for others, like Bahr, I was sure they feared a noise might wake the dead. A shadow passed overhead and Bahr fell to the ground, frantically looking up, his nerves unraveling. Circling high above us were two racaa, probably wishing we were antelope. Synové smiled when she saw them. "Move along," she ordered, motioning with her sword. Kardos eyed a decaying wagon, looking desperate, ready to pry anything loose to use as a weapon. Maybe he heard the voices too, or maybe he felt the dead clawing at his feet.

The wind rustled, the grass moving in waves, like a message being passed. *They're coming.*

Jase stopped at the bones of a brezalot, its giant bleached ribs pointing like spears to the sky. "What is it?" he asked.

Brezalots were not found on this part of the continent. "Similar to horses," I explained. "Majestic, giant creatures, for the most part wild and unstoppable, but the Komizar managed to subvert their beauty and turn them into weapons. Hundreds of them died here too."

Halfway in, we saw a rock memorial, a tattered white shirt on top of it, waving in the breeze. I watched Jase take it all in, the mass graves, the scattered human bones dug up by beasts, the rusted and abandoned weapons thick with grass, the occasional skull, grinning up at the cliffs. His eyes were dark clouds, sweeping from one side to the other. "How many died?" he asked.

"Twenty thousand. In one day. But as Sarva mentioned, this was just a spring picnic compared with what they had planned."

He didn't say anything, but his jaw was rigid. He turned, looking long and hard at Sarva, the same kind of hunger in his eyes as I saw in Synové's when she looked at Bahr.

Kardos suddenly screamed, his foot falling into the soil up to his knee. He scrambled away and looked back. It was only a collapsed burrow, but they all looked at it with horror, even the captain, waiting for a bony hand to emerge. Yes, this was a torture of their own making.

As we neared the end of the valley, we spotted riders coming toward us. I noticed the captain visibly brighten, but then he cursed. They were Morrighese troops. A low shudder rolled through Torback.

"It began with the stars," Phineas suddenly blurted out. I turned and looked at him. His eyes were glazed, his expression lost. "It was the tembris that showed us. The stars brought a—"

"Shut up!" the captain ordered.

"Why?" Phineas asked. "What difference does it make now? We're all going to die anyway."

"What do you mean, *It began with the stars*?" I asked.

"Quiet!" Torback yelled.

"We're not going to die!" Bahr growled. "There's still time!"

"It's too late," Phineas said. "It's too late for all of us." He looked at

Jase. "I'm sorry. There never was a fever cure. He knew what would make you listen. I tried to—"

"Stupid bastard—" Sarva lunged toward him. A warning arrow hissed through the air but at the same time, Bahr lunged toward Phineas too, his fist jamming into his gut. Wren, Synové, and I moved swiftly, knocking Bahr and Sarva to their stomachs and pressing swords to their backs. Eben and Natiya nocked arrows, ordering Jase, Torback, Kardos, and the captain down on their knees.

Phineas stood frozen, his mouth open, his eyes wide as if terrified by the sudden swirl of commotion. But then I saw a trickle of blood on the front of his shirt. He dropped to his knees, still unable to speak. I left Bahr facedown, ordering him not to move and went to Phineas just as he fell forward. A giant brezalot rib protruded from his back. I looked over at the captain, who had been directly behind Phineas. His expression was smug and remorseless.

We were prepared for them to attack us, but not one another.

I rolled Phineas to his side and pulled him up into my arms. His face was splotched with tears. "I'm sorry," he gasped, every word an effort. "The olives. The casks." He coughed, blood seeping from his mouth. "The room. Where you found me. The papers." He let out a long, wheezing breath.

"What about the papers?" I said.

"Destroy them. Make sure—"

His lips stilled. His chest stilled. But his eyes remained frozen on me, still afraid.

The captain didn't look smug now. I saw the sweat bead on his upper lip as the king approached. We had arrived at the encampment just outside the southern entrance to the valley. The queen's brother, Bryn, was the newly crowned King of Morrighan, his father having passed last year. He walked toward us leaning heavily on his cane. He was a young man, robust and healthy, but he'd lost his lower right leg in the attempt on his life. With every labored step, the king had a reminder of the captain's treachery. We had the prisoners lined up for inspection, but the king approached me first.

"Your Majesty," I said, bowing. Wren and Synové did the same. He stopped us mid-bow, reaching out and touching my shoulder.

"No," he said. "I should be the one bending a knee to all of you. I would, but I might not get up again." He was without pretense, much like his sister.

He smiled. I knew he was trying to pretend this moment wasn't affecting him as much as it was. He was a handsome man, but old for his years. The queen said he had once been her humorous brother, the prankster she often got into trouble with as a child. There was no humor in his eyes anymore. His family had been decimated.

He told me he would be leaving twenty soldiers with us as escort and support, and then walked with me down the line of prisoners, looking at each one as I told him who they were and what they had done. First Kardos, Sarva, and Bahr, and then we came to Torback. He had actually been one of the king's tutors when he was a child.

"You found a full snake's nest. We didn't know about him." He stared at Torback for a long while, and when Torback buckled under the heat of his scrutiny, babbling for his life, the king silenced him.

"There was another scholar," I explained. "The captain murdered him on the way here."

"So I heard," he said. "Phineas was hardly more than a boy himself when he disappeared from Morrighan. The conspiracy was a long time in the planning." He stepped in front of the captain, his scrutiny searing.

"As you well know, Captain Illarion. The one thing you will get that my brothers and thousands of others didn't is justice. Since you aligned yourself with the Komizar, you'll face Vendan judgement. My sister has a court waiting for you."

The captain stared back, silent, maybe seeing the boy king he had betrayed, maybe retracing the choices he could have made. I saw Death standing behind him, waiting to take him. Maybe not here. Not today. Maybe on a windy turret in Venda justice would be served, when the Watch Captain's neck snapped and it was time to move on to his final judgement.

"And who is this?" the king asked, stepping in front of Jase.

"The *Patrei* of Hell's Mouth," Jase answered, glaring at the king, "and I demand to be released."

The king turned toward me. "And he's here because?"

"Tell him, Kazi," Jase said. "Explain to him why I'm here and not home protecting my family and empire."

I swallowed, the answer trapped in my throat.

Griz stepped forward and answered before I could. "He gave the fugitives sanctuary and the supplies to build an arsenal of weapons."

"Then he'll face a noose too."

CHAPTER FIFTY-SIX

JASE

OVER AND OVER AGAIN AS I HAD WALKED THROUGH THE VALLEY I thought to myself, *Our weapons were not meant for this. Never for this.* I stared at Sarva, remembering when he tried to take the launcher from me, remembering all their promises, *We'll have the cure soon.* They had shown my father the ledgers of the Ancients, the magic of cures in formulas we couldn't understand, but they promised that the scholars were deciphering them and we bought it. The months were peppered with false breakthroughs and progress whenever our patience wore thin.

Sarva and Beaufort both looked far too cocky, as if there was still a chance of escape. Twenty Morrighese troops were escorting us back to Venda—not to mention the fellow named Griz, who was three men in one. There was bad blood between him and the Vendans, and he would never let them out of his sight. There'd be no slipping away, though it was still on my mind. I had to get home. Whatever league was trying to displace us, it wouldn't be long before they regrouped and came after us again. Had Beaufort been conspiring with one of them? It seemed unlikely. He'd been holed up at Tor's Watch for almost a year with no outside contact. Except for Zane. He was Beaufort's lone contact with the outside world.

Somewhere deep down, I had known they couldn't be trusted. My father knew. That's why he had sent a letter to the king's magistrate. Yet in spite of the vague reply, he still let them into Tor's Watch.

I'm sorry. There never was a fever cure. He knew what would make you listen.

How? How did an on-the-run fugitive know about my sister and brother? Sylvey and Micah died four years ago, years before Beaufort arrived at Tor's Watch. It wasn't news anymore. Somehow he'd done his research. He found the chink in our armor—the one thing that would open the door to Tor's Watch and the Ballenger purse, a wound that still wept.

I had been first among my father's sons to agree to it. The guilt of Sylvey had stayed with me, including the things I did after she died. I'd been haunted by her pleas, her fear of being trapped in a cold dark tomb, the simple promise I wouldn't give her in her last moments. Two days after her funeral, I stole her body. I did the unthinkable and desecrated her tomb in the middle of the night. No one ever knew. Everyone thought I had disappeared from grief, but I had taken her wrapped body high into the Moro mountains and buried it in the most beautiful place I could find, the kind of place she would love, at the base of Breda's Tears, just below the seventh waterfall where ferns and flowers bloomed, where the sun shone in the day and the moon glowed at night. I marked it with a single stone and the tears that wet it were not Breda's but my own.

Beaufort's false promise had hit its mark with resounding accuracy. It sickened me how well he had strung us along, how perfectly he explained one delay after another, how the others had backed him up. How humble and earnest they had all been—until the end. When they were close to getting what they wanted, their arrogance started showing.

I looked over at them, sitting together, eating their dinner. The rage in me rose. We were forced to eat with our hands shackled—a trencher of bread and meat only—no plates, no utensils, nothing that might be used as a weapon against one another. Our keepers didn't want any more prisoners dying en route.

What had they all been trying to keep Phineas from saying? The few words he said were only babble. Stars? The tembris showing him? He'd been shaken by the staggering death and destruction in the valley. I had been too. But something else ate at him. *It was just a spring picnic compared to what they had planned.*

What was it they had planned? Kazi had mentioned domination of the kingdoms. What had seemed ludicrous when she first told me didn't seem implausible now. *I'm guessing they planned to kill your whole family once you gave them everything they needed.*

I eyed Sarva, shoving the last of his dinner into his mouth. *You can't take that.* He had tried to stop me from taking the launcher because he didn't want me to be armed. Why? Because I might be able to stop him from killing my family? After seeing a whole valley swollen with dead, I knew one family was nothing to him. He licked his fingers and looked up at me. A smirk crossed his lip, *fool,* and that was all it took.

I flew across the expanse, grabbed him with both shackled hands and threw him across the clearing. He tumbled over the dirt, jumped to his feet, and I came at him again, both chained hands swinging into his gut, doubling him over. I heard the yelling, someone saying, *Let them fight.* I doubted anyone could have stopped us. He returned my blows, his shackles not diminishing the impact of his fists as they slammed into my stomach. Another powerful strike to my shoulder knocked me to the ground, but it was the words he hissed between blows when our grips strained against each other—mocking my father, my family, the things he would do to them—that blinded me with fury. I couldn't believe we'd let this monster into our home.

I jammed my elbow into his side, my forearm into his face, and when he stumbled to the side I swooped my chained hands over his head, pulling the chain tight against his neck. He choked and gasped, his fingers struggling to pull it away. "Now, let me tell you what I'm going to do to you, Sarva—"

I felt a sword at my back. "That's enough, *Patrei*. He'll die by Vendan justice, not yours." Eben ordered me to let him go. I hesitated, and he pushed the sword harder. "Now." I loosened my hold, slipping the chain free, and Sarva dropped to the ground, gasping for air.

I looked over at Beaufort with a clear message, *You're next*, before a guard hauled me away.

The Lost Horses streaked across the sky in their endless quest to find their mistress. Usually, spotting them made me think of loyalty and determination, but now they only filled me with a sense of futility, a quest that would never be realized. It made me think of my father and his deathbed wish, *Make her come*. I should appreciate the irony—I was going to meet the queen, but not in the way he had envisioned.

They had chained me over on the far side of camp, away from Sarva and the others, this time with my leg to the trunk of a fallen tree to make sure I didn't go anywhere. Natiya had come by and bandaged a cut on my arm where Sarva's shackles had slashed it. I sat on the trunk, picking at the frayed edges of the bandage, looking up at the heavens, wondering if the gods were looking back.

It began with the stars. Phineas's words were the same ones Greyson Ballenger had written in our histories. Everything began with the stars. Even—

I tried to get it out of my head, but I couldn't.

Kazi and I began with the stars.

On a ledge in the middle of nowhere, we counted the stars together and then we kissed. We became part of something as endless as a night sky, and I had believed it could be just as lasting. Even when I discovered her betrayal, some small part of me still held hope. She had loved me, I was certain, even if she wouldn't say it. I wanted to believe there was an explanation, that what we had could somehow be salvaged. I still wasn't ready to let go.

But our end was as clear as our beginning—the moment she saw Zane. It was the final blow. When she had looked from Zane to me, the look in her eyes—it wasn't hatred—I watched something in her die. Us.

I gave the ring back to you when it mattered.

She would never believe another word I said. Truth that came too late was as useful as a meal to a dead man.

"Looks like I can't step away for one minute. Getting into more trouble, I hear?"

I startled at her voice but kept my eyes fixed on the horizon. Kazi stood somewhere close behind me. I didn't answer, hoping her curiosity was satisfied and she'd go away. I couldn't trust myself around her.

My silence didn't sway her. "I was in the king's tent," she explained. "I was having dinner with him so I didn't hear the ruckus."

"Dinner with the king? You're moving up in the world. To think, just a few nights ago you were having dinner with the likes of me."

I heard the bitter implication that I cared and immediately regretted it. "I'm sorry. I'm angry about a lot of things but not that you had dinner with the king."

She stepped over the log and stood in front of me so I had to look at her.

Emotions battled inside me—anger, resentment, guilt, and surprisingly, desire. I fought an impulse to pull her into my arms, to press my lips to hers, whisper in her ear, to make the last few days disappear, to explain things that should have been explained long ago, to tell her about Zane when I knew it would only make her hate me more, because after everything she had been through it was a truth she deserved, but those same thoughts spun with others and anger pounded in my temples that I was here at all, that she had whittled her way into my life and Tor's Watch under false pretenses. That she had strung me along on a grand scale.

Her gaze was as warm as frost. "What are you angry about?" she asked.

I laughed. "Really? It's not obvious?" I rattled the chain on my leg. "I've been deceived by just about everyone I trusted or counted on—right down to the cook I hired." I stood so I was looking down at her now. "The cook I hired for you." The words were meant to stab her, but instead they stabbed me. She never promised me tomorrows, and now I knew why.

She blinked at last, the frost splintering. Emotion rushed through me again that I couldn't trust. "You should go."

She didn't move. "What's the fever cure?" she asked.

"Another thing that never existed. Please, Kazi, I need you to leave."

"I heard Phineas say 'He knew it would make you listen.' What did he mean?"

I sighed and sat back on the log. "My brother and sister that I told you about, Micah and Sylvey—" I cleared my throat. "They died from a fever. Beaufort figured it out. He found a weak spot in my family and used it to wheedle his way into our good graces. He claimed he had a cure. That was all he needed to say to make my mother invite him in. And my father." I looked at her sharply. "Yes, we wanted the weapons too. Yes, we gave him the supplies. Yes, we looked the other way to get what we wanted. Is that what you wanted to hear? We knew he was trouble, even if we didn't know exactly what kind." I raked my hands through my hair, still wishing she'd leave. Instead she sat down beside me.

"No, that's not what I wanted to hear," she said quietly.

I leaned forward and shook my head. "Why didn't you just tell me about Beaufort when you first came?"

"We didn't know for sure if he was even there, and if he was there it was obvious it was with the Ballenger welcome. If I had told you, what would you have done, Jase? Be honest. Alerted him? Questioned him so he could disappear again? Denied it? Isn't that exactly what you did when I spotted him outside Darkcottage? You claimed he was a groundsman. You lied to me and hid who he was. You saw the devastation today, and now you know their crimes even beyond that valley. These men deserve to be held accountable. I made a vow to the queen and to the gods that I would bring the captain back. I couldn't risk losing him by telling you."

"We were not going to use our weapons for that," I said, motioning in the direction of the valley. "If you ever knew me at all, you know that much."

She nodded. "It's in the hands of the queen now."

<hr />

It was late. The camp was asleep, except for the soldiers on watch—and Kazi. I had seen her pacing, watching the other prisoners as if she entrusted their care to no one else. *I made a vow to the queen and to the gods.* We may have grown up differently, but there were many ways that Kazi and I were alike.

She finally rested, propping herself up against a thin, leafless tree, but still staring into the darkness.

You asked me why an open world frightens me, Jase? Because it gives me nowhere to hide.

I thought of all the stories I had told her when we were chained together in the wilderness, the stories I could tell her now to help her fall asleep. I thought of the riddle I had promised her, the one that still circled through my head. The one I could never tell her now. I rolled over so I wouldn't have to look at her and tried to remember that I wasn't supposed to care.

CHAPTER FIFTY-SEVEN

KAZI

"And sometimes she likes to snip the eyelids away first so you have to look at her. It depends on her mood . . ."

I walked away as Synové concocted yet another punishment, describing it in gruesome detail to torture Bahr and the other prisoners. Mostly Bahr. These past weeks, she always managed to dip into a deeper well of creativity, making sure he was within earshot of her as she wondered aloud about the punishments the queen would dole out. I saw it wear on him. He no longer cursed her but listened in grim silence.

Mije and the other horses stood in the middle of Misoula Creek, drinking and cooling themselves. The sun was high and hot, the last days of summer taking a final bow. The break was a welcome respite. Even with troops to relieve us, I had rarely stepped away from the prisoners, always keeping my eye on them, wary that they would vanish before I could deliver them to the queen. The captain had a slippery history, but this wide, barren valley of sandstone and high cliffs was almost a prison in itself. He'd be going nowhere here.

I stopped at a sparkling shallow where fool's gold glittered through the clear water, and I bent down to splash my face. The caravan was strewn out along the banks of the creek, but my attention settled on Jase. His hands were unshackled for the rest stop, and he was rinsing out his shirt. He'd gotten into another fight, this time with both Sarva and Bahr. They had said something to set him off, but he didn't say what it was. It was Synové who broke up the fight, saying she wanted to make sure Bahr lasted long enough to face the justice he deserved.

Jase had gotten a bloody nose out of the skirmish and had used his shirt to wipe his face. As he washed it, I noticed a group of soldiers looking at his tattoo, probably wondering at its significance, but certainly not understanding the story behind it, not understanding the reasons he got it when he was only fifteen, not understanding anything about the man who wore it, just as I hadn't the first time I had seen it. I found myself wanting to tell them about the long history of Tor's Watch, the recent settlement that Jase had helped build, the sluice, the root cellar, the small Vendan boy he taught to dig post holes. I wanted to tell them about the ongoing power wars that threatened Jase's home, the town he kept safe, the secret enemies who battled to take it, the family who had clothed me and welcomed me to their table. Jase was more than just a prisoner they looked at with curiosity. He was a *Patrei*, and that symbol tattooed across his chest was a promise, centuries of promises, to protect. It was in his blood. His world was not our world.

But I had wanted it to be.

Now, with our days together coming to an end, I realized that with everything that I knew about him, there was still so much more I didn't know—or hadn't bothered to know. Like Sylvey. I'd heard Jase's voice crack when he said her name.

I was going to tell you, I swear I was.

Sometimes it seemed the timing of the entire world was off, our intentions coming too soon or too late, life crowding up to blur our vision, and only later when the dust settles can we see our missteps. I could have given him that ring sooner. I could have saved him the worry. But there were questions I had wanted to avoid, just as he had wanted to avoid mine.

"Stop staring and enjoy the break while you can," Wren said. I hadn't heard her walk up behind me.

"Someone still with them?" I asked, craning my neck to look through soldiers and horses for Beaufort and the others. Wren knew that by "someone" I meant one of us. It wasn't that I didn't trust the Morrighese soldiers, but I trusted us more. We were too close now to take any chances. I'd had to choose between Zane and these men—I wasn't about to lose them too.

"Relax. Eben and Synové are with them."

I looked back at Jase. After two fights, we now kept him separated from the other prisoners.

"You have to stop beating yourself up, Kazi," Wren said. "You gave him a chance to step aside. And according to Griz, it was an undeserved chance."

"I know how it looks to Griz, but the bare facts don't always tell the whole truth. I didn't give him any chance. A Ballenger never steps aside. They hold their ground. They protect what's theirs at all costs. And I knew that."

Wren shook her head. "It's that stubborn pride of theirs."

"It's more than that. It's their history. It's who they are."

We sat down together on the bank and cooled our feet in the water. "I'm still worried about what Bahr said to Phineas."

"That 'There's still time'?"

I nodded. We had interrogated every prisoner individually, but none would say a word, not even with the hope of a deal to spare their lives, as if some other hope was still out there. "It's as if they're expecting a rescue, and if they are, that means they weren't working alone."

"He might have meant there was still a chance for them to escape. They've done it before."

Possibly. I had seen them watching for opportunities, eyeing weapons and stands of forests to disappear into. "But there was one other thing—when the captain first saw troops riding toward us, his face brightened, as if he thought they were somebody else."

Wren thought for a moment. "It could be they were working with a league. Paxton maybe?"

"Yes. Or one of the others." Or worst case scenario, several of them together. I remembered Rybart and Truko walking the streets together back in Hell's Mouth.

"Even if they were working with a league to take down the Ballengers, the important thing is, by their own words, they didn't have an arsenal yet. We got there in time and destroyed their plans. We saw them go up in flames. Plus, we have the architects for those weapons in custody. Whatever plans they had are finished. Life will go on as usual at Tor's Watch."

I thought about the captain's reaction when we destroyed the plans—the piles of documents that were his key to riches. His fury at their loss was real. The same with Torback, all his work up in flames. I was certain by their reactions that they were all burned—but then what were the papers that Phineas wanted me to destroy? He had mentioned olives in his last breaths too. *Olives?* Maybe as he struggled with his last words he became confused. Maybe he meant the papers I had already destroyed.

"Break's over!" Griz called. "Let's move out."

Wren dipped her handkerchief into the water and tied it in a cooling band around her head. "I better get back before Synové starts in on another gruesome end. We'll never get her moving." But neither of us begrudged any fear she wanted to inflict. Bahr had earned it. Synové and many others would have to live with the fear Bahr had inflicted on them for the rest of their lives.

With the call to move out, soldiers began putting their boots back on and saddling horses. Jase wrung out his shirt and slung the twisted fabric over his shoulder. He sloshed back along the creek's edge with his boots in hand. His horse was tethered in the creek near mine. The axel on the wagon had broken more than a week ago, and we'd been forced to switch the prisoners to horses. While we made faster progress, it made for a tenser ride. Even with their hands tied in front of them and two horses tethered together, we had to keep a constant watch on our captives.

I waited at the bank's edge until he caught up, my toes nervously curling into the sand. It had been days since we had really spoken. The last time I tried to talk to him, he had asked me to leave. He didn't want to speak to me. I understood that.

He stopped in front me. "I get an escort back to my horse?" he asked.

I looked at his bare chest, the sweep of the tattooed wing seeming to wave me away now. I was an outsider again. I remembered when my fingernail used to outline the jagged edge of the feathers. "You should put your shirt back on so your back doesn't burn."

He stood ankle deep in the water, not moving, his shirt still dripping from his shoulder, the tilt of his head full of irritation. "What's really on your mind, Kazi?" He reminded me of how he had looked that day on the riverbank after we had escaped from the labor hunters. Then, he'd looked like he was ready to bash in my head, and I'd thought the chain was the only thing saving me. That seemed like years ago. He shifted weight, signaling his impatience.

"I was talking with Wren and Synové this morning," I said. "They're afraid that your family will retaliate against the settlement. It's my worry too. Will they?"

"And incur the further wrath of the Vendan queen? You don't need to worry." He started to walk on.

"Jase—"

He spun around. "I made a blood vow to protect them, Kazi. And the *Patrei*'s vow is his family's vow. We don't go back on our word. Call it that Ballenger pride you like to make fun of. Anything else?"

His expression was strained, as if he couldn't stand to be next to me. I thought there was nothing left inside of me to crumble, but I was wrong. His contempt was more than I could bear. "No. Nothing."

I began to step away when he lunged, pulling me with him as we tumbled to the ground. I didn't have time to yell or react. He hovered over me, his chest pounding against mine, his expression impossible to discern. "A scorpion," he explained. "You almost stepped on it." He looked at me for a second longer, and I wondered if he was thinking the same thing as me. *What happened to us? How did we get here?* But the answer was clear. Once again, we'd been shoved down an unexpected path, and there was no clawing our way back to the one we'd been on. A simple chain we had both cursed had done the unthinkable—it forced us to see the world through each other's eyes. Now we had to forget those worlds. Or maybe we would always be haunted by the memory of each other.

His grip on my arms tightened for a moment, a breath shuddering in his chest, but then he released me and stood. He grabbed one of his fallen boots then smashed it down. "It's dead. You should put your boots back on."

I got up and looked at the broken scorpion. A black ringtail. Its venom could kill you in seconds. I watched Jase walk away, uncertain if even he knew how strongly protection ran in his blood.

When we got back to where our horses were tethered, there was a commotion. Bahr had mounted his horse before his hands were chained or the horse's lead was tied to another. While some soldiers had their arrows drawn and were ordering him off his horse, Synové screamed above them. "Stand down! I have this! I said, stand down!"

Griz motioned to the soldiers, and they lowered their weapons. He knew Synové's archery skills, that she could easily take Bahr down on her own. But she didn't. She was doing the opposite. Taunting him to run like she had before. His eyes were crazed and his lips twisted. Maybe Synové's stories were finally getting the best of him. "Don't worry," she told him. "You have my word I won't put an arrow through your skull. But you're a coward, Bahr. A sniveling, weak coward who hides behind a sword. I bet you wouldn't make it a day out there alone. You'll save us the waste of a good rope if you run. Here! I'll even help you out." She tossed him her water skin, and he slung it over his shoulder. "Go," she ordered. "*Go!*"

He stared at her, uncertain what to do, freedom at his fingertips. His knuckles were white, gripping the reins.

"I won't kill you," Synové said softly. "I promise."

Griz's eyes were tight beads. He looked at Synové like she had lost her mind.

The whole camp was quiet, waiting, every breath held.

And then Bahr ran. He turned his horse and lit out as if demons chased behind him.

Griz glared at Synové. "Do something, or I will!"

Synové smiled. She walked over to her quiver of arrows and pulled out a blunt. Her movements were slow, smooth, calculated. Her chin lifted, her head turning, assessing the light wind.

Bahr was getting farther and farther away. A blunt would not stop him. She studied the horizon, waiting, adjusting the pristine glove the queen had given her, then she nocked the arrow. She lifted her bow and slowly pulled back, poised and calm as if she had choreographed every breath and breeze. Seconds passed and she finally let the arrow fly.

What was she doing?

It would not kill him. At this distance it likely wouldn't even stun him. He was at least two hundred yards away now.

I lost sight of the arrow in the bright sky, but then suddenly the water skin on Bahr's back exploded with a dark liquid.

"What the devil is that?" Griz yelled.

A chill ran down my back as Synové grinned. I knew.

"Blood," she answered. "Rich, ripe antelope blood."

It was only seconds before a dark cloud swooped across the horizon. It skimmed the parched valley floor like a winged rider heading toward us—toward Bahr, who still raced ahead. It happened fast. He was snatched up in its claws, and in seconds it was flying over us, Bahr writhing in its grip, screaming, and then, just as fast, they were both gone, the whoosh of the racaa's wings drowning out the last of his screams.

Synové's eyes narrowed, a grin still on her lips. "I guess I was wrong. He's not alone out there after all."

CHAPTER FIFTY-EIGHT

JASE

I COULDN'T SAY I WASN'T GLAD TO SEE BAHR DEPART, BUT afterward it made me think that if the queen had half the creative fury of Synové, I was in big trouble. But the queen was supposedly bedridden, so there was at least that. I had to look for whatever bright spots I could.

I wondered why she was confined to her bed. Had she been injured in the Great War? Rumor was that she was strong and had managed to bring down the twelve-foot, half-god Komizar. Maybe, like her brother, she had an injury she had never recovered from.

Griz had strong words with Synové after Bahr's departure, and she took them stoically. Apparently she had broken some rule of theirs, or maybe Griz just didn't want to arrive at the queen's doorstep emptyhanded with every prisoner snatched from his grip. Two were already dead. I noted the other prisoners had gone silent, maybe trying to avoid drawing Synové's attention. Last night at dinner, the only sound I heard out of them was a burp. In some ways, I was sorry that Griz had reprimanded her. I wouldn't have minded if she pulled that stunt at least one more time—on Beaufort.

Last night when we set camp, I had watched Kazi studying Synové, and I had wondered what she was thinking. Was she wishing she could see Zane suffer the way Bahr had? But that chance was gone. For eleven years, she had looked for him, and I had kept him out of her grasp. The right moment to tell her had never come.

Kazi told me this morning we weren't going to Venda, but to a place called Marabella. We'd be there today. I thought I'd have more time. I was caught off guard, and maybe that was the point—to keep the prisoners in the dark. I was sure the others still didn't know. She said Marabella was a former Dalbretch outpost that had been converted and expanded to serve as a place of mutual rule for two kingdoms. When the Dalbretch king and the Vendan queen married, they divided their time between the two kingdoms and also the outpost halfway between them.

Kazi was riding up ahead with Wren, Synové, Eben, and Natiya, surrounding the other prisoners. They guarded them like they were gold. I had seen the strain in her face this morning when she saddled Mije, as if she might lose them in these last hours. Ruins had become more plentiful as we traveled, and maybe that's what contributed to the tension—there were more places for bandits to hide. I was left to ride at the end of our caravan with Griz on one side of me and a Morrighese soldier on the other. If I were picked off by bandits, I supposed it wouldn't matter as much.

As we rode over a rise in the landscape someone called, "There it is!" It was still a long way off, but I caught my first glimpse of Marabella. Its high, white walls gleamed in the distance, and a city sprawled around it. Natiya had told me it was the first site designated as a settlement. I guessed there was less than an hour before we reached it.

"I need to speak to Kazi," I said.

Griz snorted, disinterested in my requests. "Nah."

"It's important."

He squinted an eye. "About what?"

"It's between me and her, you bastard; go get her." His eyes sparked and his fingers twitched and I knew I was about to get a mouthful of knuckles from a man three times my size and I added, "Please."

Kazi rode back, her face shining with sweat, a tense crease between her brows. "What is it?" she asked. "I need to stay with the other prisoners. They're jumpy."

So was she. She looked at me, waiting, impatient, and I realized what I had to say didn't really matter anymore.

"*Jase,*" she said, trying to hurry me along.

I blurted something else out instead. "Will I get a chance to speak?"

"Yes," she answered. "When you stand before the queen to answer to the charges. She'll hear you out."

"At her bedside? Is she dying?"

"What?"

"You said she was unable to travel and was confined to her bed. I thought that maybe—"

"No. It's nothing like that. Her physician ordered no travel. She miscarried her first child, and now she's expecting again."

CHAPTER FIFTY-NINE

KAZI

SCOUTS HAD RIDDEN AHEAD OF US, SO LONG BEFORE WE ARRIVED the news had spread. By the time we neared the gates of Marabella, large crowds had gathered. Soldiers lined our path to keep everyone back, but mostly the crowd was still and surprisingly silent. A deathly pall had fallen as if ghosts rode at our sides. These were not prisoners they ever expected to see. Mouths hung open. Eyes glistened. A man as big as Griz wept. They may not have recognized Beaufort and Torback, but they knew Governor Sarva and Chievdar Kardos. I watched the stunned faces fill with terror and then hatred. No doubt many had experienced loss at these men's hands or knew someone who had. Sarva and Kardos looked straight ahead, refusing to meet their gazes.

Beaufort began looking around, his head craning back nervously.

"Still expecting a rescue?" I asked.

He looked at me, and that was when I saw real terror. He'd never expected to face the queen again—at least not on her terms. He had thought his patience would pay off once more, and he would never meet his fate.

"It's over, Captain. No one is coming for you. This is the end of the line."

His face contorted as if struggling with this truth and finally his lip lifted in a snarl as he scrutinized me. He shook his head with disgust. "By worthless street trash. By a crapcake like you."

That's right. By someone like me.

A drop of sweat trickled over his half-moon scar. "It will never be over. Not now. A door has been unlocked. More like me will always come."

"Maybe so. But more like me will always be there to stop them."

He looked over his shoulder one last time, as if still hopeful, but all he saw were the Vendan crowds closing in, erasing the path behind him.

I clutched the jail log in my hand. As lead on the mission, it was my job to present it to the queen—the names of the prisoners we had delivered into the warden's custody. She would address the prisoners later.

I sat on a stone bench outside her personal chamber, waiting, my knee bouncing. I fingered the wish stalk in my pocket that I had bought from a merchant just outside the outpost walls.

A servant opened the door, and I jumped to my feet. "The queen will see you now," she said. I was escorted in and the servant left. The room was cool and dim. The sweet fragrance of roses hung in the air. With the curtains drawn, I didn't see her at first.

"Kazimyrah," she said softly, walking toward me. She was in a dressing gown and her hair was loose around her shoulders.

I dropped to a knee. "Your Majesty."

"Enough of that." She lightly touched my arm so I would stand, then drew me into her arms. She hugged me tightly, as if she'd been worried, and I found myself hugging her back, holding her in a way I had never done before, my breaths uneven, my throat stabbing, and somewhere deep within I felt a tug, like a stitch pulling tight, and I imagined its color to be silver. "Welcome home," she whispered.

When she drew away I noticed her belly. The large round bump was gone and my heart jumped. She must have seen the fear on my face.

"No. Everything's fine. Come." She guided me to a cradle beside her bed.

My chest swelled. "She—he?—is beautiful."

The queen smiled. "She. I can't stop looking at her. I watch every twitch, every smile, every pout of her lip." She leaned over and scooped the sleeping baby into her arms, kissing her forehead, then touching her tiny fingers, wonder filling her face.

"Have you named her?" I asked.

She nodded and her eyes glistened. "Aster," she answered. "I named her Aster. The saving angel." She kissed the baby again and gently laid her back in the cradle.

"And you have made her world safer, Kazimyrah. I am indebted to you and your team. A thank-you is not nearly enough."

My throat squeezed. "I am honored to serve, Your Majesty."

"Will you ever call me Lia?"

"Griz doesn't approve."

She shook her head. "Come," she said. "Tell me about your journey."

We sat on the settee beneath the window, and she poured us each a goblet of water. I presented her with the prison log, but she wanted to hear about the prisoners from me. She had already heard we had come back with more than we set out for. First I told her about the prisoners who had died en route, then Torback, and then I told her about the captain. She let out a slow breath, and I saw the relief in her face that he was finally captured. But there was also turmoil in her eyes, as if she revisited the pain he had wrought, not just upon Morrighan and Venda, but upon her family. She said she wished her father had lived long enough to see this day.

When I told her about Governor Sarva and Chievdar Kardos, she shook her head in disbelief, shocked that they were still alive. She had known them when she was held prisoner in the Sanctum and remembered their cruel, vindictive ways.

"Captain Illarion still thinks he's going to get away," I warned.

"That doesn't surprise me, but there's no chance of that now," she said. "He murdered Captain Azia, one of my husband's best officers. Rafe will probably guard Illarion himself until he sees him hanging from a rope."

She assured me that all the prisoners would remain under heavy guard while they awaited trial.

"There's one other prisoner I need to tell you about," I said. I dug my nails into my palms, trying to force the wobble from my throat. "This one may take a while."

The queen's brows rose with interest, and she sat back on the settee, curling her feet beneath her. "I'm listening."

Some said it began with the stars.

They brought a magic the world could not contain.

No, my grandfather said, *it began with the anger of men*.

However it began, we are the end. I was five when the first star struck.

I have no memory of my family, only my grandfather, one of the most powerful men in the world, the leader of a once-great nation, scooping me into his arms and running. Running is all I remember.

Years of running.

I will never run again.

—*Greyson Ballenger, 16*

CHAPTER SIXTY

JASE

By the time I got to the receiving hall, I was seething. I'd been thrown in a cell and handed a bucket, and my inquiries of when I would see the queen were met with silence. Not a word. An hour of waiting and pacing passed. And then three, sunlight shifting through the tiny window of my cell. I could be here for days, weeks. I knew the game she played. I had played it with prisoners plenty of times. Let them wait and fear the worst.

Maybe her tactic was working. Kazi said the queen would hear me out, but when? And even then, would she really listen? As far as the kingdoms were concerned, Tor's Watch was nothing but a minor speck on the landscape. All they knew about us was what the King of Eislandia had told them, and he knew nothing. I was through upholding the terms of Paxton's idiot great-grandfather—a whole town for a round of drinks. If I ever got out of here, I was taking back Hell's Mouth. We would no longer be held hostage to a gambling debt or defer to a king who had no interest in the town that he didn't bother to support. We would no longer be ignored. I felt like the voice raging in my head was my father's. After at least four hours, I was dragged out of my cell by two burly guards who again had nothing to say to me other than *shut up*. They hauled me through the outpost and threw me into an empty hall to await the queen, my hands still tied behind me. But she wasn't there.

Twenty minutes passed. Then forty. Silence ticked by. More waiting? The elevated end of the room had two passageways on either side. I waited for someone to come, but no one did.

"Where's the queen?" I finally yelled. No answer. I let loose with a litany of shouts, demanding that someone come. I heard a baby cry in the distance and then footsteps. Loud, angry footsteps. The crying stopped, but a man burst through one of the passageways, his burning blue eyes landing on me. He stomped down the steps and crossed the room, grabbing my shirt, nearly jerking me off my feet. He held me close so we were eye to eye. "The queen will get here when she gets here, but if you wake my baby daughter one more time, I'll pop your head from your shoulders. Understand?"

"Who are you?" I asked.

"A man who has had very little sleep in the past forty-eight hours. But to you I am King Jaxon."

The King of Dalbreck. I'd also heard rumors about him, another twelve-foot legend—one with a temper. Right now, he looked like an exhausted, crazed man. And a protective one. He let go of my shirt with a shove.

And then I heard a shuffle. We both turned. Four soldiers filed out of the right passageway, Dalbretch officers by the look of their uniforms, and then just behind them, more officers, but these were Vendan. Griz was one of them. They lined up on the dais, facing me, long swords at their sides, and I wondered if this was going to be an impromptu execution.

There was another shuffle of movement, this one quieter, and from the opposite passageway a woman walked out onto the dais. She held a baby in her arms. The king forgot about me and walked up the steps to meet her. His face was transformed as he looked at her, his rage replaced with tenderness. She looked at him in the same way. They gazed down together at the baby in her arms and the king kissed the queen, long and leisurely as if I wasn't there.

This was Queen Jezelia of Venda, the one who held my fate in her hands. She was younger than I thought she'd be, and softer and more serene than I'd expected. Maybe this wouldn't be so difficult after all. She handed the baby to the king, and he held his daughter in the crook of his arm, his knuckle rubbing her cheek.

The queen turned to me, and in an instant her softness vanished. The dreamy eyes she had for her baby and the king had turned hard and cutting. This was a monarch who tolerated no nonsense. She stepped to the end of the dais, confident in her stride, one brow arched in irritation. "So you're the one making all the noise."

"I'm the *Patrei* of Tor's Watch and I demand—"

"Correction," she said, briskly cutting me off. "You're my prisoner and—"

"What do you want me to do? Bow? Because I won't do that. My realm was centuries old before the first stone was laid in yours. Because—"

She put her hand up in a swift *stop* motion and shook her head. "You're going to be trouble, aren't you?"

"I was told I would get a chance to speak!"

"You will, but I get to go first, because I'm the queen, I just went through twenty hours of labor, and I'm the one wearing a sword." She wasn't wearing a sword, but I got her point. She may as well have been. "I was told you're a good listener, but maybe my source is wrong."

A good listener?

"Kazimyrah, is this the prisoner you told me about?"

I startled as Kazi walked out of the passageway. Her steps were smooth and composed. She turned to face me, her expression grim, but her eyes only looked into mine briefly before she looked away again. "Yes, Your Majesty. It's him."

The queen turned back to me. "Then I expect you to listen, *Patrei*, because my Rahtan are never wrong."

I boiled inside like an overheated kettle, but I remained silent waiting for my chance to speak. She had a guard untie my hands, then repeated the charges against me, violating kingdom treaties by harboring fugitives, in addition to conspiring to dominate the kingdoms. I opened my mouth to respond, and she shut me down with a quick glare and tilt of her head.

"*However*, as Kazimyrah pointed out to me, you have not signed a treaty with the Alliance of Kingdoms, because you are not a kingdom at all, nor are you even part of Eislandia, and yet you are steward of Hell's Mouth, which is part of that kingdom, which is all a very curious and complicated arrangement. I don't like complications. Kazimyrah explained to me how that came to pass." She shook her head. "A word of advice, *Patrei*, never play cards with a monarch. They cheat."

The soldiers behind her rumbled in agreement, and the king grinned.

"In addition, she has also made me aware that the King of Eislandia may have not acted in good faith, nor held up the tenets of the Alliance in finding suitable land for a settlement and in fact, may have intentionally chosen your land as a way to provoke you. This does not sit well with me. Using my citizens to settle grudges is not something I take kindly to. They have already been through untold hardships, and I will not suffer fools who bring them more. Nevertheless, I understand you rectified the situation by rebuilding the settlement at your own expense in a better location, and that you were very generous in the process."

I glanced at Kazi. She stood to the side of the queen, looking straight ahead, avoiding eye contact with me.

The queen walked down the steps, studying me. I wondered if I was ever going to get a chance to speak, but my gut told me to wait, because none of this was going quite how I expected it to. I was wary, uncertain if I was being led to a cliff and any minute I would be pushed over it.

"Still, you conspired to build weapons," she continued, "providing the fugitives with materials that could have brought great destruction upon the kingdoms, but my Rahtan tells me the Watch Captain deceived you and his purposes were not your purposes. That you only wanted to protect your interests against aggressors. Should I believe her?"

I started to answer, but she shut me down again. "It was rhetorical. I always believe and trust the judgment of my Rahtan. It's you I'm still leery of." She pursed her lips. "But Captain Illarion is an accomplished liar, and in fact, even my father and I were greatly deceived by him."

She walked in a circle around the room as if thinking. I looked at Kazi, whose eyes were on me now, her pupils tight beads. The king's eyes drilled into me too. Something about this was all wrong. I felt like a lone fish in a barrel, and everyone else in the room had a spear.

The queen stopped circling and faced me again. "I've also been enlightened about your family's long history, perhaps longest of any of the kingdoms. Kazimyrah says you claim to be descended from the leader of the Ancients—the first family—and she's seen some evidence of it herself."

"It's not a claim. It's the truth," I said, not waiting for an invitation to speak.

"Tell me something about it, then. I want to hear it in your own words."

"The Ballenger history?" I asked.

"Yes."

I hesitated, still uncertain where this was going, wondering just what Kazi had told the queen, because it seemed she had said a lot. The queen waited for my answer. "All right," I answered slowly. This wasn't what I thought I'd be speaking about. I started at the beginning with Aaron Ballenger, the chief commander of the Ancients. "He was forced to run, like everyone else during the Last Days, when the seat of his command was destroyed." I explained about his struggle to survive, and his final effort to get a group of children to a faraway shelter, and then his murder by scavengers. "Before he died, he passed the responsibility of leadership to his grandchild, Greyson. He was the eldest but only fourteen." I told her how he and twenty-two other children struggled to survive in the Tor's Watch vault while predators waited outside. She listened intently, but she seemed to be studying me too, and I became self-conscious of every move I made. "They finally learned to defend themselves and eventually ventured out to lay the first stones of Tor's Watch. And that was the first generation. We have centuries of history after that."

"That's quite impressive," she answered. "I have a keen interest in history. I've discovered that there are several histories on this continent, and I've learned something from them all, but yours is especially intriguing. It seems that perhaps all the kingdoms have been remiss in failing to acknowledge the place of Tor's Watch on the continent, however small it might be."

She tapped her lips, her gaze dissecting me, long seconds passing, and then her chin lifted, like a seasoned trader at the arena ready to make a final offer. "Here's what I'd like to propose, Jase Ballenger. I'd like to suggest to the Alliance that they take Tor's Watch under consideration to be acknowledged and accepted as another kingdom on the continent. However, as Kazimyrah says, your ways are not our ways and that presents a few prickly problems." She stated the things we would have to change in order for this to happen and that included ending our blatant support of the black-market trade. "It might be rampant across the continent, but it is still theft. And then there's the matter of your borders. You would have to establish clear ones."

I didn't respond, still thinking all this was some sort of trick.

"You're not willing to do this?" she asked.

"What's the catch?"

"No catch. Some things are just the right thing to do. Kazimyrah told me you understood that concept. And it would serve our interests too, to have a reliable ally in that region."

There it was. I heard the implication that King Monte was incompetent. I couldn't disagree, though it seemed Kazi had embellished the story about him choosing the settlement site. I still wasn't convinced he knew it was our land.

"And it's that simple? Just like that we're a recognized nation?"

"No," the king replied, jiggling the stirring baby on his shoulder. "It's not that simple at all. It could take months, even years for all the kingdoms to agree, and it would include several investigative trips by ambassadors. But the queen is very persuasive, not to mention she has an inroad with the King of Dalbreck. The kingdoms will go along, eventually, providing you agree to the terms."

"Fifty miles," I said. "Those are our borders. Fifty miles in all directions from Tor's Watch."

"But that would include Hell's Mouth," the queen noted.

"That's right," I confirmed. "It's always been ours. It's time to settle any question about it."

She bit the corner of her lip. "That might be a little trickier if the King of Eislandia will not willingly cede the lands to you. He is still the sitting monarch."

"We'll persuade him," I said.

"By lawful means, I assume?"

Whose laws? I wanted to ask. I had racaa and antelope blood in mind, but I answered, "Of course."

"Maybe the persuading would be better left to us," the king said, as if he had read my mind. "And considering the longer Ballenger history of stewardship of the land, it shouldn't be hard to argue for its return into your hands."

The queen nodded. "Very well, then, if the other kingdoms are in agreement, Tor's Watch will become the thirteenth kingdom."

"The first," I corrected.

The queen's eyes narrowed, but I saw a glimmer behind them. She was amused by this. "You are trouble, just as Kazimyrah warned me." She sighed. "Very well then, the first."

She said they would put me up in quarters tonight, have papers for me to sign in the morning, and then I could leave. I would hear from them in several weeks. A delivery of Valsprey and a trainer for them would be made to aid in communications. For now, they would provide me with supplies for my trip home and an escort if I required one. "You're free to go."

Go? Just walk out the door and not look back? I looked at Kazi. She was a rigid soldier, her gaze fixed on an empty wall, but her hands were fists at her sides. I had just gained everything my father had ever dreamed of—what generations of Ballengers had dreamed of—the acknowledgment of all the kingdoms that would establish our authority once and for all. We would be a recognized nation ourselves. And yet, I stood there, unable to leave. I should have felt light with victory but instead a heavy weight pulled at me.

I looked back at the queen. "Thank you," I said. I knew I had been dismissed, but I still stood there. The queen looked at me oddly as if she noticed my hesitation. She glanced at Kazi, then back at me. Her eyes suddenly turned sharp again.

"On second thought," said the queen, "it would be the height of foolishness to strike a bargain with a band of outlaws. I'm not sure I can really trust you, Jase Ballenger. You might revert to your old, lawless ways. What do you think, King Jaxon?"

He looked startled for a moment, then answered, "I completely agree." He stepped close to his wife, shaking his head disapprovingly. "I don't trust him. Look at that smirk of his. I don't think it's safe to let him go."

Was this the trick they'd been planning all along? My blood raced. "What—"

"Though I could send a trusted representative along to keep an eye on you," the queen suggested. "An ambassador of sorts. What do you think, *Patrei*? Do you think I should trust you?"

I stared at her, the air punched out of me, but then, the glimmer again—I saw the glimmer in her eyes, and it struck me. I understood what she was doing.

CHAPTER SIXTY-ONE

KAZI

THE QUEEN MADE ME NO PROMISES. SHE HAD LISTENED carefully to everything I told her, and I watched her expressions change as I spoke. Sometimes I saw anger, surprise, confusion, and sometimes I saw sadness, or maybe I was only seeing myself reflected in her eyes. I kept to the facts, only telling her things that pertained to the kingdoms and what I observed. I didn't tell her about Jase and me together, nothing about the wilderness, because that was a story that would take me a lifetime to tell.

When I finished, she told me she would consider everything I said— including what I had boldly asked for—but she had to see the prisoner for herself. She had to speak to him, look him in the eye, get a sense of who he really was, and then she would decide, but she sped up the process, calling him to the receiving hall immediately.

I was right behind the queen in the passage as she walked to address Jase, but just before entering, I stopped and pressed myself up against the wall. I couldn't go in. I couldn't face him. I'd heard his angry shouts echoing down the hallway—his resentment and bitterness. There were some things I could try to make right for him, but some things would be forever broken.

"Kazimyrah," the queen called, "is this the prisoner you told me about?"

I had no choice but to enter the room. I pushed away from the wall and created composure where there was none, molding my dread and regret into one step and then another, calling upon old tricks, fooling myself one more time that I could do this. *Juggle Kazi. Pivot.* But there was nothing left to juggle, no more directions to turn.

"Yes, Your Majesty. It's him."

I fixed my eyes on the far wall, listening to the charges, waiting. It felt like giant hands pressed down on my shoulders, like every one of my bones was about to crack under the strain. I wasn't sure how much longer I could stand, but after only a few minutes, I knew. I heard it in her voice. It was firm and familiar, a voice I had first heard six years ago when I spit in her face. *Bring her along to the Sanctum.* Back then, I couldn't hear the compassion in her voice. I was too frightened, too angry. But I heard it now, and I wondered if this was another one of those things you could only perceive from a distance.

I watched her closely as she listened to him tell the Ballenger history, gauging and interpreting her every move and blink. I knew she heard the pride in his voice, the determination, and the responsibility he bore. She was seeing all the same things in Jase that I saw, who he really was, and everything he could still be.

It was all going well, better than I could have hoped. Tor's Watch was to be recognized for what it was, the first realm of the land. I took a chance and looked at Jase. He was leaving. He was going back. It was what I had wanted, what I hoped for, because Hell's Mouth did need him. His family needed him. But then he looked at me, and my mind became a windstorm, memories whirling in a riotous tunnel, and I saw it all sweeping away, out of my reach.

Then the path suddenly veered terribly, and everything spun out of control, the storm exploding right in the middle of the receiving hall. My head pounded, trying to quickly retrace where it all went wrong.

I'm not sure I can really trust you, Jase Ballenger.

I don't think it's safe to let him go.

What do you think, Patrei? *Do you think I should trust you?*

I was frozen, afraid to move, my eyes locked on his, my breath trapped in my chest waiting for Jase's reply. *Say yes, Jase! Tell her! Tell her you'll keep your word!*

But instead he hesitated.

Tell her!

He looked back at the queen. "No," he answered. "I don't think you can trust me at all. I might slip back into my old habits."

What was he saying? Had they all gone mad?

"That's just what I thought," the queen replied. "I'm afraid I'd need someone who was equal to your sly ways, someone clever enough to keep you in line. Someone already familiar with Tor's Watch." The queen looked up at me. "What about you, Kazimyrah? Would you be willing to take on this position? Would you be willing to go back with the *Patrei*?"

I looked at her, trying to grasp what was she saying. Go back? The room bloomed with stifling heat, the air sucked out in a sudden *whoosh*. Ambassador? She didn't understand. "I'm afraid, Your Majesty, that would be impossible. I've left considerable ill feelings behind me in Tor's Watch. I wouldn't be a wise choice for a liaison." I looked at Jase, my eyes stinging. "And I'm sure the *Patrei* wouldn't want me to go back with him. Everyone there despises me by now."

There was a long, fragile silence, then Jase shook his head. "Not everyone."

He crossed the room, and no one tried to stop him. He walked up the steps and looked down at me, his eyes searching mine, and then he pulled me into his arms, crushing me, his face nestled in my hair. "I already told you," he whispered in my ear, "and I won't take it back. I love you, Kazi of Brightmist, and I will never stop loving you, not through a thousand tomorrows. Come back with me. Please."

My face buried in his shoulder, breath jumping in my throat. *Make a wish. One will always come true.* My fingers curled into his shirt, holding on to what I had thought was far beyond my reach, trying to understand what was happening, and then words tumbled from my mouth, words I didn't want to hold back any longer, no matter how risky they might be. I didn't care if every god in the heavens was listening. "*Le pavi ena.*" I gasped. "I love you, Jase Ballenger."

"I know," he said. "I've always known."

I turned my face to his and our lips met, a kiss that was salty with tears. "My tomorrows are yours, Jase. I want them all to be with you."

We held on to each other, tight, as if weaving some solid part of us together so nothing could ever separate us again, and when we finally parted there was no one left in the room but us, and I guessed the queen knew that my answer to her was yes.

Jase helped me with Mije's saddle and pack. This time on our trek across the wilderness together we would have ample supplies and boots on our feet. We'd already said good-bye to the queen and king, and Jase had signed the necessary papers to begin the process of Tor's Watch becoming a recognized nation on the continent.

He buckled the strap on my bag. "So does this mean I have to call you Ambassador Brightmist now?" he asked.

"Or perhaps Magistrate Brightmist," I answered. "I think that is the queen's intention."

He pulled me into his arms. "I'll definitely be misbehaving, just to make sure you have something to report. I wouldn't want you to lose your job."

We kissed again, like it was all delicate and new, and wondrous, a turn neither of us saw coming, and I knew I would fiercely fight to stay on this path, no matter what it took or what it cost me.

"Stop, would you?" Synové called.

Jase and I stepped apart as she and Wren walked over. Synové held up a small package tied with twine. "Just a little good-bye treat for the trail."

"I'm not sure there's room for one more thing," I said.

"Trust me, you'll appreciate it once you're out there in the middle of nowhere."

"I'll find room," Jase offered and took it from me. When he turned his back, Synové made all kinds of suggestive eye signals. Wren only rolled hers. I wished they could come back to Tor's Watch too, but the queen had another mission for them once they had rested. I also suspected she wanted to spend some time with Synové to review how Bahr met his fate. It was already becoming legend throughout the settlement.

Wren shifted on her feet. Hissed. Pulled out her *ziethe*, spun it, and shoved it back in its scabbard. She shook her head. "You sure about this? Who will have your back?"

"I'll be fine," I answered, though I was still uneasy too. I knew Wren had heard the same deadly threats I had in those first hours after we had taken Jase and the prisoners. His family had been quite articulate in their rage. No doubt the whole town held similar thoughts by now too. I would be a prime target.

Jase finished stuffing the package in my bag and turned around. "I'll have her back, and I promise you, once I tell my family everything, they'll be grateful to Kazi." Jase told me Bahr and Sarva admitted to him they planned to kill the whole family, taunting him with some of the ugly details, especially regarding his sisters and mother. It had prompted their last scuffle. Once they no longer had a use for Jase, provoking him brought them sick pleasure.

Wren still looked unconvinced, but she nodded.

Synové leaned up unexpectedly and kissed Jase's cheek. "Give that to Mason for me, will you?" she chirped. "I know he must be missing me terribly by now. Let him know I got here okay. It will be such a relief for him."

Jase couldn't suppress a grin, and maybe a bit of an eyeroll. We'd heard Mason's threats too, not to mention we'd only seen him grudgingly tolerate her attentions in the first place. "I'll let him know."

We stood there awkwardly, none of us wanting to say good-bye. I shrugged. "Then I guess this is it."

"*Nooo*," Synové said and winked. "*It* comes later."

Wren jabbed her with her elbow, then hugged me. Synové joined in. "Blink last," Synové whispered before she let me go.

"Always," I answered.

"Remember, *Patrei*," Wren warned as they walked away, "watch her back, or we'll come after yours."

Late afternoon we stopped at a spring to water the horses and to rest. We'd been estimating how long it would take us to get back to Tor's Watch. Three to four weeks at minimum, depending on the weather. The crispness of autumn nipped the air.

"First thing I need to do when I get home is to make amends with Jalaine and put her back on at the arena," Jase said. "She loves her job even if she complains about it." He paused and looked at the ring on my finger as I filled a waterskin. The gold glinted in the sun. "And you'll need to take that off before we get back."

"This?" I spun the ring on my finger. "Why?"

"You think it's wise to wear something you stole from the king? Especially when we want him in a congenial mood toward us when he receives the proposal."

"What are you talking about? I already told you, I got this fairly." I explained about the merchant who gave it to me in return for a riddle.

Jase corked his water skin and lay down on the shady patch of grass beside the spring. He folded his hands behind his head. "My mistake. Garvin told me he thought you had nicked something from the king and I assumed—"

"Well, actually . . . I did," I admitted and sat down beside him, "but it was only a piece of paper with a name on it, maybe a pig-iron dealer. I think Paxton may have given it to him. Devereux something."

Jase turned his head like he didn't hear me correctly. "What?"

"Devereux seventy-two. That's all it said."

He sat up. "Devereux? You're sure?"

"Why? Do you know him?"

And that was when he told me about Zane. Everything about Zane. That he'd been a Ballenger employee. About the setup and Gunner bringing me to the fountain to see if Zane recognized me. About the interrogation that followed. That was how Gunner was able to bring him out to me so fast that night. They had been holding him prisoner in the warehouse.

"That's why I didn't tell you right away, Kazi. I was trying to find the right words and timing once I knew for sure he was the same man you described. I was afraid I'd lose you if you knew he'd been our employee."

It took me a minute to absorb this revelation—an employee but now their prisoner. He would still be at Tor's Watch when we got there.

"You're sure Zane said the man who gave him money was named Devereux too?" I finally asked.

Jase nodded.

We discussed what this might mean. Was the man who gave Zane money for labor hunters the same man named on the king's slip of paper—the paper Paxton may have given to him? Just who did Devereux work for? These past weeks someone had been campaigning to oust the Ballengers. There were five leagues who'd had run-ins with Jase's family over the years, all of them hungry for control of Hell's Mouth and the very profitable arena. Devereux likely worked for one of them, and now the finger was pointing at Paxton.

"Maybe Devereux is Paxton's new hawker by day," Jase wondered aloud, "and by night he's taking care of another kind of business."

"What about the king?" I asked. "I did find the note on him. Could Devereux be his man?"

Jase frowned. "Not the king I know. I think Montegue would wet himself if he ever ran into someone who frequents dark alleys, never mind have the guts to hire him. And for what? He doesn't head a league. He's a farmer. He has no stake in this game."

And then we both wondered about Beaufort. Was it possible he had been working with one of the leagues? Having them undermine the Ballenger's foothold in town in return for a piece of the pie? Was Zane their go-between? Or was the scheming unrelated? One conspiring faction? Or two separate ones? Paxton's threat to me resurfaced, *Crossing the wrong person can get you into more trouble than you bargained for. Watch your step.*

Jase shook his head, thinking. I knew it burned in him that he wasn't home. "Last time I was away, Gunner managed everything well," he finally said. "He will this time too. And we still have Zane in custody. My family won't let him go. We'll get more answers out of him when we get back." He squeezed my hand. "And we'll get your answers too, Kazi. That comes first. I'm sorry for what Gunner did."

I glanced down, remembering Gunner's taunts. "Emotions were strung tight, and he was afraid for you," I replied, trying to understand, but Gunner's cruelty was still a raw wound inside me. He dangled Zane in front of me like food to a starving animal, then snatched him away. I'd been worried about the family forgiving me, but now I wondered if I would ever be able to forgive Gunner. *We'll get your answers too.* The thought chilled me. What if I was wrong? What if my mother wasn't dead? What if Death had tricked me?

Jase looked at me, his eyes dark with concern.

I blew out a long, cleansing breath. "Don't worry. We'll figure it out," I said, "but this time there will be no secrets between us, and we'll be working on the same side."

He smiled. "The Ballenger odds have just doubled." He nudged my shoulder until I was lying back on the grass, and he kissed my cheek. "Before I forget, I still owe you something."

"What's that?" I asked.

"The riddle I promised you. The *good* one. It took me a while. Turns out it's not that easy to find the right words." He lifted my hand, kissing my fingertips as if he cherished each one. "But sometimes you need to say what is in your heart while you can, because you might not get a chance later. Every word is as true as I can make it, Kazi, so I may as well tell you now."

He pulled his shirt loose from his trousers.

"Jase," I said. "Just what are you—"

"Shhh," he whispered. "Wait." He took my hand and slipped it beneath the fabric, pressing it flat to his chest. His skin was hot under my palm, and I felt the light beat of his heart beneath my fingers. "Ready?" he asked. "Listen carefully, because I won't repeat myself, Ambassador Brightmist."

I smiled. "Don't worry, *Patrei*. I'm a good listener." He began, still pressing my hand to his chest.

> *"I have no mouth, but my hunger is fed,*
> *With glimpse, and touch, and kindness said.*
> *I have no eyes, but see a soul,*
> *The only one that makes me whole.*
> *I swell beneath a soldier's palm,*
> *Its touch my breath, my blood, my calm.*
> *I am utterly lost, but completely found,*
> *Captured, taken . . . a prisoner bound."*

My throat ached. I knew the answer, but I played the game. "A key? The wind? A map?" His lips brushed mine between each wrong guess.

"It may take me a while to figure this out," I said.

His mouth was warm against mine, his tongue gentle, his hands curling through my hair. "Take as long as you like."

We were in no hurry.

We were alone, we had each other, and we had a whole wilderness ahead of us.

CHAPTER SIXTY-TWO

THE BIRD WAS DEAD. HE'D SEEN IT FALL FROM THE SKY. A DOZEN arrows had followed its flight. One had found its mark in the bird's breast. He scooped it up with his bony fingers and cradled the bird. Its neck was broken, and its head fell back in an elegant swoon over his arm. He already knew what the note attached to its leg said. He'd stood behind Jalaine as she wrote it.

> *Jase, Kazi, anyone,*
> *Come! Please! Samuel is dead.*
> *They're banging the door.*
> *I have to—*

He'd known she wouldn't have time to finish the note. She had barely had time to release the bird. He looked down to where the arrow pierced its stained breast. He gripped the shaft and pulled it from the bird. A spray of downy white feathers floated to the ground. He didn't know if it would help, but he had promised Jalaine, and he always kept his promises. He lifted the bird to his mouth and whispered against the feathers. *Not yet. Not today,* then threw the bird into the air.

Its wings snapped taut, catching the current, and it flew away from Tor's Watch.

ACKNOWLEDGMENTS

I am so thankful to the enormously talented team at Macmillan and Henry Holt: Jean Feiwel, Laura Godwin, Angus Killick, Jon Yaged, Christian Trimmer, Morgan Dubin, Brittany Pearlman, Ashley Woodfolk, Teresa Ferraiolo, Allison Verost, Lucy Del Priore, Katie Halata, Mariel Dawson, Robby Brown, Molly Ellis, Jennifer Gonzalez, Claire Taylor, Jennifer Edwards, Jess Brigman, Mark Von Bargen, Sofrina Hinton, and the army of you who work behind the scenes—from advertising to marketing, to sales and publicity, to hand-selling at every stage of the process—you make book magic happen. Without you, *Dance of Thieves* wouldn't exist, and I am grateful to all of you.

Additional accolades to Starr Baer, Ana Deboo, and Rachel Murray for careful and multiple reads and expert advice. Rachel, also extra thanks for all the hats you wear—you keep the wheels turning.

I am forever indebted and grateful to my extremely talented editor, Kate Farrell. She is so very smart, patient, always there with a listening ear, and offers up boatloads of wisdom at every turn. She is a rare gem, and I'm one lucky writer to have her.

Thanks and hugs to Caitlin Sweeny, who championed this book from the beginning and continued to support it from afar and offered the very first "review," which meant the world to me.

Keith Thompson, map artist extraordinaire, worked his magic again.

I am such a map geek, and I may have squealed when I found out he was creating a new map for *Dance of Thieves*. He brought the Remnant world and now Jase and Kazi's world alive with positive brilliance.

I am always surprised by the breadth of talent of Rich Deas. The *Dance of Thieves* cover is perhaps one of the prettiest covers I have ever seen, and with wings and swords and thannis vine, he infuses meaning and beauty into his art. The cover is everything I could have hoped for and more. Thank you, Rich. Many thanks also to Becca Syracuse, who worked on the design details and made the whole book come together in a stunning way.

I can never sing enough praises for my hardworking, wise, hand-holding, and smart agent, Rosemary Stimola. She is the whole pie with a big dollop of ice cream on top. Thank you to Ro and the Studio crew, Debra, Pete, Adriana, Allison, and Erica, for helping me navigate this wonderful but crazy business.

A bouquet of gratitude to my foreign publishers, agents, and readers worldwide who embraced the Remnant world and jumped on this book at first whisper. I hope one day I can travel to all of your amazing countries and thank you personally!

I am forever indebted to librarians, booksellers, tweeters, booktubers, bloggers, Instagrammers, and the many fans who have spread the word in innumerable and astonishing ways—from reviews to tweets, to fan art, to drop-dead gorgeous cover shots, to full-on cosplay, and even to candles celebrating the *Dance of Thieves* world. I am humbled and in awe of their talent and boundless enthusiasm, and grateful to be on this book journey with them.

I will always be thankful for so many dedicated, generous, badass, in-the-trenches YA writers. Through all the stages and the highs and lows of what we do, they keep me grounded with my eye on the story, help stamp out plot fires and character mutinies, and offer support and writing advice. Their deep wells of creativity inspire me. Thank you to Marlene Perez, Melissa Wyatt, Alyson Noël, Jodi Meadows, Susan Dennard, Jill Rubalcaba, and additional thanks to Robin LaFevers, who happened to be writing a same-universe book at the same time and mused with me on the challenges these books present. Thanks also to Leigh Bardugo for sage advice and offering metaphors about meadows just when I needed it. I owe you a bouquet of flowers. And many thanks to Tobin Anderson, who commiserated on the corners we write ourselves into and offered resources and thoughts on riddles.

My family is my rock and my joy. They keep my spinning thoughts in perspective and support me unfailingly. Thank you to Jessica, Dan, Karen, Ben, Ava, Emily, Leah, and sweet baby B, who will debut about the same time as this book. My heart is full.

And of course, my deepest thanks to Dennis, my favorite thief, and the man who stole my heart. I have danced through life "chained" to this brilliant man, who has helped me see so much of the world in a new way and is always eager to see it through my eyes too. The day we met, our world doubled. He is the best partner in crime I could have asked for and always there for me whether he is bringing me a latté, a lunch, or a listening ear to help me untangle a plot knot. He makes the writing and the books happen.

ARENA

HELL'S